MUSIC OF THE NIGHT

A Crime Writers' Association Anthology

Edited by Martin Edwards

This is a **FLAME TREE PRESS** book

Introduction copyright © 2022 Martin Edwards
Stories are subject to international copyright law, and are
licensed for publication in this volume.

FLAME TREE PRESS
6 Melbray Mews, London, SW6 3NS, UK
flametreepress.com

US sales, distribution and warehouse:
Simon & Schuster
simonandschuster.biz

UK distribution and warehouse:
Marston Book Services Ltd
marston.co.uk

Publisher's Note: This is a work of fiction. Names, characters, places, and
incidents are a product of the author's imagination. Locales and public names
are sometimes used for atmospheric purposes. Any resemblance to actual
people, living or dead, or to businesses, companies, events, institutions, or
locales is completely coincidental.

Thanks to the Flame Tree Press team, including:
Taylor Bentley, Frances Bodiam, Federica Ciaravella, Don D'Auria,
Chris Herbert, Josie Karani, Mike Spender,
Cat Taylor, Maria Tissot, Nick Wells, Gillian Whitaker.

The cover is created by Flame Tree Studio with
thanks to Nik Keevil and Shutterstock.com.
The font families used are Avenir and Bembo.

Flame Tree Press is an imprint of Flame Tree Publishing Ltd
flametreepublishing.com

A copy of the CIP data for this book is available from the British Library
and the Library of Congress.

HB ISBN: 978-1-78758-735-9
HB (Deluxe): 978-1-78758-736-6
US PB ISBN: 978-1-78758-733-5
UK PB ISBN: 978-1-78758-734-2
ebook ISBN: 978-1-78758-737-3

Printed and bound in Great Britain by Clays Ltd, Elcograf S.p.A

MUSIC OF THE NIGHT

A Crime Writers' Association Anthology

Edited by Martin Edwards

FLAME TREE PRESS
London & New York

CONTENTS

CRIME WRITERS' ASSOCIATION

The CWA was founded in 1953 by John Creasey – that's over sixty-five years of support, promotion and celebration of this most durable, adaptable and successful of genres. The CWA runs the prestigious Dagger Awards, which celebrate the best in crime writing, and is proud to be a thriving, growing community with a membership encompassing authors at all stages of their careers. It is UK-based, yet attracts many members from overseas.

INTRODUCTION

Welcome to a collection of new mystery stories written by members of the Crime Writers' Association. This year the guiding theme is music, a subject which really enthused members of the CWA and prompted a large volume of submissions. In selecting stories for inclusion, I've aimed to include a wide variety of voices and styles, showcasing the wonderful diversity of contemporary crime fiction.

If you glance at the list of contributors, you'll see that I've tried to cater to a wide range of tastes – in mystery writing as well as in music. The stories are an eclectic mix, some of them very short, some much more elaborate. Four of the authors have won the CWA's Diamond Dagger, the highest honour in UK crime writing. Although the CWA's membership is predominantly British, there are two American authors, an Irish writer, and a high-profile bestseller from Iceland. In addition, no fewer than nine of the twenty-five stories gathered here are written by people who have never previously contributed to a CWA anthology. I believe this enhances the freshness of the collection and I hope that readers who enjoy stories by writers previously unknown to them will be tempted to sample some other work by those authors.

I wasn't surprised by the number of stories that were sent in, because music is a subject that fascinates a great many crime writers, including myself, and is often touched upon in mystery fiction. After all, Sherlock Holmes was fiction's most famous violinist. In his first recorded case, *A Study in Scarlet*, he says to Dr Watson, after attending a concert: "Do you remember what Darwin says about music? He claims that the power of producing and appreciating it existed among the human race long before the power of speech was arrived at. Perhaps that is why we are so subtly influenced by it. There are vague memories in our souls of those misty centuries when the world was in its childhood." When he seeks solace after solving the mystery of 'The Red-Headed League', he finds it in 'violin-land, where all is sweetness and delicacy and harmony.'

In her youth, Agatha Christie dreamed of a musical career, and her lifelong love of music is reflected in a number of her novels and short stories. Dorothy L. Sayers' Lord Peter Wimsey was, like Sherlock, an amateur musician, with a talent for the piano, while music features prominently in any number of classic detective novels. An interesting if obscure example is *Death on the Down Beat* by Sebastian Farr (a pen-name for the music critic Eric Blom), in which a loathsome conductor is shot dead during a performance of a tone poem by Strauss; the book includes four pages of musical notation, which contain clues to the crime. Better-known is Cyril Hare's *When the Wind Blows*, where a snippet of musical knowledge proves crucial to solving the puzzle. Edmund Crispin, another accomplished author of detective novels, was a pen-name for Bruce Montgomery, whose main profession for many years was as a composer. His work ranged from church music to dozens of film soundtracks, including several Carry On movies. Naturally his enthusiasm for music is evident in his mysteries, notably *Swan Song* (a title also used by Christie for a short story with musical elements).

A fascination with music is equally evident in very different types of crime fiction, such as Raoul Whitfield's hardboiled novel *Death in a Bowl*, which sees a tough, hard-drinking private eye investigating another murder of a conductor in the middle of a performance – this time in the Hollywood Bowl. More recently, Ian Rankin's love of music has been apparent in many of his novels – and in titles such as *Let it Bleed*. My own first series, featuring the Liverpudlian lawyer Harry Devlin, took their titles and themes from 1960s hit songs including *Suspicious Minds* and *The Devil in Disguise*, while references to the work of Burt Bacharach crop up in all my contemporary novels.

Among the contributors to this book, perhaps I may highlight Paul Charles, who has spent many years working in the music business with leading acts such as Ray Davies, Van Morrison and Elvis Costello; Paul's knowledge and love of music shines through in his series of novels about the cop Christy Kennedy, who is a fan of the Beatles, the Kinks and Jackson Browne. Many of our other authors have had some kind of involvement with the world of music over the years. Their love of different kinds of music is a recurring feature of the stories presented here.

This is the first CWA anthology of brand-new writing to be published by Flame Tree Press. Its appearance was prompted by the success of a previous Flame Tree anthology, *Vintage Crime*, which celebrated CWA members' work published since the mid-1950s and traced the intriguing development of mystery writing over the past half-century. In trying to put together a book that is a varied yet harmonious whole, I've benefited from having the opportunity to work again with Nick Wells, Josie Karani, and their colleagues, and I am particularly grateful for their commitment to publishing books with high-quality production values. The CWA board has been supportive as ever, and I'd like to thank all the members who sent in stories, including those who were unfortunate enough not to make the cut.

Above all, my thanks go to you, the readers of this book. The CWA has been responsible for publishing anthologies of members' work for more than fifty years and I've been editing the collections for nearly half that time. These collections have yielded many stories that have won or been nominated for awards in the UK and the United States, by writers ranging from Ian Rankin and Cath Staincliffe to Edward D. Hoch and Lawrence Block. But the series could never have lasted for so long or enjoyed so much success without enthusiastic readers. I hope that you will find in these pages plenty to entertain you, and a number of pleasurable surprises.

Martin Edwards
martinedwardsbooks.com

BE PREPARED

Abi Silver

Masham, Yorkshire, May 1982

Campfire was the highlight of our week. It represented survival; four nights sleeping in tents, four days lugging firewood, building fires, cooking our own food and hiking and navigating our way back. Plus some healthy competition, as each patrol performed for the others. But the real joy came from staying up late and joining together, Guides, Scouts and leaders, to sing our hearts out to a variety of well-loved songs.

This year had been particularly successful, in my opinion, and I should know as I'm pretty much a veteran camper. In fact, me, Ruth and Helen, my two best friends, were so experienced, after five years in a row, that we didn't even have to be patrol leaders. Instead, we had been allowed to make up our own *senior patrol*. My mum always says that good things come in threes and that's how I like to think of us; we're a unit, a team, we complement each other. Helen is the pretty one, always beautifully turned out, hair smooth, nails polished, delicate gold sleepers in each tiny ear. She's the one the boys are always attracted to, wherever we go. And I suppose Ruth has the brains, not that I'm stupid, but Ruth is the all-rounder, the one who gets As across the board, even in Physics. I compensate though; my talent is noticing things, things that other people might not see or hear or connect.

At the age of fourteen, we were kind of halfway between the younger kids and the leaders, and we'd been allowed a few privileges this time, like no daily tent inspections; in fact, we were allowed to conduct inspections ourselves and award the marks. Danny Banks and Rob Jacobs, who were the same age as us, were definitely jealous. They didn't say anything, but we could tell by the way Danny scowled when they were sent off to bed and we, the senior patrol, were allowed to stay up for another hour. I'd known Danny at primary school, but he went to school in Harrogate now with Rob. My mum said Danny was 'a tearaway' and that was why he'd been sent to a private school, but I knew he was OK underneath.

Phil Knox and his wife, Pam, were in charge. Phil was a dentist from Leeds, oldish, probably at least fifty, and the nicest man. Pam was his receptionist. They had been running these camps for years, decades even, so I'd got to know them a bit. Phil called us all 'petal' or 'flower'. I suppose it meant he didn't have to remember any of our names, but he did it so nicely that none of us minded. I expect he would have been a pretty nice dentist too.

Pam was a fabulous cook, preparing gourmet meals for the leaders, while we languished in the shadows with sausages and beans. But every night, with limited ingredients and utensils, she made an enormous steamed pudding for sharing. This year, Pam and Phil's son, Adam, had come along too. He was in his early twenties, with lots of curly blond hair, and he laughed a lot. He looked nothing like Pam or Phil; Ruth said he was most likely adopted. Helen said maybe he was a test-tube baby, but we laughed at her then, because it was only four years before that they'd made the first one.

Colin and Carol Marsden were new on the scene. Colin had taken over running the Scout troupe a few months before. He drove a Jaguar and ran a jewellery shop in Halifax, where Helen's mum had bought a sparkly eternity ring. I don't know much about cars, but I know that Jaguars are expensive. When we arrived, I'd seen Colin picking at the mud on his tyres, as if a bit of dirt would puncture them. Carol was an optician and she worked in York. She'd been married before Colin, but her husband had died.

My mum says that sometimes you wait for things for a long time and then they disappoint you. I asked did she mean something about Dad when she said it, as he was asleep on the sofa with his mouth open, and she said I "had an aptitude for jumping to conclusions", so I thanked her for the compliment. But, anyway, I knew that wasn't going to be the case with campfire. This one was going to be the best yet.

The evening began predictably enough; the Guides were made to sit to one side, the Scouts to the other, and me, Ruth and Helen were in the middle. Pam and Phil sat on fold-up chairs behind us, the kind you might take to the beach on holiday. Colin and Carol sat opposite, behind the fire, on an upturned packing crate. Adam had disappeared into his tent in the late afternoon and not yet returned. Ruth said she thought he'd gone to sleep.

"Colin, why don't you start?" Pam called out once we were all settled, and Colin rose to his feet, with a grin as wide as a kid when the ice-cream van comes by.

Colin was a bull of a man, as wide as he was tall, with a bulging neck and enormous hands. I'd seen him earlier in the day chopping wood; legs splayed, axe raised high above his head, grunting each time the blade met resistance, patches of sweat leaching through his shirt.

"They're pulling down the Rose 'n' Crown," he bellowed and Helen, who had been fiddling with her Alice band and generally not paying attention, jumped a foot in the air.

"Booooooo," we all shouted and I was one of the loudest.

"To build a bigger one," he roared.

"Hurray," we replied.

"It only has one bar."

"Boooo."

"A mile long."

"Hurray."

★   ★   ★

The younger Guides and Scouts had begun to get the hang of the chanting and Colin was enjoying himself too. His voice boomed out across the verdant landscape, as he stalked left and right, in turns crouching and looming, owning the stage, and we responded with our alternating cries of approval and admonishment, gleefully, ecstatically, dutifully, until our young voices cracked and our throats ached.

"They don't serve beer."

"Boooo!"

"They give it away."

"Hurray!"

"The barmaids wear silk stockings," Colin continued.

"Boooo!"

"But nothing else."

"Hurray!"

*   *   *

Ruth rolled her eyes and me and Helen giggled. I looked over to where Carol, Colin's wife, was perched, to see if she was enjoying her husband's performance. She was tiny, gossamer-like, with flyaway hair and owlish glasses, which must have been fashionable, as she was an optician, so she would know. She took them off at night and hung them in a pocket on the outside of her tent, and she was forever leaving them lying around the site. And she didn't wear a fancy ring like Helen's mum; just a plain gold band on her wedding finger.

Carol wasn't very strong or resourceful, either. Once I saw her asking Phil to help carry some water from the river; another time she asked Adam to lift a box down from the pile in the store tent, and every night she complained about the cold. Tonight, she had both hands wrapped around a mug of something steaming and she wasn't joining in. It seemed strange that she'd come at all, that's what I'd said to Ruth and Ruth agreed, but maybe you don't have any choice in these kinds of things once you're married, especially if it's your second husband.

"Thank you, Colin. We all know who has the loudest voice in camp now." This was Phil taking back control, as Colin retreated and Adam emerged from his tent, yawning and stretching his arms above his head.

"Glad you could join us," Colin shouted.

Then Adam crawled back into his tent and, for a moment, we thought that was it, the extent of his appearance.

"Was it something I said?" Colin joked, and everyone laughed.

Then Adam re-emerged, guitar in hand, shaking his head, most probably to keep his curls out of his eyes. I'd heard Pam and Phil talking about Adam earlier.

"When he plays, it makes my heart sing," Pam had said.

"At least there's something he can do well, then," Phil had replied. I wasn't certain if he was joking or not, but Ruth had said Adam was working on the checkout at Safeway, so perhaps he wasn't.

Adam began with 'Sweet Molly Malone', a song about a woman pushing a barrow through the streets of Dublin, and we all joined in. It was a good choice to get everyone singing along, even the new recruits, with its lilting chorus of 'Alive, alive oh, Alive, alive oh, Singing cockles and mussels, Alive, alive oh'.

There's this bit near the end when the music moves into a minor key. I hadn't known what a minor key was until recently, even though I'd had piano lessons for years and played all the scales. It's when you drop the third note by a semitone and it makes everything sound miserable. I watched for Adam's chord change and there it was, a subtle movement of his fingers from one string to another, at 'She died of a fever and no one could save her'. A lump came into my throat, although it might have been because of all the shouting I'd done at Colin's behest, rather than the minor third or the sad lyrics.

Adam continued with 'My Bonnie Lies Over the Ocean'. Great choice for a chilly evening; all those actions to get the circulation flowing. Pam gave us a nod; me, Ruth and Helen, the senior patrol, and we went to the front to demonstrate. It was then, as I stood, waving my arms around and singing, the heat from the campfire scorching the backs of my legs, that I noticed Danny Banks wasn't joining in. He was probably still bothered by the incident with the toilet and I wouldn't blame him.

We had five toilets on site. Two for each of the Guide and Scout pack and one for the leaders, laid out in identical navy poplin tents, marking out the perimeter of our camp. Each patrol took it in turns to be on toilet duty, which involved transporting the liquid-filled buckets, one at a time, to the cesspit, emptying them into the steaming mire and conducting some rudimentary clean-up operations. On our site, the cesspit was situated just over the brow of a not insignificant hill, the same hill that provided us with shelter from the strongest winds. We, the senior patrol, had lucked out, as our duty had fallen on the first evening. Danny hadn't been quite so lucky.

Me and Ruth had just been to paddle in the river this afternoon, only in the shallow bit to the right of the bridge, as it got pretty deep on the other side. Then we'd sat down with pen and paper to put the finishing touches to our campfire performance. Helen didn't go in the water. She'd fallen in some nettles on our day hike and Danny had come bowling over with dock leaves and she'd let him rub them on her ankle until Colin shouted at him to "stop faffing around". Now she said she didn't want to irritate her stings. Anyway, we'd been lounging around, in an industrious kind of way, when we'd heard a shout. Danny and some boy in his patrol had been cresting the hill with a full bucket, when the other boy let go, the toilet lurched to one side and half its contents spilled over Danny's leg.

Carol had heard Danny too. She was in the leaders' area, scrubbing away at a cooking pot with a Brillo pad, the most exertion she had undertaken all week, and she had run up the hill, grabbed the bucket and single-handedly flung out the remains of its contents, before lugging it back down the hill, with the boys close behind.

Then, Colin had appeared and, whether he'd witnessed what happened or not, he could see the aftermath and he threw his head back and laughed, his enormous neck straining and bulging. Carol put her arm around Danny's shoulders, even though he must have smelt awful and she offered to take his jeans home and wash them, but Colin said it was too far and that we were all going home tomorrow anyway. Danny had started walking back to his tent and Colin had called after him, asked him "where he thought he was going". Danny said he was getting changed, but Colin made him finish up first, empty the other four toilets in his stinking clothes. "Just in case it happens again," he'd said. "We can't have you spoiling all your clothes, can we?"

Later on, I'd gone down to the river and I'd seen Danny's jeans, caught against the wire on the far side. I'd waded across and checked, but they were definitely Danny's because they were Wranglers and one leg was sawn off below the knee. Perhaps, this evening, Danny was worrying about how to explain his missing jeans to his mum when he got home, and he didn't feel much like singing.

We got to the last verse, the one where you have to point to yourself and circle your face and all that, in quick succession. Me and Ruth were doing fine but Helen began to get the actions wrong and collapsed into fits of laughter at her own ineptitude. When we sat down, Helen checked first with her hand whether the ground was wet or dirty, like she always did. I suppose she didn't want to get her clothes spoiled.

*   *   *

Now we were back in our places, I could see that there was this great big gap between Colin and Carol, so big I could see the woodpile in between them, the moon glinting off the blade of Colin's axe. Most of the leaders were drinking beer from bottles, except for Colin. He had whisky, which he was pouring liberally into the mug he had commandeered from day one, because it had some slogan about golf balls he liked.

Adam asked for requests for his next song and Pam called out 'The Boxer'. It was hardly *Top of the Pops*, but no one would complain as it was Pam and she had done everything for us all week, especially the steamed puddings. Ruth knew all the words, because she had an older brother, but the 'Lie-la-lies' calmed us all down after the exertions of the last song. Pam must have planned it, then. It was hardly nine o'clock and they didn't want us peaking too early. Danny still wasn't singing.

Next up Debra's patrol performed a skit in which they each pretended to be one of the leaders, and maybe that's when I felt it first. I can't be certain, but I think it was then. That subtle shift in the atmosphere from excitement and anticipation (we had told all the younger troops about Pam's legendary hot chocolate and marshmallows which would be making an appearance shortly) to apprehension tinged with menace. There'd been a taster with that minor third I mentioned in the 'Molly Malone' song, but this was a full course.

Adam had propped his guitar against the woodpile, Phil and Pam were laughing along at the jokes; Pam, politely, Phil, full-throated – and Colin and Carol? He was hugging her close and thrusting his mug, the golf one filled with whisky, into her face and she was grimacing and pulling away.

In their parody, Debra, playing Pam, was making Phil carry more and more pots, in his arms, over one foot, even on his head, till they all came crashing down. That was pretty funny. Then another girl, Susan, lay down in a hastily made-up tent, a canvas held aloft by two of the younger Guides and she made snorting noises, followed by the loudest raspberries. Debra, still pretending to be Pam, walked past, held her nose and shouted, "Colin Marsden, keep the noise down in there. Some of us are trying to sleep."

The pack screamed with laughter and even Pam seemed genuinely amused this time. But Colin's smile faded quickly and he ran his fingers across his chest and sloshed more brown liquid from the bottle. Carol murmured something to him, something which only reinforced his discomfort, before she ran off, out of the circle, past her tent, past even the toilets, just away into the night.

"If you don't like the smell, take a peg and put it on your nose," Debra continued, brandishing a wooden tent peg. No one laughed and Debra's face reddened. I felt sorry for her. It might have been funny, the fact that the peg was the wrong shape – tent pegs aren't like clothes pegs – if that bit hadn't just happened in real life, with Colin and Carol. Me, Ruth and Helen conferred and decided they deserved top marks for everything. It wasn't their fault the leaders couldn't take a joke.

"Did you see Carol went off somewhere?" Helen said, stating the obvious.

"Probably to be sick again," Ruth said.

"To be sick?"

"You must have seen her, at least twice, this morning right in front of us. She's probably pregnant. My Aunty Enid was sick every day of her first trimester," Ruth explained.

"It might not be that," I said, feeling cross with Ruth, but not quite sure why. Anyway, even if Carol was pregnant, I knew that wasn't why she had run away. And Colin wouldn't have been feeding her alcohol if she was pregnant, anyone knew that.

*　　*　　*

Adam came to the rescue then, with 'Michael, Row the Boat Ashore', an easy one for everyone to join in and kind on the ears and throat. At the end of every new line, you just had to sing 'Hallelujah', which no one could mess up and the tune was nice too; rousing but also soulful. Adam's strumming and Pam and Phil snuggling close, tapping their feet in time to the music, helped deflect attention from Colin, who was sitting alone now, swilling whisky around his mouth, gripping the edges of the packing crate, his knuckles gnarled and white. The wind had shifted and the flames were blowing in our direction and, with them, the light and heat was transposed on to us, leaving Colin truly out in the dark and the cold.

Suddenly, just as Adam reached the repetition of the line 'River Jordan is deep and cold', Colin sprang up, grabbed the guitar and flung it to the ground. Then, he picked Adam up, as if he was nothing more than a guitar himself and, letting out a primeval roar, he raced off towards the river.

Thirty-two heads on thirty-two necks switched through 180 degrees, to watch Colin, with surprising agility for a man of his massiveness, halt right on the edge without losing his balance, before opening his arms to deposit Adam into the deep water to the left of the bridge.

Splash!

Adam struggled to his feet, slipping over at least twice before he gained any foothold, as Colin roared out, in a deep baritone voice, "River Jordan is deep and cold". No one answered him. And, because he had turned around to face us all, to bask in the aftermath of his own joke, he failed to see that Adam, soaked through, teeth chattering and stumbling over the mossy boulders, had picked up a rather large rock specimen and was wielding it over his head.

Helen squeaked but Phil was there in a flash, intervening between the two men, one arm outstretched towards each heaving chest, delivering a resounding "No" at his son, which, after a second, was met with a nod of filial resignation and the low plunk of the stone being released back into the water. "He's such a bully," Ruth said, and I nodded my agreement.

"Hot chocolate," Pam called out from the fireside and thirty-two heads – actually everyone except Adam, who had slunk off to his tent again – turned around to claim our reward. The stretching of our limbs, making an orderly queue and pouring of the drinks from two gigantic kettles took quite a few minutes. Time for everyone to forget what had just happened.

When it came to Colin's turn to take a cup, he explained to Pam that it wasn't his fault if "Adam couldn't take a joke". Then I saw him searching for the golf mug. But I could see that Danny Banks had it and he was sipping from it slowly and purposefully. When Danny caught my eye, he tucked it into the folds of his jumper.

Without Adam and the musical accompaniment, we returned to less tuneful songs. Now it was 'A Poor Old Man was Crossing the Road', hardly melodious and pretty tragic too, when you analysed the words. At least Molly Malone was resurrected to carry on doing something she loved. This unfortunate pensioner was repeatedly run over by a series of vehicles; steamroller, wheelbarrow, chip potato cart, jeep – *whoo, whoo!* I joked to Ruth that it would be a good song to play when we had our session on road safety.

Pam whispered something to Phil and he got up and left too. That was disappointing. I would have liked everyone present for our big showpiece, which was coming very soon. And it piled all the pressure on Pam and, I suppose, Colin – although I hardly cared about him now – to keep things going. I gestured to Ruth and Helen and we sang louder, to help jolly things along.

Then Carol returned, all wrapped up in a tartan blanket, and sat back down next to Colin. There was no noticeable sign of nausea or sickness or pregnancy – I had a good look, which was challenging with the blanket, though I knew Ruth was wrong. But when Colin reached his hand out towards Carol, tentatively, maybe even tenderly, she edged away from him again and he didn't persist.

Now we had finally come to our turn – the senior patrol. I had written us a barnstorming medley using songs from the Top 40. The premise was that we were going to reminisce about when we were Brownies and all the things we'd learned since then. Clever, eh? We'd dug out our old uniforms, worn underneath our warmer clothes, which we were going to reveal when we got to the song 'Flashback'.

Right on cue, we began to undress. It was challenging to carry on the singing and the dance routine while taking off our coats, jumpers and jeans, but we managed it pretty well, I think. It was part-way into the next number when I noticed what Helen was wearing.

Sure, it was her Brownie uniform and we'd all grown a little in the last few years, but, whereas Ruth's tunic still fastened and finished just above the knee, and mine was tight across the chest and perhaps shorter than I'd remembered, Helen's was straining at its seams, buttons popped open to reveal the lacy edges of her black teen bra and it barely covered her bottom. It didn't help that she'd cinched it in at the waist with the regulation leather belt. OK, I admit, that was part of the original uniform, but not a necessary part, and not when your uniform was five years too short. Or that she'd chosen to accessorise the outfit with a pair of fishnet stockings – real stockings with suspenders too.

Phil had just returned with Adam, who was wearing knitted slippers which came halfway up his legs and Carol had thrust her blanket in his direction and insisted he keep it, despite his protests. He began to giggle when he saw Helen's outfit, before Phil thumped him to stop. Pam covered her mouth with her hand. But it was Colin who was the most distracting. He was staring goggle-eyed at Helen, and, when we finished and took our bows, he whistled his appreciation over and over again, his fat fingers stuffed into the corners of his mouth. I stole a look at Danny, just to see if he was applauding us, no other reason, but he was scowling at Colin. He didn't seem to have enjoyed our routine at all.

We scuttled away into the darkness to get changed, but Colin followed close behind, still cheering. He took Helen to one side and, his hand in the small of her back, spoke into her ear and pulled her away into the darkness. She joined us shortly afterwards and was unusually quiet, as Ruth and I chatted about the bits we'd done well in our sketch and the bits we'd forgotten. When we returned to the fire, Helen still didn't speak and she didn't check the grass before she sat down, and when I looked over she was biting at her nails.

Carol and Adam collected the hot chocolate mugs up, Carol from the Scouts and Adam from the Guides, and then Colin took centre stage for the last song, with a feathered head-dress on his head and his arms horizontal, one on top of the other, at chest height. Then he lifted his right hand, hinged at the elbow, turned the palm towards us and uttered the deepest "How" I have ever heard.

Everyone laughed. Well, everyone except Helen and, now I think of it, Adam and Phil and Carol and, although I didn't see, I expect Danny wasn't laughing either. Colin stooped down and picked up ash from the edge of the fire, wiping it across his face. For a moment, I saw him look across at Helen and she looked away. Then he began to sing.

"We are the red men tall and quaint,

In our feathers and war paint,

Pow wow, pow wow.

We're the men of the Old Dun Cow.

All of us are red men, feathers in our head men,

Down among the dead men.

Pow wow."

*　　*　　*

Somehow, with Colin's song, everything seemed returned to how it was before; before Carol ran off and Adam was dumped in the water and Colin had whispered in Helen's ear and Danny had stolen the whisky. Colin was so thoroughly enjoying himself, playing the part of the chief, head thrown back, chest puffed out. When he thrust his thumbs downward at 'Down among the dead men' like a Roman emperor sentencing a gladiator to death, everyone joined in. And when he swiped his index finger across his neck with a cutthroat gesture and an accompanying '*Cth*' noise, immediately afterwards, the youngest Guides and Scouts were ecstatic. Adam, cajoled by Pam, started to strum along, even Carol was swaying her head from side to side, and Phil had his arm around Pam's shoulders.

It must have been the song? I'd read, I'm sure, that the pow wow was all about peace and reconciliation. I truly believe that, as the smoke rose high into the clear Yorkshire sky, and our voices rang out over the rolling hills, someone, some god of the Native American Indians, heard our song and granted our prayer and all that earlier stuff was forgotten.

It was nearly ten-thirty when the campfire finally came to an end; two of the youngest Guides had fallen asleep, cross-legged, propped up in the middle of their peers. There was a rush for the toilet and then Pam asked us, the senior patrol, to check everyone was safely in bed.

"Did you like our act?" I asked, and she frowned and didn't reply.

"Colin said he liked it," Ruth said. "He asked if we would perform it again, just for him."

Helen's face crumpled for a moment, as if she was going to cry.

*   *   *

After we'd carried out our senior patrol duties, we hovered on the threshold of the leaders' camp, not sure if we were welcome to stay or not. Phil had settled himself down in a folding chair, drawing it close to the fire, and he had poured himself a tumbler of whisky and was holding it up to the flames. Pam had the tartan blanket over her knees. Adam was smoking a funny cigarette I'd seen him rolling earlier. So he had at least one other skill his father didn't know about.

"Maybe it's time for you three to get to bed too," Pam said. "There's… a lot to do tomorrow to clear up camp." Just for a moment, I had a feeling that she was going to say something else.

As me, Ruth and Helen undressed, I heard Adam strike up the guitar again. Now he was wending his way through a Beatles' playlist; 'I Wanna Hold Your Hand', 'Help', 'Can't Buy Me Love'. Actually, now I thought about it, they were all pretty appropriate songs for how the evening had progressed. Ha! I thought about sharing that with Ruth; she would understand, Helen wouldn't, but when I turned my head, which was all I could turn once I was pinned into my sleeping bag, I saw she was already asleep.

"Will you swap places with me?" Helen asked, as she yawned the widest yawn.

I was a bit annoyed as I was all cosy, but given what I was planning, it was probably better to be next to the door and I was pleased Helen was talking again.

"Please," she said, when I didn't immediately reply. So, after a bit of wriggling, I obliged.

*   *   *

After twenty minutes or so, once Helen was also asleep, I left the tent. I wasn't spying or anything. I just didn't want things to end quite yet. I snuck back to the periphery of the leaders' area. Adam was sitting on the grass, still playing guitar with Pam listening, and the flames had gone from the fire leaving the embers glowing orange. I spent a while just watching, letting the music fill me up inside. Then I heard voices coming from Colin and Carol's tent and I moved closer.

"Did you want Colin?" Carol was saying, her voice breathy and more high-pitched than usual. "He's just this second gone for a walk, down by the river." Her voice tailed off.

"I... just wanted to check you were OK. You went to bed early." It was Phil's unruffled voice in response and, as I shifted around, crouching low to the grass, I could see his boots sticking out of the side of the tent.

"Yes, yes. All fine," Carol replied, although her staccato delivery suggested something else. "I was just a bit tired. It's a lot of hard work, this camping."

"But you've enjoyed it?" Phil asked.

"Enormously," Carol said. "We were just saying, Colin and I, that we'd love it if we could come next year." Now she sounded more positive, as if she was convincing herself too.

"Oh, well, I'll leave you to get some sleep now."

I noticed that Phil didn't make any promises to her. My mum always says never to make a promise you know you can't keep, even if you do it to be kind. I retreated to the cover of the nearest tree, to ensure I was well and truly out of sight, as Phil raised himself with a groan and trotted back towards his family group.

I heard a rustle and there was someone outside the nearest boys' tent. Danny, torch lodged between his front teeth, was unzipping the canvas, poised to climb back in. As I watched, he sat himself down on the inside ground sheet, pulled off his boots one at a time and deposited them under the fly sheet, as we'd been taught. I saw his face, only for a second, before he extinguished the light, but he seemed to be smiling for the first time that evening.

I had seen enough now to know that I wasn't missing anything. Things were well and truly winding down and what Pam had said was true. They would need us, the senior patrol, to help supervise the packing up, once it was light. I headed back towards my tent, the one I shared with Ruth and Helen, but I decided to walk the other way around the site, past the supplies and the woodpile, just for a bit of variety.

Then I saw it; a figure lying in the grass. Well, at first I just saw the legs, pointing towards me at an acute angle. A couple of steps more and I identified him, because it was certainly a him: Colin, lying on his back, motionless, the axe embedded deep in his forehead, blood streaming through his hair and onto the grass, feeding the earth below.

I wanted to say his name; it fluttered across my lips, but no sound came out. I moved towards him and even the wind held its breath. I knelt down and prodded at his arm, but there was no response. He was well and truly dead. Helen would definitely have screamed but I didn't. Instead, I did what I like to do; I investigated.

I swept my torch the length of Colin's body. About half his shirt buttons were undone and he was wearing only one shoe, and a dart of the light around the surrounding area didn't reveal the missing one. Otherwise, he was fully dressed, the string of feathers wound around the fingers of one hand. As I stood up, my foot knocked against something, something which made a soft clinking sound. It was Colin's golf mug, the one Danny had pinched. 'It takes a lot of balls to golf like me', the slogan read. Not so funny after all. And then I remembered that when Carol had collected in the mugs, in contrast to those of the other Scouts, she hadn't touched Danny's. Instead, she'd lowered the tray and very deliberately pushed it towards him and he'd obliged by nudging the mug to the centre. I'd wondered then if Carol knew Danny had stolen it and she was trying to reassure him, with her gesture, that his secret was safe with her. A further search of the grass revealed a cigarette end. I held it up to my face and the sweet smell confirmed it as one of Adam's.

A person without my superlative sleuthing skills might have concluded, then and there, that Danny or Adam or even both were the culprits; a confrontation between Colin and Danny over the whisky which got out of hand or Adam taking revenge for his earlier humiliation. But I knew better. Even as I scooped the mug off the grass and shoved it back on the tray with the others and pocketed the cigarette butt, pretending it was instinctive – we'd spent the whole week tidying things away which might harm the marauding wildlife - I knew that Carol Marsden had killed her boor of a husband and it was up to me to ensure that neither Danny nor Adam would take the rap.

It was all clear to me now; the pretence at physical weakness, when, caught offguard in the toilet incident, Carol could clearly lift considerable weights; the oversized glasses, so often set aside, a useful adjunct; the sickness, clearly feigned – if you wanted to keep it private, why throw up in full view? – and her panicky chat to Phil just now, in which she'd lied. I'd been hanging around at least fifteen minutes before Phil's arrival and Colin had been distinctly absent. And, if Colin had been going for a night walk, why were his buttons open and where was his shoe? They must have argued when Colin was getting undressed, he had retreated outside and she'd followed him over to the woodpile and decked him with the axe. I could imagine him facing up to her, daring her, never imagining that someone so diminutive could hurt him in any way at all. In fact, on closer scrutiny, and, to be fair, it was a bit hard to be sure because of all the blood, Colin's features, in death, more than hinted at it all having come as a total surprise.

I was about to leave the crime scene, having at least in part thwarted Carol's plans, when I focused for a second on Carol herself. I thought about her first husband having died and her plain ring, even though Colin was a jeweller with a Jaguar, and Danny and the toilet and Colin soaking Adam in the river, and Colin's hand against Helen's back and whatever he had muttered to her in the darkness. And I remembered all the times this week when Colin had ordered Carol around or stopped her from doing something fun or made a joke at her expense, and how she'd complied and said nothing and how her voice had been shaking just now, when she tried to cover up what she'd done. My mum sometimes says "all's fair in love and war" but Colin's behaviour this week didn't seem all that fair to me.

I crept back over to Carol's tent and started to hunt around under the fly sheet. I had to be as quiet as a mouse, as I could hear her inside the tent, rustling around. And then I found it; Colin's shoe. I returned to his body, placed it on his foot and closed the buttons on his shirt.

Only then, when I'd done what little I could to protect Carol, as well as Danny and Adam, did I burst into the remaining group of leaders, seated around the fire. Everyone turned to look at me and, before I spoke, before I said "Colin's dead" and the whole place erupted into pandemonium, I remembered there was one old favourite we hadn't sung this year and I was cross we'd missed it out. The one everyone knows, the one everyone sings, the one in the key of C major which always raises the spirits.

'Campfire's burning, campfire's burning,
    Draw nearer, draw nearer,
    In the glowing, in the glowing,
    Come sing and be merry.'

A SHARP THORN

Alison Joseph

It was the ringing of the landline that shook Emma Collett out of her habitual reverie.

"I'm phoning from Petherick Lodge Care Home. In Truro." The voice was female and polite. "Robert needs to see you. Robert Sinclair."

The name meant nothing.

"He's not got long, to be honest. Dear Bob, he's been asking for you, and I said I'd give you a ring."

"I've never heard of a Robert Sinclair. Who is this?"

"Petherick Lodge—"

"I think you've got the wrong number."

"Is that Emma Collett? In London?"

"Yes."

The voice gave her address. "You worked at Arden-Hanley music publishers?"

She was aware of a nervousness, a quickening of her breath. "Yes," she said, again.

"Robert would so love to see you."

"Really, I've never heard of him."

"You're in the notes. The person who needs to hear his last wishes. For all I know you're in his will as well. Please come. He's a lovely man, we all adore him. He had his seventy-sixth birthday last week, we were so glad he got that far. But he's been ill for a long time."

"Why—" She gathered her thoughts. "Why has he only chosen now to contact me, this Bob, whoever he is?"

"Oh, he said, she won't want to be bothered by me. He's been saying that for a while. But last night..." The voice shook slightly. "Last night, he turned to me and said, please call her. So I am."

"But why…" She stopped. Why everything? Why me? How does he know about my job, my address? Why Cornwall? "I've never been to Cornwall," she said.

"Oh, he's not local. As you know, he retired here, after the move from Kent. He had a happy few years, until the diagnosis. And even then he had a good couple of years after that too. But with the secondaries…" There was a tone of exasperation. "You must know. He's talked of you several times. He said you were all friends. All pottering around old harpsichord workshops, as he put it. You and him and Edmund, you know, Edmund Rundell."

The name caught at her throat, stopped her breath. "I know him. Of course. I knew him very well…"

"Well, then. You will come, won't you?"

"I – I'll ring you back. As soon as I can—" make arrangements, she was going to say, but of course she wasn't going to Cornwall, a dying man had made a mistake, there must be two of us with the same name, it's out of the question…

"Thank you." The voice was warm. "Thank you so much. You've got the number here. My name's Sylvia." A hesitation. "Please – please don't tarry."

A *click.*

Tarry. An old-fashioned word.

Emma hung up. She stared at her phone in its polished cradle on her polished desk. The low sunlight of the London afternoon warmed the deep brown mahogany. Polishing, she thought. Not much else to do these days.

Old harpsichord workshops.

Edmund never 'pottered around'. Edmund went to war, with a sword-sharp resolve. He would prepare, as if for battle. He'd have read an auction house listing, or he'd have had a tip-off from a dealer. He would be quiet, for days. She would put meals in front of him, and he'd eat, distracted, brooding, silent. Then he would disappear for a day or two, and some time after that, there would be a delivery, a lorry appearing at the warehouse gates, an unloading. And then she wouldn't see him for a week or so, as he stayed at the gallery, sleeping on a camp bed, admiring his new acquisition. He'd return home, cheerful, chatty, even. For a while, at least.

★   ★   ★

And anyway, she thought, that part of my life is over. No Edmund. No work, since Arden-Hanley decided it didn't need an archivist anymore. Just a small pension, my visits to the library, and my bi-weekly visits to Mother, Wednesdays and Sundays. No social life. Apart from Georgie, my best friend really, the only other person in the archive department of Arden-Hanley until he managed to escape: "Only due to the death of an aunt, dear girl, I can live in faded splendour for the rest of my days. As those lifestyle coaches always say, there's no such thing as failure, merely opportunity…" Just Georgie. And Mother over in Harrow. Mother who is bored. Won't knit. Won't sew. Won't read. "Oh, these novels you keep giving me, all so sentimental, those ladies in frocks trying to get a husband. And that modern one, that Russian man stuck in a room somewhere, couldn't get on with it. Or was he Ukrainian…? And as for that detective thing, can't remember the story but everyone ended up dead. Apart from the detective. And he was so very dull, it would have been better if he was dead and everyone else was still alive…" Typical of your mother, Georgie said. "If it's not complaining about poor dear Dostoevsky, it's nagging you about dripping taps…"

She stared at the notepad beside her phone.

Sylvia. Petherick Lodge.

It makes no sense at all.

She picked up her phone, clicked on Georgie's number, about to call.

And what would I say?

I'm thinking of going to Cornwall.

She put her phone down.

Ridiculous. Some crazy mistake. I shouldn't let it upset me like this. I've got enough to get on with.

There was a cobweb in the corner of the window frame. She got to her feet, went to find a duster.

"Out to grass," Georgie had said. "Never mind. Something will turn up. Life is like a jigsaw, as I always say. The missing piece always appears just when you need it. Mind you, what do I know? I've got that bloody *View of the Lagoon* painting sitting in bits on my coffee table, been there since my sister gave it to me last Christmas, haven't a clue, frankly, that tiresome Venice sky is all the same shade of blue…"

The cobweb had a spider at its centre. As she touched the thread's edge, the spider uncurled, clawed her way sideways.

She put down the duster.

Her phone pinged with a text. *I assume you've been in touch with the plumber about this tap and just failed to tell me…* She sat down, fired up her laptop, clicked on *Search*. She typed *Robert Sinclair. Truro*.

There was very little. A young CEO of a transport company. An American, author of a novel about the cotton fields of Arkansas, written in 1949. An obituary of a Wiltshire clergyman, dated 1890.

Robert Hugh Sinclair, she read. An entry at Companies House.

Click.

R H Sinclair Ltd. Property services.

There was an address in Chatham, Kent. 'Ironmongers Yard.'

Her hands were tight fists against the keyboard edge.

Ironmongers Yard, Chatham.

How did he – how was that possible?

She remembered it. A cul-de-sac, behind the old dockyard, just off the Gillingham Road.

She searched for the address, found photographs, three luxury flats for sale, a roof terrace, balcony gardens, fabulous estuary views.

It was the same building. Beautifully restored.

She checked the dates. He must have done it up and sold it on. And then retired to Cornwall.

She pushed the laptop away from her as if it was too hot to touch. She snatched up her phone, dialled the number, asked for Sylvia.

"It's me," she said. "Emma. This Robert – when did he say he'd met Edmund Rundell?"

"Well…" A pause for thinking. "He only mentioned you all quite recently. But then, it's like that if you know you don't have long. People want closure."

"Making amends?"

"Amends?" Sylvia laughed. "He's the sweetest, loveliest man. I can't imagine there's anything in his life he would regret."

"Can you ask him, why he wants to see me?"

"Of course. He's asleep at the moment, but we'll bring him a cup of tea later, I'll say we've been in touch, I'll ask him then. He'll be so pleased…"

She rang off. She looked again at the Companies House entry.

Company dissolved seven years ago. He'd bought the old warehouse in Chatham five years before that. She checked the date. April. About fourteen months after…

After I left Edmund.

I wonder why it was sold.

She had a sudden image of the old workshop. High-ceilinged, tall leaded windows, the warm oak tones of the heavy beams, whitewashed walls, rough wooden floor. She remembered slanting afternoon sunlight, a sense of calm, the river not far away.

The wiry, grey-haired man, standing by the instrument. He'd introduced himself as Meyer, "Heinrich Meyer, known to my friends as Harry." He'd talked about the instrument, "A Couchet. Almost certainly Jan Couchet. It's dated 1649…"

Edmund, tall and broad in his black tailored suit, expensive brogues, loud-voiced and adversarial. "I got wind of it through one of my contacts," he said.

"Of course," Mr Meyer had said. "I never advertise."

The harpsichord was beautiful. Delicate, glowing. She saw marbling black and white, exquisite carving, the line of the keys, a glimpse of blue in the decorated lid.

"You have the right space for it?" Mr Meyer said.

Edmund stooped to examine the strings. "I have my collection rooms. Temperature-controlled, electronic blinds…"

"You mean – You won't—" Mr Meyer straightened up. "You won't play it?"

"Play it?" Edmund managed a smile. "My wife here, she'll play it. Won't you, dear?"

Sometimes one of the instruments would be on display at home. She would study the pretty mouldings, the painted wreaths and gilded roses. She'd run her fingers over the delicate keys, careful not to make a sound.

She used to play, early in their marriage. She'd practise, for hours, on her Goble spinet. But Edmund had made her sell it: "A modern travesty," he'd called it. "It offends the eye…"

Now she thought about sitting on a train. Cornwall, she thought. All that coast, that wide-open space.

When she'd left Edmund, she had gone from a well-appointed

Kensington mansion flat, with its white-painted interiors and well-tended gardens, to this. Two small rooms in Belsize Park. "I can't imagine what you think you're doing," Mother had said. "You're not going to find anyone else, not at your age…"

There was no point explaining how it was. That however scared I was of leaving, I was more frightened of staying.

"… All that money from his father's bank. You'll be in poverty the rest of your life. You've never known what's good for you…"

Now she picked up her phone, dialled Georgie, got his voice message. "I need to see you," she said.

"It's like you've slipped into a parallel universe," Georgie said next morning, as he stirred sugar into his black coffee. "None of it makes sense."

They were sitting in an upstairs room in their favourite Soho haunt, Georgie, in his crisp white shirt and worn grey Savile Row suit, on first name terms with the waiting staff as usual: "Guido, dear boy, how are things, did you ever manage to get rid of the puppies, how the hell were you to know that ghastly fluffy thing was female and not a male… ah, well, pedigree at least, I bet that makes up for the pittance that Antonio pays you here…"

He turned to her. "Have you booked your train?"

"No, of course not."

"You should. Nothing to keep you here. Think of it as a holiday…"

A holiday. She'd spent the evening before on her laptop, searching train times, ticket prices, seaside hotels, car hire… "But what am I going to say to him?" she said. "He's a dying man, he'll set eyes on me and realise he's made a terrible mistake, it's not me he wants to see at all; there's a muddle with the names or something, it'll be awful, embarrassing, and so unkind to the poor man too…"

"But if you don't – you'll never know. Ooh, it's all so interesting. So – this property man ended up with the old piano mender's workshop. Perhaps he's going to leave you his fortune."

"Of course he isn't. He doesn't know me. And anyway, I don't want it. I was perfectly all right before that phone call."

"If I may say so, I don't think you are. Look at that, the best brioche in town and you're leaving it untouched. I think you're furious. With our ex-employers. With Edmund, given that he ended up with everything. With your mother. Just because you've spent your life feeling that you don't deserve to be happy—"

"Georgie—"

"Well, it's true." He took a cigarette out of its packet. "Edmund always did mistake possession for love. True of you. True of his priceless collection of instruments. Which I'm sure he's still got. Wherever he is now. Brazil, was it? Croatia?" He placed the unlit cigarette between his lips. "You were brave to escape."

"And you were brave to help me."

He nodded. "True that. I mean, I know we're old friends but as for laying down one's life…"

She laughed. "I'm fine as I am. I don't mind my own company."

"No, of course. But have it by the sea. Coastal walks. Borrow a dog. Get one of Guido's ghastly fluffy puppies…"

"Don't be silly—"

"OK, not the dog. But give yourself a break. Put this weird thing to rest. Then, you can come back to London and get on with the rest of your life."

On Wednesday morning Emma Collett boarded a train at Paddington Station.

"Business?" her mother had said, on the phone. "What kind of business can you possibly have in Cornwall?"

She had found herself being accountable, again, stuttering, again. "An old colleague, from the music publishing days…"

"Oh, it's all moved on since then," her mother had said. She could see her, in her high-backed armchair, the airy wave of her ringed hand, her nails still painted scarlet. "I can't imagine anyone will take you seriously now, someone like you… Still, if that's preferable to coming to see me, it's up to you, I suppose I'll manage till Sunday…"

Someone like me, she thought. She could see her reflection in the train window, a flickering, muslin-thin image, the collar of her pale blue jacket, her favourite ceramic beads at her neck. Smooth grey hair, lined face…

It's not a bad look, Georgie would often say. "Flinty survivors, both of us. There are worse looks."

The hired car was a Vauxhall Corsa, compact and silver. She put her small neat case into the boot and set off into town.

I haven't driven a car for years, she thought.

On the ring road out towards the suburbs she almost exceeded the forty-mile-per-hour speed limit.

Petherick Lodge Care Home had an ornate wrought-iron sign and a wide gravel drive.

She got out of the car.

The air seemed salty, the sunshine brighter.

She thought about Venetian blue skies.

She walked up the steps, with their pots of bright flowers either side, violas and primroses. She rang the bell.

Sylvia was round-faced and broad, with tight black curls of hair, edged with grey, and eyes that were wet with tears.

"Oh, my dear, I'm so sorry. 'He's – oh, dear. We told him you were coming, but… Sometimes it's just too late."

She showed her into a lounge. There were turquoise armchairs with golden yellow cushions, a sprawling lily in a pot that was too small for it. A flat, low sunlight filtered through the dusty air.

"Such a lovely man," Sylvia was saying. "At least he knew you were on your way." She dabbed at her eyes. "You're very welcome to see him, if you like. He's in our chapel of rest."

Robert Hugh Sinclair was wearing his pyjamas. He lay under a neatly folded sheet, his hands resting on the edge of it. His eyes were closed, his mouth slightly open, his skin flattened out, as if something had departed from him, closed him down. His pyjamas were high quality, she thought, grey with a maroon stripe. He had been tall, she thought, lean.

"He looks good, doesn't he," Sylvia said. "He died peacefully. Breathed his last. A good man. It shows on their faces," she said.

Emma turned to her. "Thank you," she said. "I'm glad to see him."

"He wanted you to have this." Sylvia pressed a CD into her hands. "Music. It was important to him. He said it was important to you too. There's a photograph too."

Emma looked at the CD. Harpsichord music, the name of a performer she didn't know. Merullo. Frescobaldi.

She turned the photograph over in her fingers.

"Oh—"

The photo showed a harpsichord, standing in a workshop, its lid open. The harpsichord had a sledge hammer driven into its centre. Strings hung loose, strips of wood cut jagged-edged across the gaping hole.

She couldn't speak.

"There's the funeral, of course," Sylvia said, as they walked back along the corridor. Emma concentrated on putting one foot in front of the other.

"Mr Sinclair's solicitor here is organizing things; here's his number. I'm sure he'll want to hear from you…"

On the doorstep they shook hands. "Thank you," Emma managed to say. "I'm so glad to have seen him."

"A lovely man. We'll miss him." Sylvia briefly touched her arm, then turned and went inside.

She drove fast, reached the coast. She parked in a windswept and deserted car park at the back of a caravan site. She switched off the engine, leaned back against the seat. The sun had disappeared. The sky was heavy with rain.

She stared at the photograph.

Robert Hugh Sinclair. A man I never met. What did you know?

She put the CD in the music system, pressed *Play*. The notes filled the air around her.

Frescobaldi. *Toccata Terza*.

On the rocks beneath, the sea raged against the shore.

Thirteen years ago. They had driven to Kent, together. We'll do it in a day, Edmund had said, no need to stay over, I'll beat the man down, we'll get the sale, drive back the same day…

Why do you need me there, she'd wanted to say, why not go alone as usual? Edmund had said something about a softer approach, I know what this Mr Meyer will be like, I've met his kind before…

"You need me to play," she'd said. He'd laughed, his empty, brittle laugh.

"My captive songbird," he'd said.

She switched off the music. She got out of the car, walked across the car park. She sat on a rock, watching the crashing of the foaming waves, feeling the cold rain against her face.

Mr Meyer had taken her by the hand, sat her down at the harpsichord. "Your husband says you will play."

Her fingertips felt their way to the bone-white keys, the dark bog oak sharps. In spite of the clench of fear, she began to play.

"You play very well," Mr Meyer said. "The *Toccata Terza*. Not many people can play as well as you."

Edmund was smiling his false indulgent smile.

Mr Meyer sat down next to her, placed long fingers on the keyboard. "A meantone temperament... Of course, the lowest note, here, looks like bottom C but sounds bottom F – you'll know this, of course. It gives you the perfect major third..." He played a few notes, his hands caressing the keys. "And the painting in the lid," he said, "almost certainly Italian – this instrument had a cultured journey. And it's an external scene, unusual for an Annunciation..."

Robert Sinclair, lying there in his pyjamas. Wanting me to hear this music, again. An ordinary, sweet businessman, retired to Cornwall. What did he know?

She thought about Georgie and his missing jigsaw piece.

She jumped up, chilled by the rain, by the memories. She went back to her car. She shook out her wet hair, pulled out her phone, dialled the solicitor's number and spoke to a young woman who promised to pass on her details, Mr Lethbridge is arranging everything, "a small funeral, a cremation, probably on Friday..."

She drove to her hotel in silence, with only the rhythm of the windscreen wipers against the driving rain.

A flash of memory. Cleaning Edmund's shoes. Scrubbing the black leather, the mud that wouldn't come off.

The Wyndham Guest House had a bright conservatory breakfast room. Emma ate an uncharacteristically large plateful of eggs, bacon and mushrooms, and felt her spirits lift in spite of the chill and drizzle of the Thursday morning. "Well, you're on holiday now," Barbara said as she brought in more toast. Barbara ran the guest house with her husband

Kevin: "We retired from Wetherby four years ago, never looked back. I know I'll always be a Yorkshirewoman, but what with my joints I decided it were better to be a Yorkshirewoman in Cornwall…"

★   ★   ★

Later that day Georgie rang. She was walking along the high street, wondering about an ice-cream.

"What are you doing with yourself? How's the jigsaw?"

"Nothing but blue sky," she said. "You'd hate it."

He laughed. "Found a Chihuahua yet?"

"I don't need one. I walk. I think. I admire the shops. Lovely ceramics. A very good cake shop. And a florists, I keep nearly buying myself flowers."

"All very healthy. All that sea air. You're eating?"

"Yes. And the sun's come out now."

"And – Mr Sinclair – now dead, according to your text—"

She sat on the wall by the ice cream shop.

"Mr Sinclair left me a photograph of the harpsichord that Edmund tried to buy, that time in Chatham. But – it's got a hammer through its innards."

"Whoah."

"Exactly."

"That is weird."

"The lid's open. The painting inside seems unharmed. I remember it, I remember from when I was playing it for that dealer, with Edmund standing there pretending not to mind that I was touching the keys…"

"He can still get to you, can't he?"

She was silent. She could see the beach, hear the barking of two dogs as they chased each other round and round.

"He was sweet, that restorer," she said. "Heinrich Meyer. Slight German accent, I remember." She took a breath. "The thing is, Georgie – I keep having this memory," she said. "Afterwards. When Edmund went back, a few days later, to try to get Mr Meyer to change his mind… It's worrying me."

"Dear girl, it's a jigsaw. Enjoy it. And you'll be at the funeral?"

Stuart Lethbridge had phoned that morning. "It'll be a direct cremation, all arranged, so glad you'll still be here, it'll be nice to have someone in attendance even with no service or anything, although we are hoping to play some of his favourite music…"

"Yes," she said. "The funeral's tomorrow. I'll come home on Saturday."

"Ah. In time to see Mother on Sunday. How many missed calls so far?" he said.

"Three," she said. "But I haven't answered yet."

"That's the spirit."

She laughed, then, as a third dog joined the chase, accompanied by the shouts of hapless owners.

That evening she sat in her comfortable room, her laptop open, looking at Italian religious art. The sea was a distant, calming whisper, and the air was warm. She put on the CD, and the Frescobaldi filled the air.

"Play some more," Mr Meyer had said. She played the notes of a madrigal, something she'd learned years ago. *Tra le rose d'amor, pungente spina.*

Mr Meyer looked at her. "A sharp thorn amid love's roses," he'd said. "Also by the master."

A woman came into the room. She had dark eyes, long black hair tied back, a long black dress over which she wore a white linen apron. She stood, silent, as Emma continued to play.

After a moment Emma glanced up at Edmund. He stood rigid, blank-faced, fists clenched at his sides. She stopped playing.

Mr Meyer got to his feet. He looked straight at Edmund. He closed the lid of the instrument.

"I won't sell," he said. "Not to you."

"What do you mean, you won't sell?" Edmund stepped towards him. "I came here to buy it. Name your price."

"It has no price," Mr Meyer said.

The woman was standing to one side, silent.

Mr Meyer faced Edmund. "We are only the guardians," he said. "We are the guardians of the things we love. Possession is nothing. Without love, there is nothing."

Edmund opened his mouth to speak.

Mr Meyer turned to her. "I'm sorry it can't be yours," he said to her.

"I would like the thought of you playing it each day. But I know that while you are with this man it cannot be like that." He turned back to Edmund. "I cannot sell it to you."

There had been shouting, then, as Edmund grabbed her arm, pulled her to her feet. "We're going," he'd said, dragging her towards the door. "We're not staying here with this phoney restoration merchant, who doesn't know what he's dealing with—"

She remembered his rough grip on her arm as she was dragged out of the door.

She remembered the housekeeper, her silent, fearful look.

She had looked back at Mr Meyer. He'd clicked his heels and bowed, a calm smile in his blue eyes. She knew then, that he had seen things for what they were. She knew, with a strange and sudden certainty, that she would leave Edmund.

On the morning of the funeral, she went to the florists and bought a large bunch of white flowers, lilies and roses.

The brick walls of the crematorium were bright in the sunlight. As the bearers lifted the coffin from the hearse, she placed the flowers on top of it.

There were two other mourners, a man she assumed was Stuart Lethbridge, and Sylvia from the care home, who nodded a smile at her. They took their seats. A young woman appeared and sat down quietly at the back.

The music began to play, an aria from Bach's *St. Matthew Passion*, '*Erbarme dich, mein Gott*'. Emma looked at the coffin and found herself weeping. For a man I never met. Or for myself, she thought.

The music came to an end. After some minutes of silence, the coffin slid away and the curtains were drawn. Mr Lethbridge turned to leave. The young woman approached him, and they engaged in muted, affectionate conversation as they walked out into the cloister.

Outside in the sun, Emma introduced herself. "Mr Lethbridge?"

"Ah, Miss Collett. I'm glad you could be here. He often spoke of you towards the end. This is Mairead Kelly, his cousin's daughter, his next of kin."

The young woman had tousled blonde hair, a blue floral dress. She gave a shy smile. "I always say I'm his niece, it's easier. And he was like an uncle to me."

"She knows all about Mr Sinclair's last wishes."

Mairead looked up at her. "Shall we go for coffee?"

The café on the high street had a terrace with red-and-white-striped parasols. They sat in silence. Mairead had a large mug of coffee with a pile of whipped cream on the top. "I don't really like coffee, that's why," she said. "Lots of cream. And sugar." She looked up at Emma. She took a deep breath. "What made you answer his call?" she said.

"Because," she began. "Because there's something he knew, that I also need to know."

"The harpsichord," Mairead said. "It's at his house."

Emma put down her cup.

"My uncle – he loved buildings. He'd wanted to be an architect but his family were poor. So he went into business, created his own property company and did very well, and I guess his love of buildings was expressed that way…"

Mairead was still talking, about how her uncle had paid for her studies, how she was doing History of Art, and now he'd left her his house, how kind he was, how much he'd given to charity, to Sylvia at the care home…

In her mind, Emma could see the shoes. Edmund's black brogues. Scrubbing and scrubbing. The mud that wouldn't come off.

"Come on." Mairead got to her feet. "Let's go."

*   *   *

The harpsichord stood in the centre of the room. The floor was polished wood, the walls painted a deep blue-grey.

She ventured towards it.

"Still broken, of course. But no hammer now," Mairead said. "Robert removed it when he found it all those years ago."

Emma sat at the stool. The wood was splintered, the strings ripped apart. She touched a key, and a hoarse croak sounded in the air.

She looked up at Mairead. "I know," she said. "I know who broke it."

*   *   *

Edmund had dragged her out of the workshop, down the stairs, still shouting. "What the hell did you think you were doing, flirting like that, madrigals about fucking roses…" He'd pushed her into the car, driven back to London with his foot on the accelerator and his hand on the horn. She had felt sick with fear, a fear that didn't leave her in all the days that followed, as she quietly met his needs, quietly made her secret plans.

The following Sunday, he said he was going back to Kent. He had to have that Couchet, he'd said. It went with the Ruckers, the Andreas double.

That night he was away. She had sat, alone, in the dark chill of their white-painted bedroom. She remembered Mr Meyer's bow, his bright blue gaze, as she had been dragged out of his workshop.

A captive songbird.

At the end of the next day, Edmund had come home.

She had put dinner in front of him, a risotto. She'd poured him a glass of Amarone. He was tense, agitated, his breath short, his hair awry. "He wouldn't sell," was all he said. "He refused to sell."

Later she had found his shoes, left on the shoe rack behind the door, his trousers hung on the coat hooks. They were wet up to the knee. She had dried them out, pressed them. She thought about the harpsichord, and Heinrich Meyer, and his refusal to sell.

*　　*　　*

And now she sat by the same harpsichord, and touched the soundless keys.

"The shoes," she said. "Edmund's shoes. I couldn't get them clean."

Mairead was standing by the window. She turned to Emma. "My uncle used to say, every building tells a story. It's written in the bricks, in the cracks in the walls, he'd say."

"But how—?"

"Mr Meyer had a housekeeper," Mairead said. "Chesa. She was still there, when my uncle bought the building. She was kind of hiding out. She wasn't legal, she'd come from the Philippines, Mr Meyer had given her a home, but she didn't have any papers. She was terrified. But my uncle employed her, sorted out all her citizenship, she grew very fond of him. She married in the end, an Englishman, they settled in Broadstairs.

We're still in touch, Christmas cards, you know, photos of her kids... But – when he started on the conversion of the workshop floor, she wouldn't go near it. 'Very bad thing,' she kept saying. She talked of evil spirits. Ghosts, she said. Hauntings."

Emma felt cold, in spite of the sunlight in the room. "I remember her," she said. "Chesa. I met her."

Mairead gave a brief nod of her head. "My uncle asked her about it. Of course, it was where he'd found the broken harpsichord, with the hammer still embedded in it. But she was never very clear. She said, a man came. Very angry man. Shouting. And then one day he came back. But she said, on that day, she wasn't there. Church, she said. And when she got home her employer was nowhere to be seen, and the harpsichord had a hammer in its midst. After that, she had nowhere to go, so she stayed.

"My uncle acquired the building about a year later. It had been repossessed by the owners, they sold it on. Mr Meyer was thought to have gone abroad, he had a place near Genoa where he'd often stay. Robert and Chesa made enquiries but couldn't trace him. But he couldn't forget the moment when he unlocked the workshop, when he found the harpsichord with the hammer still in it. He said, he had a feeling that someone had got away with something."

Emma's fingertips were numb as she stroked the keys.

Very angry man.

"I should have known," she said. "I knew what Edmund was capable of, when thwarted." She shivered. "I should have called Mr Meyer, checked he was all right."

"But – how could you have known?"

"Because – because it was Mr Meyer who set me free. I owe him a lot."

She stood up. She went to the lid, studied the painting. She turned to Mairead. "But – how did your uncle track me down?"

"Chesa had kept the records of the visitors to the workshop, a kind of visitors' book. When my uncle retired, he brought the harpsichord with him, and also the book. So, when he didn't have long, he asked me to go through the names in the book, from around the time that Heinrich Meyer disappeared. And we tracked you down. Amazing, what the internet will tell you. And he decided to get the home to phone you.

Nothing to lose, as he said. That's what he was like. Interested, curious. He said that every brick is part of a story, like doing jigsaw puzzles."

"He would have liked my friend Georgie," Emma said.

Together, they lifted the lid. The painting, undamaged, shone outward. Our Lady, receiving flowers from the Angel Gabriel.

"Mr Meyer said it was Italian," Emma said.

"Bologna, I reckon," Mairead said. "One of those women, school of Elisabetta Sirani. It explains the joy of it, that earthy-looking woman in that plain blue dress with that beautiful villa. And the flowers…"

The Virgin was holding a rose, with a thick stem.

A sharp thorn amid love's roses.

"All that blue sky," Mairead said, and Emma smiled.

"Still there, then," Georgie said on the phone, two days later.

She was sitting on the wall, by the paved path which led to the beach. "Lovely weather," she said. "And Sunday, all the church bells ringing…"

"What did Mother say?"

"Nothing. Shock, I think. I told her I'm thinking of settling here."

"Speechless? Heavens, that's a first. Well, dear girl, whatever cottage you buy has got to have a clear white wall for that painting to look its best. And as for space for the harpsichord—"

"The funny thing is, Mairead has done some research, and we think it might be a fake."

"A fake? After all that?"

"She thinks Mr Meyer was testing Edmund in more ways than one."

"Poor man," Georgie said.

"Poor man." She watched a group of children who were running in and out of the red-and-white parasols. "Robert Sinclair worked out that Edmund must have driven a hammer into the instrument, and then felled Mr Meyer too, in his terrible rage. And then somehow driven the body out to the estuary, and disposed of him there. But Mairead has an ex-partner in the police, she said. Still on good terms. She's going to make some enquiries. Missing persons, unidentified bodies. Criminal harpsichord collectors in Rio de Janeiro, that kind of thing."

"If he's still alive," Georgie said. "Well done you for being a flinty survivor—"

"And the funny thing is," she said, "Robert Sinclair had all the clues. Like a detective, only he was the one who was dead."

"Well, I guess your mother will be pleased about that, at least."

She laughed, promised to ring soon, put her phone back in her bag.

And now, she walks along the sea shore. She thinks about the cottage she might buy. A slate roof, a little garden, a sea view. The painting, in splendour, on a plain white wall.

All that blue sky.

She thinks, perhaps I'll get a dog after all.

With thanks to Tim Boon and Christopher Clarke

WRONG NOTES

Andrew Taylor

"And what about the concert at the High School?" Amy Gwyn-Thomas asked.

"We'd better send someone," Jill Francis said.

"Jim Potter's ill. And David has the parish council in Trenalt."

"I can't go," Jill said firmly. "The Cub can do it."

"The Cub?" Her secretary compressed her lips. "Do you think he's up to it?"

"He's keen enough, isn't he? We may as well get some use out of him."

"He's very *young*."

"He's all but eighteen. Plenty of teenagers start work when they're much younger than that."

"But he can't even make tea properly. The only thing he's done is set fire to the wastepaper basket. He could have burned down the whole building."

"He's wondering about becoming a journalist after he's done his National Service," Jill said. "He could do worse. This will be good practice."

Amy snorted. Somewhere in the building a telephone was ringing, and a typewriter was spraying letters like bullets at unseen targets.

"Tell him to come and see me at twelve o'clock," Jill went on. "I'll make sure he knows exactly what he has to do. Now may I have my letters, please?"

Amy gave a start, remembering why she was here in the first place. She put down the morning's post on the desk and automatically tore a page from Jill's desk calendar. Thursday, 5 July 1956.

Jill lit a cigarette while Amy retreated to her own office next door. To some extent, she shared her secretary's reservations about the Cub, but someone had to cover the concert. She was damned if she would do it herself. Being the editor of the *Lydmouth Gazette* had one or two perks, and delegation was one of them.

*   *   *

The Cub's name was Roderick Hanbridge. He had left his boarding school abruptly in the middle of last term, after what Charlotte called 'an incident'. The nature of the incident remained mysterious, but it provided Amy with ample opportunity for pleasurable speculation. Charlotte, who was friendly with Roderick's mother, had asked Jill as a favour to take the boy as an unpaid trainee for a few months. Since Charlotte was the major shareholder in the *Gazette*, a request from her was tantamount to a command.

Before his abrupt departure from school, Roderick had been studying for his A levels in English and Art. The boy was not academic, Charlotte had confided, but English had been his best subject at school, so far as that went. However, even his mother admitted that it would have been a miracle if he had achieved a pass in either subject. Rather than send him to a crammer, Charlotte said, his parents felt that working for a few months in the Real World would be a more valuable preparation for Life. The words were Charlotte's, but Jill added the initial capitals in the privacy of her own mind.

"His mother tells me he's learning shorthand already," Charlotte said. "So he's obviously as keen as mustard."

*   *   *

The Cub sauntered into Jill's office at four minutes past twelve.

"Sorry I'm late," he said, treating her to a smile.

She waved him towards the visitor's chair. He sat down, crossed his legs and looked about him. Unlike most teenagers, he seemed fully formed, rather than a work in progress. He was a good-looking boy with thick dark hair, clear blue eyes and regular features. He was conservatively dressed in a blazer and flannels, with a knitted tie and a pair of gleaming Oxfords.

"How are you getting on?" she asked.

"Fine, thanks. It's awfully good of you to let me work here." He gave her a rueful glance. "I'm afraid I made a bit of a fool of myself yesterday. Did you hear about the wastepaper basket?"

"We all make mistakes. Are your lodgings all right?"

He nodded. "I've been working on my shorthand in the evenings, as you said. I've started dreaming it now. All those little squiggles marching down the pad. Why's it always easier to write it down than to read it back?"

"That's always the way. Now – it's time for you to do some real work."

His face brightened. "A proper job? Real reporting?"

"Are you free this evening?"

"Of course. Any time. What is it?"

His eagerness was endearing. Jill wondered how long it would last. "There's a concert at the High School. I need three hundred words by tomorrow morning. We'll be sending a photographer along as well. It's the first concert they've had for a year or two, and so it's quite a big occasion for them."

"I used to sing a bit myself, actually, when… when I was at school."

"You need to get down as many names as possible. For heaven's sake, make sure they are spelled right. The headmistress is Dr Margaret Hilly – she'll be there, and she'll probably say something. Get a quote from her, and perhaps from the music mistress. Say what's on the programme. 'Something for everyone' is always a good line to take. Oh, and try to find out if Lady Ruispidge is in the audience. Local worthy, always gets a mention if she's there."

"Lady Ruispidge?" The Cub grinned at her. "I think she's some sort of cousin of my ma's."

Ah, Jill thought, that explains why Charlotte was quite so keen to do your mother a favour.

*   *   *

The main entrance of Lydmouth High School for Girls was in Narth Road. Roddy strolled along the pavement, admiring the legs of two girls walking ahead. He lit a cigarette. It was a fine, warm evening and he was in good time. He had taken the precaution of fortifying himself with a quick pint in the Bathhurst Arms beforehand.

It was an awful pity that he had to go into the army for a couple of years. But perhaps learning shorthand would come in handy. They had newspapers for the Forces, didn't they? So they must have their own journalists. If he played his cards right, he could come out of National Service and walk straight into a good job in Civvy Street.

To his surprise, Roddy was enjoying shorthand. Who would have thought it at school? He felt a pleasing superiority to his former friends, trapped in that ghastly prison where the only females were Matron and the maids, who were all at least forty and as ugly as sin. Here he was in the real world, a free man with beer in his belly, a cigarette in the corner of his mouth, and two nice girls almost near enough to touch.

Finally, he thought, he was getting somewhere, after all the confusion and uncertainty of the last few months. Getting booted out of school might turn out to be a blessing in disguise. This journalism business had a lot to recommend it – variety, meeting interesting people, being the first to know what was going on. Jim Potter wasn't much older than he was, and already he was earning decent money.

But if Roddy was going to be a journalist, he needed to show people that he was up to the job, keen to succeed. Starting tonight. This was his first story, his first chance to show what he could do.

People and cars were turning into the school drive. To the left was a long block of what were probably classrooms. To the right were two other buildings, together with a cluster of small ones. Beyond them stretched the playing fields.

As Roddy walked up the drive, slowing his pace to keep behind the two girls, a Daimler glided past them. All was not well with it. An ominous rumbling mingled with the soft growl of the engine. The rear offside tyre was flat. Through the open windows came the sound of voices, a man's and a woman's. The man was muttering something inaudible, but the woman's crisp, powerful tones effortlessly drowned his words.

"I'm sorry, but it's simply not convenient to leave now…"

The Daimler passed on. It came to a fork and continued to the right, towards the large freestanding hall that seemed to be everyone's destination. The car came to a halt, temporarily blocking the drive.

A plump, middle-aged woman walked rapidly over the grass towards it. Adults and parents scattered before her. A man beside Roddy said something under his breath and looked at his watch with a swift, impatient movement of his arm. He was spare and middle-aged, with a lean face and greying hair. He looked blankly at Roddy for an instant, as if Roddy wasn't there at all, and then made a curving detour across the lawn towards the entrance of the hall.

After a moment, Roddy followed. They joined the queue by the door. Two older girls in yellow sashes were taking the tickets. Prefects? The one on the left was nothing in particular, but the one on the right was quite a looker.

"Yes, she's already here, Mr Thornhill," the nothing-in-particular girl was saying to the man ahead. "She left your ticket with us. She's near the front, I think – she was early."

The man thanked her. He crossed the foyer and went through the double doors beyond. Roddy showed his press ticket to the girl on the right. She looked up at him, and he saw her eyes widen, just a fraction. Here was another advantage of being a journalist. You were someone. Girls noticed you. She waved him forward.

"Thanks," he said, lingering. "Are seats reserved for press or can I go anywhere?"

"Front row. The photographer's already there. Would you like a programme?"

"Please."

She gave him one, and their hands touched for a quick, electric moment. The programmes were sixpence each. "On the house," she said.

He looked into her eyes and said with his best smile, "Thanks so much."

She coloured slightly. She had big tits, too. He would have liked to prolong the moment, but people were pressing behind him. Perhaps he'd find her later. His mind filled with vague but pleasurable possibilities.

The hall was already crowded. There was a stage at the far end. The curtains were open, and an upright piano stood to one side. Music stands had been drawn up in two lines across the stage as if to repel an attack. The air was full of conversations, shuffling feet, coughs and, briefly, a solitary bray of laughter. The windows were open.

Roddy made his way down the central gangway. Ahead of him, the man called Thornhill was edging himself along a row about halfway down, murmuring apologies, and causing a ripple of movement like wind in the corn among the people he disturbed. A woman looked up at him with a smile. A girl was sitting next to her, apparently absorbed in the programme on her lap. Just a kid; too young to be interesting.

Many of the seats at the front were already occupied. The others had *Reserved* signs. At the far left, a man in a corduroy jacket was fiddling with an open camera. Roddy approached and cleared his throat. The man looked up.

"Hello – are you the photographer from the *Gazette*?"

The man nodded and bent his head over the camera again. He was feeding a film onto the spool.

"I'm Roddy Hanbridge." He wondered whether he should start calling himself 'Rod'. 'Roddy' sounded a bit schoolboyish. "I'm here to—"

"I know – they told me." The photographer closed the camera back and thrust out a hand. "Steve. I won't stay long after they start. I just need a few pictures, and that's me done." He grinned. "But you're here for the duration, eh? Poor sod."

He went back to his camera, leaving Roddy to his own devices. On this side of the hall, the windows looked across a small car park to the green sweep of the playing fields. One of the cars parked on the tarmac was the Daimler. The driver had climbed out. He was a brawny man wearing a chauffeur's uniform. He removed his peaked cap, revealing close-cropped hair and small ears that stuck out at right angles. With jerky, overemphatic movements, he unbuttoned his jacket and put it in the car. Next, he took out the spare tyre and a set of tools. He propped the tyre against the wing of the car, chose a spanner and crouched down to loosen the wheelnuts.

As Roddy watched, a girl with a yellow sash approached the Daimler. He couldn't see her face, but he was almost sure that she was the nothing-in-particular girl who had been taking the tickets in the foyer. She stopped beside the chauffeur, who looked up at her.

Whatever she said to him, the chauffeur didn't like it. He straightened to his full height. The girl shied away. The man spat and threw the spanner on the ground with a clatter. He reached inside the car for his jacket, from which he removed his wallet and cigarettes. He walked off, leaving the car windows open, the spare wheel leaning against the wing, and the tools scattered on the tarmac.

That girl brought him a message, Roddy thought, probably from the woman he was driving, and it made him even more pissed off than he was already.

Another part of him thought: I'm already acting like a real reporter.

*　　*　　*

When Richard Thornhill sat down, his wife smiled at him over the top of Elizabeth's head. She was relieved to see him. They both knew that police work was by its very nature often unpredictable. He hadn't been sure he would be able to come. If the truth be known, he hadn't wanted to, either. But he knew that this occasion meant a great deal to Edith, though he couldn't really understand why. She said that parents had an important role to play at a school like this.

On Edith's left was a couple, presumably parents, whom Thornhill didn't recognise. The boy he had seen by the Daimler was walking along the line of reserved seats in the front row. He was carrying what looked like a shorthand pad. Thornhill watched him shaking hands with the *Gazette* photographer. A reporter? He didn't look old enough to shave.

"Terribly stuffy, isn't it?" Edith's neighbour fanned herself with the programme.

"Isn't it?" Edith said. "Is your daughter singing tonight?"

"Yes, she is. And yours?"

"No. She's joining the school next term, aren't you, dear?"

Elizabeth pretended to be absorbed in the programme. The tip of her ear was pink. She had been even less enthusiastic about the concert than her father.

A clatter outside made Thornhill look to his left, towards the open window. The Daimler's chauffeur slammed the car door shut and strode off. He looked overheated too.

"Ah," the woman said. "At last. Here's Dr Hilly."

The headmistress marched onto the stage. Behind her drooped the tall, thin figure of the music teacher: patches of sweat were already visible on her dress, which was made of an unfortunate chintzy material that gave her a passing resemblance to an upended sofa. She was followed by nineteen girls, who varied widely in size and shape. They took up their position behind the music stands.

Silence rolled swiftly over the audience like a depression over Dogger Bank. Dr Hilly briskly thanked everyone for coming and Miss Furnish, the music teacher, for organising the concert.

"The school's musical tradition is very important to us all. It's delightful that our concerts have started again, and for this we must thank Miss Furnish."

The music mistress stared at the planks at her feet, as if hoping they would open up and permit the comfortable darkness beneath to swallow her.

"And we have a very special guest with us tonight," Dr Hilly went on. "I shall leave you all in suspense as to his or her identity. But I believe I have persuaded this— this guest to perform for us at the end of the evening, with a little assistance from Miss Furnish."

At this point the music mistress emitted a muffled but perfectly audible squawk. Her expression suggested that the alteration to the programme had come as a surprise to her as much as to everyone else. After a few more well-chosen words that left no room for disagreement, Dr Hilly promised them all a feast of song and marched down the steps from the stage.

"Poor Miss Furnish," the woman whispered. "They say she's had her troubles, and this won't help."

One of the girls sat down at the piano. The music mistress raised her baton with an air of supplication rather than command. The piano struck an opening chord, and the singers launched into a reedy and sorrowful rendition of 'Begone, Dull Care!', followed (according to the programme) by Morley's 'Now is the Month of Maying', during which the singers sounded confused about who should be singing which part. Next came Campion's 'Never Weather-Beaten Sail'. That was the point when it became apparent to almost everyone in the hall that the piano was no longer quite in tune.

"It's so unfair," Edith's neighbour whispered. "You can hardly hear Jean at all. She's the little one at the end. It's the fault of that red-headed girl beside her. She's shrieking away at the top of her lungs, and she can't even hit the high notes properly."

At last it was time for the interval. With indecent haste, the audience poured out of the hall in search of refreshments, a quiet smoke or merely a little peace and quiet. The Thornhills joined the exodus. Edith went in search of the lavatory while Thornhill and Elizabeth joined the queue for coffee and orange squash. He noticed the baby reporter deep in conversation with one of the yellow-sashed prefects. Elizabeth caught sight of a girl she knew and sidled away to talk to her.

A few minutes later, Edith returned. "When I was in there," she murmured to Thornhill, "I couldn't help overhearing Dr Hilly talking to Miss Furnish. It was most embarrassing. The window was open, you see, and they were just outside. It was very odd. Miss Furnish sounded quite upset."

"About the piano? Or the singing?"

"Partly. But more because of the guest. It's completely messed up the programme. This guest – it's a she, by the way – wants Miss Furnish to accompany her on the piano. But the poor woman hasn't practised the pieces, and anyway she was saying that it wouldn't be fair on her girls. And of course there's the problem of the piano. Which is all Dr Hilly's fault, because she wouldn't let them hire a decent grand. Miss Furnish sounded distraught. In the end, she said she wouldn't play."

"Poor woman," Thornhill said. "But why's it so odd?"

"Because of what Dr Hilly said next. She said, 'Yes, you will. You're still on probation, after what happened last term.' And then someone banged on the door of my cubicle, and I had to go."

Half a dozen prefects were now circling the audience like sheepdogs, driving them back into the hall and sweeping the Thornhills along with the rest of their flock. Among them, Thornhill saw with faint surprise, was the Daimler's chauffeur. He was in his shirtsleeves and he had lost his tie. His face was red, and he smelled strongly of whisky and mints. He shouldered his way to the back of the hall and leaned against the wall.

The second half of the concert opened with Farmer's 'Fair Phyllis', which to everyone's relief was sung without piano accompaniment. So too were the Negro Spirituals that followed. The singers went down by the riverside, where they asked for some of that old-time religion and later urged Michael to row the boat ashore. Returning to dry land, they swung low in the sweet chariot. Finally, this section of the programme concluded with 'Dem Bones', the prophet Ezekiel's guide to human anatomy.

Perhaps it was the absence of the piano. Perhaps it was the tunes. Perhaps it was a kindly impulse of sympathy. Whatever the reason, the audience responded with more enthusiasm than they had yet shown, and Miss Furnish looked almost happy.

Then Dr Hilly marched up the steps to the stage, followed by a large lady with tightly permed dark hair. She was carrying a folder of music under her arm.

"What a splendid concert this has been," Dr Hilly told the audience.

"A round of applause for Miss Furnish and her girls." When the clapping died away, she continued, "Now we move away from the programme for a very special treat. Ladies and gentleman, girls and boys, let me introduce my old college friend, the mezzo soprano Miss Hermione Pilton. I know most of you will have been delighted by her voice already, because she regularly broadcasts on the Third Programme. She dropped in to see me this afternoon on her way back from a private performance in Cardiff, and I prevailed on her to sing for us. More than that, she has agreed to talk to the entire school about her life and work tomorrow morning after assembly."

To express her gratitude, Dr Hilly began to clap, and the audience, cowed by her personality, joined in. In the middle of this, a door slammed at the back of the hall. Thornhill turned in his seat. The chauffeur was no longer leaning against the wall. The two prefects guarding the door to the foyer were whispering to each other.

When the applause had petered away, the headmistress went on, "The girls will leave the stage now, while Miss Pilton explains the accompaniment she needs to Miss Furnish."

Miss Pilton, Thornhill guessed, hadn't yet had the privilege of hearing the strange, discordant sounds that came from the piano. He watched the two women conferring, while Dr Hilly left the stage and sat down again in the front row. Miss Furnish's appearance underwent a rapid change. Her face became not only woebegone but increasingly pink.

Meanwhile Miss Pilton's powerful voice was becoming steadily more audible. "…and after the second verse, it's imperative that you come in on the second beat of the bar, and not a fraction sooner. Got that, dear?"

Miss Furnish said nothing. She sat down at the piano and leafed through the music. The marks of perspiration on her dress had grown steadily larger. Wisps of lank grey hair had escaped from the pins at the back of her head and were now trailing down her neck. Miss Pilton faced the audience and gave it a wolfish smile.

"Among all the wonderful composers for the human voice," she began, "I find myself most at home with Schubert. Dear Schubert. We shall start with the lovely 'Nacht und Träume'."

Miss Pilton glanced towards the piano. Miss Furnish did not look at her, but she lifted her hands above the keyboard, ready to play. Miss Pilton turned back to the audience and raised her arms as though she wished to embrace it.

Miss Furnish played the opening bars of the lied. Miss Pilton frowned. She was peering down at the audience, the crease of a frown between her heavily marked eyebrows. Was she frowning at the sound of the piano, Thornhill wondered, which had slipped even further out of tune? Or at something in the hall?

Miss Furnish stopped playing. Someone coughed. Miss Pilton seemed to recollect herself. She gestured towards the piano, and the music mistress played the opening bars again.

"No, no, no!" Miss Pilton cried, turning suddenly to glare at Miss Furnish. "That piano belongs on a bonfire, dear, not a stage. You must have it tuned. It's quite unplayable. Surely you can hear that?"

A scarlet stain swept like an invading army across the skin of Miss Furnish's face and neck. She turned away from the audience. Her shoulders were shaking.

Oblivious to this, Miss Pilton went on, "I shall sing *a cappella* instead." The wolfish smile reappeared. "A professional musician must be prepared for anything."

After 'Nacht und Träume', she gave them Dorabella's aria from *Così Fan Tutte* and 'Habanera' from *Carmen*. No one could deny that her voice was impressive; indeed, the performance left the audience in a stunned stupor. After a second of silence, Dr Hilly leapt to her feet and clapped frenziedly, and everyone else joined in.

Everyone, that is, except Miss Furnish, who had remained at the piano for the brief recital, staring at the sheet music before her. During the clapping, however, she rose to her feet and slipped into the wings.

With Dr Hilly behind her, the smallest member of the choir scrambled up the steps to the stage and presented Miss Pilton with a bouquet of overblown roses.

"Look at Jean!" Edith's neighbour whispered, clasping her hands. "Oh, I do wish she'd straightened her tie."

Petals drifted to the floor as Dr Hilly made a brief speech of thanks. Afterwards, Miss Pilton left the stage to retrieve her coat and hat from the music room. Prefects opened the doors, including the fire exits.

Dazed and overheated, the audience stumbled from the hall. Edith, who had a wide acquaintance in Lydmouth, showed a disposition to linger and chat, but Thornhill and Elizabeth almost dragged her away. They joined the stream of concert-goers walking down the drive.

"I thought it was going on forever," Elizabeth wailed. "And that woman at the end made my head hurt. I won't have to join the choir, will I? Please not."

"It did go on rather," Edith conceded. "But Hermione Pilton! The Third Programme! That's the sort of thing that makes the High School what it is."

"I agree with you there," Thornhill said, wondering if there was any beer at home.

Immediately after the words had left his mouth, someone screamed.

Thornhill stopped. Elizabeth bumped into him. Edith looked at him, her face worried.

There was another scream. And a third.

"You two had better carry on," he said. "I'll join you later."

*　　*　　*

The evening sun slanted through the windows of Jill's sitting room. When the phone rang, she was sitting at the bureau and trying to balance her cheque book. She picked up the receiver with her free hand. She'd hardly begun to recite her number when she was interrupted.

"Miss Francis? Is that you? This is Roddy, Roddy Hanbridge. Oh, God, something awful's happened. The singer – she's dead."

"Slow down," Jill said. "Where are you?"

"At the school – this singer was there, Hermione Pilton, she's famous. I went to see if I could interview her after the concert, and she… she's dead." There was a whimper on the other end of the line. "And it was me that found her."

Heart attack? Jill wondered. She said, "Slow down. Has someone rung for an ambulance?"

"The policeman did."

"What policeman?"

"He was in the audience. He's with her now. There were… there were rose petals everywhere."

The Cub sounded distraught, and no wonder. Poor kid, Jill thought – something like this on your very first assignment. "Are you all right?" she said. "Find somewhere to sit. I'll be with you in ten minutes or so."

"Miss Francis, the thing is – I'm not sure it was an accident."

"What?"

"I think someone killed her."

*   *   *

Roddy's hands were trembling badly, and his skin was slippery with sweat. The receiver slipped from his hand and clattered onto the desk.

He picked it up and put it carefully on the rest. He took a deep breath to steady himself. He was in the headmistress's study, one of a set of school offices near the hall. From the windows, he could see the door to the music room, where that woman's body was presumably still lying, her eyes still open, still staring. She had been using it as a dressing room before the performance. One of her shoes was lying on its side on the floor. The bouquet was next to her body. There were rose petals everywhere.

His heart was still pumping so violently it seemed about to burst from his chest in a great spray of blood. *Oh, God, don't think about blood.* There had been blood on the side of her head. Not much, but enough. It was a relief that the man he'd seen in the drive, the one who had gone into the hall just in front of him, had turned out to be a policeman in mufti. He had taken charge of everything.

Roddy swallowed and squared his shoulders. His shorthand pad was on the desk beside the telephone. The sight of it reminded him that he was supposed to be a reporter. *That's why he was here.*

He had rung Miss Francis, his editor. That was good, that was what a proper journalist should do. Now he should go outside and wait for her. In the meantime, he could poke around, maybe, keep his eyes open. See who was there. Talk to people. Make notes. It might come in useful. This might even be an opportunity, his chance to make his mark as a reporter right away.

Outside, the elms were throwing long shadows across the playing fields and the air had grown appreciably cooler. He walked slowly and unsteadily towards the hall, his eyes moving skittishly from side to side.

Most people had left. Someone had given Miss Furnish a chair; she was sitting outside the fire exit. She had her head in her hands and she was crying: ragged sobs that made her shoulders shake. Dr Hilly was standing on one side of her, and a burly young woman on the other. It struck

Roddy that they weren't so much looking after the music mistress as guarding her like a pair of prison warders.

The police officer was talking to the chauffeur, who was standing by the Daimler with hands on his hips and his head hunched forward as though he wanted to butt somebody. A police Wolseley was nosing up the drive. Behind it came another car, a green Morris Minor. Roddy felt a warm, almost shameful rush of relief. Miss Francis was here.

Everything was going to be all right.

*　　*　　*

It was a long night for Thornhill.

One of the first people he talked to was the headmistress. If Dr Hilly was in shock, she didn't show it. Perhaps her grief would come later. But in the immediate aftermath of the murder, her predominant emotion was outrage that someone – anyone – should have dared to murder *her* friend in *her* school.

"I hate to say this, Chief Inspector," she said as they faced each other across the desk in her study, "but if I were you, I should look very closely at Miss Furnish."

The music mistress had been the first person to see the body after the young reporter had raised the alarm. She had become hysterical. The doctor had examined her and sedated her.

"Why in particular?" Thornhill asked.

"I fear she's mentally unstable. She has a history of violence, too. Last term, a fifth former accused her of slapping her and using bad language. Unfortunately, there were no witnesses, and there was a touch of doubt about the girl's veracity. Enough for me to put Miss Furnish on probation, rather than dismiss her outright. To tell the truth, I felt sorry for her."

"There's a big difference between a possible slap and killing someone with a spanner," Thornhill pointed out.

"I wish now I'd asked her to resign," Dr Hilly continued, as if he hadn't spoken. "She couldn't even control her classes. I suspect her very public failure this evening tipped her over the edge. She must have felt that Miss Pilton had humiliated her. Did you notice – she sneaked off the stage before anyone else had left the hall? I think she snatched up the spanner from the tools near the car, and laid in wait for Miss Pilton in the music room." She wagged her finger. "She made sure she was the first person to see the body after that boy raised the alarm. No doubt she wanted to make sure she'd left no traces behind her."

"She says she went because she's trained in first aid. To see if she could help."

"I wish I could believe her."

"Thank you, Dr Hilly. We'll need to talk to you again in the morning, and to Miss Furnish. In the meantime, no one must use the hall, the music room, the car park or the area between them. I'll make sure that two officers keep an eye on them overnight."

Dr Hilly snorted, like an aggrieved tank engine confronted with an impossible load.

★   ★   ★

The chauffeur's name was Bob Cartwright. The police talked to him in an interview room at the station. He was the next best thing to drunk, and inclined to be truculent.

"You going to let me go? You got to let me go if you don't arrest me. I know my rights."

"How long had you worked for Miss Pilton?" Thornhill asked.

"She hired me and the car from the agency for a week." The chauffeur put the agency's card on the table and slid it across to Thornhill. "She's been doing a tour of Wales and the West – wanted to impress people, I guess. She was that sort of person, you know – snobby as they come. I know, she's dead, poor cow, and I shouldn't say it. But she was a real Lady Muck."

"You had a puncture this evening," Thornhill said in a neutral voice.

"Final straw." Cartwright took out a cigarette packet and discovered it was empty. "Just after that she told me she wanted to stay a few hours longer in Lydmouth, and drive back by night. That was bad enough. Then – just as I was about to change the tyre – she sent a girl out to say we were going to spend the night here. She'd squared it with my boss and there was fuck all I could do about it. But I need to get back tonight – it's my parents' golden wedding party tomorrow. I'm the bloody host."

"In cases like this, Mr Cartwright," Thornhill said in a gentle voice, "we have to look at all the possibilities. Miss Pilton was killed with your spanner, which you say you left on the ground by the car, along with the rest of your tools. After that girl told you about the change of plan, you walked off. Where did you go?"

"I went down town. Had a scotch or two. And I bought a half-bottle while I was there. Why not? I'd had a bugger of a day, and I wasn't driving anywhere. When I came back, I went inside the hall for a bit. But I couldn't face seeing any more of that woman, let alone hear her squawking... So I went out again and lay on the grass for a bit. Must have nodded off. Next thing I knew there was all this shrieking going on."

They had found the bottle in his pocket. It had been three-quarters empty.

"In cases like this," Thornhill said again, "one of the things we do is ring round to see if any of the people involved have a criminal record. Nothing personal, Mr Cartwright. Just procedure." He paused. "We find out sooner or later. But it does make everything easier if we can short-circuit the process. Easier for everyone."

He stared at Cartwright. The silence stretched between them. The chauffeur dropped his eyes.

"GBH," he said. "About nine years ago. Look, I was young. I'd just come out of the army. I'd had a few drinks, and I got in a fight with a couple of Geordies. They were asking for it." He swallowed. "It wasn't my fault, not really. Honest."

*　　*　　*

Jill Francis pressed the button on her intercom. "Amy? Would you tell the Cub I want to see him? Right away."

In the office next door, her secretary's footsteps retreated. Jill bowed her head over the typed copy before her. The Cub must have stayed up half the night to write it. The piece was single-spaced on paper so flimsy that the typewriter keys had punched dozens of black holes through it. The Cub couldn't spell. His grammar was erratic. And his typing was truly atrocious.

To his credit, the boy was trying as hard as he could to do his job. You couldn't fault his keenness. Perhaps he would learn the rest in time. He must have had a terrible shock, too. He was young to see his first dead body, not even eighteen, and especially in those circumstances. Jill hoped that writing it all down had at least been a form of therapy.

There was a knock on the door, and Jill told him to come in. The

Cub was carrying his shorthand pad. He looked peaky, which wasn't surprising, and he'd cut himself shaving, which was ironic because he didn't need to shave in the first place.

"Did you get any sleep?" she asked.

"Not much," he said ruefully.

"What about breakfast?"

"There wasn't time. I was writing." His eyes strayed to his copy in front of her. "Have you read it? Is it all right? Will it be in the paper?"

"We can't use it, I'm afraid, not as it is." She watched his face fall. "It needs editing. Everyone needs editing. And in a case like this, where there's been a suspicious death, we have to be especially careful what we say."

Roddy put down his pad on the desk. He rubbed his bloodshot eyes. "Yes. Of course. I see that."

"Also — some of these details — the exact words you quote people as saying, for example — are you sure you're reporting them accurately?"

"I couldn't read back my shorthand," he blurted. "Not all of it. So I thought it would be all right to…"

"To make things up? No, it's not all right."

"But it's more or less what they said—"

"More or less won't do. It's never all right for a journalist to make things up. And it's not all right to do the work of the police for them. You actually say, in black and white, that someone killed the poor woman with a spanner, and that it was probably either her chauffeur or the music mistress." Jill paused, reining back her irritation. "That amounts to libel. If we were sued, it could bankrupt us."

The boy looked on the verge of tears. After a moment, he said, "Shall I rewrite it?"

"No. Leave it with me. I need to talk to the police first in any case. Go home. Have something to eat. Try and catch up on your sleep. I'll ring you later this afternoon and see how you are."

Roddy rose to his feet. He swayed slightly. "Sorry."

"Don't be. Just treat it as useful experience. You did well, you know. You kept your head."

He blundered from the room, fumbling with the doorknob as if it were a potentially hostile device. Jill sighed. She had already written a brief, sternly factual report about yesterday's concert and its unhappy aftermath. She would check it with the police before filing it.

She was about to pick up the phone when she noticed the Cub's shorthand pad, which was still on the corner of her desk. She drew it towards her and flipped it open. Inside were the usual pencilled scribbles. Exercises, mainly.

Dear Mr Smith, Thank you for your letter of the 18th inst…

She riffled through the pages. The Cub had admitted that he wasn't very good at reading back his shorthand. On the evidence here, he hadn't entirely mastered writing it either. She studied the content of the last few pages. In time, words and phrases began to emerge.

Big tits.

She reached for a cigarette. Adolescent boys, she thought ruefully. She struck a match.

The Hall full. 19 girls. Piano out of tune?

That was better. She turned a page.

Fair Phyllis…

Jill's eyes skipped to the bottom.

Oh, God…

Jill yelped as the flame burned down to her fingers. She dropped the charred remains of the match in the ashtray. She turned the pages of the pad with increasing urgency, deciphering perhaps seventy per cent of the symbols.

She picked up the phone – not the office one, the private line. She rang the familiar number of the police station and asked for Chief Inspector Thornhill.

*   *   *

When Jill returned home that evening, later than usual, she hardly had time to wash and change before there was a ring at the door of her flat. It was a mixed pleasure to find Richard Thornhill waiting outside. As ever, encountering each other in the present instantly conjured up the uneasy ghosts of past selves, past possibilities.

"Sorry," he said. "Perhaps I should have phoned first. But I thought you'd want to know at once. Easier to do it face to face."

"You'd better come in."

He prowled around the sitting room while she poured sherry and shook a packet of peanuts into a bowl. He drank half the glass in the first swallow.

"Well?" she said.

"You were right. Hanbridge was in such a state he was scribbling on his pad automatically. Afterwards he couldn't read back most of his notes."

"Shorthand's like that."

"He's at the station now. We've sent for his parents, and they're driving down tonight. Their solicitor's coming in the morning."

"Has Roddy actually admitted it?"

"Oh yes. He blurted everything out as soon as we started questioning him. I think he was glad to get it off his chest. If you hadn't untangled at least part of the story from his notes, he could have got away with it." Thornhill finished the rest of his sherry. "He recognised Miss Pilton when she was up on the stage looking down at the audience. And I'm pretty sure she recognised him. I noticed her face change, and he's a distinctive-looking boy. As soon as the second half was over, he left the hall and followed her to the music room where she'd left her things. He picked up the spanner on the way. I don't think he planned it. Spur of the moment."

"But why did he do it?"

"He said she'd been unfair to him once. Then he clammed up." Thornhill rubbed his temples with the tips of his fingers. "But I got the name of his old school out of him and rang the headmaster. It turns out that he was in a party of boys that went to sing with the choir at the local girls' school. It was a big concert, with professional soloists, and there was some sort of party afterwards. That was when he followed a fifteen-year-old girl into her classroom and assaulted her. Luckily she started screaming."

"Dear God. He's seemed such… such a nice boy."

"Perhaps he is, most of the time. But hormones do strange things." He paused. "It only took him a moment to try and rape an underage girl. It only took him a moment last night, too."

"I assume Miss Pilton was there when he tried to rape the girl?"

"She was one of the professional soloists. She opened the classroom door and found them. The lad was terrified when she recognised him in the front row last night. She'd already got him chucked out of school and ruined his exams. He thought she'd tell everyone in Lydmouth and ruin the rest of his life."

"Sex," Jill said, lighting a cigarette. She blew out smoke and squinted at him through a shifting blue-grey haze. "It makes people act out of character."

"Yes," Thornhill said. "And no. I noticed him before the concert. He was really enjoying staring at the schoolgirls. Sometimes sex just makes people more themselves."

THE MELODY OF MURDER

Antony M. Brown

A knot of visceral dread tightened in the pit of my stomach as I sped through the streets of Westminster. The initial description of the crime scene sounded eerily familiar and I knew the timing was about right: two months from the last one. This would be the third.

I was heading up Operation Treadmill, London's biggest murder enquiry in years. It was May 1982 and the news was dominated by events thousands of miles away in the Falklands. A thin-lipped man from the Ministry of Defence appeared daily on television, grimly imparting the latest from the South Atlantic, although my teenage son was more concerned that we would be forced to pull out of the upcoming World Cup in Spain; there was the unthinkable prospect of England facing Argentina on the football pitch as well as the battlefield.

I swung my red Volvo 244 behind a fleet of police vehicles, their flashing blue lights reflecting on the elegant Georgian façade of the Academy of Performing Arts. The first hacks were already milling outside and, leaning against a wall, a paparazzo taking an early-morning drag was reading the *Daily Mirror*. 'HMS SHEFFIELD SUNK' screamed its headline. Seeing my arrival, he thrust the paper inside his jacket and readied his camera. I cut the engine and hurried up the stone steps of the imposing portico as the photographer fired off a salvo of shots.

Crossing the vestibule, I passed students and staff, visibly upset at the loss of a young life and the shocking interruption to their own. Beyond them, standing by open double doors, a just-out-of-college constable was acting scene guard. He entered my details in the logbook and directed me to the rehearsal studio. I stooped under a ribbon of police tape and walked down a dingy corridor plastered with colourful posters for West End plays and musicals. There was a hubbub of conversation from a gathering of waiting officers. It was the usual work banter, mundane gossip about *Wogan* and the Snooker World Championships, far removed from the scene awaiting me in the adjacent room. The noise petered out as I approached. For a senior investigating officer the first question at a murder scene is always the same: "Has death been certified?"

"Yes, sir," came a reply. "The doctor has just left."

"And the pathologist?"

"On his way."

The small crowd parted to let me through and I stopped in the doorway of the studio. It was an elegant but sparsely furnished room with tall sash windows letting in a diffused light. A Steinway took centre stage with other instruments and equipment scattered around. A police photographer was pointing a 35mm camera mounted on a tripod towards the body of a young woman sprawled across the floorboards in the far corner. She was clothed in a black top, split side skirt and fishnet tights. Her head rested on her right arm, which was outstretched towards the centre of the studio, palm down and fingers apart, as if she was trying to haul herself across the room in a desperate bid for freedom. Her eyes were wide open, staring at infinity in a lifeless gaze. Along her back was a cello on its side, mirroring her body, its neck pointing towards the centre of the room. But, most noticeably, her left arm was raised, holding the end of the bow which stood vertically about two feet from her side.

"Do we know the record cover?" I asked; a surreal question, I know. Typically we would first enquire about the victim's identity, but this was not a typical murder enquiry.

"Yes," replied the photographer, without moving his face from the camera's viewfinder. "It's 'Babooshka'. I bought the single a couple of years back." The shutter clicked and the darkest recesses of the room lit up in a flash of light.

"Love Kate Bush," muttered one of the scenes of crime officers as he bent down beside the body.

I knew the song but was unfamiliar with its picture cover, and instructed one of my team to get a copy. "And I want the names and addresses of every student and member of staff. I need to know who was on campus over the past few days."

"Got it," one of my detective constables replied.

I approached the body, careful to remain out of everyone's way and not interfere with the processing of the scene. "It's the most elaborate staging yet," I remarked. "How has that bow remained vertical?"

After a few moments of inspection, a SOCO replied, "From what I can tell, its tip has been modified and tacked to the floor, the victim's hand placed around the handle and..." He tugged at it, but the hand remained stubbornly in position. He crouched down, peering at the palm. "Superglued, I think, but we'll know for sure after a proper analysis back at the lab."

I watched the officers go about their painstaking task of collecting evidence. As the cello and bow were dusted for prints, the pathologist arrived; in fact, I heard him long before I saw him. He wheezed and gasped as he heaved his large frame down the corridor, his walking stick tapping out a lumbering rhythm on the floor.

"Rupert Templeton-Jones," he announced grandly, his mellifluous voice pinched with a public school accent. "From the Home Office." His wiry, white hair was in full retreat, the last wisps standing vainly on his crown, compensated for by wild eyebrows that dangled like old cobwebs over his eyes. He stared at the body, scratching his dimpled chin, which had sunk almost without trace into his bloated neck. "By Jove, what a show the killer's put on!" He set down his case and, with some difficulty, knelt by the body. He lifted the right arm. "No rigor."

He peered at the face. "The lips look a little swollen." He moved even closer, scrutinising the eyes. "And there appears to be petechiae around the lids."

"Strangulation?"

"Possibly, old boy. Let's see what delights the post mortem offers, eh?"

I was beckoned to the door by Eve Daley, a tenacious and enthusiastic DC who was a bit too clever at times but immensely likeable. The only woman on my team, she had sacrificed a family for her career. She merited a rank of sergeant or inspector, and though had been continually overlooked for promotion, remained remarkably sanguine. "The deceased is Anna Kaminski, a nineteen-year-old cellist at the academy. She's an international student – from Poland. We're contacting her next of kin."

"We need to trace all her friends and classmates," I instructed. "Find out when she was last seen alive." Although a laborious and boring task, it was often the most reliable method of discovering an approximate time of death.

"Who found her?"

"The caretaker when he was opening up this morning," Daley replied. "He didn't have much else to say except that clock is new." She pointed to the corner of the room behind the body. I spun round and saw the antique Westminster wall clock. "It wasn't there yesterday evening when he locked up."

"Get that clock dusted and sent to forensics," I instructed. "It might be part of the staging."

Later that afternoon, as the undertakers discreetly removed the body through the back entrance, a team conducted a fingertip search of the studio, bagging any potential evidence. One item of interest found near the body was a piece of rubber from the sole of a trainer. It could have been debris unconnected to the crime – but it might have come from the killer.

As I left, a scrum of reporters surged up the steps, phones and cameras thrust in my face. Being on TV was not a new experience for me, but this level of media interest was far higher than anything I had experienced before. Through the ruckus, a male journalist shouted, "Has the Picture Cover Killer struck again?"

"I can only confirm that a body has been found in suspicious circumstances and our enquiries are continuing."

"What's the record this time?" another shouted.

"No comment." My tone was brusque.

"What was found at the scene?" I pushed my way through a barrage of similar questions, giving the same short response each time. With camera motor drives whirling in my ears, I dived into the sanctuary of my car and headed to the mortuary.

The post mortem confirmed that manual strangulation was the cause of death, estimated to have occurred thirty-six hours prior to discovery. The lividity – the discolouration of the skin due to the settling of blood following death – was incompatible with the position of the body at the crime scene. The deceased had been prone for some hours after death and the body moved. One curiosity: the victim's right hand had a single staple in the middle of the palm. The injury was inflicted after death, so torture was ruled out, but its presence was something of a mystery.

When I returned to the office, I was handed a copy of 'Babooshka'. The crime scene was remarkably similar, right down to the detail of the wall clock in the corner. I pinned the cover to the large display board in the conference room and drew a line to the location of the Academy on a central London map. How many more would there be?

Over the following weeks, the red tops devoted page after page to shrill headlines and outlandish theories. The previous two killings, both raw and recent, were regurgitated in detail. The first was dubbed the 'Ashes to Ashes' murder. In early January, the body of eighteen-year-old Dave Duffy, an unemployed school leaver, was found in the loader bucket of a JCB digger at a retail building site. He had been dressed in a blue Pierrot costume and conical hat, his face neatly shaved and painted white, and his lips glossed with cherry red lipstick. In his right hand, pressed to his ear like a phone, he held a silver shoe. It was a recreation of the cover of David Bowie's number one single, with the digger a reference to the song's famous video.

The second victim was found at the end of March. The day after SDP co-founder Roy Jenkins won the Glasgow Hillhead by-election, the body of twenty-three-year-old Barry Robinson was found hanging in a Battersea storage unit. His head tilted to his left, he stood tiptoe on a clear Perspex cube next to an old-fashioned electric fire. The scene was a visual replica of the slow suicide on the cover of 'Can't Stand Losing You' by The Police, with the Perspex replacing the block of ice in the original. As in the cover, the victim held an album in his right hand; Ike and Tina Turner's *Nutbush City Limits*, fixed in position with superglue. It was evidently murder, and Treadmill had turned into a serial-killer investigation.

We could find no connection between the victims. They all appeared to be loners, with few family or friends in the capital, and we suspected they had met or befriended their killer shortly before their deaths. We believed they were first drugged or incapacitated, strangled and then possibly kept in a warm location to allow rigor mortis to pass more quickly. The bodies were fastidiously dressed and made-up before being moved to the crime scene, almost certainly in a van. The 'Babooskha' murder in particular required significant reconnoitring to know how to get inside the Academy late at night without attracting attention.

As for the killer, a psychological profile suggested he was a white male, twenty-five to forty years old and intelligent, possibly educated to degree level. He would exhibit psychopathic tendencies, probably with a seductive but superficial charm. In fact, his greatest disguise would be his sheer ordinariness. But a profile is only of limited use, and no substitute for suspects or leads, and we were fortunate that the 'Babooshka' murder brought our biggest break yet. Forensic analysis revealed the partial rubber sole was from a New Balance 620 trainer, manufactured in America. The Enquiries Team had questioned a second-hand record dealer who had recently sold a *Nutbush City Limits* album. He remembered the customer because he had complimented him on his stylish footwear: expensive blue and grey trainers embossed with a large white 'N', the logo of New Balance. This was our best lead: a facial composite and description of the customer and the trainer were widely circulated.

Everyone working on Treadmill was buoyant, confident that we were on the trail of the killer, but progress remained agonisingly slow. The weeks rolled by: the Union Jack flew again over Port Stanley, the IRA bombed two London parks, an intruder broke into the Queen's bedroom and Princess Grace of Monaco died in a car crash. And early one Monday morning in September, Eve Daley knocked on my office door with a startling discovery.

"Can I have a word, sir?"

"Come in, close the door and take a seat."

She entered, sitting pensively on the other side of my desk, which was littered with case notes and files. "What can I do for you?"

"I might be overanalysing this, but…" She paused, pursing her lips, unsure of how I might react.

"Go on."

"In the 'Ashes to Ashes' murder, the victim held a Copeland shoe. The staged cover in the second murder was by The Police." She paused. "The drummer in The Police is Stuart Copeland."

"Oh, God," I interjected, closing my eyes. "I think I know where this is going."

"In the second staging the victim was holding a copy of *Nutbush City Limits*."

I sighed. "And the next was Kate Bush."

"Whatever the victim holds in their hand is a clue to an artist, and the next murder will be staged recreating a single cover of theirs."

"And in the 'Babooshka' murder?" Suddenly the penny dropped. "The stapled palm!"

"Yes." Daley took a deep breath as she prepared her reveal. "I can only think of one musician who fits: Neville Staple of The Specials."

I leaned back in my chair and ran my hand down my face. It was the sort of clever, cryptic clue that was awash in crime fiction but had nothing to do with real detective work. Yet the connection was undeniable.

"Sir, it's exactly how a killer with above-average intelligence might toy with us. He's already planned his next murder. He's telling us he is going to kill again."

I snapped forward in my chair. "Get every single by The Specials pinned up on the board right away. And get the team together. Let's see if we can get one step ahead of him this time."

That afternoon the back catalogue of The Specials blasted out from a cassette recorder while we pored over the covers. Most of their singles were released in simple record company sleeves but were instantly recognisable, featuring a black-and-white cartoon-like man dressed in a shirt, tie, sunglasses and pork pie hat. Some of the team thought this was how the next victim would be staged, but I was sure that the killer was escalating the grandeur of his grisly art and would settle for nothing less than a royal variety performance. My eyes were fearfully drawn to the cover of their biggest hit, 'Ghost Town', which depicted a skeleton playing at an upright piano like a scene from a Ray Harryhausen movie. It was now a race against time: either we caught the killer, or a macabre recreation of the 'Ghost Town' cover was going to appear somewhere in the capital. Every time I heard that haunting song, I felt the same knot of visceral dread tightening in the pit of my stomach.

The next few weeks saw the Soviet leader Brezhnev die and Henry VIII's warship raised from the bottom of the Solent, but office gossip was dominated by an androgynous pop star on *Top of the Pops*. The reaction was jaw-dropping incredulity: was it a man or a woman? The clue was in the name: Boy George. And his hit was playing on the radio when I received an urgent call to go to the Tate Gallery.

When I arrived uniformed officers were shepherding a crowd outside the entrance. I was taken straight to an exhibit hall. Among the modern art sculptures stood a black upright piano with inverted coloured keys and a Samsonite suitcase beside it. Sitting on a bare wooden stool and hunched over the keyboard was a figure in a top-to-toe skeleton suit, his forehead pressed against the upper panel. On the rack was the sheet music for 'Ghost Town'. An accompanying sign read:

Melody of Murder
Gerald Radford, 1982

For almost a day, crowds of art-loving visitors had milled around the exhibit, thinking the figure was a mannequin. They had taken pictures and enthusiastically discussed 'the art'. It was not until the exhibition manager arrived in the afternoon that the cuckoo in the nest was detected. When *Melody of Murder* was investigated more closely, it was found that the skeleton's glassy, staring eyes were all too real – and inert. The alarm was raised and the floor immediately evacuated.

"The doctor's on his way," Eve Daley announced before I could ask. "Looks like you were right, sir."

"You were, you mean." I scanned the sign. "Is Gerald Radford an artist?"

"Not one that anyone has heard of. But there is a technician who works here with that name."

"Right, we need to speak to him. See if he can shed some light on this."

We were interrupted by a small, balding man with a shaggy, grey beard and circular spectacles who introduced himself as the police surgeon. It did not take him long to certify death. "Full rigor has set in, I would say, but I'll leave that to the pathologist." The photographer and scenes of crime officers swept in.

"Take a look under his hands when you get a chance, would you?" I received a frown from one of the officers and had to wait until the body was removed to discover nothing was there. It was a detail that had not been made public and the possibility of a copycat flashed across my mind. Or was this the Picture Cover Killer's grand finale?

We did not have to wait long to find Gerald Radford: he was identified that evening on the mortuary slab. The post mortem revealed he had died from asphyxiation and the pupils were severely contracted, mere dots in the iris, consistent with a morphine overdose; a fact confirmed by toxicology. A new cause of death and a named victim at the scene; it was clear this killing was different to the others.

Gerald Radford was twenty-nine years old and had worked at the Tate for about a year. He was described by colleagues as an introvert who shut himself away in the world of his Walkman. He had no family or friends and went largely unnoticed; he was the archetypal loner living vicariously through his music, although fate was slowly robbing his life of meaning. Suffering from otosclerosis, the bones of his middle ear had fused together, causing hearing loss. It had spread to the bones of his inner ear and he was slowly descending into total silence.

Radford had moved with his family to London in the late 1950s, only to lose both parents in a car accident while he was still a child. In later life, he was an Academy of Performing Arts dropout – a connection we duly noted – and held a string of menial jobs, including a stint as a porter at a local hospital. He had applied for jobs at the Tate Gallery several times, before finally securing his position with the help of a government job scheme.

An examination of the suitcase found it contained neatly folded clothes and a pair of New Balance trainers. Conspicuously, the right shoe had a section of tread missing. The only other item was a used syringe containing traces of morphine. We found no more of Radford's possessions; his dingy bedsit had been cleared and his Ford Transit van sold days before. This did not so much raise a red flag as sound a klaxon – it looked as though he was anticipating the end of his life. Piece by piece, the jigsaw took shape, but it did not show a picture of a victim. Rather, to our consternation, Gerald Radford was our killer.

For his own death, placing the piano in the exhibition hall was hardly difficult – it was part of his job. We surmised that after the gallery closed its doors, he remained in the building, out of sight, drinking steadily – not only for Dutch courage but also to intensify the deadly effect of the opiate he was about to take. He returned to the exhibit hall under cover of darkness and changed into his skeleton suit, placing his clothes into the suitcase. In the silence of the small hours and by the dim glow of the security lights, he sat at the piano and injected himself with a lethal dose of morphine. He calmly finished his remaining tasks, including hiding the syringe in the suitcase, and hunched over the piano, resting his tremulous hands on the keys. Perhaps he even played some music as he waited for the end. We can only imagine his last thoughts as he slowly slipped from the blur of torpor into unconsciousness. Finally, his breathing stopped and his life's work was completed by death, rigor fixing him in position for when the doors opened that morning. The murders had merely been a preparation for his artistic coronation, providing notoriety that a suicide alone could never attain.

The remarkable denouement to the Picture Cover Murders astounded the world. It still does to this day. Many refuse to accept that a serial killer would make himself the final victim. The scepticism of armchair detectives has only grown over the ensuing years, especially with the advent of social media. GERALD RADFORD WAS INNOCENT! they shout, pointing out that the last murder was so different to the others and the trainers left in the suitcase just too convenient. Conspiracy theorists take it further, claiming the murders were perpetrated by the son of someone famous and covered up by making Radford the fall guy. His death, like good art, was ambiguous and open to interpretation.

To others, Gerald Radford was a great but evil artist, a genius who created the ultimate expression of self-reflexive art. The plight of his victims is scandalously rationalised: they also received immortality in return for their sacrifice. I guess it's true that the world would never know the names of Dave Duffy, Barry Robinson and Anna Kaminski had they not met their ends in the way they did. Would we know anything of the pitiful lives of Elizabeth Stride or Mary Jane Kelly if it was not for the Ripper?

Many books have been penned on the Picture Cover Murders; more will undoubtedly follow, and there was a Hollywood movie in the 1990s. It completed an ironic circle: art inspiring murder inspiring art. Indeed, the lines between entertainment and crime are now hopelessly blurred. Murderers are feted like celebrities, their crimes treated like bestselling novels. And now Netflix has commissioned a major drama series. I suppose that's the denouement of an infamous murder nowadays; life and death streamed on demand in an age of unconstrained leisure. Just how Gerald Radford would have wanted it.

LOVE ME OR LEAVE ME: A FUGUE IN G MINOR

Art Taylor

1

Garrett heard the music the first time moments before sunrise – if *heard* was the right word.

He was caught halfway between sleeping and waking, not quite himself but drifting uncertainly, trying to find some steady path out of the dying echoes of troubled dreams and towards the new day. In the middle of all that: faint music. Ten notes, maybe twelve. An extra one or two sliding around somewhere? Some fragment of a melody.

An earworm, he thought, rousing himself slightly. A song he'd heard on the car radio or a TV commercial or Spotify – stuck in his head, bouncing around. A DJ in his mind, spinning tunes – that's how he'd sometimes imagined it. The song had shown up in his dreams, and the dreams had carried over into waking.

But then it also seemed the notes were outside of him, a kind of... humming? Like the hum of an electrical line?

A hidden alarm on his phone maybe? Or Tess's? He fumbled in the darkness to pick his up, tapped the screen, checked for notifications. Nothing.

His girlfriend kept her phone on her nightstand. Sometimes it glowed in the middle of the night, waking him up, but right now that screen was dark too.

Tess slept soundly. In the light creeping around the blackout shades, her hair flashed red, then quickly back to its honey blonde.

He shook his head.

The music persisted. Faintly, but... there.

Weeks since he'd moved in, but he was still getting used to her apartment. Their apartment. It felt strange wandering around someone else's space, living in it. The paint colour kept surprising him. When he sat on the couch, he sometimes felt like a visitor. He still had trouble finding the right tools in the kitchen.

Was the battery dead on the smoke alarm?

"Did you hear that?" He nudged Tess, her back to him. "Music?"

She lifted her head, looked towards the clock. "Do you know what time it is?"

"That's what I'm saying. Why would there be music so early?"

She waited – clearly listening. He listened too.

The notes floated at once near and far away. Maybe something from the neighbour's place? He'd been surprised at how thin the walls were, how sounds carried. Or from the closet, was that it? He remembered the keyboard propped at an angle in the back, some preset tempo playing itself out? But it wasn't plugged in, he realised, with a chill. He'd never liked that keyboard, the way it had been stuck back there.

"You're hearing things." Tess pulled the covers tighter. "Go back to sleep."

Listen! Garrett could feel the word in his throat, and anger behind it now – chill to heat, a sudden blast of it – because if the situation had been reversed, if *she* had heard a noise, he would've been interested, wouldn't he? If she loved him enough, then—

He fought the urge to shake her.

Because he loved her, he did. He'd been feeling this more than ever lately. That was a true thing.

And she loved him too.

And anyway, the music had faded away.

* * *

Until it came back the next morning. And the next. And the next.

Like a warning. Like it was calling to him.

Like he should answer it.

* * *

"It was kind of like a *da dum-dum dum-da-da da-dee-dee dee-da-da*," Garrett told Tess at breakfast one of those mornings, trying to bring it up again, moving his fingers up and down to demonstrate the higher and lower notes. "Like that."

Tess stood at the counter, slid her toast from oven to plate. He'd already mixed his oatmeal.

"You know those games," she said, sitting down with him, "where you have to hum a song and your teammates have to guess what the song is?"

"Yeah," even though he didn't.

"You wouldn't be good at it."

She winked at him, flipped the top off the margarine tub, same as if nothing was wrong.

He watched her butter her toast, tried to focus on sipping his coffee, tried not to think about how late it was getting, how he needed to get to the print shop.

"So, you don't recognise it?" he said.

"OK." She sighed. "Do it again."

He did.

She shook her head.

"And you haven't heard it, not at all?"

She bit her toast – chewed it. Chewed thoughtfully, it seemed. He didn't look at her, looked instead at her bread plate, the half slice of toast sitting there, cut on the diagonal, the angle of the butter knife perched on the edge. He listened to the room, the silence of it, the sound of her swallowing.

"Remember right after you moved in, that ticking you heard?" she said finally.

Garrett's turn to shake his head. "This isn't like that."

"You searched and searched. Standing in this part of the room, that part of the room, listening to the walls, listening to the floor."

"But I *found* that." He tried to keep his voice steady. "I Googled it, remember? HVAC ducts. They expand and contract."

"Exactly. No big deal in the end."

She raised her hands, a 'whatever' gesture, a small shrug. *What matters?* That was one of her phrases, one he'd understood, but hadn't really.

"So?" he asked.

"So, let this go. You'll find it."

"Or I won't."

"In which case…" An arch of an eyebrow. *What matters?*

The woman I love – that was how he'd taken to thinking about her, what he reminded himself of again now, even if the idea had left him anxious. And here was one of the things he told himself he'd loved about her from the first, her steadiness, her practicality, how calm she tried to make him feel, even if right now it didn't hit him as something he appreciated.

He ticked through the other things he loved about Tess:

The curve of her smile, and the smell of her hair.

He liked that she worked in the library, that she liked to read, liked to lose herself in a book.

She never judged him for his own work, clerking at the print shop.

And he'd never felt suspicion or jealousy about her, never had to ask about the men she knew or the time she spent with them, or how far things had gone, never had to ask, "Who was—?" or "What the hell were—?"

Because he did. He did love her. This was *the* true thing.

But sometimes, he felt like he didn't know her at all. Sometimes he looked at her and thought, "Who are you?" and not only like he was surprised by something she'd done or said or thought.

Garrett could see what they might look like from the side, from a distance – the happy couple at breakfast, chatting, start of the day, him leaning forward, her leaning back.

But seeing them like that, they seemed like strangers to him – the way you get so used to someone that you don't notice them really, or yourself either. The same way you say a familiar word over and over until suddenly it's just sound – and a sound you don't recognise. Or stare at something ordinary until your focus blurs. And then those things *didn't* seem true anymore.

Sunlight through the window. The fern on the table.

Yesterday's mail. This morning's paper.

Tess chewed her toast, smiled some mysterious smile, tucked a strand of red behind her ear.

He tried to fight the urge to shout *Why aren't you listening?* To snatch that toast from her hand. To—

No, wait. Not red.

The sunlight again?

Looks deceived.

He hardly recognised himself either.

Who are *you? What am* I *doing here?*

Awareness, Garrett thought, snapping himself back to himself.

But again, the next morning, *What is that music? Where is it coming from?*

★ ★ ★

"Likely a case of auditory pareidolia," Dr Bitterman told him.

"Sounds serious." Garrett felt a sudden fear grip him. He pictured a brain tumour, growing.

It wasn't an official visit. They were standing in the parking lot at the print shop. Dr Bitterman was one of their customers, had come in to pick up a new batch of business cards: *Dr Marvin Bitterman, Psychologist.* Garrett had been the one who'd printed them, serendipity, and he'd already held a card back, planning to call. When Dr Bitterman had come to pick them up, Garrett had been standing at the printer watching three hundred copies of a concert flyer roll out of the machine. It was only a last-minute impulse that sent him rushing out after him, to talk to him in person. No harm in that, right? Unless it *was* something to worry about.

"I wouldn't say serious," – Dr Bitterman glanced at his nametag – "Garrett. It's more like an optical illusion. Let me guess. You use a sound machine at night? White noise?"

"Tess does, yeah. My girlfriend. Helps her sleep. Me too, I guess."

"That's what does it. White noise, the hum of an air-conditioner, running water, that kind of thing. We humans, we like patterns – we're pattern makers, in fact. And if a pattern isn't there, our imagination *makes* one for us to find. It's like a Rorschach test, to use another analogy – random, nothing definitive pictured, but people see things anyway. Some people have heard voices in white noise, conversations even. Hearing music wouldn't be too far-fetched."

"So that's... normal?"

A shrug. "It's not entirely uncommon. And if that's it, then nothing to worry about."

"If?"

Dr Bitterman gestured to the parking lot around them. "Hard to do an official diagnosis here. Other conditions are possible. Hearing damage, brain damage, some forms of epilepsy…"

Garrett shook his head at each one.

"Well, if you *are* concerned…" Dr Bitterman handed him one of the cards he'd just picked up.

Now Garrett had two. And he wouldn't need either if Dr Bitterman's explanation was right.

"Auditory pareidolia," Garrett said aloud, trying to remember it.

"Turn off the noise machine." Dr Bitterman smiled. "See if that doesn't clear it right up."

But when Garrett did – waiting till Tess was asleep herself before switching it off – he still heard the notes the next morning, same as always.

*   *   *

Garrett began to search more purposefully, then earnestly and frantically and desperate to keep Tess from seeing him. This wasn't like the ticking of the vents at all.

He searched the bathroom. The electric toothbrush. The countertop dehumidifier. Inside the cabinets, inside her toiletry case and his too.

He stared out the window, put his ear hard against the shared wall with the next apartment.

He checked the smoke alarm in the hallway, the cable box on top of the dresser, the DVD player too.

He searched around her nightstand, the mess on top, the pile of magazines on the small shelf beneath, within both drawers, expecting some stray bit of electronica tucked away inside. He searched her phone while she was in the shower, remembering the code he'd glimpsed once before, suddenly certain that the mystery lay within, an alarm she'd set and neglected to turn off, an app that she'd used and forgotten, or maybe messages coming through, text or Facebook or Twitter, something persistent – or someone?

Scrolling through posts and emails, he found himself stung by a jealousy he didn't recognise, overwhelmed by it, certain suddenly that it wasn't the phone but Tess herself hiding something, hiding some*one*, and if he could find the right post or message, he'd find out who it was.

He could hear the song even now, distant, dimly, swelling up as he hunched over her phone. He scrolled fast and furtive, focused on screen after screen of texts and emails. But he stayed on guard in other ways too – suddenly seeing how he would look to her if she stepped out of the bathroom. Paranoid, intrusive. It was as if he could see himself through those eyes, gazing at himself from behind or above, hardly recognising himself. Then he saw her too, looking down from above at her as she hunched over the same phone, tapping messages, hiding from *him*, some brand of déjà vu in what he was watching, familiar and disorienting. Her red hair glowed, flamed with the same burning rage he felt building inside himself, and—

"Stop it," he said – out loud, jerking himself back to reality, thrusting the phone down. "She's not, she wouldn't." The shower was still running. She was humming, happily. "I love her, I do."

But he could still hear the music. Not her humming. Not the phone. Something elsewhere. Haunting him. Taunting him.

★   ★   ★

No answers then, and the music was coming at other times of the day now too.

It was strongest in the morning, that same dim twilight, that same woozy awakening, that same brief wondering where he was, even who he was, as that same sun peeked around the edges of the blackout blinds, and that same *da dum-dum dum-da-da da-dee-dee dee-da-da* sounded somewhere in the near distance, and he clutched those same sheets beneath his fingers, searching for steadiness.

Until the morning that he woke to himself, walking through a kitchen he didn't recognise, a house he didn't know, with unfamiliar fingers clutched around a knife – a knife that was the one thing that he *had* seen before.

2

1. Bowl (*absence of*)
2. Knife (*presence of*)
3. Car (*absence of*)
4. Messages (*unanswered*)
5. Toothbrush (*dry*)

These were the items Tess ticked through as she gradually realised that something was wrong – that Garrett hadn't merely left but was, indeed, gone.

*   *   *

It hadn't been unusual for her to wake up to an empty house. Garrett was an early riser, usually let her sleep late. More unusual for him to wake her up, like he'd done a week or so before with whatever he'd been hearing.

Most days, Garrett liked a morning walk before work. He said he had a wanderer's heart, said it cleared his head.

She'd learned he was a creature of habit, brushing his teeth first thing, weighing himself, then out the door and around the neighbourhood. He would come back hungry – a big bowl of oatmeal always, a small coffee with honey, strict in all routines.

He hadn't had his breakfast yet, she saw that morning – the morning he disappeared. No bowl in the sink, rinsed and sitting the way he left it, no spoon at its sharp angle. Only a knife out on the counter, and it looked clean. Not like he'd cut anything, and odd for him to leave it out. He was 'fastidious' – his word, some pride there. She slid it back into the block.

A half-hour passed and then forty-five minutes. Had he left for the print shop? She glanced out the window. No car in the driveway, so he must have.

But skipping breakfast. That wasn't like him.

She texted him then, but he didn't respond. Not even a *delivered* notation popping up. Just a blankness at the end of the message chain. No answer when she called either. It didn't ring, just went straight to voicemail. The same things each time she texted, each time she called, each voicemail she left.

She tried the print shop too, something she never did – she hardly knew anyone there, Garrett rarely talked work. But the woman who answered said he wasn't in yet, they'd expected him, she wasn't sure where he might be.

His wallet was gone from the nightstand where he always kept it. With a sudden worry (irrational, she thought), she checked the closet, but his half was still full of clothes – his suitcase there too. The small shaving kit was there where he'd tucked it under the sink when he moved in. His toothbrush was propped in its stand, but when she touched the bristles, they were dry.

Definitely not the Garrett she knew.

*　　*　　*

Despite first instincts, she didn't call the police.

Not that she hadn't gone halfway in that direction – more, in fact. She'd Googled the non-emergency number, picked up the phone, dialled most of the digits, then held back, hung up. Too many reasons against it.

1. She hadn't heard anything earlier – no shouts, no struggle
2. The front door and porch door were both locked, no sign of a break-in
3. The car was gone

It was mostly the car that stopped her – the absence of it.

If the car had still been there, that might have been one kind of evidence, but the fact that he'd driven it away was another.

Unless someone had forced him into the car, that is – an idea that had her dialling the numbers again, and then hanging up again. She couldn't seriously imagine that.

Garrett had left abruptly, yes, but of his own free will.

Another text – *G? Where r u?* – before she headed to the library and a long, distracted shift ahead.

*　　*　　*

Had there been a problem between them? Had she done something to drive him away? Sitting at the breakfast table each morning before work, staring at the empty space across from her, she kept revisiting the same questions, kept coming back to them again and again through the day, talked about them sometimes with Carla, her best friend at the library.

It had happened before with previous boyfriends, she'd told Carla – unlucky in love, no doubt about it.

1. She was too independent
2. She was too practical
3. She was too distant

Still, she couldn't remember anything that might have triggered him to run. No arguments over the last few weeks. No friction really. None that she was aware of.

At least nothing that *Tess* had done, Carla clarified – and Carla had heard already all the ways that the relationship had indeed changed even over such a short time.

In the beginning, Garrett had seemed intense and enigmatic – a good thing then, the attraction, the fun. She'd met him in the psychology section at the library, trying to find a book about dreams and what they mean. Tess had helped him locate it, helped him check out. He'd been nervous when he asked her out. But on the date, he'd been focused, interested in her. He asked questions, he leaned in, he listened.

Tell me about your parents, what were they like? What did you dream about as a kid? Did you always want to be a librarian?

She didn't answer that last one at first – only several dates later, a night at her apartment. "The truth is, I always wanted to play piano," she'd told him, showing him the keyboard in her closet, the one she'd gotten as a teenager, put away a long time ago, then salvaged again from her mother's house a couple of years ago. A second attempt to learn – this last time by watching YouTube videos – before she'd stuffed it away again.

The sight of it, the story behind it, seemed to upset him. Empathy for her failed ambitions?

"I wasn't very good," she explained, but his forehead stayed crinkled. Maybe poor talent wasn't any better than failed ambition.

*　　*　　*

These were the positive traits about him – traits she'd written down in her notebook, weighing her attraction.

1. He listens when I talk about my mother, about how I felt like I'm disappointing her
2. He was concerned, empathetic about my piano playing (lack of)
3. The first time he said, 'I love you', I could feel the weight of it, the thought behind it
4. His hand in mine feels strong but gentle

5. The mistiness in those blue eyes of his, smokiness even –
    <u>mysterious</u>! (She'd actually underlined that word, in a good way.)

Honestly, she'd thought it might be the start of something, date
after date.

Too soon, of course, to think of marriage, of children (though her
clock was indeed ticking, she felt that all too well). But the possibility was
there, the possibility of a future – first time she'd felt that, felt it strongly
enough that she'd let him move in, after all.

But then, same page, column B – counterpoint after counterpoint:

1. He never talks about his own family – what really do I know?
(a) Mother was a singer (part of his reaction to my piano playing?)
(b) Stepfather 'a hard man' (no elaboration on what that meant)
(c) Both of them lost in an accident G doesn't want to talk about
    (had he been in the car too?)
2. Wasn't his reaction to her piano playing a little neurotic?
3. *Every* time he says, 'I love you', I can feel the weight of it, the
    hesitation behind it
4. His hands always seem to be clenching and unclenching, like he's
    squeezing an invisible stressball (am I the stress?)
5. <u>Mysterious</u> ➔ <u>maddening</u>

Question piled on question:
•   Why did he never talk about that family?
•   Why didn't he have any friends he kept in touch with?
•   Why didn't he get together with anyone from work?
•   Were all his strange routines normal? That 'fastidiousness' of his?

His OCD-ness, Tess thought, call it what it was. I mean, *she* liked
order too – writing things down, seeing them clearly, mindful, aware –
but bowl in this place, spoon at this angle, coffee with *exactly* this much
honey, hunting the house for that ticking in the HVAC, and then this
new 'music' she was supposed to be hearing?

She'd been patient, though, hadn't she?

He couldn't have left because of anything *she* did. Could he?

(No, Carla kept saying, but did Carla really know?)

*　　*　　*

Tess kept coming back to how she'd made fun of him for the sounds he'd heard, for being out of tune.

But her intentions had been good, hadn't they?

1. Levity can lighten a situation
2. Best to downplay his urgency
3. Other times he'd gotten so wound up he'd lost himself (example, HVAC)

Still... maybe she'd been wrong to dismiss him.

What was the song? And where was he hearing it?

From her closet, she pulled out her old keyboard, set up the stand, plugged it in – regretting now she didn't do this when he'd first asked about the notes.

She began to finger the keys, trying to piece together whatever he'd hummed. *Da da da dum da da da dee? Da dum da dum da dee dee da?* A higher note or two first before a lower one, that was clear, but what *was* that first note? And how many of them? And what was the jump to the lower one? Had the note after that been the same note or a higher one again? What was the rhythm?

The truth was Garrett *hadn't* been very good at humming it – and even if he had, she'd never been good at naming that tune.

Which circled her back to her own reaction and how that might have driven him away:

1. Mistaken thought: Levity can lighten a situation
2. Incorrect assumption: Downplaying...
3. Etc.

But no, that wasn't it. It was just another relationship gone south, another boyfriend walking out. Sometimes things didn't work out – that same old song.

Same old song. She laughed – a good sign, she thought.

She started to shut down the keyboard, but instead began playing the scales she'd memorised so long ago. Even though she missed some of those notes, it felt good, her fingers against the keys.

She pulled out a music book from her old lessons, tried to brush up on reading the notes. Every Good Boy Does Fine – she'd always fumbled through that. FACE had been the easier one. A memory for faces instead of names, that thought flitted through her mind.

She surprised herself by how naturally some of it came back, some motor memory, and other memories too.

1. How much she'd wanted to learn piano, and her mother stressing the cost and how Tess had to stick with it because if she didn't practice practice practice…
2. How she'd wanted to learn 'Tiny Dancer' but her teacher Mrs Goolrick said she had to learn 'Chopsticks' and 'Twinkle, Twinkle' and 'Happy Birthday' and 'Für Elise' first.
3. The way Mrs Goolrick kept her drapes closed and that small sliver of light through the crack.
4. The way Mrs Goolrick smelled – sickly sweet mothballs, stale coffee, hairspray – and how her mother had said Tess was just trying to find a way out of it all.

Despite her fumbles now, Tess had to admit the music sounded good. Before she knew it, she'd been playing for an hour – no longer trying to get it right but just enjoying herself.

She ended up leaving the keyboard in the living room, began playing every day.

Maybe she'd take up piano for real. Or those pastels and watercolours stuffed away in the same closet. Maybe learn to bake finally.

Maybe she'd go wild. Shake up her style.

1. Take up piano again
2. Cut her hair short like she'd always wanted. Dye it red
3. Learn to surf

She'd always wanted to surf, she realised.
No limits really to who she might be.

*   *   *

Several weeks later, after Tess had stopped mentioning any of it to Carla, after she'd stopped noticing the clothes still in the closet except to think about whether she should box them up and donate them somewhere, Tess's phone dinged – an incoming message. Garrett.

Got your texts. Saw your name. May be strange to hear maybe, but not sure who you are any more. Or this 'us' you said. Or me really. Though I know who you are, I mean, I saw you that morning, so I remember that. It made me afraid, all of it – not of you, but of me. We must have meant something, I know I loved you, I must have. I don't want to hurt you.

*   *   *

Didn't want to hurt her? Tess shook her head.

How many times had she heard that?

- It's not you, it's me
- I'm not ready for a relationship right now
- I need some space
- You'll make someone really happy someday
- Etc. All that. More.

Then a second text a few minutes later.

Whatever's happening needs to be with someone I DON'T love.

She read that one a few times, not sure what to make of it. But here was the curious thing: she didn't feel disappointed anymore.

After the initial surprise of Garrett's disappearance – the suddenness of his absence, the totality of it – a second surprise had gradually crept up on her:

- I don't actually miss him

Tess felt relieved by this thought really – lucky now, thinking back on his quirks and obsessions, like she'd dodged some trouble she didn't need.

3

EXCERPTS: CASE FILE ON GARY BELL, OFFICE OF DR SEYMOUR BITTERMAN

[Standalone notation; no heading]

For documentation and insurance compliance, notes will use Gary's legal given name and surname. In session, patient has requested use of the name Garth, request with which I have complied. Both are in contrast to the name by which he was introduced in first unofficial meeting. Variety of names seem not evidence of schizophrenia or of multiple personality disorder but of serially progressive dissociative fugue.

*　　*　　*

Notes on third session, 27 May 20—

Gary reports some progress since last session, including returning to his workplace, though he has explained that transition as 'bumpy'. He retains some mechanical memory of how to do his work – the printing software, printers and copying machines – but he does not recognise his co-workers and continues to feel that he is pretending to be someone he is not. This provides further evidence of the dissociative fugue he has been experiencing, conclusions also based on the many instances he's described of watching himself from some distance, as if he is a stranger interacting with co-workers who are also strangers – awkward and alienating, as he himself describes it.

While he claims to be unable to access any memories of who he is, he continues to make efforts to reconstruct elements of his life both from the items in his possession – wallet, identification, credit cards, insurance card, the business card that brought him to me – and from search through his phone – contacts, emails, messages, social media. He also reports that he has reached out to his girlfriend in response to her text messages, which he called 'puzzle pieces with the picture slowly coming into view'. Still, he remains reluctant to return in person to see her or to enter the house where he had been living. He is also reluctant to use the word 'home' at all. He continues to live in his car.

While I've tried to encourage him in other directions, Gary has continued to focus on the musical notes he claims to hear, not only at sunrise now but increasingly at random throughout the day. Gary has picked up my term 'solution to self' from previous sessions, and he has insisted that the song may provide such a solution. He believes that understanding this song will help him 'cut through to the truth', even as he has simultaneously resisted discussions of childhood and family relationships which to my mind might identify the trauma that I suspect to be at the root of Gary's fugue state. (My job is to listen and lead, clearly, not discover and explain.)

As in previous sessions, we played the notes as he'd best determined what they were using trial and error and an app on his phone: several notes of higher C, several of lower, then stepping up to three at D and two at E, all played in various rhythms, fast, slow, etc. But today I proposed a new approach – hypnotherapy – and suggested that the combination of hypnosis and playing the notes might help to unlock further clues to counteract the fugue state and help trigger a return to self (though question of self remains layered, e.g. Gary and Garrett).

Gary agreed to my recommendation, and I induced a hypnotic state, relying on both metronomic ticking (courtesy of my own phone app) and verbal repetition to induce. The results were revealing if not entirely complete.

While under hypnosis, I asked Gary what he remembered about his time immediately before his first visit to me – the time between first hearing the musical notes and his call to me to make an appointment. No narrative details emerged; Gary returned to images familiar from previous sessions. Darkness and twilight. A woman lying in bed, with her back to him, humming. Himself standing somewhere in relation, but with his own back to himself – perhaps the initial presentation of the fugue state? There was another image of a kitchen, of standing at a kitchen counter, and of a knife stationary before him.

When I played the musical notes, Gary seemed to become anxious, hunching slightly and curving his shoulders inward while drawing his knees closer – foetal, clearly. But some of the images became clearer, both in more definite focus and in terms of content, angle and setting.

The woman he was watching was his mother (childhood memory, as anticipated), a beautiful woman with bright red hair (beauty and hair colour emphasised twice). He explained that she was a singer, information he had not related before. In new images, instead of lying down, she either stands facing him or crouches with her back to him. When standing, she holds a microphone close to her mouth, singing into it, words indistinct but the melody Gary has been hearing. When crouching, she hums the same song, but on the other side of a large room encompassing both a kitchen (same kitchen as aforementioned?) and an adjacent living area. According to a skewed angle of perception, Gary sits at a table at some distance from his crouching mother as another figure steps in between them. At first, this seemed to be a second self (himself watching himself), but upon questioning, Gary said that this was his stepfather and explained that the stepfather was humming the same song as his crouching mother.

Gary's posture continued to retract – evidence that we were perhaps tuned into the trauma scene at the source of his fugue. I have recreated a transcript of our discussion – a pivotal moment, in my professional opinion.

Q: What is your stepfather doing?

A: He's humming.

Q: Is he humming the same song as your mother?

A: Yes.

Q: Do you know what the song is now? Can you identify it?

A: No. He's reaching down towards her.

Q: Is this a gesture of warmth and tenderness? Of aggression and anger?

A: Her hair is like fire. Her mouth is open. [Here Gary formed his own mouth into a wide O.]

Q: Is your mother singing? Is she saying something?

A: She's quiet now.

Q: She didn't make any sound?

A: My father is the one talking.

Q: Your father?

A: Stepfather.

Q: What's he saying to her?

A: [Here Gary's voice shifted to become more gruff and husky, mimicking stepfather, it seems] 'How far...? Who was...? What the hell...?'

Q: What were these questions in reference to? Were these accusations?

A: He's talking to me. [Returning to his normal voice.]

Q: He's asking those questions of you?

A: No.

Q: OK. What's he saying to you then?

A: 'Love 'em and leave 'em.' [Gruff and harsh again, followed by a sound that seemed half laughter, half spitting.]

Q: Your stepfather was talking about women?

A: Sluts. [Still the gruff, husky tone.] Redheads the worst. Don't let 'em get in.

Q: Did your mother say anything in response?

A: ___

Q: Garth?

A: 'Don't let 'em get in.' [Then a return to his own normal tone.] He pointed at his head when he said that.

Q: With his finger?

A: ___

Q: Garth?

A: ___

Q: Gary?

A: No. The knife.

Q: He used the knife on himself?

A: ___

Q: On your mother?

A: It was an accident.

Q: What was an accident? What happened, Gary?

A: ___

Q: Gary?

A: Garth.

Gary didn't answer any further questions after that. It's worth noting that during the course of the questions and answers above, his body relaxed its foetal crouching, and Gary ultimately seemed more at ease.

After Gary emerged from the hypnotic state, I asked what he remembered. He returned to the images which have become common in our sessions: same light and darkness, same red-haired woman crouching then lying down, more of himself watching himself, same bed, kitchen, knife.

I moved then from specific questions about the memory to more general questions. What is love? How do you treat someone you love? How do you expect them to treat you? Do you believe people are innately good or bad? Do you believe in choice? In free will?

Gary became agitated anew at these questions. He wondered aloud if any of this was working. 'What matters?' he asked. He ultimately cut the session short, though he accepted the reminder card for our next meeting.

*   *   *

[Standalone private addendum: no heading, not for official documentation]

Nagging concerns about discoveries during hypnotherapy. Consulted Dr Meriweather to discuss. Consult: Focus on sexual and violent imagery (open mouth, microphone and knife as phallic), intensity of watching (stalking?), latent Oedipal fixations (mother as consistent motif) and related obsessiveness about musical notes.

Location of key trauma in Gary's early life seems potential clue to resolving fugue and identity issues. Question persists whether abuse → abuse, witness of violence begets violence? Sudden appearance/persistence of mother's song, visions/revisions of violence witnessed as child, unresolved trauma = potential danger? To Gary? To others? Possible concern that Gary may replicate behaviour?

Argument to Meriweather: If Gary can remember/recognise/resolve trauma, then healing can begin, healthy relationships will follow.

Meriweather counterpoint: If traumatic episode remains submerged/repressed, can fester, or perhaps find outlet in further violence, catching Gary unaware.

Q for Meriweather: His honest professional opinion or merely devil's advocate?

Upshot: Concern about Gary's own potential violence – unclear. No explicit suggestion of violent behaviour, either past or future from Gary himself – no ticking time bomb, at least no clear evidence to believe so. But Meriweather consult confirms need to document discussion separately – premature perhaps but liability concerns if potential subpoena of notes, god forbid any reason to.

Despite discussion, remain personally confident, however, of Gary's own fear of violence, fear of hurting someone he loves. So long as love is present, love will prevail? Optimistic perhaps. Will explore more fully in future sessions.

*   *   *

[Standalone memo; no heading]

Fourth scheduled session – patient did not show, no sufficient cancellation notice.

Bill insurance per office policy.

4

Psst. Steph?
You up?
Sorry! Early I know!

> 3 dings
> your worse than my alarm

Haha! Sorry x2

> sorry not sorry obvs
> whassup pheebs?

I am!
Not just awake.
Feeling good, I mean.

> u met someone

How'd you know?

> again

LOL!

> & its love at first sight

This one seems nice. Different.

> so much in love he already
> whipped out a ring and proposed

Stop it! We just met....
though he's still here.

> so he did whip something out

LOL!!

> whats his name?

Garth? Gareth?

seriously phoebe?
u dont know his name??!

LOL! I did ask, but it was loud.
We were at the club.

obvs
he couldve written it down
his name

No paper.
Took me awhile to get it out of him anyway.
He was like 'What's in a name?'

real romeo
rose by any other

And I'm like 'Well, you have to have one, yeah?'

and its garth

Or Gareth

old guy name
he married too?

Was.

filling my bingo card pheebs

Or maybe just serious relationship?
Either way, not now.

rebound

'Fresh start.'

and your the fresh

You sound like my mom.

u know how guys are
prolly a thing for redheads

STFU.

just sayin

He was nice. He listened. He was there.

there?
like 👻   he was there so y not f him?

No.
I mean there like present.
In a real way. Intense.

so... stalker
beware

I'm gonna phone another friend.

> ghead

You don't want to hear more?

> im here

Seriously.

> seriously

I'm saying he paid attention. He focused.
He was there.

> got it
> he listened
> but u couldnt get his name

Please?

> Sorry

It was the club.

> k

Electronica. Heavy beat.

> got it

They played that song you hate.

> the ticky one?

Yeah. That's how I met him.

> ticky ticky ticky ticky ticky
> awful

Middle of that song, and here's
this guy drifting my way.
Never seen him before,
maybe part of the allure.

> stranger come to town

Exact.

> same old story
> like a xerox

Not always.

>

Anyway, here we are dancing near one
another and then dancing WITH one another.
Then it's like we're in rhythm.

> ticky song got no rhythm

You just have to listen to it.

And here's the thing. He WAS listening.
First thing he says, he leans in and says,
'Do you hear it? Those notes.'

> ticky song got no notes

Well HE heard them.
And he was trying to get me to hear them too.
He's moving his hands up and down like he's
IDK
Conducting an orchestra or something.
And like he was humming but I couldn't hear it really.

> the club
> the ticky

He tried to hum it again later,
last night in bed.
All hmm hm hm hum hm hm hum.
And I'm listening to it, but whatever
he heard
it didn't sound like that to me.
'It's there,' he said.
'You have to listen.'

> somebody had too much to drink
> why didnt you ask him his name in bed?

Embarrassed I didn't
know it by then.

> for real

Anyway, we had fun.
I liked him. It felt good.

> so true love again?

LOL! NO!

> swept off your feet?
> dreaming bout happily ever after?

THAT'S NOT WHAT
I'M SAYING!

> all caps
> ease up

Just saying I had fun.
And different this time.

But different in a different way —
about me, not him.
And trying to share that news with
MY BEST FRIEND.

> appropriate use of caps lock
> finally
> and ty

You know how everybody pretends they're
looking for someone?

> yeah

The thing is he said straight out he just needed
someone.
He said he couldn't love anyone, not then.
But he needed someone.

> honest at least
> on his side
> did he say he needed a red-head in particular?
> cause fetish on bingo card too

Hush. That's the thing.
I felt OK with it.

> you'll still fall hard

Maybe. Maybe not.
But that's the thing, what we talked
about last night. He was telling me all
about that ex. Ex-wife, ex-girlfriend,
whichever. She had cheated on him, cheated
with many people. A singer, he said, so you can imagine.
Band, travelling probably, sleeping around, broke his heart
Left him hurt and angry, too angry to see
straight, that's what he said, said he doesn't
even know how he ended things, what he said,
how he got out.
And so he said straight out that the next
woman in his life needed to be someone he didn't love —
because he needed to figure out what love is anyway,
what to do next, who to be next.
Deep really. But here's the trick. How he said it,

it made sense. Because who knows what's next?
I mean you could find the love of your life
tomorrow or you could find that what you
wanted yesterday isn't what you want any more
and you could die tomorrow, so enjoy today, right?
Let the future take care of itself?
Live in the moment instead of worrying
about everything
Like I usually do – I can hear you saying that.
Which is why bringing him home last night
felt different than other times because he was clear
about not loving me and I was clear about just
wanting what felt good at the time.
No love.
And if it's right tomorrow then it's right and
if it's not it's not and if I DO decide love that's
fine and if I decide to leave that's fine and if
I were to get hit by a bus or whatever at least
I had what I chose in the NOW, you know?

tl;Dr

Asshole!
I was saying I was fine NOT having love at first sight.
Or love at all.
Live for the moment!
It was an EPIPHANNY!

spellcheck

Jerk.

we are who we are

Anyway I'll fill you in more later.
Sounds like he's getting up.

yep
be a good wifey
make him big hungry man breakfast

Bagels and cream cheese.

apron and nothing else

T-shirt and sweats TYVM.

give it a few minutes

He said he'd slice the bagels for us.
A gentleman!

                                    mansplainer

Hush.

                                        🐦

And he's humming again! So cute!

                              happily ever after

Whatev.
L8R?

                                          sure
                        cant wait for all the gory details
                        meet for coffee early pm, k?

                                      pheebs?

THE SCENT OF AN ENDING

Brian Price

It started with a tickle. A faint irritation in his chest. Then his eyes began to water and he started to cough. He had no idea he was dying.

"Bloody Julia," muttered Keith Watts. "Giving me her sodding cold. And it isn't as if she was standing anywhere near me."

Feeling the need for something loud, Keith eased a rare, signed copy of Pink Floyd's *The Piper at the Gates of Dawn* from its place on the shelf, removed the disc from the sleeve with cotton gloves and placed it reverentially on the turntable. He sat back to listen, immersing himself in the psychedelic swirls and crazy lyrics of his favourite band.

By the end of 'Interstellar Overdrive' Keith was beginning to feel quite unwell. His breathing was painful and his chest was tight but swallowing a couple of paracetamol tablets made no difference. Realising he was seriously ill and needed help, he tried to open the door but the key wouldn't fit in the lock. Something had jammed it. Shouting or banging on the door would be pointless as Emily and Julia wouldn't hear him – his den was soundproofed extremely well. He could reach the windows, if he stood on a chair, but they were too small to climb through and no one would hear him if he opened them and shouted for help.

Perhaps he could Skype or WhatsApp Emily? He staggered over to his laptop and switched it on. *No Internet Connection* flashed up when he tried to log in. Panicking, he stumbled to the door and tried once again to get the key in the lock. No joy. By now he could hardly breathe. He vomited, coughed up bloody mucus and collapsed on the floor. Ten minutes later, he took his last agonising breath.

★ ★ ★

Keith Watts's death had been reported by his wife, Emily, at 10:40 that morning. He hadn't appeared for breakfast and, getting no reply by hammering on the locked door of his den, Emily had stood on a ladder, peered through the window and shouted to her sister, who was holding the ladder.

"Get an ambulance. He's on the floor, not moving."

With Emily's permission, the paramedics had forced their way in. Keith was lying near the door, a small pool of vomit by his, obviously dead, body. A repetitive *hiss, click, hiss, click* was emanating from the enormous speakers at the back of the room as an LP rotated on the turntable, the music long since finished. A paramedic switched it off, checked for signs of life and called the doctor.

★   ★   ★

The faint smell of new-mown hay tickled Dr Singh's nostrils, reminding him of summer holidays in the country. Odd for December, he thought, but dismissed it from his mind and focused on the corpse in front of him. After examining Keith's body, he closed his briefcase, straightened up and addressed a weeping Emily sympathetically.

"This is very strange. It doesn't look like a heart attack, stroke or seizure. I really can't say why he died. There will have to be a post mortem, I'm afraid, and we'll know more then. I'm very sorry."

Emily's sobs echoed down the hall as the doctor arranged for Keith's body to be moved to the mortuary.

★   ★   ★

"What is it, Nick? Tell me you've got a tricky murder or an armed robbery for me."

Detective Inspector Matilda Barrett, tired of reading budget projections and yet another force mission statement, welcomed the interruption when Detective Sergeant Nick Lane poked his head round the door.

"There's a message from the pathologist. Could someone go down to the mortuary and look at a suspicious death?"

"Gladly – I need a break from this bloody computer. I joined to catch criminals, not sit in an office all day."

Stepping into the shoes she had kicked off under her desk, she straightened her jacket, smoothed her skirt and strode down the corridor.

★   ★   ★

"Good afternoon, doctor," she said as they shook hands. "I gather you're worried about a recent death?"

"Yes, I am. A Mr Keith Watts. Came in yesterday. I've not seen anything like this before. I first thought it may have been an asthma attack, precipitating heart failure. When I opened up his respiratory tract, however, I saw extensive damage to its lining and fluid in the lungs. I was puzzled so I rang up a friend of mine, a lung specialist. He said it sounded like poisoning with phosgene – a First World War gas. When I mentioned Dr Singh's comment about the smell of hay in the room, he was convinced."

"What does phosgene do?"

"In a layperson's terms, it wrecks the lungs. It smells a bit like cut hay but Mr Watts wouldn't have noticed it. His GP notes mention that he suffered from anosmia – he had no sense of smell.'

"Phosgene sounds horrible."

"It is. Anyone handling it needs specialist training to avoid killing themselves."

"So he couldn't have come across the stuff by accident?"

"No, certainly not. I can't give you an estimate of time of death, I'm afraid – we don't know how warm the room was throughout the night. From what Dr Singh said, he was probably dead for at least six hours before he was found. Anyway, I'll email you my report tomorrow."

"Thank you, doctor. I'll look forward to it."

Barrett phoned Superintendent Arnold as she walked to the hospital car park.

"We have a suspicious death, sir. Keith Watts. I'll notify the coroner and put a team together."

★   ★   ★

Two hours later, scene of crime officers were busy in Keith's den. A red-eyed Emily showed Barrett into the untidy kitchen, a scrunched-up tissue dangling from the sleeve of her cardigan and her hair in a mess. Declining coffee, Barrett offered her condolences and began gently.

"I'm afraid I have bad news, Mrs Watts. It looks like Keith was poisoned. We need to search the premises, if that's all right with you, but we'll do our best to avoid making a mess."

Emily paled and collapsed into a chair.

"Oh my God. Poisoned? I don't believe it."

"I know it's difficult for you, but can you tell me how you found Keith?"

"He didn't come down for breakfast. He usually needs his caffeine fix before ten so I went looking for him. He wasn't in his bed – we have separate rooms – but I thought he could be in his den. He sometimes falls asleep there."

"Were you worried? Did you think something had happened?"

"No, not really. I just went looking. I banged on the door of his den but he didn't answer, so I looked through the window. I knew something was wrong as soon as I saw him. An ambulance came quickly and I got the paramedics to break open the door."

Emily sobbed.

"It was horrible. He was lying by the door, his face all twisted and his eyes streaming. He'd been sick. I'll never forget how he looked as long as I live."

"It must have been dreadful for you. I'm sorry to add to your grief but can you tell me more about Keith's habits?"

"Keith collects, I mean collected, old records. They were his life and he was never happier than when playing them in his den. It was his private space, away from the rest of the house, and only he had the key. He would stay there all day sometimes and hated being disturbed, so I didn't knock on the door when I went to bed."

"What time was this?"

"About ten-thirty, I think. The central heating had stopped working during the afternoon, and we couldn't get an engineer to come until today, so I wanted to be somewhere warm. Keith had a portable gas heater, so he was comfortable in the den."

"Who else was in the house?"

"Only my sister, Julia. She came to stay that morning."

"Has anything in his den been touched?"

"Not since the doctor left. I couldn't bear to go in there again."

Emily fiddled with a bracelet as she spoke.

"Can you help me by running through everything that happened during that day?"

"I'll try but I'm not sure I can remember everything. It's been such a shock. Julia was helping me in the workshop during the morning. I restore furniture for a living. We went off to the garden centre for lunch, I suppose about twelve. We bought some plants and got back around three. Keith was in his den with two fellow record collectors, Simon Napier and Jimmy Chandler."

"Did Keith know the others well?"

"Fairly. They were friends but also rivals, each trying to outdo the others by acquiring the most obscure rarities. Keith was very good at that."

"What time did they leave?"

"Napier around five, I think. Chandler about forty minutes later."

"And then?"

"Keith stayed with his records until dinner, around seven. Afterwards he tried to restart the central heating, but couldn't, and then went back to his den. I never saw him alive again."

Her voice caught in her throat.

"Can you think of anyone who would have wanted to harm him?"

"God, no. He didn't have any enemies. There was friendly rivalry, as I said, but no hatred. Thinking on it, I did hear an argument in the kitchen, later in the afternoon."

"What was it about?"

"Oh, I couldn't catch it all, but it seemed to be something about low numbers."

"Low numbers? Numbers of what?"

"I've no idea. Something to do with records, I expect."

"Did you hear any noises in the night?"

"No, nothing. But Keith's den was soundproofed so he could listen to his music, as loud as he wanted, without disturbing the rest of the house. Also, so I wouldn't disturb him."

"Did you have a key to the den?"

"Definitely not. Keith wouldn't let anyone else in the room alone. He kept both copies in his pocket."

"I see. One last thing. Have you seen anyone suspicious around the house at all?"

"No, Inspector. No one. But our security lights aren't working so I can't be sure there was no one out there."

"Thank you, Mrs Watts. That's all for now. I'll need the addresses of the two collectors before we go. I'll arrange for a family liaison officer to support you and we'll need your fingerprints and a DNA sample for elimination purposes. Here's my card. Please get in touch if you can think of anything that might help us."

⋆   ⋆   ⋆

In the lounge, a brisk Julia had little to offer DS Lane. Smartly dressed, her business clothes contrasting with Lane's casual jacket and chinos, she was clearly irritated about being interviewed. Her elegant appearance was marred somewhat by a red, runny nose which she continually wiped with a tissue.

"I'm staying for a couple of days while they replace the boiler in my flat. Ironic, isn't it – I leave a freezing flat for a house with no heating. And I've got a cold. Anyway, I didn't see much of Keith. Apart from helping Emily in the morning and going out for lunch with her, I was working on a case. I'm a barrister. You can check my internet use if you need proof."

"I hope that won't be necessary. Did you see anyone else around the house?"

Julia sneered slightly.

"Only those collectors. Nerds like him with their boxes of records and one-track minds."

"I take it that you weren't fond of Keith. You don't seem distressed at his passing."

"No. If you must know, I disliked him."

"Why?"

"He was a creep. We all went on holiday once and he was forever ogling me and 'accidentally' brushing against me. I stopped wearing my bikini when he was around. I'm sure he would have made advances if Emily hadn't been there."

"But he never actually tried it on?"

"I didn't give him the chance. I avoided him whenever I could."

"I see. Anything else you can tell me?"

"'Fraid not. Can I go now? I do have work to do."

"Yes, thank you. We'll need your fingerprints and DNA and may need to talk to you again, though," Lane called, as Julia left the room abruptly.

$\star$ $\star$ $\star$

Keith's den was the epitome of tidiness and organisation. Records were arranged alphabetically on shelves around three walls. An expensive audio system took pride of place against the fourth wall and everything in the room was spotless. The only things out of place were the record sleeve, which belonged to the album still on the turntable, and a white double album which lay on the desk, with three pairs of cotton gloves next to it.

"That Beatles' *White Album*," said Lane, "is worth a fortune. Hence the gloves."

"What's so special about it?" queried Barrett.

"I collect vinyl. Each of these albums was individually numbered and very low numbers go for massive prices. This is number twenty-seven – it's probably worth three grand if it's in good nick. I bet he's got a few more treasures on those shelves."

Barrett whistled.

"Amazing. I didn't realise you were such an anorak. You can drool over the rest later. Right now, we have to work out how Watts was poisoned, in a locked room to which no one else had access."

Between them they went over every inch of the room, checking for holes through which the gas could have been injected. They found none. There were no suspicious cylinders, canisters or bottles in the room. The small, high-up windows were all locked securely, although a trapped green leaf suggested that one had been opened and closed recently. The only oddity was a large, roughly rectangular, mark on the varnished floorboards beneath the gas heater.

$\star$ $\star$ $\star$

As they were leaving, Barrett stopped to talk to a heating engineer, who was just getting into his van. She then caught up with Lane at the car.

"I don't understand why he didn't call for help when he started to feel ill," said Lane, as they drove back to the station.

"Perhaps he couldn't. Maybe someone stopped him from opening the door," Barrett speculated.

"Yeah. That's a thought. Did the SOCOs find anything?"

"Nothing obvious. We're still waiting for reports. We'll send his laptop and phone to IT forensics. There are some paper financial records but a quick glance suggests nothing unusual. I'll talk to the record collectors this evening and get their fingerprints. In the meantime, find out what you can about phosgene. Get someone to look into the family background. I'll send DC Richards to check the outside of the house for signs of intruders. Team briefing tomorrow at eight a.m."

*　　*　　*

When Barrett, accompanied by a detective constable, visited Simon Napier he was rubbing down a stripped-back door frame, his muscular chest stretching a faded Grateful Dead T-shirt. He showed her to a study lined with shelves of records and sprawled into an armchair, inviting Barrett to sit in its twin and leaving the DC standing.

"Can you tell me your exact movements at Keith Watts's house, sir?" she asked, after showing her warrant card.

"Sure. I arrived about two, the same as Jimmy. We talked records over a few beers and discussed our latest finds. I left about five, got home around half-past. I was shocked when I read about Keith's death on my newsfeed this morning. He seemed fine when I left him."

"Did you go anywhere else in the house?"

"Well, I went for a pee at some point. Otherwise, no."

"Where was Mr Chandler while you were doing this?"

"In the kitchen with Keith, getting beer."

"Were you alone at any time?"

"Only in the toilet."

"I understand there was an argument."

"Jimmy said that Keith had paid too much for a low number Beatles' *White Album*. Keith was furious and argued that it was a fair price and that low number examples would only increase in value. I didn't get involved. They calmed down eventually."

"Can you think of anyone who might want to harm Keith?"

"No, not really. He was a bit odd. No one really liked him that much but he knew his stuff. I don't think anyone actually hated him."

"Odd? How do you mean?"

"He was just so paranoid about his records. He seemed to think people would want to tamper with them. No one was allowed in his den alone. He went spare when a key was missing a few weeks ago, although it turned up again shortly afterwards."

"I see. Well, thank you, sir. I'll be in touch if I have any more questions."

*   *   *

Pale of complexion and nervous of manner, Jimmy Chandler wasn't just a record collector. The table in his hobby room was littered with model cars, some freshly painted and some taken back to the metal for repainting. More were displayed in cabinets on the one wall not occupied by records. Chandler stammered slightly but his answers were similar to Napier's. He confirmed that there'd been a disagreement – 'Nothing serious' – and said he waited in the hall while Keith saw Napier off. He, too, had used the toilet and was adamant that he hadn't been anywhere else in the house. Jimmy agreed that Keith had been odd. He also described him as being rather obsessive in his search for bargains, which he would crow about to others.

*   *   *

The chatter in the incident room subsided as Barrett started the briefing.

"Keith Watts, avid record collector, died in his vinyl sanctuary between about eight p.m. on Tuesday and four a.m. on Wednesday. His portable heater was switched on but the gas bottle was empty. He died from phosgene poisoning but the chemical couldn't have been injected into the room. He was found by his wife, Emily, on the floor near the locked door, with one key in his pocket and the other close to his hand. The windows were locked and there were no signs of anyone trying to open them from the outside. The ground was hard, so there were no shoeprints. If Keith had called for help, no one would have heard him as the den is soundproofed.

"The couple had no children and there are no offences on record, apart from a speeding ticket each. Keith wasn't well-liked but no one seemed to hate him, although there is rivalry among record collectors. He had no obvious reason to commit suicide. That's our starting point. What have we learned since?"

DS Lane spoke first.

"Keith's collection is worth a couple of hundred grand. It's full of highly collectable rarities."

"Inheriting that lot could be a motive for murder," said Barrett, "although his wife isn't short of money. She restores antique furniture and has an excellent reputation. All the big museums and auction houses use her. They have separate bedrooms so there could be some marital issues there, which we haven't discovered yet. Other collectors might like to see Keith's treasures come on to the market but, surely, they wouldn't kill for them? Anything else?"

"DC Wyman found these among the LPs, next to the Jefferson Airplane."

Lane held up a large envelope and tipped out its contents. Two dozen photos of a woman, in various states of undress, fell onto the desk. Some were shot through a bedroom window and others were taken on a beach, where she was changing into swimwear.

"That's Julia," said Barrett.

"She told Nick that Keith had been pestering her. Maybe it went further than that. He could have been blackmailing her. Putting naked photos of her on the internet wouldn't exactly help her legal career. She would never be appointed as a judge. A motive for murder, perhaps?"

"So we have four potential suspects for now," said Lane. "What about means and opportunity?"

"We need to work on those. What did you find out about phosgene?"

"You can't buy the stuff but it's made when some solvents are burned."

"Which solvents?"

"One used to strip paint, mainly. Something called dichloromethane. It was banned a few years ago but is still permitted in the US."

"But how could someone burn it and get the phosgene into the room?"

"Well, they couldn't," replied Lane. "There was no point of entry to the room. We looked everywhere. If a window had been opened and the gas pumped in, Keith would have noticed. Anyway, they were all locked from the inside."

Barrett frowned and thought for a minute. Then she smiled.

"Got it! It was the heater! The killer must have poured paint stripper onto a shallow vessel of some sort, perhaps a plate or dish, and slid it underneath. Some spilled, which accounts for the mark on the floor. As the stuff evaporated, the gas flame did the rest."

"Lucky for the killer that Watts used the heater."

"Not luck. Planning. I talked to the boiler repair guy and the timer was disconnected. It's unlikely to have happened by accident."

"Did the SOCOs find anything?"

"Not much. A few scratches around the lock on the inside of the door. No unidentified fingermarks – just Keith's, Emily's and the two collectors'."

"Why didn't Keith phone or email for help when he started to feel ill?"

"Good question," replied Barrett. "Get on to his internet service provider and see if it was working. And check his phone records."

Barrett summarised her conversations with the record collectors and continued.

"Of the four, only Julia has a particularly strong motive – and that assumes Keith was blackmailing her, or had assaulted her. All had access to the boiler, it's in a cupboard next to the toilet. All four could have possessed dichloromethane. There must be old stocks around and you can buy it as a pure laboratory chemical on the internet. Napier is doing some house renovating, possibly using old paint stripper. Chandler could use the stuff on his model cars. Emily probably used it for removing varnish from furniture and Julia helps her from time to time, so she would have known about it, too."

"But would they know how to turn it into phosgene?"

"That we don't know. Might be worth looking at their internet searches, if we can get a warrant to look at their computers. We'd need stronger evidence first, though."

She continued.

"A key disappeared some weeks ago. Emily or Julia would have had plenty of opportunities to copy it and one of the collectors could have taken it on a previous visit and replaced it later. A bit risky but feasible."

"How did the killer get the stuff under the heater?"

"Julia or Emily could have put it there around dinner time. The collectors both brought those large LP carriers which would easily hold a plate and a can of paint stripper or a bottle of the chemical. Chandler could have nipped in while Watts was seeing Napier off. Napier could have done the same while the others were arguing in the kitchen. The heater wasn't switched on until after they left and Keith wouldn't have noticed the smell of the stripper or the phosgene because of his anosmia."

* * *

When Barrett returned to the Watts house the following day, Julia had gone home and there was no answer when Barrett rang the bell. She walked round the side of the house and found Emily in her workshop, no longer red-eyed, French polishing a fine old writing desk. The workshop smelled pleasantly of wood dust, polish and wax. Tools were arranged neatly on hooks on the wall and shelves carried jars holding screws and nails. Brass fittings lay on a plate on Emily's workbench and a row of glass bottles held mysterious liquids.

Emily looked up from her work, visibly irritated.

"Can I help you, Inspector?"

"A few more questions, if I may."

"OK, but I need to keep polishing this piece. Concentrating on work helps me cope."

Barrett wondered if that was an excuse to avoid eye contact.

"Could anyone have copied Keith's key?"

Emily started. "No, certainly not. He had two copies which he never let out of his sight."

"I see. Do you use dichloromethane in your work?"

"I wish I could, but those strippers have been banned for years. For some woods they were the best you could get."

"So what's in the bottles?"

"Various polishes and stains I've mixed up – my own recipes. Take a look if you like."

Barrett declined.

"You said Julia helps you."

"Yes. She's quite useful and she says it makes a nice change from the stress of the courts."

"I see. How did you get on with Keith?"

"OK. We basically led separate lives. He was obsessed with his records and had little time for me. I have my restoration work. Still, we rubbed along and remained good friends."

"Did he support you financially?"

"He didn't need to. The mortgage is paid off and I earn enough from this. He was an accountant but was made redundant when his firm downsized. He got a decent pay-out and made some profitable investments."

"How about Julia?"

"What do you mean?"

She coloured and her hands gripped the desk tightly.

"I gather she didn't like him and thought he fancied her."

"She avoided him. She's younger and prettier than me so I suppose he did look at her, that's all."

"Was he blackmailing her with those embarrassing photos?"

Emily blinked.

"Photos? I don't know what you mean, Inspector. I haven't seen any embarrassing photos. Look, I don't want to be rude, but I must finish this desk. Is there anything else?"

"No, you carry on. I'll see myself out."

Barrett walked slowly back to her car, something niggling at the edge of her mind, something she'd seen. But what was it? She returned to the station for lunch, all the while worrying at her memory.

*   *   *

Talking to Lane in the canteen, Barrett ranked the suspects in reverse order.

"Least likely are Napier and Chandler – weak motives and not the easiest of opportunities. Also, they couldn't have retrieved the plate without help from someone in the household. Forget about them. Emily seemed to be indifferent to her husband, rather than hating him, although she did seem distressed when we first met her. She was nervous during our conversation today, especially when I asked about dichloromethane. But if Julia was being blackmailed, she had the strongest motive, so we'll have a serious chat with her. She could well know how to tamper with the boiler. Her own was being replaced, which is why she stayed with

Emily. We'll pick her up at her home address this evening. Did you find out anything about Keith's phone and internet use?"

"Yes. The router was switched off for several hours during the night, so he couldn't email, WhatsApp or Skype out. There's no mobile reception or landline in his den either."

Barrett stared thoughtfully at her empty plate and recalled her interview with Emily. She stood up suddenly.

"It's not Julia. It's Emily. Bring her in and caution her. I'll get a couple of DCs to search the workshop and any other outbuildings for old paint strippers. I need to collect something."

*   *   *

Barrett repeated the caution, switched on the recording equipment, identified those present and started the interview with a defiant Emily. A smartly suited solicitor sat next to Emily, making indecipherable notes.

"Thank you for coming in, Emily. We'd like you to clarify a couple of points for us."

"I didn't have much choice and I don't know why I'm here. I've got better things to do than answer yet more questions. And my solicitor is costing me money."

"We have reason to believe you were involved in Keith's death."

"Absolute rubbish."

"Then let me outline the case against you, Emily. Keith was killed with phosgene, produced from a plateful of dichloromethane which you placed under his heater. For the benefit of the recording, I am showing Mrs Watts a rectangular sandwich plate, which I retrieved from her workshop. The base matches a mark found under the heater in Mr Watts's den. Although the plate has been cleaned, there are some small brown marks on the bottom where the glaze is missing. We believe that tests will show that the stain is from varnish on the floor.

"You copied the key to Keith's den some while ago. Last Tuesday evening you tampered with the boiler to make sure he would use the heater. You slipped into his room, probably while he was finishing his dinner, and turned it into a gas chamber. We know that Keith couldn't get help – you switched the router off and he couldn't phone. He couldn't get out because you had jammed your key in the lock."

"Pure speculation, Inspector," interjected Emily's solicitor.

Barrett ignored him.

"In the morning, holding your breath, you retrieved the plate and opened a window to allow the gas to escape. Before staging the discovery, you shut the window again, trapping a leaf which you didn't see. Despite your efforts, a few traces of gas remained, which Dr Singh noticed.

"We found an old can of dichloromethane paint stripper hidden under the floor of a garden shed, with your fingerprints on it. I've no doubt that your internet searches will show us how you found out about phosgene. We also found a key to Keith's den, hidden in an empty soup tin and left in your recycling box."

As the evidence against her accumulated, Emily's despair grew. Her defiance evaporated and she crumpled in her chair, crying quietly. Barrett gave her a few moments to compose herself.

"So, why did you do it?" Barrett asked, her tone now sympathetic.

"It was for Julia," Emily sniffed.

Ignoring her solicitor's warning look, she continued.

"I found the photos on the printer a couple of months ago. The filthy pervert didn't know I was at home and hadn't retrieved them. When I challenged him, he blustered but I knew he was planning to blackmail her into sleeping with him. I saw how he lusted after her.

"I'd saved up some old paint stripper for my work and a warning on the can led me to find out about phosgene. I realised how I could kill him. Stupidly, I hoped it would look like a heart attack or something else natural. I copied the key a few weeks ago, planning to use it when I had the chance. I thought he was going to make his move while Julia was staying, so I had to act then. Julia knew nothing about it, I swear."

Emily sobbed as Barrett charged her with Keith's murder and handed her over to the custody sergeant.

"A devious murderer and a nasty man, Nick," sighed Barrett. "But at least she confessed. Our evidence is pretty circumstantial."

"Mixed feelings, boss?"

"No, not really. He may have been a creep but Keith Watts didn't deserve to die, certainly not like a gassed soldier, trapped in a First World War trench. No one deserves that."

"True enough. Pub time, then. Your round or mine?"

MIX TAPE

Cath Staincliffe

She made him mix tapes in the beginning. Musical love letters. Eclectic selections of three-minute sonnets.

Sitting cross-legged beside the boombox, wreathed in smoke, a can of Special Brew to hand, listening to the John Peel show or Ranking Miss P, fingers poised over the *Record* and *Play* buttons.

She spent Saturday afternoons flicking through the stacks at the second-hand record stalls in the Corn Exchange. Touring Piccadilly Records and Spin Inn for new releases, seeking out the tunes they danced to at the university disco, the West Indian Centre, at benefits for the Miners' Strike and Greenham Common.

★   ★   ★

After it was all over he made a tape for himself. Titled it *Our Soundtrack*. He even decorated the cardboard insert like she used to do with bright felt tips. And carefully labelled the tracklist. He played it often. Sometimes maudlin weeping through the drink, photographs scattered about. Other times angry, raving for all they had lost.

Side A

'Hey There Lonely Girl' – Eddie Holman
'Can't Take My Eyes Off You' – Frankie Valli
'I'm a Believer' – The Monkees
'You Really Got Me' – The Kinks
'Let's Get It On' – Marvin Gaye
'My Baby Just Cares For Me' – Nina Simone
'Going to the Chapel' – The Dixie Cups

'Lovely Day' – Bill Withers
'Let's Stay Together' – Al Green
'God Only Knows' – The Beach Boys
'The Power of Love' – Frankie Goes To Hollywood
'When a Man Loves a Woman' – Percy Sledge

Side B

'I Heard It Through the Grapevine' – Marvin Gaye
'Suspicious Minds' – Fine Young Cannibals
'You Don't Love Me (No, No, No)' – Dawn Penn
'I Would Rather Go Blind' – Etta James
'Walk Away Renée' – Four Tops
'The Sun Ain't Going to Shine (Anymore)' – The Walker Brothers
'Cry Me a River' – Ella Fitzgerald
'Paint It Black' – The Rolling Stones
'Nobody's Baby Now' – Nick Cave and the Bad Seeds
'Have You Seen Her' – The Chi-Lites

They came for him years later.

By then everything was MP3s and streaming. Though there was talk of a cassette revival. Same as had happened with vinyl.

He heard their words overlapping. Each one a hammer blow.

Remains discovered... serious anomaly... given your last statement... claimed not to have seen her for months... DNA traces... sole of her boot... consistent with your blood... shoes only bought a week before she went missing.

Doc Martens, fourteen hole. She always wore Docs.

She'd kicked out hard, smashing her heel into his face. His nose spurted blood. Fuelling his rage.

*   *   *

There was space on the tape for a final track, he realised, as they locked the cell door.

And he knew exactly what it should be.

She'd leap up whenever it started. Those familiar falling notes of the bass line, the bright tambourines joining in with their jaunty beat. He never danced to it. Thought it was cheesy. But she'd stomp around, hand on one hip, finger pointing in accusation, singing along and threatening vengeance. Vowing that one of these days she would deliver retribution.

Tongue in cheek, he'd thought back then.

Oh, the irony.

Side B: final track

'These Boots Are Made For Walkin'' – Nancy Sinatra

THE LAST GREEN BOTTLE

Catherine Aird

The time when a funeral commences is quite easy to determine. It's when the cortège reaches the entrance to the church and the congregation, very much on the alert for the arrival of clergy, coffin and family, then struggles to its feet. The moment when the ceremony can be said to be finally over is less easy to determine.

Some mourners, those not very close to the deceased or too busy to spare the time to contribute to the final part of the obsequies, will often take the opportunity to slide away at this point in the proceedings. Others dutifully follow the coffin out of the church and into the churchyard and thence to the graveside.

On this particular occasion the officiating clergyman, the Rector of St. Anthony's Church, Pevington, in the county of Calleshire, said a few more words of comfort and hope while young Tod Morton, the undertaker, began to offer a handful of loose earth from a shovel to those assembled round the graveside who wished to cast it down onto the coffin, murmuring 'Earth to earth' in undertones as they did so. The origins of this ancient and quite possibly pagan practice being lost in the mists of history, Tod Morton took care not to offer his loaded shovel to anyone present who hung back.

He had already caused the headstone of the double grave to be moved to one side, and would have quite some work to do reinstating it afterwards. It was an interesting one, as it was composed of white marble and had been carved in the shape of an open book. On the right-hand 'page' of this was already inscribed the name of *Sheila Mary Burwash, beloved wife of Colin Burwash*, and the date of her death some five years before. Under this were inscribed in inverted commas the words 'Until the Day Dawns'. It was into the newly dug space alongside this earlier grave that the coffin of Colin Burwash had just been lowered.

A tall, well-dressed elderly man, still of upright bearing, who had been standing on the fringes of those grouped at the graveside, was one of those who had eschewed the ceremony of casting the earth. He had waited long enough, though, to make his move out of the churchyard until just after the last handful of earth had been scattered over the coffin. Anyone who had happened to turn round shortly after that could have seen a sleek grey Jaguar car being driven away from the church car park, but no one did, being now more concerned in the exchanging of suitable pleasantries with the others there.

It was little more than half an hour after that when Detective Constable Crosby burst into Detective Inspector Sloan's room at Berebury police station and announced breathlessly that there had been a murder reported in the village of Pevington, some miles beyond Berebury, and well out into the Calleshire countryside.

"Just reported, sir. A man called Burwash of 24 Church Road there did it, the message said. A Colin Burwash." He frowned and peered at his notebook. "Then he said something I didn't quite get about there having been ten green bottles hanging on the wall but there weren't any more now."

Sloan, never a man to waste words, immediately joined the constable in the police car and did not ask for further details until they were well into the traffic stream and speeding in the right direction.

"That's all that the man who rang in said, sir," answered the constable. "That a man out there called Burwash had murdered someone and then he went on about some green bottles which I didn't understand. After that he rang off without saying who it was that he'd murdered."

"It hasn't caused a sensation here yet," observed Detective Inspector Sloan mildly, confident that the call could be traced easily enough. They had turned into Church Road at Pevington without seeing anything to indicate which house there was number 24 or that all was not well there. There was no cluster of ghoulish sightseers, no twitching curtains and, more importantly, there was no one standing anxiously outside in the road on the lookout to guide police and ambulance to the right house – always a sure sign of an emergency.

"Wait until we get inside, sir," forecast Crosby.

He was destined to be disappointed. The two policemen tumbled out of their car when they found number 24 but were diverted from going to the front door by the sight of a young woman pegging out clothes on a washing line in the back garden. A toddler was pummelling a slightly older brother while a sleeping baby was parked in a pram under the shade of a tree.

"Police," jerked out Crosby in a manner derived from the silver screen.

The woman gave a quick glance in the direction of the family car standing safely on the garage apron before saying, "Something wrong, then?"

"Murder," said Crosby impressively.

This time she looked in the direction of the house. "You'd better come in then and have a word with my husband." In her book murder was clearly a male preserve. "Jason," she called to the eldest child, "don't do that or you'll wake the baby." She turned and looked at the two policemen again. "You did say murder, didn't you?"

Her husband seemed equally unalarmed. "Someone's been having you on, mate. Leastways, if there has been a murder here no one's told us anything about it, and we live here."

"You can look round the house if you like," offered the young woman, while still keeping a wary eye on the children in the garden.

Her husband endorsed this, waving an arm. "Feel free," he said.

"And you said your name was Pearson?" said Detective Inspector Sloan, writing down what he had told her.

"Not Colin Burwash?" asked Crosby.

"It's Pearson," repeated the man firmly. "Kevin Pearson," he said, adding sardonically, "or so my father always led me to believe. More to the point, so did my mother."

"He's got his father's eyes," contributed the woman, not quite grasping the import of this exchange.

"I don't know of anyone in the street of the name of Burwash," said Pearson.

"Neither do I," said his wife. "Mind you, we've only been here since we got married and we don't know everybody."

"Old Mrs Sykes next door does," said Pearson, adding feelingly, "And everything about them."

"Do you know anything about Ten Green Bottles Hanging on a Wall?" asked Crosby.

"Now it's me you're having on," growled Kevin Pearson.

Detective Inspector Sloan, a conscientious man, decided that no harm would come from having a word with old Mrs Sykes next door. He was prepared, though, for her not to be all that old. The Pearsons were young enough to think of forty as being almost over the hill. In the event he was wrong about this. Old Mrs Sykes was old, but very sharp.

"We've had a report of a murder hereabouts," began Sloan.

"From the newspapers, are you?" she said unexpectedly. "Or is it for a book?"

"From the police," said Crosby, stung.

"They write stories, too," countered old Mrs Sykes.

Since this was undeniable and even considered by some members of the force to be unfortunate, too, Crosby asked what did the police writing stories have to do with a murder.

"Research," said the old lady. "They used to say that Dolores's death was Calleshire's very own Red Barn murder."

"Dolores who?" asked Sloan immediately.

"Dolores the Dire was what they always called her round here. She was the woman who was murdered in the hayloft at Brambles Farm just outside the village. I misremember her surname now." She looked appraisingly at the two policemen. "Before your time, I daresay?"

Detective Inspector Sloan could stand just so much surrealism, but no more. "This murder," he began crisply, putting Maria Martens and her murder in the Red Barn out of his mind.

"Manslaughter, they called it in the end," she said, "because she might just have fallen from the hayloft onto the barn floor like he said."

"Who said?" asked Sloan, the phrase 'one green bottle accidentally fell' coming to mind.

"The man who did it, of course. An army man, he was, and they know how to kill, don't they?"

"I should hope so," murmured Crosby, who as a schoolboy was brought up on comics. He was young enough still to have a video-game idea of warfare – and never to have known the actuality.

"When was all this?" asked Sloan pertinently.

She frowned. "Must be the best part of twenty years or more ago by now."

As they thanked her and took their leave Sloan casually asked old

Mrs Sykes if she remembered the people who had lived next door before the Pearsons.

"'Course I do. The Burwashes," she replied promptly. "Sheila and Colin. Sheila, she died 'bout five years ago. He went to live over Calleford way after that and then they said he'd had to go into a care home on account of their not ever having had any children to look after him. She really minded about that, did poor Sheila. I did hear that he'd died, too, not that long ago."

"Did you ever hear anything about Ten Green Bottles Hanging on a Wall?" persisted Crosby.

"Sung it at school," said Mrs Sykes succinctly. "A right daft song if you ask me. Teaching kids how to count they said it was."

"Crosby," said Detective Inspector Sloan as they walked back to their car, "did you turn over two pages or something?"

"Two pages?" echoed Crosby richly, "more like twenty, sir, if you ask me."

"Are we being led up the garden path then, do you suppose?" asked Sloan, since this was not unknown even in the detective branch.

The constable said dubiously, "The man who rang in didn't sound phony to me, sir."

"Since, Crosby," said Sloan, "we don't either of us know precisely what someone trying to lead us astray should sound like, perhaps you'd better take us to the newspaper office instead. At least," he added ironically, "they're not likely to mistake us for gentlemen of the press there."

The pages of the old copies of the *Berebury Chronicle*, sere and yellow though they were, were still legible. The first mention of a death in a barn at Pevington was a brief report stating that the police had been informed and were making enquiries.

"I'll bet they were," said Crosby.

The next week's issue included a two-page spread topped with a blurred photograph of the face of the woman found dead. A post-mortem examination had revealed that the woman had died from multiple injuries and was five months' pregnant. Inspector Walter Wilkinson had been put in charge of the case at the time and a former serviceman was helping the police with their enquiries.

"Nothing changes, sir, does it?" Crosby remarked to Sloan.

"Walter Wilkinson got to be Assistant Chief Constable before he retired," said Sloan. "I did hear he's living somewhere on the coast these days."

The following week's edition of the frail newsprint was much more specific. Christopher Martindale, of the next village to Pevington, had been charged with the murder and committed for trial at the Crown Court in Calleford.

★   ★   ★

"Of course, I remember," said Walter Wilkinson, pouring the two detectives cups of tea in his trim bungalow by the sea at Kinnisport. "Martindale's defence was that he and Dolores had been romping about in the hayloft and she had rolled off over the edge and fallen down onto the barn floor. He could see that she was dead and that was why he had automatically pulled a tarpaulin over her. Proper Amy Robsart affair they made it out to be."

Detective Inspector Sloan nodded intelligently, the one green bottle that accidently fell coming into his mind again. "And did she fall or was she pushed?"

"Neither," said the old policeman. "According to the doctor, that is. He wasn't at all happy about some bruises round her neck and in a lot of other places he wouldn't have expected from a fall, as well. But the doubt about it all did serve to get the charge commuted to manslaughter, which was something."

"I wouldn't have thought that an old soldier would have panicked," observed Sloan judiciously.

"That's what the Prosecuting Counsel said, too," said Walter Wilkinson. "And went on saying. But there was a lot of sympathy for men home from the Falklands War in those days. And not a lot for pregnant girls," he added thoughtfully. "Dolores, in particular."

"You knew her then?" said Crosby.

"Only too well, my boy. We all did in 'F' Division. In any case we never thought murder would stick but there was always the risk that it might. His distinguished war record helped. The man had been decorated for bravery, too. Twice. That really helped a lot."

"So what did he get?" asked Crosby, beginning to lose interest.

"Seven years. Or it might have been ten. I forget now."

"Ten," said Detective Inspector Sloan firmly, light beginning to dawn. "It would have been ten."

"I don't remember exactly," said the former detective, looking up. "Is it important?"

"Not any longer, but it was murder, though, wasn't it?" said Sloan, who had got the old man's drift even if Crosby hadn't done.

"Oh, yes," said the old policeman placidly. "It was murder all right. Dolores was a really bad lot. She had it coming to her, if any woman did. That was only a matter of time. Dolores the Dire was what everyone called her in those days, and she really was. Another cup, either of you?" He picked up the teapot. "Getting it off his chest now, is he? In my experience they all want to do that in the end."

"We don't really know," said Sloan, sinking the tea and then rising to go, "but we intend to find out."

Walter Wilkinson saw them to his front gate. "By the way," he said, "there was a young constable on the force in my day who thought rather a lot of himself. Name of Leeyes. Did he ever get anywhere?"

It was actually to Police Superintendent Leeyes that Sloan would be reporting presently, but not until he'd found Christopher Martindale. The superintendent didn't like half a report.

"I want to know where a man called Christopher Martindale lives," Detective Inspector Sloan said to the member of 'F' Division of the Calleshire County Constabulary who specialised in the tracing of those who, usually with good reason, did not wish to be traced. "If he's still alive, that is."

"As long as he's not called Smith or Jones, I'll do my best," said the man, adding lugubriously, "I'm not very keen on looking for Browns either."

"And one called Colin Burwash, who is said to be recently dead," went on Sloan, undeterred.

"That'll be easier," said the man. "The dead don't move."

"Except to the cemetery," muttered Crosby under his breath.

In the fullness of time came the reply from the man that Colin Burwash had died last Saturday week...

"Like Solomon Grundy," muttered Detective Constable Crosby, another nursery memory surfacing.

"And," continued the man, "your other fellow wasn't difficult to find, either. Here's his address."

Christopher Martindale lived in one of Berebury's best streets, a quiet backwater of good houses. His surroundings were on the affluent side of comfortable and Sloan hoped he hadn't learned the wrong ways of achieving these in those years in prison.

"I'm sorry we've taken so long to get here," began Sloan, who believed in taking the initiative where possible.

"There was no hurry, Inspector," said Martindale politely. He seemed to have been expecting them. "After all it was a long time ago now."

"You wanted to set the record straight, I suppose," said Sloan.

"You could say that, I suppose," agreed Martindale equably. "But it wasn't what William Shakespeare said about conscience making cowards of us all."

"No?" said Sloan.

"No. Now just seemed to be the right moment."

"So, Dolores was murdered, then?" said Sloan, opening his notebook.

"Oh, yes, Inspector. Definitely." He remained quite calm, his whole bearing still that of a man totally relaxed.

"She was pushed, you mean?" asked Detective Constable Crosby, anxious to get one thing quite clear. "She didn't fall?"

The older man's face twisted wryly. "You could say that in a manner of speaking she fell first and then she was pushed."

"The bruises," persisted Crosby. "They said there were bruises."

"The doctor was quite right about those," agreed Martindale. "He wasn't at all happy about them but as the accused had pleaded guilty the medical evidence didn't get much of a look-in."

"Blood always tells, though," said Sloan sedately. "You can usually count on it. It was said at the trial that the accused had blood matching that of the deceased on his clothes."

"Very true. He had."

"But not who the father of the baby was. That wasn't mentioned in the report of the trial."

"Just as well, Inspector," said Martindale. "In the circumstances, that wouldn't have done at all."

"I understand that there's been quite a lot of progress in that field since then," remarked Sloan with apparent inconsequence. "DNA is the police's friend these days."

"Science marching on and all that," contributed Crosby helpfully.

"In those days," said Martindale, "you should remember that a man was completely at the mercy of the mother and what she chose to say about who the father was."

"Quite so," said Sloan. "Could one suggest perhaps that there was some doubt in the case of Dolores?"

"I think one could say, Inspector, that there was absolutely no doubt at all." The man Christopher Martindale still appeared quite relaxed and was quite unhurried.

"You mean she wasn't pregnant?" asked a confused Crosby.

"No, Constable, I don't mean that at all." Martindale turned towards him. "Dolores was certainly pregnant. There was no doubt about that. It was just that the wrong conclusion was drawn."

"I see," said Sloan. A lot of murderers said that by way of exculpation. The law naturally took a different view. "You just felt that the baby wasn't yours?"

"I knew it wasn't mine," said Martindale. "That wasn't the point, Inspector."

"Ah," said Sloan alertly. "Then tell me why…"

"Actually, it mightn't have been Colin Burwash's baby either but he couldn't be as sure as I was."

"Colin Burwash?" echoed Crosby, frowning, the memory of a voice coming back to him. "You mean the man you told us in your message – it was your message today, wasn't it? – was the murderer?"

Christopher Martindale nodded. "That's right. Colin killed Dolores because she was threatening to tell Colin's wife Sheila about their affair and the baby."

Detective Inspector Sloan said, "And where did you come in, then?" He thought about saying something about the crime of aiding and abetting a murder but changed his mind and thought about ten green bottles instead. He knew where they came in now: one for every year of a prison sentence.

"Colin rang me in a panic that night, Inspector. He said he knew I would know what to do seeing that I'd been in the army."

More than eight hundred years had made no difference to the way in which a fighting man thinks of a civilian. Or a civilian of a fighting man, presumably. Unbidden, Henry Vth's speech before Agincourt about 'gentlemen now abed in England thinking themselves accursed they were not here' floated into Sloan's mind, and was gone as quickly.

"So?" Sloan said instead.

"So, Inspector, I made sure I got some of Dolores's blood on my hands and clothes and then went round to the Royal Oak pub shaking like a leaf and had three double whiskies in quick succession, while Colin went home, had a bath and went to bed with his wife."

"Colin Burwash?" asked Detective Constable Crosby, still puzzled. "You mean the man who's just died?"

"It was the Last Green Bottle Hanging on the Wall," said Sloan, putting his notebook away.

"Sheila loved him, you see," said Christopher Martindale by way of explanation.

"Sheila?" echoed Crosby, still confused.

"His wife. My sister."

TAXI!

Chris Simms

His good eye narrowed. A possible had appeared in the side street opposite. From the unlit interior of his Nissan, he watched her unsteady progress. She came to a stop, pressed a palm against the wall and swallowed back a few mouthfuls of air. She was wearing a skirt. He liked them in skirts; made things easier. Was she going to be sick? He hoped she wasn't. Or maybe it would be better if she was. Didn't want anything like that happening if he got her into the car.

Behind her, a speaker above the doors of the nightclub blared out music. How he hated the stuff these people listened to. Brash, monotonous drums. Words practically shouted. No subtlety or depth.

Her hand dropped to her side and she stood motionless, feet planted a little too far apart. She focused on the pavement before her, as if willing one of her legs to work. Definitely a possible, this one.

A group were on their way towards the doors she'd just emerged from. Talking loudly, they started to go round her. But then one of them – a female with braids of yellow hair coiled on her head – looked back. She said something to her companions. No, no, no. Don't try and help.

They gathered round her in their skimpy clothes and oversize heels. Light was caught in the glitter on their faces. They had the painted lips of harlots. One laid a hand on her shoulder. In response, she made a flicking motion with her fingers before managing a few tottering steps. They watched with concerned expressions. Something was called to her, but she repeated the gesture while continuing towards the main road. Closer to his parked car.

The only male in the group said something and, reluctantly, the three women turned round and followed him towards the glowing doorway. Good little girls, listen to the man. In you all go.

She was now at the corner. Her head made a jerky swing as she tried to survey the main road. He was deep in shadow, safely tucked in behind another parked vehicle. What are you thinking? Will you turn left or right? Which will it be?

The local news came on the radio. A few headlines that held no interest for him. Then an update on the series of attacks on women in the Manchester area. He eased up the volume. The latest victim had died of her injuries that morning. The presenter went on to say that, following the murders of Caitlin Meredith in May, Lorna Reeve in June and Vanessa Baxter in August, four women aged between eighteen and twenty-three had now been killed. Of the four, he could remember Caitlin Meredith most clearly. But the first always would be special, wouldn't it? How nervous he was, wondering if his half-formed plan would ever work. The amazement when it did. Police were urging those enjoying a night out to stay in groups and only use pre-booked taxis.

Lights in his side mirror. Several cars were heading along the road. She raised a hand as they sped by, not a taxi among them. Are you that drunk you can't even tell? She set off in pursuit, weaving from one side of the pavement to the other, a look of grim determination on her face as their rear lights shrank into the distance.

He waited a little while longer before starting the engine and turning on the lights. As he struggled to get the seatbelt across his huge belly, he couldn't help licking his lips. He had a feeling this one was more than just a possible.

*   *   *

"Where are you going?" I called through the open passenger window. She blinked stupidly at my car, as if not quite believing it had pulled over. "You a taxi?"

"Yeah! Where are you going?"

Her hand was still held out. "Towards…"

Why do they get themselves in such states? It's disgusting. "Towards?"

"You know, there." She gestured down the road with a forefinger.

We were on the Chester Road. Carrying straight on would lead to Sale. "Jump in, then."

She went to open the front door, then hesitated when she saw the debris I'd carefully arranged on the front seat. Coins, CD cases, sweet wrappers and a little notepad real cabs used when the passenger wanted a receipt. "Better in the back. More room, too."

"'K."

As she lurched towards the rear door, I quickly checked the road. Nothing coming in either direction. My heart was thudding. Once in the back, the tinted rear windows would ensure no one could see her. The door opened and she practically fell into the vehicle. I observed in the rear -view mirror as she twisted her torso, reaching across to slam the door shut. Firm little breasts. Fair hair, like the first one's. Caitlin.

"So, you're wanting to go to Sale?"

"Alty," she said, giving up on trying to find the seatbelt and slumping into the corner.

"Altrincham?" That's where the first one had been going, too. Another little rich bitch. Even more fun.

*   *   *

It was his half-closed left eye that made me think. What do they call them? Lazy eyes, that's it. I made a show of losing my balance as I got in his car. It was important that he believed I was drunk. He was watching me in the rear-view mirror as I got myself back into a proper sitting position, reached for the door and slammed it.

He asked again where I wanted to go and seemed pleased when I said Alty. Probably thinking how lucky that was. Another pissed blonde-haired girl going to Altrincham. That's if it's even him, of course.

He had music playing, but not the Bhangra style I'd been expecting. This was softer, more gentle. I scrabbled about in the pockets of my jacket, knowing his eyes were still on me.

"Whereabouts in Altrincham?" he asked.

Frowning now, I continued my search. "Can't find my phone. Shit, can't find my phone!"

"Try your handbag."

"Mmm?" I looked about. "Oh, no, where's my handbag? Where's—"

"On the seat beside you."

I looked down to my right. Acted surprised to see it lying there. "It's here! Thank Christ." I lifted it on to my lap. "What's this playing?"

"I can change it if you want me to."

"It's fine." As the car started moving, I slipped my phone out. Using my handbag as a shield, I brought up my sister's last messages. The ones she'd sent me on the night she was killed. There was the final one.

Ranga!

It was one of our little jokes. A sisters thing. I'd got things mixed up once and called the fast-moving dance music you sometimes heard coming from the city's shisha lounges Ranga, not Bhangra. So, when she'd sent the message, I'd assumed that was the music playing in the vehicle she'd climbed into.

But now I wasn't so sure. Maybe she'd meant the driver had a lazy eye – like that comedian off the telly. The one whose series was called *The Ranganation*. Is that what her message had meant? Her driver had a lazy eye?

"A good night, then?"

I lifted my chin, and widened my own eyes for an instant, as if having trouble focusing. "Good night? Yeah."

"That's good."

Nodding in agreement, I stifled a fake yawn. My mind went to what I'd told the police. Because of me, they believed the man who killed Caitlin – and the others – was probably young and of Pakistani heritage. But this man must have been over fifty. And he had pale skin. In fact, he looked more Caucasian than South Asian. Maybe Turkish or Syrian? The music he had on could have been Turkish. Were the instruments those long-necked lutes?

Caitlin would have known. There wasn't much about music she didn't know. My darling little sister. I pulled my collar right up so it formed a barrier between my head and the window. As if settling down to sleep. Then, keeping my phone hidden, tapped out a message to Flynn.

I thought about the detective's face when she realised what I was doing. Good. It would finally force them into actually doing something.

*   *   *

I eased the heating up a few notches so warm air began flooding the back of the car. Not long and she'd be asleep; she'd already yawned once. Soon, her body slumped lower, head sagging to the side. I kept a nice steady pace.

After a few more miles, I tried the first test. A little jink of the steering wheel. It rocked her body slightly, but her head just slid back against the window. I made the swerve a bit stronger. But she just sank lower, both eyes definitely shut.

I began to consider the best place to take her. It had its advantages working as a delivery driver during the day; there wasn't much of Manchester I wasn't familiar with. The dead-end lane beside Sale Water Park was a no-no. That's where I'd taken the very first one and the police could have set up a camera there or anything. I scanned through other options in my head. Sale Cemetery? That was a couple of miles further along the A56. The recreation ground behind the big school off Harboro Lane? I checked the time: just after midnight. People could still be up in the houses bordering it. Too risky taking her there. Then I had an idea. It meant ignoring a one-way sign, but the turn-off was only a short way after it. This time of night, the chances of a car coming the other way were tiny.

*   *   *

I kept the tiniest crack of my eyes open. Through the hazy veil of my eyelashes, I could just make out my phone's screen. I scrolled up to read once again the last of Caitlin's messages. She'd spent her final day in college. A few on her course had gone to a concert in the main performance hall at the Royal Northern College of Music. A Russian pianist, her message had said. Obviously influenced by Rachmaninoff, but very impressive all the same. How she could even tell those things, I had no idea. After that, they'd gone for noodles then cocktails in the Northern Quarter. Later still, they'd been heading for more drinks in The Sky Bar. Somewhere between the two, she'd become separated from the rest of the group.

Her aim was to complete her Bachelor of Music degree and then apply for a Masters in Composition down in London. We'd already discussed me going to stay with her. The two of us jumping on the tube, seeing London's sights, maybe picking up cheap seats for a West End musical, then the bars and clubs of Soho.

He'd destroyed all that, the man who murdered her. Snatched something beautiful and kind from the face of the earth.

The car moved left and then immediately right, as if he was steering round something in the road. I used the opportunity to tilt my head back a fraction. Now I could see his hands on the steering wheel. Stubby fingers with thick patches of dark hair above the knuckles. The police had told us she'd been strangled. Had those hands squeezed the life from Caitlin? Did it happen right here, where I'm sitting?

The car jinked again and I could feel his stare in the mirror. That left eyelid permanently half open. Stuck in an eternal leering wink. He's making sure I'm asleep. This is him. After so much wandering around late at night, I think I've finally found him. I didn't need to actually see my phone to type another message to Flynn.

Blue Nissan. Still on A56. Could be going to same place as Caitlin. Hurry.

★   ★   ★

Time for the second test. I turned in my seat and, keeping my voice low, I said: "I need to stop for some fuel. OK?"

Nothing. Fast asleep.

A pair of headlights were a few hundred metres back but catching up fast. I double-checked my speed. Thirty-two. Nothing to concern any patrol car. Was it a patrol car? I tried to make out what was behind those two glaring points of light. Impossible to tell. It got closer and closer and then flashed past. A black VW doing over sixty. Risky, this time on a Saturday night.

I reached across to the glove compartment and partially opened it. Just enough to make sure the gaffer tape and plastic ties were in there. As if I'd forget to pack them! Right: the turn-off I wanted was about a mile ahead. I wondered if it was too early to switch music. She was totally out of it. I could probably have it on full volume and she wouldn't know.

★   ★   ★

Detective Flynn's message appeared a few seconds after he changed the music.

Tell him you feel sick. Ask him to pull over. Exit the car immediately and stay on the main road.

I wondered what to reply. Part of me wanted to point out that, if their investigation hadn't been so fucking useless, maybe I wouldn't have had to be here. First, they'd spent days looking into Ben, Caitlin's boyfriend, even though the thought of Ben being able to... it was just stupid. Next, they started asking Dad questions. Dad! My seventy-year-old Dad. More time wasted.

But what pissed me off the most – and I know it's a stupid thing, I really do – was Caitlin's possessions. Her phone had been smashed, stamped on. But they took three days to find her college bag, even though it was in the undergrowth a few metres from where she'd been found. Human error, Flynn had mumbled. Whatever that bloody meant. We'd told them again and again she would have had it with her. Caitlin had a mild form of OCD. She wouldn't have left it in the cocktail bar, or in Wagamama's or beneath her seat in the RNCM's concert hall. When they searched the lane again and finally hooked it out, rain had ruined everything. The folder with the velvet cover I'd bought her when she won her place: all her score sheets inside were mush. The final piece she was working on, lost forever. And they never even found the present Mum and Dad had given her: a Kaweco stainless-steel pen for when she was writing music. They'd even had it engraved with her name.

I thought about that pen a lot. A really lot. Had he kept it as some sort of trophy? Was that where it was? Hidden in a box beneath his floorboards, now among other items he'd kept from the other girls whose lives and futures he'd also stolen? Did he lift the lid every now and again? Take it out and caress it? The thought of that made me want to scream. My counsellor kept saying I had to explore those feelings. That it was the only way I could start to move past the anger.

A *click-clock-click* of the indicator. He was leaving the main road. But he didn't turn left, like I was expecting. Sale Water Park was left. What was he doing? I didn't dare turn my head to see exactly where we were. But the road was suddenly much darker.

I probed the outside of my handbag, felt the contents through the thick fabric, quickly located the fat cylinder inside. Mace. The moment he got close enough, the contents were going straight in his face.

Feeling sick with nerves, I realised I hadn't replied to Flynn. Told her that we weren't on the main road anymore. There was a pause in the music. I don't know how, but in that moment of quiet, I could tell trees were now on either side of the car. Something about how the noise of the tyres was reflecting back differently. More muffled. The car tilted as I started to type. He must have been driving down quite a steep slope because the reception abruptly got worse. Five bars to four, then three. Oh my god: the last ones were also starting to vanish. Two, then, suddenly, just red letters in their place: *No Signal*.

*   *   *

As I turned into the single-track lane, I had to grin. This was a stroke of genius. At the bottom of the dip was a tunnel that ran beneath the railway line. Forty metres long, maybe. I could park with her side of the vehicle within inches of the wall. Close enough so her door wouldn't open if she woke up before I was ready. I checked the rear-view mirror another time. She was still like a sack in the corner, but something about her made me wonder if she was awake. The lane was pretty bumpy and she'd lost that floppiness. The slight lolling of the head. Not that it really mattered any more. We were in the tunnel now and no one would hear a thing.

The music was building beautifully, too. We'd arrived at the main part of the song; the tabla and harmonium were picking up pace as the singer's voice started to soar. A drip flashed through the headlights like a miniature comet. I drew softly to a stop and turned the lights and engine off. Another landed on the car roof with a metallic *bink*. I breathed deeply then lowered the glove compartment door and removed the ties and tape. This was it. Hardly a sound as the car door opened. Before climbing out, I checked her one more time. Still hadn't moved. These girls: they made it so easy.

*   *   *

As soon as he got out, I looked quickly to the side. So dark! The blackness was pressing against the glass. Shit, we were in a tunnel. The sense of being trapped was making it hard to breathe. I reached quickly into my bag and closed my trembling fingers round the can of pepper spray, flipped the lid back and placed my thumb on the button at the top. Steady, I said to myself. Steady. Wait until his face is close, then spray his nose and mouth and that horrible drooping eye.

The rear door opened and the ceiling light came on. He studied me for a second then reached beneath the empty seat. There must have been a lever because the back of it sank to an almost flat position. From the corner of my almost-shut eyes, I watched him haul his bulk inside. Kneeling beside me, his gaze never left my face. I could see the glistening wetness of his lower lip as he started reaching round my lower legs for my seat's release.

I hadn't planned to yell, but that's exactly what happened as I whipped the can out. I thrust the nozzle up at his face, my thumb pressed down and... nothing happened. I tried again but the plastic didn't give. The lock was in place. I hadn't turned the plastic band at the nozzle's base! Then a big hand slapped it from my grasp and the back of the seat collapsed.

* * *

I thought she was pretending to be asleep. Little bitch, trying to be clever. The strength of her shriek took me by surprise, though. And then she was holding something in my face. I hit out at her hand, heard something tinny bounce off the side window. Soon as her seat released, I used all my weight to pin her down. You're not shifting me, little lady. She was putting up a good struggle, though. Kicking those legs back and forth and shouting *bastard!* over and over. She hadn't realised all that noise was only using up her air. Not easy taking in breath with eighteen stone on top of you. I let her struggle on while working my face into the soft skin of her neck. She smelled of cardamom and patchouli. I wanted to lick her, so I did. Soon, her energy would run out. Already, the kicks were getting weaker. Just a little longer and I'd get her other arm up and bind her wrists together.

* * *

It was like being crushed by a bear. Stale coffee breath bathed my face. I felt his wet tongue probe my ear. Heard it moving about. He'd bent my left arm above my head, wrist crushed by his huge hand. My right arm was pinned by my side. I tried to lift it, get my nails to his face, but his body was just too big.

The music was reaching a crescendo, hand-drums and clapping getting faster and faster, the torrent of singing other-worldly. Almost religious. I'm going to die in here. Just like Caitlin. The little light in the car roof was floating away. Smaller and smaller.

The fingertips of my right hand fluttered uselessly in the gap between the seats. Something moved. Something thin and hard and cold. Immediately, I knew what it was: Caitlin's pen. I could even feel the grooves where her name was engraved in the steel.

He shifted his weight to the side, free hand searching out my right arm. I let him lift it from beneath him. Soon as it was clear, I wrenched it back and drove the pen into the side of his head. It was like an electric current going through him: muscles stiffening as a little noise sounded deep in his throat. Then I was stabbing again. Again and again, back and forth as hard as I could. The singing was now a high ululation, the claps a rhythm for each stab. His back arched and his face lifted, the droopy eye unchanged, the other rolled back and totally white. Dark droplets flew out each time I pulled the pen clear to plunge it in again. Spots were pattering down on my face. The pen was warm and slippery. Air came out from between his clenched teeth in a slow hiss. He collapsed onto his side and I was able to wriggle out from under him. His head was twisted and I could see blood pumping from the cluster of holes in his temple. A galaxy of black dots peppered the heavens of the roof above me. Drips of it were running down the windows. Pen still poised to strike, I pulled my skirt back over my knees before scrambling across his lower legs. Then I was out, running down the tunnel with Caitlin's pen like a dark wand before me, that frantic music pouring from the car and bouncing off the bricks.

SOME OTHER DRACULA

Christine Poulson

> 'There seemed a strange stillness over everything;
> but as I listened I heard, as if from down below in the valley,
> the howling of many wolves. The Count's eyes gleamed,
> and he said: "Listen to them – the children of the night.
> What music they make!"'
> *Dracula*, Bram Stoker

The man lay sprawled at the heart of the maze. The faint strains of music playing and laughter and voices were borne on the still night air, but he knew nothing of that. There was a dagger in his chest and his white waistcoat was drenched in blood. His black cloak, lined with red silk, was spread out beneath him. The red and the black made a stark picture against the snow that covered the ground and the hornbeam hedges of the maze.

From somewhere in the distance came the muffled sound of a church clock striking midnight.

*   *   *

It was earlier that evening.

Stephen's voice floated out of the bathroom. "I suppose it's too late to cry off."

"Of course it's too late!" I was standing in front of the bedroom mirror trying to adjust my wig. "Anyway, we've paid a fortune for the tickets. Oh, hell, I just can't get this right."

Grace, our teenage daughter, appeared at the bedroom door.

"Give me a hand with this, could you?" I said.

"Oh, wow, cool. Are you going as Marge Simpson? But shouldn't the wig be blue?"

"No, no, it's a Halloween party, remember? I'm going as the Bride of Frankenstein."

Grace seized the wig, tugged it one way and then the other, and stood back to consider the effect. "Yeah, that's fine now. Hey, Mum, you're looking good."

As Halloween costumes go, it was pretty flattering, I had to agree. The long white flowing dress and the filmy sleeves concealed a multitude of middle-aged sins.

"I'll do your make-up for you, shall I?" Grace said. "Hey, if you're going as the Bride of Frankenstein, does that mean that Dad's going as—"

"No, no – he's—"

From the bathroom came an eerie, long-drawn-out howl like the cry of a wolf.

Grace looked at me, open-mouthed. A few seconds of silence and then Stephen appeared at the bathroom door, his hand to his ear. "Listen to them," he said, "the children of the night. What music they make!"

He had taken Bela Lugosi as his model. He wore a red-lined cloak over evening dress. His hair was slicked back and a white mask covered the upper part of his face. Bloodstains were painted round his mouth. He snarled, revealing fangs, and advanced on Grace, his hands crooked like claws.

Grace squealed in horrified delight. "Dad! Stop it!"

"Not Dad, my dear, but Dracula! *Count* Dracula!"

*   *   *

"Now you've got your taxi booked for coming home, haven't you?" Grace said as she saw us off.

My eyes met Stephen's and his lips twitched. That could have been me speaking. The tables were turned and she clearly considered us barely fit to be let out alone.

I had to admit that, like Stephen, I was feeling that I would have preferred a night in reading a good book, or watching *Money Heist* on Netflix. But it was all in a good cause, the Cambridge Literary and Philosophical Society, a wonderful subscription library dating from the mid-nineteenth century. As Vice-Principal of a Cambridge college, where I specialise in Victorian literature, I am more or less obliged to be on the board. Like many independent libraries, the Lit and Phil struggles to balance the books. Six months ago, when Sir Robert Morgen was elected on to the board, our finances were in a parlous state. He brought to the problem the razor-sharp mind that had made him a fortune as a software developer in Silicon Fen. The Halloween masked ball, held at his own house, Hamberly Hall, was the result. Robert explained, "What we are trying to do, is raise the library's profile and make it a place that people with money and status will want to support. The ball will get us plenty of publicity."

It would do that all right, as it turned out, though not quite in the way any of us had anticipated.

★   ★   ★

Hamberly Hall is a fine William and Mary house of around 1700. It's grand, yes, but not so grand that you couldn't imagine living in it. The gardens, restored by Robert, are stunning: terraces, parterres, a ha-ha, even a hornbeam maze. Everything that money could do had been done.

The taxi drove round the carriage sweep and dropped us outside the portico. Snow was falling, big soft flakes that spiralled slowly down.

I shivered as I got out of the car. "I hope we're going to be able to get home."

Stephen said, "I checked the forecast and it's supposed to stop by ten o'clock – at least for a while."

At the door Sir Robert and his wife were receiving the guests. I couldn't be sure it *was* Robert until he spoke. He was wearing a black top hat and a full-face skull mask. His closely fitting black frock coat had a skeleton design on the front and back, and his tie, also black, had a line of white vertebrae running down it.

His wife – his much younger second wife – was a spectral bride in a white lacy low-cut gown. Her face was painted white and her lips and eyelids were black.

Standing a little behind them, dressed as the Phantom of the Opera, was Ronan, Robert's personal assistant, suave and elegant in evening dress and a mask that covered just one eye. He had done the heavy lifting of organising the ball, hiring the catering company, planning the decoration of the hall. He ticked us off his guest list and when he leaned forward to kiss me on either cheek, I inhaled the scent of some delicious lime-based cologne.

★　　★　　★

We left our coats in the cloakroom and emerged into the huge central hall, already thronged with guests. The air was warm and scented and the lights were dim. Fake cobwebs and bats dangled from the ceiling. The rhythmic strains of a merengue band drifted in from the ballroom. Everyone was masked, but I didn't expect in any case to see many of my friends – not with tickets at that price. Robert, I knew, had twisted the arms of the great and the good in Cambridge. Was that a Nobel laureate that I spotted over there, dressed as a werewolf? And that svelte figure in a black cat costume – I was pretty sure she was a well-known poet who sometimes came to High Table at my college.

Marcus approached with a tray bearing drinks. He runs the domestic side of Robert's life. I'd only ever seen him wearing jeans and a tweed jacket, but tonight he was dapper in a proper butler's outfit. "In my penguin suit tonight," he joked. He offered me champagne or a sinister-looking cocktail – "Black vodka and pomegranate juice," he explained. I settled for champagne.

A buffet supper was laid out in the dining room. After we had eaten, we headed for the ballroom. The party was going with a swing. The leader of the band, who had a green face and a bolt through his neck, explained how to dance the merengue. "It's easy," Robert had told me. "Only takes a few minutes to learn." I'd been sceptical, but he was right. Stephen and I quickly got the hang of it and we were soon whizzing round the dance floor.

When Stephen went off to the loo, I looked at my watch and I was surprised to see that it was already eleven o'clock.

A man wearing a broad-brimmed black hat and a white mask with a long curved beak stepped in front of me and bowed. Without waiting for permission he seized me and swung me into the dance. I gave a little shriek.

"Cass, you idiot, it's me! Giles!" he said.

I relaxed and let my hand rest on his shoulder. We were old friends from the days when Giles had been librarian at the Lit and Phil, before he moved on to bigger and better things at the British Library.

"Surely I told you I was coming as a plague doctor?" he said.

"I'd forgotten about the bird's head – it's so sinister, like one of those surrealist pictures by Max Ernst."

Giles was an enthusiastic if erratic dancer.

As he rocked me round the dance floor, he said, "Did you see the *Financial Times* today?"

"Not my regular read. Why?"

"Sir Robert's got his hands full. Seems to be some sort of scandal brewing."

Out of the corner of my eye I saw that Stephen had returned. He was standing by a drinks table on the other side of the room.

The music ended. Giles released me and was immediately accosted by a woman dressed as Morticia in a figure-hugging black dress and a long, black wig. The music started up again and the woman swept him away.

"What sort of scandal?" I shouted after him.

He mouthed something over her shoulder. I strained to hear and thought I heard 'industrial espionage'. Typical of Giles to offer that tantalising titbit and leave me in suspense! I'd catch him later.

I went over to Stephen and put my hand on his shoulder. Except that when he turned round, it wasn't Stephen. It was some other Dracula. This one was wearing a grey-streaked wig with a widow's peak and a full face mask complete with bloody fangs, more Christopher Lee than Bela Lugosi.

He must have misunderstood my gesture and thought I wanted to dance. He hesitated for a moment and then held out a hand. Well, why not? I let him lead me onto the dance floor.

Conversation wasn't easy over the music, but I made an effort. "Are you enjoying the ball?" I asked. He nodded, but didn't speak. Only his eyes were visible in the narrow slits in his mask. His hand was unpleasantly clammy in mine. He was a decent enough dancer, but why was he so silent? I became more and more uncomfortable and I wasn't sorry when the music ended.

He clicked his heels together, bowed, and still without a word, walked away. I found myself wiping my hand on my dress.

Stephen appeared at my side. "Who's the other Dracula?" he asked.

"No idea! He didn't introduce himself."

"I've checked the weather. It stopped snowing a while ago. We shouldn't have a problem getting home before it starts again in the early hours."

But we wouldn't be leaving just yet. The invitation had said, 'Carriages at 1 a.m.,' and besides, we were having too much fun.

Some time later, Stephen said, "I need a break. Let's wander round for a bit, maybe find somewhere a bit cooler?"

We made our way up the great staircase and then up a smaller staircase that led to the top floor. The hubbub died away and now that we had left the crush of guests, the air was fresher. We found ourselves next to a window at the side of the house. Light spilled out into the garden, illuminating a monochrome world, as still and silent as a woodcut. The lawn was an unblemished carpet of white and beyond it the maze too was coated with snow. A few papery copper leaves remained, and the branches formed a kind of trellis with glimpses into the interior. Unusually, the heart of the maze was close to the entrance, rather than in the centre, though you had to go all the way round to reach it.

I leaned my forehead against the window, relishing the coolness. I was, I realised, rather tipsy. Very faintly, far off, a church clock was striking midnight.

I turned to Stephen and we embraced. My head swam and it wasn't just the champagne.

I was just thinking, *Yes, there is something erotic about being kissed by a vampire*, when Stephen said, "That's funny."

"What?" I murmured.

He was looking over my shoulder. "If you stand here at this angle, look—" He turned me towards the window.

The light through the snow-laden hedges of the maze created a dappled effect and at first I didn't know what I was supposed to be looking at.

"Tilt your head a bit to the left," Stephen said.

I saw what looked like a black trouser leg and the gleam of a black patent leather shoe in the heart of the maze.

Stephen said, "I wonder, can we get this window open?"

It was an old-fashioned sash window and stiff, but we managed to pull it up and cold air poured in.

Stephen leaned out and shouted, "Hey, you there! Are you all right?"

There was no reply and the foot didn't move. Stephen called again, and still there was silence.

"'There's something wrong," he said. "I'll go and find Robert. You wait here."

Ten minutes later I saw Robert and Stephen and Ronan, now without masks, arrive at the maze. They conferred at the entrance and then Robert went in alone. I saw the beam of his torch bobbing along as he wound his way through and at last reached the heart of the maze. He directed his torch to an area that was in shade and illuminated a masked face. I gasped. It was the other Dracula, the man I had been dancing with less than an hour ago.

⋆ ⋆ ⋆

"Some of you will no doubt have already heard that there has been a… someone has very unfortunately…" Robert's voice trailed away. The situation was taxing even his savoir-faire. "I am afraid there's been a death," he concluded firmly. "The police will be arriving shortly. However, it so happens that we have Chief Superintendent Allen here as one of our guests and he is taking charge in the meantime."

We were all assembled, guests and staff alike, in the ballroom. Masks had been removed. Ceiling lights were on, casting a harsh light on tired, middle-aged men and women, with untidy hair and smudged make-up. The party was well and truly over.

Chief Superintendent Allen stepped forward. He'd been dressed as a voodoo witch doctor, but had taken off his frock coat, top hat and skull mask, and was in shirt sleeves.

"The dead man is John Morrell," Allen said. He was a tall man with an imposing presence and a Scottish accent. "Morrell was on Sir Robert's staff as head of security. His body was discovered outside a short time ago. I have to ask you all to remain at Hamberly Hall until statements have been taken."

There was a low murmur of voices.

"Is that really necessary, Chief Superintendent?" said the guy dressed as a werewolf. He was indeed a Nobel laureate, as I'd suspected earlier. "Does this mean that you regard his death as suspicious?"

Suspicious? Well, yes, I thought grimly. Robert had told Stephen, who had told me, that it looked as if the man had been stabbed through the heart.

"That is so," Allen said, "and we are especially interested in establishing the dead man's movements during the first part of the evening. He had attended the party alone. He was dressed as Dracula and was wearing a full face mask."

★　　★　　★

"I don't know about the first part of the evening," I said. "But I was dancing with him at eleven o'clock."

Stephen and I were in the study along with Robert, his assistant, Ronan, and Chief Superintendent Allen.

Allen stared at me. "That's not possible. Morrell must have been dead by ten o'clock. That was when it stopped snowing. If he had gone out after that, we'd have seen his footprints in the snow – those of his killer, too."

Of course! I remembered now that we had looked down on smooth virgin snow from the window above.

"He may have been dressed as Dracula," the Chief Superintendent continued dryly, "but he can hardly have changed himself into a bat and flown there."

"Then who was my wife dancing with?" Stephen asked. "I saw him, too."

I thought of the man's clammy hands, his silence – had there been a very faint musty smell or was I imagining that? – and then his abrupt departure when the dance was over. A crazy thought flashed across my mind. Had I been dancing with a dead man?

It was as if a shadow had fallen over the room. I looked at the others. We were rational, well-educated people, but just for a few moments I think we all felt a superstitious thrill.

Then the Chief Superintendent spoke. His dry, matter-of-fact tone broke the spell. "There must have been a third guest dressed as Dracula."

Robert shook his head. "My wife and I greeted all the guests and there were only two, Stephen here and John Morrell. Ronan had a list and also made a note of their costumes. We were planning to give a prize to the best."

"'That's right,'" Ronan said. "I ticked people off as they came in. Only two Draculas."

"Then there is only one explanation," Allen told me. "The man you danced with was the killer dressed as Morrell, trying to establish that Morrell was still alive. It was just his bad luck that you and your husband spotted the body when you did. Snow was forecast again for the early hours – in fact it's started now – and that would have accounted for there being no footprints, when the body was eventually discovered. No doubt the killer would have had an alibi for the later time."

I thought back. "I see now that he didn't want to dance. It was more or less forced on him, when I mistook him for Stephen. And as I *did* mistake him for Stephen, he must have been about Stephen's height and build."

"Did he say anything?"

"Not a word. I thought it was strange at the time."

"What can you tell me about him?"

"His hands were clammy."

"Aye, no wonder," said the Chief Superintendent. He didn't need to spell it out. The man I'd danced with had not long come in from the cold after killing a man. Of course he was nervous.

"Anything else? The colour of his eyes, maybe?"

"I think they were brown... I don't know for sure," I said, feeling useless.

"Maybe something will come back to you."

*   *   *

Back in the ballroom, Stephen and I waited for our statements to be taken. Ronan with his usual efficiency had arranged sandwiches and hot drinks and he was going round the room himself, checking that no one needed anything.

When he reached Stephen and me, he bent over me to say that Robert was very happy for us to stay the night if that would make things easier.

"Thank you, but no." I stifled a yawn. "I just want to be in my own bed, however late it is."

"Of course. Let's hope it won't be much longer."

He walked across the hall, still in his Phantom of the Opera cloak. He stopped to confer with Marcus, who was pouring out coffee at a side table, and that was when it came to me. I knew who I had danced with and how easy it had been for the killer to transform himself into Dracula.

I got up and walked across the hall to where Ronan and Marcus were standing.

Ronan looked round and there was a question in his eyes. I moved past him and put my hand on Marcus's shoulder.

"It was you," I said. "You're the man I danced with. You were the third vampire."

★   ★   ★

"I'm not sorry!" Marcus said. "Morrell deserved what he got. Dressed as a vampire! He really *was* a vampire. He was draining the life blood from me, the bastard!"

We watched as he was led away in handcuffs.

The Chief Superintendent said, "I'd already fixed on those two guys as prime suspects for the same reason that you did, one in his Phantom of the Opera costume and the other in his butler's outfit. All either of them had to do was slip into the cloakroom unobserved, change the black bow tie for a white one, and put on the mask, the wig and the cloak."

"It could be done in a minute or two," I agreed. "Easy to switch between identities as often as he needed to establish that Morrell was still around."

"Yes, indeed. But what made you settle on the right one?"

"Ronan's aftershave. Even by the end of the evening, it was still pretty strong. I smelled it when he bent down to speak to me. I couldn't have danced with him without being aware of it, so I knew it wasn't him."

We learned later that Morrell as head of security had discovered that Marcus was selling information that he had gleaned in his privileged position in the household. But instead of telling Robert, Morrell had been blackmailing Marcus.

★   ★   ★

Never had I been so glad to get home.

I eased off my Bride of Frankenstein wig with a sigh of relief. "What a night! Can you help me out of this dress, please?"

"We really should have guessed earlier," Stephen said, as he unzipped me.

"We should?"

"After all," he went on thoughtfully, "it *is* the classic solution, is it not?"

I looked at him warily. Years of marriage had warned me that a bad-taste joke was coming.

"You mean—"

"That's right. The butler did it."

VIOLIN – CE

David Stuart Davies

Yes?

I have to speak with you. I need to come in.

Do I know you?

Not yet. This is very important.

(*Hesitation*) Very well, come in.

Thank you.

What is this all about?

I've come for the violin.

What?

You're not deaf, are you?

No.

So… I've come for the violin.

What violin?

Not deaf but a bit dim, eh? *The* violin.

The violin?

Look, don't take me for stupid. You know what I mean. I want the Stradivarius. I need you to hand it over.

That's impossible.

No, it's not. This gun proves that.

Heavens! You mean to shoot me.

Not necessarily. I just want the violin. I want it badly. I have dreamed for ages of possessing it. Its beauty, its delicacy, its fucking history. I want it. I need it! I've watched you many times on stage with that instrument, the pale wood catching the light while it gave forth such glorious tones.

You are a player yourself?

Heavens, no, but I don't need to be to appreciate the wonder of the Strad. The fine construction, the superb veneer. I want to touch it, to stroke it, to feel it in my hands. Holding it close to me will bring all the music I will ever need. I just want it. Can't say it more simply than that.

How do you know about the violin?

You're Andre Gardner, aren't you?

Yes.

Well, you've been playing the bloody thing for years. In concert halls and on numerous CDs. It's always mentioned in the sleeve notes…

You know of my work?

I just said so, didn't I? I'm a fan.

A fan?

I've followed your career for ages. I even came to your farewell concert at the Albert Hall.

Really?

Yeah. Loved your Bruch concerto.

Thank you, that is kind.

You played it like a dream. A fine mix of the sentimental and the mathematical. The precise but elegant, emotional fingering… superb.

You are a music critic?

No. I just love the sound of that violin. It makes angel music.

A nice phrase.

So, I want it. Hand it over. I'd rather not hurt you, but I will if you make it necessary.

You are serious, aren't you? You mean to steal it. And you are prepared to shoot me, to kill me to get it.

Bullseye, Andre. I mean to take it, yeah.

I'm sorry, but I can't let you do that.

(Chuckle) Oh, yes, you can.

No, no. That violin is part of me. Any success I've had as a performer I owe to that instrument. I could not live without it.

Well, that could easily be the case. See this gun, nicely loaded and ready for action? It can either blow your bloody head off and I can find the fiddle for myself or you can hand it over and you'll get by without a scratch.

Why, why would you do this?

I've told you. Because I want it, to take possession of its beauty and magic. I've wanted it for a long time but I curbed my impatience while you were still performing… while I could still hear the music that it makes. But now… now that you have retired… Make no mistake, I have no conscience about this affair. Get me the violin or else.

(*Long pause*)

(*A long sigh*) It seems I have no choice.

No choice.

Very well…

Good man.

Here… here it is. Could I ask a favour…?

What?

I would like to play it one last time. It has been my friend, my inspiration, my solace for many years.

OK – but make it short and sweet.

A little Mendelssohn.

Sure.

Thank you.

(*He plays*)

You *are* good. That was peachy. Now hand over the violin.

No, I cannot. It is mine. It is part of me. It would be like tearing out my heart. I may be retired but I play it every day. Without it my life would be meaningless.

Death is sort of meaningless, too. For the last time, hand it over.

Sorry, but no.

Very well, face the consequences.

(*Fires pistol*)

Heavens… you really meant it…

(*Falls to floor, gasping for breath*)

I warned you. (*Snatches up violin and examines it.*) At last. Hey, this isn't a Strad! Of course not. It never was. How could I afford a Stradivarius when I began playing solo? I lied about it and the lie stayed with me and became part of my career. Still, I played sweet music with it… as good as a Stradivarius … didn't I? Didn't… I…?

THE SOUND AND THE FURY

Dea Parkin

She drove fast, but not fast enough to invite attention. The motorway was quiet at 10 p.m. and the miles hurtled by; so many amber streetlights misty in the haze of the evening, so many bridges, illuminated signs, strings of cat's eyes. And the soundtrack, angry and vicious, tearing a melody that was hard and uncompromising from heavy bass, synth guitar. The perfect accompaniment.

Focus on driving, on the next mile, the next junction, the next services. A hundred miles, but she was nearly there. Off the motorway now, through a town, then out on the side roads. Time for just one more track on her 'Murder at Midnight' playlist. The one with the tune that haunted her and the lyrics she loved.

There's a devil in the air and damnation in the fire

Her breathing quickened as she pulled into the tranquil cul-de-sac. Maybe she should have spent the driving time planning this rather than deliberately escaping into her music and allowing the passing streetlights to hypnotise her, like a child with a winking Christmas tree. But no, if she'd allowed herself to think for one minute about what she was going to do, and what had brought her to this decision, she'd have resisted the lure of those unremitting cat's eyes and run into a bridge. Or split off at a junction and turned for home. No, not home. Home was before her now, not behind. Maybe.

The sound of her car door slamming shattered the silence of suburban middle-class bedtimes. Did she have the nerve for this? She thought about how she was hurting and for no good reason. She could make this right. She patted her pocket. Deliberately slowed her breaths. Walked up the path, the rhythm of that last song a timpani in her head. Raised her fist and knocked loudly on the door, echoing the beat.

It's do or die tonight, our fate says it's you and me

The sudden quiet of activity disturbed. The TV had been on, now it was turned off. She heard low voices, then footsteps approaching the door. Well, at least they weren't in bed. She wasn't sure she could have faced that. The door opened and her heart juddered. He looked taller than she recalled as she gazed up at him, the doorstep giving him the advantage despite her killer heels. The shock on his face was gratifying.

"Good evening, Keir."

He didn't say anything, didn't move. Her hand went to her hip pocket again, but the element of surprise was all she needed. She planted her hand on his chest, pushed, and as he took a step back she strode into the hallway.

A high-pitched voice from another room. "Who is it, Keir?"

Nemesis, the Furies, retribution. All at once.

He came hurrying after her. "Gina, what are you doing?"

Answer him or go and find her? Go find, he'd get his answer soon enough.

She marched into the room on the left. It was a living room, generously proportioned. A large TV, an enormous sofa. And half-rising from it, a girl, ridiculously young, with wispy blonde hair curling round her shoulders and wide blue eyes looking up in puzzlement. This was going to be so easy. But she was so young. Oh, Keir.

She looked at the girl, whose perplexity was transforming into anxiety and whose eyes were seeking Keir's as he entered the room behind her. Time to do the deed.

You know that doom is in your blood, you know it's destiny

"Get your stuff and get out."

"Pardon?" The girl looked up at her like she'd spoken in a foreign language, before her eyes sought the man hovering beyond her shoulder again. Alarm inflected her voice. "Keir?"

"I've left my husband and I'm moving in. You're moving out."

Now at last Keir spoke.

"Gina? You've really left him?" She faced him and his eyes focused entirely on hers. The pathetic little wimp on the sofa couldn't even get his attention, though it tried.

"Keir? Who is this?"

She turned to the girl.

"Dim as well as desperate." She took a step towards her and the blonde immediately retreated. "I'm lover boy's lover. His real lover, not some temporary inadequate bedwarmer. Now get out."

The blonde went pale. Trembling, she appeared transfixed. "Keir?" she repeated, voice quavering.

Keir's height and his breadth too were suddenly between her and the girl. She wanted to reach out and touch him. It had been too long.

"OK, Gina. Calm down."

She laughed. "I'm perfectly calm, thank you, sweetheart. Now tell this bitch to leave."

Keir sighed. "Gina…"

She cocked her head, dark hair swinging. "What? Here I am. Should have done it ages ago, but I'm here now. All yours. Just get this scrubber out the door."

The girl with the pixie face gasped, and if it were possible for her to go whiter, she did. The last time she'd seen someone so colourless, she'd been a corpse.

"Keir, what's going on? You can't!"

She smiled, nastily she knew, but this cow had no right to be here. "I want someone to watch TV with," Keir had whinged defensively. "You won't leave him, and I'm lonely. What do you expect me to do?" Well, she'd not been prepared for how she felt, a blowtorch of agony, and suddenly loyalty had seemed like yesterday's yellowing newspapers, and her decision to stay in her marriage a wanton sacrifice of life. Keir was the man she loved, and it had overwhelmed her from the start. And that had been years ago. He was the man for her, and she was the woman for him. They both knew it.

"Gina." Keir's tone was gentle. "Let's sit down. Let's talk."

She laughed again and this time the advance she made towards the slut didn't halt until she grabbed her arm. She yanked the girl towards her, knowing she could break her whenever she wanted. She deliberately tightened her fingers and the girl squealed.

"Ow. Let go! You're hurting me." She tried to bring up her other hand to strike but Gina grinned, blocking her with a gym-solid arm that she brought hard across the girl's face before shaking her away. The girl lost her balance, fell to the hardwood floor and started to cry. Keir made towards her, stopped as he met Gina's eyes.

"Are you really leaving him?"

"My suitcase is in the car." She stretched up, kissed him on the lips, lingering. Excitement shot through her, and the hand that was stroking his cheek dropped to his crotch to feel his, too. It never failed. Then the girl on the floor sobbed and she felt it dwindle. The little trollop was an impediment to the reunion of the century and she needed her gone.

"Blondie. What's your name, Adele? Come on, I don't want to hurt you, though fuck knows your existence has hurt me enough. Come on, game's over and you've lost. Go get your things and get out of our hair."

She laid her hand on Keir's arm and looked down at the girl. God, how old was she? The tear-blotches were livid on the pale face. She made no effort to get up but gazed up past Gina at her treacherous man.

"Keir? Is she for real? Are you going to let this happen? She hit me!"

Keir made an indistinct noise. Again he inched towards the girl on the floor. Gina's grip tensed on his arm.

"She's all right. I didn't hurt her."

But the view of that wet face with the blonde hair criss-crossed over it and the knowledge that Keir was looking at the girl, maybe wanting to comfort her, maybe remembering the touch of her body, flicked at the flame of anger inside her and it surged into her stomach and across her skin in burning waves, fiery into her mouth. This was the whore who'd moved in with her man. Her man whom she could hear fidgeting right beside her, undecided where his own loyalty lay. He'd better decide soon.

I'm gonna ramp up the venom, the poison is mine

The sound and fury of the last track she'd listened to reprised, and soaring synths and thudding drums powered through her nerves and her veins. God, she hated this woman. And if Keir lifted a finger to help her, she hated him too. He'd done this to her, he'd screwed her up, changed who she was. Well, fuck them all.

"Oh, God," the bitch on the floor cried, and she realised she'd slipped her hand in her pocket and pulled out the flick-knife, and snapped open the sweet cold hardness of her blade.

She leaned forward and smiled. Stared into the girl's eyes. Held her down easily, knee across her legs, arm fixed across her neck restricting any movement of her upper body. She was too terrified to move anyway. So feeble, a piece of trash.

A dagger making claims in your smile

She cut off a huge hank of blonde hair, letting the steel nick the tip of her ear, caress her throat. The girl's sobs mingled with the melody pounding through Gina's head as she kept her elbow on the narrow neck.

And you know it's murder, it's murder at midnight

Keir's breaths were harsh behind her, but he didn't intervene as she brought the blade up to the girl's face and slowly incised her cheek. Blood spurted a little way into the air, then rained down in fine warm droplets across Gina's hands, harmonising in some strange dance with the music in her head, and she smiled again.

Behind her, she felt Keir's horror, and his arousal. Soon, they would make love and it would be spectacular, the best ever. Her blade slashed open the girl's blouse. The song was blazing its climax in Gina's head, and frantic screams urged her on. She dipped the knife into skin, slitting through into soft pink flesh, and pushed down.

A VULTURE SANG IN BERKELEY SQUARE

Jason Monaghan

I could hear the song once the traffic of Piccadilly faded behind me. A man's voice, a decent tenor, was part-way through a ballad. His tone rose and sang of bravery. He could have chosen a position by the Underground station at Green Park, but then the cars and buses would drown out the sheer beauty of his voice.

"Bravo," I said.

The young man gave a nod of his head towards his cap that lay next to where he sat, and I dropped sixpence into the change already there.

"Your voice is excellent – you should be on the stage."

"With these?" Now his head twitched to indicate two crutches propped up on the wall behind him.

"Were you injured in the War?"

"Oh, aye," he said.

"May I ask how?"

He smiled. "I'll trade a secret for a secret."

"I'm on the way to my club. We have a dining group we call the Thursday Club."

"Because you meet on Thursdays?"

"Now, that's two secrets. Tell me about those."

"I crashed my Spitfire," he said, in a brogue that suggested he hailed from Ireland.

As I made my way to my club, he began the popular song one would expect to hear in Berkeley Square.

"Excellent, isn't he?" I commented to the doorman. "Crippled Spitfire pilot."

"He tells that to everyone, sir. He's never flown in his life."

The next time I heard that voice singing 'The Minstrel Boy' I paused and listened to the whole song. I dropped a shilling into the cap.

"I used to sing in the choir, at my school," I said. "Sing for me again, sing the whole song."

The young man complied and I started to hum along, joining in for the first two lines then listening intently to the rest. For those two verses I was captivated by Irish courage and Irish loss, and the harp that would no longer play – then dropped in another shilling. "You didn't fly Spitfires," I said.

"No, no, I was joking."

"So how did it happen?"

"A secret for a secret. What did you do in the War?"

"I'd like to boast that I won the Victoria Cross storming the beaches at Anzio." I paused. "But I was unfit to serve. There, it takes a man to admit that. I found employment on the Home Front."

At first I had been rated as too old, then too frail to fight for my country. Luck was with me as my frailty allowed me to turn a financial advantage during a time when everything was in short supply.

"So tell me the real story of the crutches."

"I was on the stage," the young man admitted.

"I always wanted to go on the stage," I said, then hurriedly stopped myself as I had wasted a secret.

"Do you remember the bomb that hit the Windmill? That took my legs away. They're useless props now. But tell me what you did on the Home Front?"

"One secret at a time," I said.

I sensed this would become a ritual. The singer would be there as I walked to the Thursday Club, but never by the time I came out. Singing in the dark would constitute a nuisance – it is best left to nightingales. He judged his timing right for men and ladies of quality to pass by on their evenings out. Perhaps he told them all about the bomb that struck the Windmill, at which no male singer was injured.

"The Minstrel Boy to the war is gone…"

"Mr Home Front," he said with a smile as my shilling dropped into his hat.

"My name is Thomas Peyton Legge," I said. "That's my secret up front, and I know you can't have been injured by the Windmill bomb. That's just another story."

"But we all love stories," said the young man. "I sing stories all evening."

"Will you tell me your secret? An honest one?"

"But if a man has only one story to tell, when is it right to tell it? To be sure I lost my legs in the War, and I'm sure we've met before."

"I'd know that voice. You sing like an angel, but I'll wager you've never dined at the Ritz."

He laughed. "You're a gent of quality, Mr Thomas Peyton Legge. And no, I've never dined at the Ritz and I've not heard a nightingale since the sirens stopped. There, two secrets for you."

"We could play this game all summer," I said.

"Every Thursday," he said. "I'm going nowhere."

I warmed to the game. Fencing words with the beautiful yet maimed man was no more than a little fizz to start my evening, but it was providing an *hors d'ouevre* to Thursday nights' dining. I started to plan my secrets in advance, and wonder what I could pry out of him, as thus far I'd learned nothing beyond the fact that nightingales do not habitually sing in Berkeley Square.

"Let's try 'Minstrel Boy' again," I said. I had almost mastered the first verse and loved the rousing way the song rose in the fifth line. "Land of song! said the warrior-bard..."

"You're getting it, sir," said the man.

"Tonight, you must tell me your name."

He shook his head.

"It's only fair, I've told you mine."

"You don't live close by," observed the man, looking back down from the square towards Green Park. "You come up from the Underground station."

"It's only a couple of stops from Knightsbridge. I rent a house in the Mews near Brompton Oratory. There, that's my secret for tonight, and no more fibs. I'm not going to believe you lost your legs in a duel with a Prussian prince or had them snapped off by a crocodile."

"You set me thinking," he said, "of the secret I'd reveal tonight. And you know what it is?"

"I'm all ears."

"We were in the same trade, in the War."

"I doubt it."

"I saw you, Piccadilly Circus. Talking to the fine ladies and the city gents on their way home. Nylons."

I could have struck him. That was my secret, not his. "I've moved on. We all had to make a living. What was yours? Cigarettes, whiskey? That's Irish whiskey with an e."

He put up both hands in surrender. "As you say, we've moved on."

I dropped half a crown into his hat. Perhaps he would turn to drink and forget me. Yet, I was not forgetting him, not for a moment. Even if there were no Thursday Club the next week I would be drawn back. Perhaps before autumn I would have a name. I had no memory of ever seeing that man in Piccadilly or anywhere else. If he thought I'd been a common spiv like him, he'd been wrong about the common. Men who attended schools like mine were never called spivs. I was a merchant.

Arriving early one evening, after an appointment with a prospective buyer close by, I saw him limp into position at his usual pitch. The crutches were no lie, no cheating route to easy sympathy. He moved awkwardly, sat down even more awkwardly and massaged first one knee then the next.

I would be spoiling the routine if I turned up too early, so I took a turn around the streets. I did make sure I was in good time, though. I would master 'Minstrel Boy' before going on to supper. He let me sing alone and applauded at the end. A well-dressed couple were clearly amused and tipped us a shilling.

"We could go into business," he said, "you and me."

I laughed along with him. "A jolly idea, but I don't sing for shillings."

"But you've come up in the world, and it's my wager you no longer sell nylons."

"Antiquities," I said. "Fine *objets d'art* to men and women who appreciate quality. Now that counts as my secret."

"It does. *Objets d'art* is far and away a world above nylons."

"I must say, I have enjoyed our chats, but we…" I paused now. I wanted to cement our friendship beyond merely dropping coins in a hat, but I could never invite my singing companion across to the club. The chaps would never understand. "Oh, dammit, give me your secret."

"We have a mutual acquaintance."

"I doubt it. And that's only half a secret, if it is true you must tell me the name of this… acquaintance."

"Danny McGuire."

My heart sank and I could have fled from the spot at that moment.

"What do you know of Danny McGuire?"

Slowly he raised a finger and pointed back to the crutches.

"He?"

"I couldn't pay the man, so he took my knees."

And so 'the Minstrel fell'. But even Danny McGuire could not drag his soul under.

"I'm sorry," I said. Some criminals could be gentlemen, but McGuire was a monster.

"It wasn't you with the hammer."

"I'm late, I'm sorry." I searched my pocket for change but all I carried was two florins and four pennies. All chinked into the hat.

My evening was ruined. What a terrible coincidence it was for me to meet a man who was aware how I spent the War. Then, I must walk past a hundred men each week, singing songs, playing an instrument, begging pennies or shining shoes. Each of them must watch thousands pass by, and every now and again spot a face they knew. It was not coincidence, but fate.

The game must end that next Thursday, I resolved. Matters were going too far and the man clearly knew too much of my real self. I never had very much money to hand, or even banked, as I made every pound work. I could hardly offer the minstrel boy an Etruscan vase or a repeater wristwatch that once belonged to a maharaja. I did not possess a harp to give the minstrel, nor my father's sword he could gird about him, I thought, with a smile at my own wit. Still, I might scrape together twenty-five pounds as a gesture in the earnest hope he would forget me. Then I must forget him.

I made sure not to arrive early, nor late. As the distance between myself and the square narrowed I should begin to hear his song, but alas, the angel had flown. His usual pitch was empty and I could not hear him singing from another corner of the square. I felt downcast, yet strangely relieved. Perhaps he was no more part of the real London than the mythical nightingale.

I enjoyed the dinner of roast pork and stayed late with my friends who commented that I seemed distracted of late. I was better now, I assured them. So confident was I that I hailed a cab and just before midnight rode back to Knightsbridge rather than shuffle down to the Underground.

My door did not seem quite closed. It opened to the touch and I ventured inside, clicking the hall light switch and automatically reaching for the coat stand with my hat. It was not there. Nor was the gilt-edged mirror or the elephant foot umbrella stand, and not even my umbrella with the ivory handle remained. The sitting room smelled of men's sweat and disturbed dust. Everything bar the curtains was gone, with scuffs on the wall being the only reminder of those artworks I most favoured while waiting to find the right buyer. The kitchen had been ransacked, and someone had found my small cache of money and taken the Italian silver cutlery. An hour passed before I dared walk up the stairs, and there was no need for me to unlock my back room where the boxed antiquities once sat awaiting their owners.

The smallest mercy was that the thieves had not stolen my bed, so I collapsed on it, head buzzing even without the copious amounts of alcohol swimming there. Could I call the police? How legitimate were the items I bought from middlemen, no questions asked? The police would no doubt ask questions.

"Hey, you." The voice awakened me, and with effort I opened my eyes to see Danny McGuire standing over my bed. A man I had never seen before stood behind his shoulder. Daylight pierced the slit between the badly drawn curtains.

"I heard you were doing a flit," McGuire said. "Looks like I caught you just in time."

"No, I—"

"Three hundred and sixty-four pounds," he said. "So let's call it four hundred with interest."

I eased up into a half-sitting position, still in my evening wear. "I've been robbed. They took everything."

"Everything? In the lorry that was parked here all evening? You're sure that wasn't your own lorry you loaded with all those sparkling trinkets bought with my money?"

"Of course not, I've been robbed, I tell you!"

"Well, they won't have robbed your bank too. Why don't we just walk around there when they open, and you can pay me the four hundred."

"I don't—" Of course I tried to explain, and of course I pleaded, but

Danny McGuire was not interested in my tale of a minstrel boy, now gone to war for all I knew. That damned fallen angel had strung together my secrets and robbed me of everything.

Down came the hammer. And again.

My friends would not want to know me now. I had nothing, less than nothing once those debts were accounted for, and Danny McGuire and the other sharks would add interest every day until kingdom come. I had no trade, and who would employ a man with broken knees whose only skill was his voice?

"Thy songs were made for the pure and free."

At the corner of Berkeley Square, a vacant pitch awaited a minstrel.

NOT A NOTE

Kate Ellis

26 May 1953
An elderly man was attacked during a robbery at his home in the Withington area. The victim was taken to the Manchester Royal Infirmary and is said to be in a serious condition. Police have warned the public to be vigilant.

* * *

Four o'clock on Wednesday; almost time for my piano lesson. I walked out of the grammar school gates with my satchel on my back, every step feeling like an effort. I was keen to delay my arrival at Miss Jessop's house for as long as possible. But it couldn't be avoided, because Mummy had arranged it.

My music teacher lived in a shabby house in Acacia Close with brown varnished wood and a faint scent of cooked cabbage. At that moment I resented Miss Jessop even though Mummy kept saying she was the best teacher around and that some of her pupils had gone on to study at the Royal Academy of Music. Mummy had studied there once and she'd decided that I would do the same. Mummy had never asked what I thought but Mummy wasn't someone you could argue with.

Everyone at school was talking about the new queen's coronation in a week's time. My history teacher, Miss Parr, said it would be the start of a second Elizabethan age and I imagined a future filled with brave explorers and wonderful theatres; an age of vivid colour replacing the drab post-war years with their shortages and bomb sites. I loved Miss Parr and I loved history and I'd longed to stay on after school for a meeting of the new History Society. However, my lesson with Miss Jessop took priority over everything. According to Mummy, playing beautiful music was far more important than living in the past, so I'd had to tell Miss Parr I couldn't make it.

Acacia Close was five minutes from the school gates if you walked briskly, but I always dawdled so it usually took me ten. The house can't have changed much since it was built in the 1920s. It had dark green paintwork and net-curtained windows and a dull stained-glass sunrise set into the front door. I didn't think Miss Jessop had lived there long and it was still an old person's house, just as its previous owner had left it. I couldn't help comparing it with my friend, Marie Dubois', house with its modern wallpaper and pale, sleek furniture. Marie's dad was French which, to us rain-accustomed Northern girls, seemed glamorous and exotic. Mr Dubois was something to do with import and export and his job must have been well paid because Marie's mum had all the latest gadgets; a refrigerator; a washing machine with a built-in wringer; a telephone. And Marie's dad had even bought a television so they could watch the coronation.

Miss Jessop's doorbell bore the word 'press' in bold black letters so I did just that, harbouring a faint hope that it wouldn't be working. But to my disappointment, Miss Jessop opened the front door, a hesitant smile of greeting on her thin face. Her brown hair was scraped back into a neat bun as usual and she wore a tweed skirt, twinset and sensible shoes. Mummy said she wasn't as old as she appeared but to my fourteen-year-old eyes she seemed ancient.

"Hester, dear, come in. I do hope you've been practising that Chopin prelude we started last week." She looked at me quizzically over the small glasses perched on the end of her nose, but I didn't answer.

I followed her into the front room where the grand piano occupied most of the available space. I'd never seen the back room or the kitchen but I had been to the old-fashioned bathroom upstairs. While I was there I'd yielded to temptation and peeped into the bedrooms. Miss Jessop, I learned, slept in a back room filled with dark heavy furniture. The lacy dress hanging on the wardrobe door looked like a relic of her youth and I was surprised to see the top of the dressing table filled with bottles of cologne and jars of face cream. Next to these stood a photograph of a dark-haired young man, posing like a pre-war film star. There was something familiar about him but I couldn't think what it was. I could see a pot of rouge beside the picture and in my mind's eye I imagined Miss Jessop shedding the tweed, donning the flimsy lace and flouncing around with her phantom lover. The thought brought on a giggle and I was tempted to look for more evidence of her secret life, but my time upstairs was limited. I quickly peeked into the other two bedrooms and found them sparsely furnished, the beds stripped as though they hadn't been used in ages. As I came downstairs I felt pleased with myself, like a spy who'd successfully completed a dangerous mission. Discovering Miss Jessop's little vanities gave me a feeling of power.

My brief visit upstairs had whetted my curiosity about Miss Jessop's life and I suspected that, if it weren't for Mummy, I might even have liked the woman. But, as it was, I hated her and everything she represented.

⋆　　⋆　　⋆

"How did your lesson go?" Mummy looked anxious as though she was awaiting life-or-death news.

"All right," I said as I began to make for the stairs.

"Did Miss Jessop mention your exam?"

I didn't reply because I knew the answer was one Mummy wouldn't want to hear.

"Hester. Did she say anything?"

"Sorry, Mummy, I've got a lot of homework tonight," I said, before disappearing into my bedroom and shutting the door behind me.

I knew Mummy, like any good interrogator, would carry on until she got to the truth. But I'd inherited her stubborn streak and I was equally determined to keep my silence.

⋆　　⋆　　⋆

Daddy said little at the dinner table that evening. He was a silent, long-suffering man who travelled to his city-centre office at eight each morning and returned home at six-thirty. After dinner he always read the newspaper by the fire, then listened to the wireless before retiring to bed. He and Mummy rarely spoke, although he always asked me how school had been.

"Never mind school," said Mummy when the inevitable question was asked. "What about her music exam? Miss Jessop really should have entered her by now. She's got to do well in the next few grades if she's to get into the Royal Academy."

I caught Daddy's eye and saw him wink. "Leave her alone, Mavis. The poor girl's had a hard day at school."

Mummy began studying her hands, as she always did when she was agitated about something. Staring at the stumps where the third and fourth fingers on her right hand used to be. The accident had put paid to her budding career, destroyed all that talent and promise the instant the train door slammed shut on her hand. But I knew she wanted me to achieve the golden prize that had been snatched from her.

I needed to change the subject before Mummy really got the bit between her teeth. "Have you heard about the burglary in Mimosa Road? Someone at school mentioned it."

Daddy looked up from his newspaper and frowned. "When was this, darling?"

"Yesterday evening. The burglar attacked an old man and he's in hospital. There was another one last week too. Jasmine Drive. He injured a woman when she confronted him."

"I don't know what the world's coming to." Daddy looked at Mummy. "We'd better make sure we lock up properly tonight, dear."

But Mummy wasn't listening. She had other things on her mind.

* * *

2 June 1953
Today the nation gathers together to celebrate the coronation of our new queen. The police, however, are concerned in case people let down their guard at this time of national rejoicing and allow the criminally inclined to take advantage of the situation.

* * *

Coronation Day was a public holiday and this meant a day off school. My family had been invited to spend the Big Day at Marie's house next door but one. Marie's parents were graciously allowing the neighbours to watch the ceremony on their newly acquired television. Although I did suspect that Marie's mum regarded it as an ideal opportunity to show off.

Mummy, Daddy and I arrived at Marie's at ten o'clock and most of our immediate neighbours were already there, packed in like sardines and staring at the tiny black-and-white screen inside a dark wood cabinet standing in the corner. Extra chairs were brought in and cups of tea served as everyone awaited the Great Event. Marie's dad sat in the corner saying little, going outside at regular intervals for a cigarette. I supposed, being French, the coronation of a British monarch wasn't as significant for him as it was for the rest of us.

Marie's mum was in her element, showing off her latest acquisitions, the tiled coffee table and the new moquette three-piece suite. And the boasting didn't stop at her possessions and the fiddly little snacks she called 'hors d'oeuvres'. She told everyone loudly that Marie was top of the class in maths and that Miss Jessop had entered Marie's brother, Stephen, for the highest grade in his piano exams. Stephen was a genius, of course; both her children were. Miss Jessop said that she'd never had such a promising pupil. The boy was a prodigy, a second Mozart, she added with pride.

Out of politeness Mummy made approving noises but I knew she was seething inside. This report of Stephen's sickening talent was sure to ruin her day, and it was hard to concentrate on the grainy ceremonial playing out on the little screen because I kept glancing at her face. How long would it be before Mummy discovered the truth about me? And how would she react when her dreams of my greatness were shattered?

Stephen, the prodigy, was a year older than Marie and I, but somehow he seemed younger as he sat cross-legged on the floor in his grey flannel shorts wearing a smug expression on his plump face. When I left the room to visit the bathroom I resisted the temptation to tread on his outstretched fingers as I passed; wrecking his brilliant future just as Mummy said hers had been wrecked.

After the coronation ceremony we had a street party. Trestle tables laden with sandwiches and cake were set up in the middle of the road. There was lemonade for the children and beer for the grown-ups but Mummy didn't stay long, claiming she had a headache. She wanted me to go home with her to practise my scales but for once Daddy stood up to her, pointing out that it wasn't every day the queen was crowned. My scales could wait for tomorrow.

*   *   *

3 June 1953

A callous thief took advantage of the national celebrations last night and broke into the home of an elderly lady who was attending a party at a neighbour's house in Didsbury, stealing valuable jewellery and antiques. Police believe it was the same thief who committed last week's burglary during which an elderly gentleman was viciously attacked. That victim sadly died in hospital yesterday and the police say the culprit must be stopped before he strikes again. They urge the public to exercise caution.

*   *   *

According to Mummy, Daddy had too much to drink on Coronation night. He went to the Rose and Crown to drink a 'loyal toast' to the newly crowned queen and Mummy wasn't pleased. But then Mummy rarely was.

As I left school that Wednesday afternoon the streets were quieter than usual, probably because people were recovering from the night before. I walked with Marie to the school gates but we wouldn't go home together as usual because I had another lesson at Miss Jessop's.

"Your brother's doing well with his piano lessons," I said to Marie before we parted. "Looks like he enjoys it more than I do."

Marie shrugged and gave a secretive smile. "Mummy says he's destined for greatness," she said with a roll of her eyes. "You'd better get going. You don't want to be late for Miss Jessop."

I began to walk towards Acacia Close. I'd practised the Chopin prelude a lot the previous week – apart from the day of the coronation when the usual drudgery of life was suspended for a few glorious hours. But however hard I tried my heart wasn't in the task and each section, practised over and over again until any magic in the music was destroyed, felt like purgatory. But Mummy insisted everything would be all right if only I made more effort. With determination, she said, I would surpass even Stephen the prodigy. I was destined for a wonderful career as a concert pianist; the career she herself had missed out on because of her accident. It was no use trying to make her see the truth, and Daddy wasn't any help. He always agreed with Mummy; anything to keep the peace.

When I reached Miss Jessop's house that day all the curtains were closed, which was unusual, and as I rang the doorbell I noticed that the door was slightly ajar. I pushed it open and called out Miss Jessop's name.

There was no reply and it took my eyes a while to adjust to the gloom. The door to the front room was open and I crept towards it on tiptoe, calling Miss Jessop's name for a second time. Again there was no answer but I thought I heard a sound upstairs, a faint creak like a soft footstep on bare floorboards. I froze and listened but I heard nothing.

The room was in semi-darkness and it took me a few seconds to spot the figure of Miss Jessop, seated on the piano stool and slumped over the keyboard as though she'd fallen asleep in mid sonata. I twitched the curtain aside to allow more light into the room and saw that her eyes were wide open, staring in astonishment at the diplomas hanging over the fireplace. Her glasses had slipped off and lay on the piano keys, and some of those keys were stained with some dark substance I assumed was blood.

For a while I stood there looking around the room, noting everything, including the bloodstained poker lying on the floor at Miss Jessop's feet. Then I took a deep breath. I couldn't leave the woman lying there. Something had to be done, so I ran next door.

*　*　*

It didn't take long before a plump uniformed constable with a reassuringly avuncular manner arrived. He asked the next-door neighbours, a middle-aged couple who had a little dog with a deep and vicious bark, to look after me and give me a cup of hot sweet tea for the shock. The neighbours seemed more shocked than I was but I accepted the tea anyway and said nothing. It seemed an age before another constable came over to take my statement. This policeman seemed very young, even to my fourteen-year-old eyes, and I could tell he was nervous. I wondered whether this was the first murder he'd had to deal with and I almost felt sorry for him.

Why was everyone treating me like a delicate creature when all I felt was curiosity blended with excitement? Of course I didn't say this to the constable and I even made a great effort to cry, hiding my dry eyes with the clean handkerchief Mummy had given me that morning. I'd liked Miss Jessop, I said. She'd been a kind, patient teacher and I couldn't think of anybody who'd wish her harm – except perhaps the burglar everyone was talking about.

This seemed to satisfy the constable who offered to walk me home and explain the situation to my parents. I accepted his offer because I wanted to escape the neighbours' cluttered, oppressive front room and the irritating barking of their silly little dog.

As I left the house I overheard two policemen talking and I caught the words, "No sign of a break-in, so maybe it was someone she knew."

*   *   *

Mummy's reaction surprised me. When the nice young policeman who escorted me home broke the news, Mummy looked annoyed, as though she'd received poor service in a shop. I'd expected her to be upset, maybe to rush to Marie's house to share the terrible news. But instead she seemed distracted, as though she was working out a difficult problem.

An hour later she came upstairs to my bedroom where I was working on a history essay.

"We have to find you a new teacher sooner rather than later. I must find out what Mrs Dubois is going to do about Stephen." She looked at the open books on my bed as though she'd caught me doing something shameful. "If you leave that you can get an hour's practice in before dinner. We won't let this little setback affect your future."

I slouched downstairs and took my place on the piano stool in the cheerless little dining room at the back of our house. Even though it was June I was cold and my fingers felt stiff. But it was no use telling Mummy that.

"There's supposed to be a B flat in bar five," she barked after I'd completed the first section of the Chopin prelude. "Chopin intended it to be slow and delicate. You're playing it like an ape in mittens. Get some feeling into it, Hester. Concentrate."

I felt tears stinging my eyes. I'd thought Miss Jessop's death would put a stop to it all. But it looks as though I was wrong.

*   *   *

4 June 1953

The police have issued a statement about the discovery of a woman's body in the Withington area. The deceased is Miss Lavinia Jessop, who taught at the Conservatoire in Paris before returning to England three years ago to care for her widowed mother in London. A year ago Miss Jessop moved to Manchester where she became a highly respected piano teacher. The police are treating her death as suspicious but they refuse to confirm any link between this incident and the recent spate of violent burglaries in the area.

*   *   *

On Saturday morning I sneaked round to Marie's for half an hour to ask her about my maths homework while Mummy was out at the shops: Marie was good at maths, unlike me. She said Mummy had asked her mother earlier that morning about her plans for Stephen the prodigy's musical education now that Miss Jessop was no longer with us. I don't know what Marie's mum told her but when I arrived home for lunch Mummy seemed more irritable than usual.

She sent me to the dining room for my piano practice as soon as we'd finished eating, even though I said I had homework to do. I perched on the stool staring at the notes on the stave, wishing Daddy would see his wife's obsession for what it was. But he was an easy-going man who took refuge at his golf club to avoid his controlling wife whose sole ambition was for me, her only daughter, to achieve the musical career that had been so cruelly snatched from her.

Daddy always went to the golf club for a drink on Saturday evenings, claiming that meeting people socially away from the office helped him to establish all sorts of useful business contacts in the world of textiles. Mummy never objected. Perhaps she hoped that, if her husband's efforts bore fruit, they'd eventually be able to afford the modern luxuries enjoyed by Marie's family next door but one.

That evening I wrote the first part of an essay on the causes of the Civil War before going to bed at nine. From my room I heard the faint sound of the wireless drifting up from the front room and I knew Mummy was in there reading while she waited for Daddy's return. The coronation had given everyone a break from routine but it was surprising how soon things returned to normal. And yet my Wednesdays would never be normal again – not now Miss Jessop was dead.

When I was lying in bed I heard Mummy's footsteps on the stairs, followed by the distant smashing of glass, and voices. Then I heard a thump, as though someone had dropped something, followed by the sound of the front door opening and Daddy shouting my name.

I ventured onto the landing, and when I looked over the banisters Daddy was standing there in his overcoat – and Mummy was lying at his feet at the bottom of the stairs.

*   *   *

8 June 1953
On Saturday night a woman was found dead at her home in Withington and the police believe she was attacked by the same man responsible for the spate of recent burglaries. Shortly after the incident a man was arrested near the scene.

*   *   *

The glass in our back door was broken. That was how the intruder had got in but nothing had been taken and the police said Daddy had probably disturbed him. Mummy had obviously fallen downstairs after confronting the burglar, who'd then fled, leaving her crumpled body lying in the hall.

It was Sunday but church was off the agenda. Nobody would expect us to be there after what happened. Besides, the police hadn't finished with us. They still had a lot of questions to ask.

First of all they wanted to know whether I'd heard anything and when I told them I was asleep they believed me. But the truth was that I'd heard Mummy on the landing and I'd pretended to be asleep in case she came into my room to nag me about my piano practice. It was something she did regularly when Daddy was out and I dreaded it.

When the police finally left I went to my room again and lay on the bed. Mummy had gone and so had Miss Jessop. And I couldn't see Daddy insisting that my lessons carried on. At last I was free to do as I pleased. Free to go to the Wednesday afternoon History Society if I chose.

I began to laugh, softly so Daddy wouldn't hear me.

*   *   *

First thing on Monday the police came back again. I hadn't gone to school because Daddy didn't think it was appropriate in the circumstances. He said everyone would understand.

The policeman who arrived wasn't in uniform. He wore an old raincoat and a trilby hat and he introduced himself as Detective Inspector Jones. He smelled strongly of peppermints and he seemed very old, and when he removed his hat his grey hair stood on end like a hedgehog's bristles. Daddy invited him to sit and told me to make a cup of tea. When I returned with the cups and teapot, I sat down quietly. I wanted to hear everything Inspector Jones had to say.

"We've charged the man. Picked him up a couple of streets away shortly after he broke in here. He was armed with a jemmy." He glanced at me and lowered his voice. "He claims your wife confronted him. Said she was shouting at him from the top of the stairs then she suddenly fell. Claims it wasn't his fault."

I saw Daddy bow his head, lost for words.

"He's put his hand up for all the recent burglaries and the murder of that elderly gentleman and we're pretty sure he was responsible for your wife's death as well, however much he denies it. He's bound for the gallows, don't you worry." He suddenly frowned, as though he'd just remembered something that might ruin his moment of triumph. "When I say he confessed to all the crimes, I mean all but one. But it's only a matter of time before he coughs to that one as well."

"Which one's that?" I couldn't resist asking the question.

The inspector looked at me as though he'd only just realised I was there. "That piano teacher – Miss Jessop. He swears he went nowhere near her house – not that I believe him."

I poured the tea, playing mother in my own mother's absence, and mulled over what I'd just heard.

That afternoon at four-thirty I knew Marie would be home and, after spending all day with Daddy, I wanted the company of someone of my own age.

*   *   *

Marie wasn't in because she'd gone to her grandmother's for tea. But I didn't want to go back home. I needed some time away from Daddy because I wanted to think. I wasn't sure of my feelings. Was I shocked? Did I feel liberated, free at last to follow my own path? I felt as though a weight had been lifted from my shoulders but I wondered if things would seem different once the reality of my mother's violent death sunk in.

I couldn't stop thinking about what Inspector Jones had said. The burglar had denied having anything to do with Miss Jessop's death.

I suddenly wanted to take a look at the scene of her murder for myself so I walked to Acacia Close. I knew Miss Jessop kept a spare key, rather unimaginatively, under a plant pot beside the front door but I half expected to find a policeman guarding the door, thwarting my plans. However, when I got there the place was deserted and there wasn't even any sign of the neighbours with the barking dog.

I let myself in and returned the key to its hiding place, grateful that high hedges separated the front gardens. Once inside the house I shut the door and crept into the front room. The first thing that caught my eye was the brown staining on the ivory piano keys. I'd seen the bloodstained poker on the floor that day and the local newspaper had confirmed it was the murder weapon. A frenzied attack, the report said. I remembered Inspector Jones saying the burglar was armed with a jemmy when he was arrested, presumably the same one he'd used to attack the unfortunate elderly man. But if he was in the habit of carrying a weapon with him, why would he use the poker?

I tore my gaze from the piano and began to look round. Sure enough the thing I'd noticed last time I was in there was still leaning against a chair leg in the corner, looking so unremarkable that it probably escaped the notice of the police. It was a black leather music folder, exactly what you'd expect to find in a piano teacher's room.

The sound of the front door opening made me jump. The police were back, which meant I had to come up with a rapid explanation. But as the door closed again I knew I was wrong. No policeman would move so stealthily. And I probably wasn't the only one who knew about the key. Any of Miss Jessop's pupils would have been told it was there in case they had to let themselves in. And the police clearly knew nothing about it or it would have been moved.

Perhaps I should have had the presence of mind to hide behind the piano but I stood quite still, paralysed with fear, as I wondered whether the killer had returned to the scene of the crime. I looked round and saw, to my relief, that the poker had been taken away, no doubt as evidence. It was just me and whoever was out there. And I had the advantage of surprise.

The door was opening slowly and the last thing I wanted to show was fear.

"I wasn't expecting you," I said as soon as he stepped into the room.

Stephen stood there with his mouth hanging open. "What are you doing here?"

"I could ask you the same thing."

I could see he was searching for a plausible explanation. "I left something here. My music folder. My mum sent me to get it."

"Has she found you a new teacher yet?"

He didn't answer.

"When I found Miss Jessop dead I noticed a folder on the floor. But I've only just realised it's yours. I recognise that railway badge pinned on it."

The boy's eyes were glowing with fury. Marie had always said her brother, the prodigy, had a terrible temper. Her mother indulged him, she said, treated him like a little god who could do no wrong.

"I'm going," he said.

I knew I couldn't stop him physically. But I could keep him talking.

"Is your mum as bad as mine was?" I said, hoping it would encourage him to be open with me. "Is she pushing you to get your exams even though you don't really want to?" I could tell he was bursting to tell me something and I waited for him to answer. Then, as I watched him, I suddenly realised the truth. I'd wondered why that photograph of the man on Miss Jessop's dressing table had seemed so terribly familiar. The man in it was the image of Stephen. The resemblance was remarkable.

I decided to take a chance, knowing I could be wrong. "Did your dad know Miss Jessop – before she came here, I mean?"

"What if he did?" Stephen might have only been fifteen years old but he was a big lad, powerful like his father.

"I saw a picture upstairs in her bedroom. That's your dad when he was younger, isn't it? You're very like him. Was your dad Miss Jessop's sweetheart?"

Stephen bowed his head. "My mum heard about this brilliant music teacher who'd come to live nearby and she wanted the best for me," he said. "Then during my last piano lesson Miss Jessop dropped a bombshell. She said she was my father's real wife."

"Why would she say that? She must have been lying."

Stephen ignored me and carried on. "She wasn't lying. She showed me the marriage certificate. She came up to Manchester to find my dad but he told her to keep away because he had a new life now. Can you imagine how shocked he was when Mum told him the name of my new piano teacher?"

"So Miss Jessop and your dad got divorced?"

He shook his head. "There was no divorce. They were Catholic, so it wasn't allowed."

"You mean your dad had two wives and he never thought he'd get found out?"

"He married Miss Jessop while she was teaching in Paris in the early thirties, then they split up and he came to England to work. When the war broke out he joined General de Gaulle's Free French but they'd lost touch by then. He thought that if she'd stayed in Paris she'd probably been killed in the war, so when he met Mum he thought he was free to marry. He only discovered Miss Jessop was still alive when she came to live in Manchester after her mother died, and she found him."

"Your dad told you all this?"

"No. She did. She said nothing until that day she was... found. I'd thought for a while that something wasn't right. She used to watch me all the time and stroke my hair as if I was her pet. She told me how handsome I was and kept asking about my father. She knew my school finished early on a Wednesday, so the day it happened she told me to come for an extra lesson, but she asked me not to let my mother know I was coming because she had something to tell me and she wanted it to be a surprise. I thought it had something to do with the exams but as soon as I turned up she came straight out with it. I'm married to your father. She said I should know the truth and she said she was going to tell my mum because it was her duty – the right thing to do. I told her she was a liar but she wouldn't stop."

"Did your dad kill her to stop her telling your mum?"

Stephen hesitated. Then he raised his hands, and I suddenly knew it hadn't been his father who'd killed the woman who'd turned up so inconveniently to turn his world upside down.

"I couldn't let her tell Mum, could I? And she said Dad could go to prison if anyone found out. I had to get rid of that marriage certificate… I couldn't let her talk."

He took another step towards me and I found myself leaning on the piano, unable to retreat any further.

"Hello," said a voice from outside in the hall. Whoever the woman was she didn't sound sure of herself. But I was glad she'd arrived.

Stephen made a feeble attempt to stop me but I pushed past him and rushed out into the hall. The next-door neighbour who'd looked after me that day was standing on the threshold, and as soon as her little dog saw me it began to bark, and I made a decision.

"I'm calling the police," I shouted. "Can you stay here with the dog and make sure no one leaves."

I hoped the noise made by the diminutive guard dog would be enough to trap Stephen in that front room until help arrived.

*　　*　　*

That evening I saw a police car outside Marie's house and I felt a twinge of guilt. I'd never particularly liked Stephen or his mother, but I felt sorry for Marie – and even for her father, the bigamist who might now go to prison for his crime.

It was the talk of the Avenue, of course, and the net curtains were twitching like flags in the breeze.

Inspector Jones turned up the following day with more questions to ask. But rather than asking about Stephen, who'd apparently broken down in tears and confessed to everything, he wanted to talk about the night my mother died.

"The burglar said he saw somebody behind your mother at the top of the stairs. Someone in a pink nightdress," he said, watching my face closely. "He thought your mother was pushed and that's why she went flying. He swears he never touched her."

"He would say that, wouldn't he?" I replied, confident that he'd believe a grieving daughter over a hardened criminal.

And he did.

*   *   *

Three weeks later the headmistress caught me in the corridor and gave me a smile full of sugary sympathy. "How are you, Hester?"

"Fine, thank you, Miss Smithers." I knew she was thinking of my mother's death but I could hardly tell her that I was more upset about Marie moving away from all the wagging tongues to live with her mother's parents in Bedfordshire. I was missing her terribly.

"That's good to hear. If you need more time to do your homework or… if you need anyone to talk to."

"No, honestly, Miss Smithers, I'm all right. My father and I are looking after each other."

She paused and I wondered what was coming next. I was soon to find out. "We need someone to play the piano at the school concert and someone suggested you. I believe you're rather good."

I shook my head. "I'm afraid not, Miss Smithers. I can't play – not a note."

HIS GREATEST HIT

L.C. Tyler

Intro

It's where we all end up, I suppose. In a box in the ground. You can't take your royalties with you. You can't take the stretch limo. You can't even take your secrets.

First verse

"So, when he did that last farewell tour, he really meant it," said the man standing next to me.

The open grave left neither of us in any doubt of that. The coffin was already partly obscured by the handfuls of earth that the vicar had politely encouraged mourners to scatter over it. Not many handfuls. There were few of us gathered today at this grey, pebble-dashed church, overlooked by the wide, purple Cumbrian fells and the cloudless spring sky. It was, by any standards, a small funeral. Very small indeed for somebody of Tony McGarva's former eminence and street cred. Some family were there. A couple of old friends. And, for reasons I was still trying to guess at, my agent had generously consented to come with me. I couldn't quite place the man who had just spoken, though his face was sort of familiar.

"Yes," I said. "That third farewell tour really was the final one. I don't think they made much money on it. Musical tastes had moved on. And now, sadly, Tony has too."

"They had to get permission to reopen the grave," he said.

"Whose idea was it to bury him with his first wife?" I asked.

"Her sister's, I think. His second wife's still alive, of course, so that was never really an option. Not that she'd have been keen, even if she was dead."

"Two wives, two divorces," I said. "Quite restrained for a rock star."

"How did you know Tony exactly?" he asked.

I laughed. It was clear to both of us that I didn't quite look as if I belonged to the world of rock and roll; but nor, to be fair, did he. "We were at university together," I said. "Then for a while he was just somebody I read about in the newspapers. Later I met him at a college reunion and he invited me up here to stay every now and then. I think – recently anyway – he was a bit lonely in a Cumbrian village with one pub and no shops. It's a while since he wrote anything or recorded anything. They still occasionally play his stuff on the radio, of course. At least, that big hit he had in the late nineties – 'Stolen'."

He nodded. I don't know if you can nod bitterly, but if you can then that's what he did. Maybe he thought 'Stolen' was overrated. Some people do.

"My name's Ethelred," I said, since we had not yet introduced ourselves. "Ethelred Tressider."

He nodded again.

"I write crime novels," I added. "Nothing to do with the music industry at all."

He didn't offer his own name in return. He seemed to think I should know.

"That song – it was about his first wife's death, of course," I said. I thought I should show that I wasn't totally ignorant of the music scene, however much of a mystery writer I was.

I wondered if he'd say any fool knew that. I wondered if, like a lot of people, he'd add that 'Stolen' was a bit too macabre, a bit too personal for his taste. But he did neither. What actually happened was that he burst into song. "She was by the bright waters," he crooned softly. "In the arms of her killer. She was sleeping so gently. In the arms of her killer."

As ever, I was left feeling that the line 'in the arms of her killer' was slightly awkward, a bit too contrived. The harsh words jarred with the gentle melody. You felt that there were better lyrics in there somewhere that Tony had failed to locate. But it was well sung by the man I had still failed to recognise. Whoever he was, I had to give him credit for that.

"Wow!" I said. "You're good. That might have been Tony himself singing. You should have taken it up."

"I did," he said.

"Hang on," I said. "I know who you are. You're Zak…"

"Frimley," he said. "Zak Frimley."

"Of course," I said. "I remember you from…"

"The nineties," he said. "I had three hits back in the nineties. Not as big as 'Stolen'. Not remotely as big. But I did OK. For three years I did OK."

"Was it that long ago?"

"Trust me. You don't forget the brief moment the spotlight shines on you."

To be honest, as I think I said before, it was difficult imagining him under a spotlight at all. He was quite short and plump. The collar of his white shirt was very worn. The cuffs of his clerical-grey suit were slightly shiny, where they had clearly rubbed against the surface of a desk. He had the face of an irritable ageing cherub. Until he announced his name, I had him down as a teacher at a rural prep school.

"Why did you give it up?" I asked.

He paused for a long time. "I'd said all I had to say. I knew I'd never write another song as good as the last one I'd written. So, I stopped."

"What do you do now?"

"I teach music in a prep school in Kent. It's what every rock star dreams of doing."

"Ah," I said.

There was another long pause, then I said: "I know the stretch of river where Silvia drowned, of course. I know it well. It's just up the valley from here. She and Tony were walking together – by the bright water, as the song goes – and she somehow slipped and fell. She couldn't swim and was swept away by the current… and then over the waterfall. Horrible, really. Nightmarish. Doesn't bear thinking about. That's why there's that bit about the brutal rocks. How did it go?"

"Brutish," said Zak, somewhat testily I thought. "The brutish rock. People always get that wrong."

"OK," I said, cautiously. It was clearly something he felt more strongly about than I did. "Anyway, he found her in the pool at the bottom of the fall. She'd apparently hit her head on a… rock. A brutish one, if you say so. He had to wade in up to his waist to get her. He tried to resuscitate her but it was much too late."

"I know," said Zak. "I was there."

"You actually saw her swept over? That must have been awful for you."

"No, not that. I mean I was staying with Tony and Silvia at the time. There was a whole party of us. Me. Tony and Silvia. Silvia's sister and the sister's husband. And Vanessa."

"Vanessa? Tony's second wife?"

"She was his PR in those days. She'd come up from London with something he needed to work on. I don't know what it was that couldn't wait a day or two. Still, it was nice that she was on the spot. To console him when Silvia died. Very convenient."

"So, Vanessa and Tony…"

He looked at me as if I were an idiot. "They married a year or so after Silvia's death. It's probably safe to assume they were an item long before that. But I can tell you Tony and Silvia were already pretty much finished by then. They'd have split up sooner or later, with or without Vanessa. Silvia became a beautiful memory only when Tony saw how profitable that would be. The perfect wife that had been snatched away. Stolen by the river."

I felt disloyal before I even asked my next question, but I couldn't stop myself. "The rumour at the time was that she hadn't fallen," I said. "Some people thought that he pushed her in. When Tony wrote 'in the arms of your killer' he didn't mean the river as some fanciful personification of a murderer – he meant himself, pulling Silvia out of the water at the bottom of the fall."

Zak's reply confirmed how tasteless my question was. "We all heard the rumours, but Tony was a good friend. So, I've always chosen not to speculate. OK?"

"No. Of course," I said, also a friend, though evidently a less good one than Zak.

"The police questioned us all," he continued. "As you would imagine. And they concluded that only Tony and Silvia had been there when she fell in. But there were no charges. No question of charges. It was an accident. End of."

"I didn't mean that's what I thought myself," I said.

"Whatever," he said.

"Sorry – it's simply that, as a crime writer, I guess my mind works that way…"

"I'm sure it does. Now, if you'll excuse me, I just need to go and talk to somebody," he said.

"Of course," I said.

Chorus

I've noticed it before. After a funeral, there's a sense of relief. People say things they wouldn't say otherwise. Sometimes things that were better not said.

First bridge

"Well," said Elsie, glancing briefly down into the grave. "Not exactly a rock-and-roll interment, is it?"

"No," I said.

"Scarcely worth the effort of dressing up for it."

My agent was attired in a manner suitable for a rockabilly funeral circa 1955. The shiny black skirt was well supported with petticoats. The bodice was as tight as could be managed until her current diet had started to kick in and deliver results. The sunglasses were perched on top of her head. The lipstick was scarlet.

"I said it would be a small affair but you were very welcome to come with me," I said. "I definitely didn't promise you the great and the good of the rock world. Tony had been out of all that for a while. He'd lost touch with the sort of people you were hoping to get a selfie with."

"I came here *entirely* to support you, Ethelred. In your very understandable grief. You know that."

"Thank you," I said.

"Is that Mick Jagger over there?" said Elsie, searching her handbag for her phone.

"No, just a fan who happens to live nearby and found out from somewhere that the funeral was today. A couple of them seem to have cottoned on. I saw them surreptitiously taking pictures of each other. But they will sadly realise their error when they post on Twitter."

"You're sure he's not Mick? There aren't many people that wrinkled."

"I've spoken to him. He's a plumber from Windermere. But that was Zak Frimley that I was talking to a moment ago."

"Really? *The* Zak Frimley? In that Oxfam suit? God, he's aged. I didn't recognise him at all. He was pretty hot in the late nineties. Then we had the Millennium and it was all about Eminem for some reason."

"Zak now teaches at a prep school in Kent."

"Why not carry on performing?"

"He told me he'd nothing new to say."

"You don't have anything new to say, Ethelred, but you carry on writing crime novels. I mean, it's fine. Your readers don't like new stuff. It frightens the shit out of them. But you have to admit that your last four or five books haven't exactly broken new ground."

"Do you think I should?"

"Hell, no. Not at your age."

"Thank you," I said.

"My pleasure," she said. "You know they reckon your mate Tony bumped his first wife off, by the way?"

She showed no sign of worrying whether this remark was insensitive. She obviously reckoned my grief was up to it.

"If so, he made a decent profit out of murder," I said.

"Which is more than you do," said Elsie. "Have you got the car keys? There's a bar of chocolate in the glove compartment that needs my attention."

Second verse

I wasn't sorry to be left in contemplation of a perfect Lake District spring afternoon. The blossom was just making its appearance on the trees in the churchyard. Primroses grew in profusion around their roots. But I was not to remain alone for long.

"Well, that's done, Ethelred. It could have gone worse, eh?" Marion drew on her cigarette and exhaled a stream of grey smoke. I had met Tony's sister-in-law – Silvia's sister – when Elsie and I arrived at the church an hour or so before. In the absence of any closer family, Marion had taken charge of proceedings, vetted and tracked down possible attenders of the funeral, made a firm and binding decision not to invite Vanessa or to inform the press of anything. She was dressed simply but expensively in a well-tailored black dress and a large black hat. Her hair was midway between blonde and grey. It suited her.

"Yes," I said. "It's all been very organised. It was good of you to do it."

"Good of me because Tony bumped off my sister?" she asked. She flicked some ash carefully into the grave.

"Yes... I mean, no... do you really think he did?"

She laughed. "It was a very odd weekend, that one. Relations between Tony and Silvia were at rock bottom. She was carrying on with anyone and everyone – Tony must have told you that. My brother-in-law, for a rock star, was sweetly but unnaturally monogamous. He wanted somebody who would unquestioningly return his love and devotion. He should have bought himself a Labrador but he inadvisably married my sister instead. Marry in haste, and so on. Most of the time he just about kept the lid on it all. Then, out of the blue, Zak showed up. That was one thing too many."

"Zak Frimley?" I said, a bit unnecessarily.

"Zak may be a portly music teacher now, but he was a rising star then. Awarded Best Newcomer at one or other of the big awards ceremonies and with a couple of mega-hits under his belt."

"He said three big hits."

"Well, two big hits and a little one to follow them. But he was very excited about his next project. He saw Tony as a bit of a mentor. He wanted to talk things through with him – run some thrilling new idea past him. But Silvia had different plans for little Zak. And Zak took a much more heavy-metal approach to infidelity. He was well up for it."

"And Tony caught them together? Is that what you mean?"

"I've no idea. Anyway, Zak was only a snack – a naughty nibble on the side. In those days, Silvia had my husband down as the main course. You've met him, so it will be as inexplicable to you as it was to me, but there it is."

I tried to remember his name. As Marion had said, we'd been introduced. "Robert?" I said.

"I usually call him 'Rock'," she said.

"Rock as in…?"

"The brutish Rock in the song? The one that did for Silvia? Yes, I've wondered about that too. Odd wording. If it was aimed at my unintelligent husband, then Tony undoubtedly knew for certain what I merely suspected. Silvia told him everything, of course. She was always happiest when being cruel to be kind."

"So, if jealousy was the motive for murder, then it may have been your husband that excited it?"

"My husband and excitement rarely occur in the same sentence, Ethelred. But I think that he in some way played a part. Or Zak the snack. One or the other. Or both. It was supposed to be a nice relaxing country house weekend, but the atmosphere was pretty tense all round, I can tell you. As the very last straw, that bitch Vanessa showed up on her motorbike – all shiny leather, sweat, Chanel Number Five and bright red lips. Tony suggested we all went for a walk, to clear our heads. We started as a fairly coherent party, but we took our respective grievances with us into the fells, and one by one people peeled off and went their own way or turned back towards home. Tony and Silvia were still together, chatting amiably, by the time they reached the river above the falls. Or that was what the police concluded. I missed the action myself."

"So you didn't see Silvia fall? You don't know that he killed her?"

"Look, Ethelred: my sister had found herself a good man and then decided to cheat on him on an industrial scale. All I know is that, if I'd been Tony and I'd been sure nobody was watching, I'd have pushed her in. Maybe I'd have given her a good whack with a brutish rock first, just to make sure. They never could prove what she'd hit her head on or when."

Marion flicked the cigarette butt onto the top of the coffin. It landed on the brass plate. You had to admire her aim. "You'll come back to the house for a sherry or something? There's beer and Cumberland sausage available too for all bona fide mourners."

"Who could resist an offer like that?" I asked.

Chorus

I've noticed it before. After a funeral, there's a sense of relief. People say things they wouldn't say otherwise. Sometimes things that were better not said.

Third verse

"Is that a cigarette butt on the coffin?" asked Robert, looking down. "Some folk have no respect."

He lit up his own cigarette anyway and drew deeply.

"Think of it as a libation," I said. "Like the wine the Romans poured onto the ground."

"Did they? Seems a waste."

I wondered if this was professional concern. Tony had told me once that Robert worked in the drinks industry – he was the regional manager or deputy head of sales or something for a distiller. From Tony's description, I'd always envisaged Robert in a tweed jacket, propping up the bar in some thatched pub. Now I'd actually met him, it still seemed likely his typical working day was exactly that. I couldn't see that the nickname 'Rock' had been applied to him in anything other than a spirit of extreme irony.

"Sort of placating the spirit of the deceased, I suppose," I said.

"It should have been a joint in that case," said Robert. "Was that young Zak I saw you talking to earlier?"

"Yes," I said.

"Surprised he made an appearance. I mean, he attended Silvia's funeral, obviously. He was pretty cut up about it all. But I hadn't expected to see him here. Laying a few ghosts to rest perhaps."

"Zak and Silvia were close?"

"You might say that. She had a habit of picking up nice young men, toying with them for a bit and then dropping them. Sadly she died before she could dump him properly. So he continued to believe that it might have all worked out for them. He probably thought it was only a matter of days until they could both run off to some rural idyll, where he would gaze lovingly on her while she baked seeded batch loaves and stitched samplers."

"Your wife said that Tony and Silvia were close to splitting up."

He shook his head. "Marion and Silvia's father manufactured petrochemicals, until he was bought out by some Americans, leaving the family with more money than it knew what to do with. When he died, it all went to the girls. But, knowing they might marry losers like me and Tony, their father ensured it was mainly held in trust. In the event of a divorce, the ex-husbands would get nothing. Shrewd old bird, Marion's dad. Liked him a lot. Tony's career was very much in the past at that stage. He needed every penny he could get from the trust. Of course, he didn't know then what a success 'Stolen' was going to be. If he had, he might have been less keen to keep patching things up with Silvia. Not making a fuss about all the other men in her life."

"But he knew what was going on?"

"She always told him. Honest as the day is long, that Silvia."

"What happened if she died?"

"Oh, I know the answer to that. I'm on the same terms and conditions of service myself. If Silvia died before Tony, he'd receive an income from the trust for life."

"And there were a lot of other men around her?"

"I'll say."

"Including you?"

"Ah, you had a longer conversation with my wife than I'd thought. Nothing in it, old boy. Silvia issued me with an invitation, if I can put it like that, but I never RSVP-ed. Too risky. Silvia would have told Tony, Tony would have told Marion and I'd have never seen another trust fund cheque for the rest of my days. I've never claimed to have been the brightest of my year at school, but I've always known which side my bread was buttered on. Didn't stop me winding up young Zak, of course. I dropped a lot of hints there." He smiled, as if at a distant memory of something rather good.

"So, it would have suited Tony if Silvia had died rather than divorced him?"

For a moment Robert looked thoughtful, then he smiled again and shook his head. "I suppose so, but I don't think things were really that bad between them just before Silvia died – I mean that particular day. Tony was actually quite cheerful. I heard him singing before breakfast – it was that thing about the bright water and so on – the one that he ended up selling millions of."

"But he wrote that *after* his wife's death," I said. "It came from the grief he felt."

"So he always told people," said Robert. "But you're not under oath when selling rock music. Obviously, he didn't grieve that much. Not in real life. And Vanessa was right there to help with the grieving process. More a PR thing really – Tony's grief. Selling gin, selling music – it's all a bit hit and miss what catches the public's imagination and what flops. You need a unique selling point, and a dead wife was almost as good as it gets. But you're right. He must have already more or less written that song before she died – words and music. Not that it makes much difference one way or the other. Not now."

Chorus

I've noticed it before. After a funeral, there's a sense of relief. People say things they wouldn't say otherwise. Sometimes things that were better not said.

Fourth verse

The churchyard appeared to be empty. All of the mourners had departed, feeling the chill in the air, or maybe tempted by the offer of Cumberland sausage. Then I saw a slight figure walk through the gate and stride purposefully towards me. She wore a black leather jacket, black leather trousers and was carrying a large pink motorcycle helmet. I didn't doubt for a moment that this was Tony's second wife.

"You missed the service," I said.

"That cow of a sister-in-law didn't tell me," she said. "I got it off Twitter – some fan had turned up and posted a picture of a guy they thought was Mick Jagger. As if. Fortunately I only live fifteen minutes away, so I got on my bike. Why are there two cigarette butts on the coffin?"

"A double libation," I said.

"If you say so. I'd have called it a bit of a liberty myself. I see they buried him with her, then?"

"Yes," I said.

"There were always three people in our marriage," she said, "even if one of them was dead. When your whole image is a man distraught at the death of your first wife, your second wife gets pushed into the background a bit. Then pushed right out of the marriage. I blame myself."

"Do you?"

"Oh, yes. 'Stolen' – that was my idea. He'd already written this song, see? Don't know when he did it but it was OK. Better than his other stuff. A bit of a departure in some ways. Anyway, day or two after she died, I said to him – if you just changed a line or two, that new thing you've done could be about Silvia, know what I mean? And he said, no. And I said, yes, it could, straight up. We could make a bit of money there, Tony my boy. Here's the story: she died and you came back here and wrote the song on the first bit of paper you could find – let's say that. He said, what bit of paper? So I got him an envelope out of the bin and said, just copy it down on that, Tone. Then leave it to yours truly. I know what I'm doing. Do you know that very envelope eventually went for over twenty thousand at auction? For charity, of course. We didn't need the money. Not with the royalties from the song and with the trust fund still paying out."

"Did Tony ever tell you exactly what happened that day?"

"You mean did he kill her? I already knew the answer to that. He was with me when it happened. We'd stopped – getting to know each other better, you might say. The others had pressed on. Marion, Robert, Zak, Silvia – they were all up there somewhere. Anyway, we heard a yell. Tony said that was Silvia and went running off up the hill."

"So they weren't walking by the river when she slipped?"

"Not even close. He did drag her out of the water below the fall, though. That's the one true bit of the song."

"So why did he tell the police – and everyone else – he'd been walking with her and she'd fallen accidentally?"

"Well, like I say, it did make a much better story – how she was literally snatched from his hands. But you'll realise that can't be *why* he did it, because we hadn't done the envelope thing when we were first interviewed by the police. I sometimes wondered if he was protecting somebody, but I can't think who. Maybe it was just that he didn't want people to know that, when his wife fell in the river, he was being rather naughty with another woman. For a rock star, he was a very private person."

"He wasn't protecting you?" I asked.

"Only my reputation, darling. Only my reputation. I couldn't have got up that slope anyway – not in the shoes I was wearing."

"Didn't the police think you had a motive for killing her? You did marry him soon after."

"We all had a motive, sweetie. Me. Marion. Zak. Maybe not Robert, but you never know, do you? Depends how much he and Silvia really got up to. Tony swearing he saw Silvia fall in rather saved everyone from too much interrogation. And Tony's dead now, so there's no chance to question him again."

I looked down at the coffin. "That certainly is true," I said.

Chorus

I've noticed it before. After a funeral, there's a sense of relief. People say things they wouldn't say otherwise. Sometimes things that were better not said.

Second bridge

"Just because you're a crime writer, you don't have to look death in the face for hours on end," said Elsie. "I think you can stop staring down into the grave now. If you were hoping for any chocolate, by the way,

I'm deeply saddened to tell you that it is now all eaten. But there is sausage available back at the house."

"I'm sure that Silvia was murdered," I said. "I just can't work out which of them did it."

I ran through what each of the mourners had told me.

"Depends a bit on whether anyone was telling you the truth," said Elsie. "People do lie to you, Ethelred. You're much too trusting. Take your ex-wife, for example—"

"Can we leave my own love life out of it? At least that bit?"

"It wouldn't take very long if we included all of it, but as you wish. The two most important clues seem to me that the song was written before Silvia died – no doubt about that – and that Tony lied about witnessing Silvia's fall into the water. I mean why would he do that? What was in it for him? Also, as Vanessa hinted and as I could have told you myself, 'Stolen' was quite different from Tony's earlier stuff. When I first heard it, years ago, I thought I was listening to a Zak Frimley number."

"Zak seems quite bitter about the song but, at the same time, quite sensitive to any errors I made when quoting it."

"Exactly. He's bound to feel quite protective, seeing it was his own composition – albeit subtly altered by Tony and his PR on the back of an envelope. How can I be so certain it was originally Zak's? We know that Zak had come up here very excited with something he had written and that he wanted to show it to Tony. But Zak never had a hit – big or small – after Silvia died. So, where did that little number go? And you say that Robert – or Rock, as I like to think of him – heard Tony singing the song in question early that morning."

"You mean it was Zak singing it?"

"It doesn't really matter. It may have been Zak or it may have been Tony, having had the song played to him by Zak the day before. But I think we can assume Tony knew about the song and liked it very much. His own stuff hadn't made much impact lately. He was well jel, as Vanessa would say. So, choir practice over, they all headed off up into the fells for a jolly day out. Zak was madly in love with Silvia and had not reached the state of complete disillusionment that comes with being dumped by an attractive older woman – a state, Ethelred, that you are very familiar with yourself."

"Not that familiar."

"Familiar enough. We know that Robert, who was also somewhere in the frame for Silvia's favours, had been cruelly winding Zak up. Poor Zak was beginning to suspect things were not quite as they seemed. On the walk he stuck closely to Silvia – where else could a besotted lover possibly be? In this whole mass of speculation, the one thing of which we can be absolutely certain is that, when Silvia got to the banks of the river above the falls, she and Zak were together. It would have been easier for somebody with a pocket full of dog treats to shake off a Labradoodle puppy. I would suggest to you that Zak asked Silvia about his prospects, perhaps mentioning stuff Robert had let slip. She gave him a straight answer, in much the same way as she did to her husband. In terms of truthfulness, at least, she'd have made a very good Boy Scout.

"A few minutes later Silvia was in the bright water. I can't say whether Zak hit her with a rock or pushed her or, in the course of a lively and frank exchange of views, she just slipped and fell. She let out a yell, which Tony, Vanessa and perhaps others heard clearly. Zak would have been much too useless to save her. Tony came running and, the current being quite fast, found Zak already alone and his wife long since vanished downstream. They made their descent to the rock pool by a safer route than Silvia's. Again, I'm sure of that: Zak would never have permitted a rescue of Silvia that he was not an integral part of. But she was already dead. And that was when they did The Deal. Tony would cover up for Zak – he'd say that he'd seen Silvia fall in accidentally – but there was a price to pay. The price was Zak's new song, which, thereafter, would be known as Tony's new song. A distraught Zak, scarcely able to assemble his thoughts, was willing to agree to anything."

"So that's why the song was called 'Stolen'?"

"Your friend Tony was a bit of a card, no? Of course, Zak later regretted it. The stolen praise that should have been his. The stolen royalties that should have been his. And the hideous changes they'd made in order to make the words fit Silvia's death – that line about 'in the arms of her killer' always felt sort of wrong. I wonder if it was originally 'in the arms of her lover' or something like that? And he knew he'd *never write another song as good as the last one he'd written*. Wasn't that what he told you? Was it surprising that he quit the world of rock and went to work as a prep-school teacher, where he'd never have to meet anyone cool ever again?"

"I see nothing wrong with being a prep-school teacher," I said.

"Exactly," said Elsie. "My point in a nutshell."

A small cloud passed over the sun. Suddenly it felt very much colder.

"There's nothing to be done about it," I said. "We don't have the sort of proof the police would want. And Zak could reclaim what was his only by admitting it was blackmail."

"If Zak had been my client, I'd have advised splitting the royalties fifty/fifty," said Elsie. "Unless Tony had photographs, in which case I'd have gone seventy-five/twenty-five. Shall we head straight back to London, or do you fancy a sausage before we go?"

"Straight back, I think. I don't really want to make small talk with the others. Sometimes you can know too much about something for your own good."

"After a funeral, there's a sense of relief," said Elsie. "People say things they wouldn't say otherwise."

I nodded. "Sometimes things that were better not said."

"Depends who you tell," said Elsie. "I can keep a secret. Possibly."

I didn't have a cigarette butt to add to the collection, but, as the shadows lengthened over the graveyard, I gave Tony a parting wave, and I think he understood me.

Outro

It's where we all end up, I suppose. In a box in the ground. You can't take your royalties. You can't take the stretch limo. But occasionally, very occasionally, you get to keep one of your secrets.

REQUIEM

Leo McNeir

A Marnie Walker short story

If they had known how the first day of their winter break would end, Marnie and Ralph would probably have opted to stay at home. As it was, they were lured out by crisp, bright winter weather and decided on impulse to brave the season and take a few days off from work. A weekend cruising the Grand Union Canal would surely blow away any cobwebs and refresh their spirits in the run-up to Christmas at the end of a busy year.

The facilities on Ralph's *Thyrsis* were superior to those on Marnie's *Sally Ann*, which simplified the choice of boat for the journey. The bonus of efficient central heating backed up by a cosy wood-burning stove, plus a modern (if sometimes cramped for double occupancy) shower cubicle, won the day. And so it was that at first light on the first Saturday in December, *Thyrsis* slipped her mooring in Knightly St. John and pointed her bows northwards with Marnie at the helm, the first boat to disturb that stretch of water for a week or more.

They chugged on through bleak chill countryside brooded over by the occasional solitary heron, too idle to stir from its vigil. Somnolent fields devoid of crops or livestock extended away to the horizon in both directions, bounded by hoarfrosted hedges punctuated by leafless trees. Marnie blew into her gloves to thaw her fingers, and was more than pleased to see Ralph emerging from the cabin armed with a tray bearing steaming coffee mugs and a plate of warmed croissants. A second breakfast was more than an indulgence. It was a necessity.

Later in the morning the village of Yore came into view. Their first sighting was the four spirelets on the church tower, pale grey filigree stone pointing up into a wispy blue sky. Most of the village was hidden away among trees and folds in the landscape, but the churchyard was bordered by the canal that clung to a contour line skirting the perimeter like a bend in a river. The bulk of the church provided shelter from the chilly breeze that had sprung up and turned Marnie's nose pink. A short stop for an early lunch seemed a good idea.

They had brought with them ready-prepared meals that only required heating up for lunches. Their intention was to stop overnight and have dinner both evenings in canalside pubs while the wood-burner prepared a warm welcome for their return. Lunch that Saturday was smoked haddock chowder with crusty French bread followed by gooseberry fool. By the time the soup was ready to serve, Marnie wondered if it was mild enough in the lea of the church for them to eat up front in the cratch with the side curtains removed. It took Ralph no more time to prepare the prow than for Marnie to lay the tray.

Marnie and Ralph ate in silence, resting against thick cushions, gazing out over rolling meadows, the soup bowls warming their hands, their cheeks glowing. The scene laid out before them had probably not changed in centuries, and a flash of movement caught their eyes as two woodpigeons flew across their field of vision like illustrations from a medieval manuscript. Their eyes met and they shared the moment without the need for words.

Ralph was setting his bowl down on the tray when he noticed that Marnie had cocked her head on one side.

"Can you hear something?" she said.

Ralph strained to listen. "What is it?" he asked.

Marnie raised a finger to her lips as Ralph closed his eyes to concentrate.

"I'm not sure I can—" He stopped. "Ah, yes. There is something…"

A sound was carried towards them on the breeze, faint, sporadic and ephemeral. Marnie picked up her dessert and listened again. Shaking her head, she reached for a spoon. After a few mouthfuls she stopped.

"What d'you think it is?" she asked.

"I'm pretty sure it's gooseberry," Ralph said, deadpan.

Marnie grinned at him. "Idiot! I meant the sound, of course."

"Hard to tell. It's so intermittent. Could it be coming from the church, perhaps?"

"That's what I was wondering."

"One way to find out," Ralph suggested.

"OK, let's finish these and explore. We can have coffee when we get back."

It was just a short walk to the churchyard gate and, turning on to the gravel path, they were surprised to see a large number of cars parked along the village street. The church was unlocked and, as they pushed open the heavy door and stepped inside, they became aware of muted voices and the scraping of chairs. Down towards the altar a small crowd was assembled. Some were holding musical instruments: violins, violas, cellos.

Marnie and Ralph took their seats in a pew near the font and looked on, curious to see the proceedings. One man in particular was obviously in charge, and he spoke quietly to various others in turn before positioning himself in the centre aisle facing towards the east window. His voice sounded down the nave loud and clear.

"OK, everybody, shall we take it from the top, one last time?"

There was a wholesale regrouping as the majority of those assembled spread out in a line behind the chairs, while the musicians took their places in the foreground. The man in charge held up his arms and everyone fell silent. Bows were raised, throats were cleared and all eyes focused on the conductor. As he began conducting, a most extraordinary thing happened. The church was transformed, and Marnie and Ralph were transported to another place, first by the strings and then by the voices swelling to fill the air. It seemed astonishing that such a volume of sound could be created by so small an ensemble. Marnie and Ralph were enchanted. After just a few minutes the conductor brought his charges to a unified halt.

"Well done, everybody. That was wonderful. I think that's it for today. I want you here by ten o'clock on Monday and we'll have a final run-through. Does anyone have any questions or problems? No? Good. Thank you all."

Marnie turned to Ralph and spoke softly. "That was *brilliant*."

Ralph nodded. "The 'Lacrimosa' from Mozart's *Requiem*."

"Yes. We must have heard them rehearsing it when we were in the cratch."

They neither noticed that, as they spoke together, the conductor was making his way down the centre aisle towards them. He paused as he reached their pew. They stood and faced him.

"That was a beautiful experience," Ralph said.

Marnie added, "I hope we weren't intruding."

"Not at all. It's nice to have an audience, though in fact I didn't even know you were there."

"Were you rehearsing for a concert?" Marnie asked. "I can't imagine you're preparing that piece for the first Sunday in Lent."

The conductor's expression clouded over. "Ah… you're not from the village, obviously."

"Just passing through on the canal," said Ralph.

"We live in Knightly St. John," said Marnie. "We're obviously missing something."

The conductor led them aside as the members of the choir and musicians began passing on their way out. He looked from Ralph to Marnie.

"You didn't know Florence Whittaker?"

"No," Marnie replied, "but the name sounds rather familiar."

"We – that is, the choral society and a section from the county sinfonietta – we're performing that part of the *Requiem* at her funeral."

"It was a favourite of hers?" Ralph suggested.

The conductor said, "It's very poignant. Yes, a great favourite. Florence was secretary of the choral society, a fine contralto in her own right. Her name is probably familiar to you as she was… murdered."

"Of course," said Marnie. "Now I remember, but it was some time ago, wasn't it?"

"It was. It seems she disturbed an intruder one evening, a month or so ago. Her body has just been released for burial."

Marnie grimaced. "How awful."

"Absolutely. Her husband told me she'd been listening to music when it happened. She had a large collection of vinyl. He told me she'd been listening to Mozart's *Requiem*, in fact, the piece we've been rehearsing."

"The 'Lacrimosa'," Ralph said.

"That's right. It's quite appropriate in more ways than one."

"How do you mean?" Marnie asked.

"You possibly know that Mozart had reached that part of the *Requiem* at the time he died. It was then completed by another composer who admired him very much."

"Probably Süssmayr," Ralph murmured.

The conductor nodded once. "Probably. Monday, the day of Florence's funeral, is the fifth of December, the anniversary of Mozart's death."

"Her husband was unharmed?"

"He was away on business at the time. He told me confidentially that he knew what she'd been listening to because he found the record on the turntable. She loved the recording by Karajan and the Berlin Philharmonic."

"Do I remember rightly that the murderer hasn't yet been caught?" said Marnie.

"That's right. The family made a special request so that her funeral could take place. The police raised no objection, so the service can now go ahead."

"I'm sure you'll do her proud," Ralph said quietly.

"It will be a great comfort to her family," Marnie added.

The conductor sighed. "I fear nothing will ever bring them comfort. While the crime remains unsolved, they'll probably never be able to have closure. I can only hope that by our efforts we'll at least give her a good send-off."

"No doubt about that," Marnie said. "And your music is very well chosen."

"Yes. Florence was a huge fan of Mozart."

The conductor shook hands with them both and walked out. Marnie and Ralph sat down for a few moments' reflection. Now the church was empty; the chairs used by the musicians had been stacked neatly to one side. An atmosphere of loss, sadness and anti-climax seemed to have descended on the building.

Marnie turned to Ralph. "Despite what he said, I'm sure that lovely music will bring at least some comfort to that poor woman's family."

"I don't see how it could fail," Ralph agreed. "Shall we get back?"

Marnie stood up. "I know it's for a sad occasion, but that music was very beautiful."

Outside, Marnie waited while Ralph carefully closed the door behind them. The chilly breeze had died away, leaving a hint of warmth in the air.

"Unusual these days not to keep the church locked," he said. "Perhaps someone will be coming to do it."

Marnie took his hand as they set off walking slowly back along the path towards the lychgate.

"I think the *someone* is already here," she said, looking ahead of them.

Halfway down the path a man was sitting on a bench. He was finishing a sandwich and stuffing the empty packet into a paper bag. He looked up as they drew near.

"Nice day," he said.

"I hope we haven't held you up," Ralph said. "Have you come to lock the church?"

"No. I just like to come here from time to time, when the weather's mild enough, to have a spot of lunch and a quiet think."

"We didn't mean to disturb you," said Marnie.

"Not a problem." He glanced towards the church. "You wanted your own quiet time, no doubt."

"Actually we came to investigate the music. We caught snatches of it from our boat. We tied up over there for lunch and heard it faintly."

"Music?" said the man on the bench.

Ralph said, "You must have seen the choir and the musicians coming out. They left a few minutes before us."

"Oh, yes, I did. There were quite a few of them."

"We listened to part of their rehearsal," said Marnie. "They're performing at a funeral on Monday."

"Florence Whittaker," said the man on the bench. "A sad business altogether."

"An unsolved case, but I'm sure the music will be a solace to her family." Marnie squeezed Ralph's hand. "What we heard was quite lovely."

"What were they performing?" asked the man on the bench.

Ralph said, "We heard an excerpt from Mozart's *Requiem*... the 'Lacrimosa'."

The man looked thoughtful and said quietly, "That's quite appropriate in a way."

"She was particularly fond of it, we understand," Marnie said.

"She was, yes, but I was just thinking it was the last piece of music she ever heard."

On that sombre note Marnie and Ralph said goodbye and walked on. They were looking forward to coffee and the next leg of their journey, already mentally calculating the lock-miles to their destination for that evening. Ralph was fumbling in his pocket for the key to the boat when he noticed Marnie's expression.

"Are you all right?" he asked.

Marnie stared at him for a few seconds before replying. "I'm not sure."

"That breeze is picking up again," Ralph said. "Let's get you in the warm."

Marnie shook her head. "It's not that."

"What, then?"

"That man just now… what he said about the last music she heard."

"The *Requiem*."

"Yes. How did he know what she was listening to?"

Ralph pondered the question. "There could be any number of reasons. It might be common knowledge round here."

"I can't imagine why it should be. You know, Ralph, I can't get the idea out of my head. It's bothering me."

"We could ask him," Ralph said, "if it's so important to you."

"Let's do that. D'you mind?" Marnie turned and set off at a brisk pace.

Ralph strode along behind her, and they reached the lychgate in less than a minute. Hurrying onto the path they saw that the man had gone. All that remained of his presence were a few breadcrumbs lying on the empty bench.

THE CRAZY CRIES OF LOVE

Martin Edwards

As darkness fell, they started up again, those crazy cries of love.

Gordon smiled to himself, remembering the past, as the girl next door reached an ecstatic crescendo. He couldn't make out the words – she wasn't speaking English – but nobody could doubt her sheer joy in being alive and in love.

It took him back, took him a long way back. Not that he was jealous or bitter. Perish the thought. There wasn't much to be said for growing old, but he loved these fleeting reminders of what it felt like to be young. Inevitably, the girl next door made him think about Millie, never mind that twenty years had somehow slipped by since his wife's passing.

The girl next door. It was the literal truth – Rula and her partner lived in the other half of this rambling old house – but somehow the phrase wasn't right. A girl next door, in Gordon's book, was someone familiar, dependable, anything but exotic. Like Millie, but not at all like Rula. She came from Kraków, and boasted a strange spiky haircut, as well as multiple piercings and a neck tattoo. She talked so quickly and in such fractured English that he found her hard to understand. In their occasional brief conversations, he usually replied with a nod or a half-smile. She struck him as excitable. Not only in bed: from time to time he heard voices rising in temper. The walls separating them were paper-thin; this had once been a single dwelling. In the old days, it was the local stationmaster's house; scarcely imaginable now that the village once merited a station of its own. So it wasn't surprising that the two houses were far from soundproof. Not Gordon's fault. He couldn't help overhearing.

Despite the increasing frequency of their quarrels, Rula and Tomasz weren't unhappy together, in Gordon's opinion. They were just passionate, the way he and Millie were, all those years ago. Rula and Tomasz cared deeply for each other. To prove it, after each and every quarrel, they were quick to kiss and make up. Gordon liked that. It wasn't prurience that caused him to enjoy listening to them. He wasn't a dirty old man, whatever Rula and Tomasz might think if they ever found out that he was eavesdropping. He simply liked happy endings.

Rula and Tomasz had moved in six months ago. They'd come round to introduce themselves, a neighbourly act that he appreciated, even though he probably seemed a surly old curmudgeon. He was always tongue-tied on meeting strangers, and since retiring, he'd spent little time in other people's company. Even in the old days, when Millie made sure he got out more, he'd had little or nothing to do with foreigners. Millie had come from Inverness, and the Scottish Highlands seemed exotic enough to him.

Soon, all was quiet again, and he was left in peace with his thoughts and his memories. It had taken years, but he'd come to terms with the loneliness of the vast double bed. It was a four-poster, a present he and Millie had given themselves to celebrate their first anniversary. He still missed her so much. Time's a healer, people said, but the scars of loss never stopped itching, and every now and then, he'd go all the way downstairs, and hold an imaginary conversation with her. Usually he talked about something and nothing, like whose turn it was to do the washing-up, but even that was better than the aching emptiness of bereavement.

Since the arrival of Rula and Tomasz, he'd found himself reflecting on the past. Something about the young couple made him think of his younger self, and Millie. It wasn't that he and Tomasz had anything obvious in common. The Pole was tall and skinny, with an intellectual's creased brow; he lectured in geography at a college five miles away. Gordon had always struggled with his weight, and now his sandy hair had almost disappeared. He'd spent his life working as an insurance broker. Tomasz invariably dressed in black, while Gordon favoured cardigans bought from a catalogue. Sometimes he still wore a collar and tie; old habits died hard.

One characteristic they did share was a tendency to defer to the women in their lives. When he'd first met Millie, she'd been delightful to look at, with much the same bone structure and face-framing fair hair as her favourite singer, Joni Mitchell. Gordon loved Joni too. A beautiful woman as well as a gifted musician.

Not that Millie was quite such a free spirit as Joni; she was a woman of strong opinions, and never afraid to voice them. Educated in a convent, she hadn't been cowed by the nuns. An only child, she was used to getting her way. That was why they'd never had children of their own; she had no maternal instincts, and found the very idea of giving birth repellent. Wasn't it enough that they had each other? Gordon hadn't argued, but now he wished he'd put his foot down. Life would have been so different if they'd had a child. Someone to share his life with after losing Millie.

There was no question about who wore the trousers next door. Tomasz might be the breadwinner, but he was under Rula's thumb. She wasn't an educated woman, as far as Gordon could tell, and she certainly didn't have a proper job. He never saw her wearing a wedding ring, and it crossed his mind that she might have come into the country illegally. So many people did, if the newspapers were to be believed, but he wasn't judgemental.

Rula earned a bit of cash in hand by walking dogs for people in the village. Shortly after their arrival, Tomasz had mentioned that if Gordon was looking for a cleaner, she'd be glad to help out. But Gordon didn't want a cleaner, and Rula seemed less than thrilled by the suggestion anyway. Glancing, as he did from time to time, through the bay window of the house next door, Gordon suspected that cleaning her own home wasn't a high priority. She didn't seem house-proud. Not like Millie. As he drifted off to sleep, the last image that floated through his mind was of his late wife, in a garish pinny, brushing the carpet in the hallway like a woman possessed, and wanting to know why he'd forgotten to wipe the mud off his shoes before crossing the threshold. It happened time after time, even when there wasn't a trace of mud to be found.

When he awoke, and pulled back the curtains, he was greeted by a bright autumnal morning. A year ago, he'd suffered a heart attack, and his doctor had told him to get more exercise. Having digested his breakfast – porridge and a cup of strong tea, same as always – he picked up his walking stick and set off on his usual, circular route. It took him along a rough path that ran by the railway track, past the edge of the village, and then back down the lane that led to the house.

As he turned into the lane, he passed Rula. She was heading in the opposite direction accompanied by a playful collie belonging to an elderly couple in the village.

"Lovely morning."

Rula, although wrapped up in a padded coat and large mitts, shivered theatrically. "Cold!"

Gordon decided to make a special effort. "You'll be glad to get back home, and put your feet up in front of a blazing fire."

She scowled. "We need central heating. I tell Tomasz."

"You do that," Gordon said benevolently. "I'm sure he'll be putty in your hands."

Rula's response was a scornful grunt, and she set off at a brisk pace, pulling the reluctant dog along after her. Gordon watched her retreating back for a full minute before setting off for home.

The lane was deeply rutted, and petered out into a muddy dead end, yards short of the old embankment. At this time of year, the pot-holes became dirty pools of water. Any car bouncing along its unreliable surface risked damaging its suspension. Gordon owned an ancient Ford, which he hardly ever drove nowadays, and was thinking of selling. Not that he'd get much for it. But money wasn't a worry. His pension was modest, but a maiden aunt who doted on him had made him her heir. When she'd died a couple of years ago, he'd been astonished to find himself a rich man. She didn't have much in the way of savings or investments, but her little house was in a part of Islington that had become fashionable lately. There was no question of his moving in there, of course, but the price it fetched was enough to make your eyes water.

Almost all the money was still sitting in the bank. Gordon didn't want to jet off on exotic holidays, or indulge himself with lavish treats. Not for him the palaver of looking after a dog or a cat. He was content to remain behind closed doors, with his memories of the good times with Millie. The pleasures he took were simple enough. Telly, radio, a spot of plain cooking. He'd always enjoyed music, and his solitary extravagance was a new state-of-the-art music system. Very often, he wore headphones to listen. It wasn't so much that he was afraid of disturbing his next-door neighbours, as a wish not to have them realise how audible loud sounds were on the other sides of the dividing wall.

The day passed uneventfully, like so many others. He didn't yearn for excitement; perhaps it was his age. Rula must find life here deadly dull. She'd seemed bright and cheerful, that first time they'd met, but lately she'd seemed bored. It wasn't much of a life for a young woman. Back Lane was almost cut off from the village, let alone the rest of the world. At least Millie had something to do; she'd worked behind the counter in the post office – in those far-off days when the village actually had its own post office. Not the most exciting job, but it brought in a few bob, and gave her an interest, until she had a row with the postmistress, and resigned in a fit of anger. She'd gone so far as to consult a solicitor in Oswestry about bringing a claim of constructive dismissal, but his pessimism had dismayed her, and nothing came of it. After that, like Rula, she was at home all the time. It wasn't ideal. Her health suffered, and so did her temper, but despite Gordon's endless pleas, she persisted in refusing to consult a doctor. For all her virtues, Millie could be a stubborn woman, there was no denying it.

Shortly after five o'clock, he heard Tomasz's old Vauxhall rattling down the lane, and made his way upstairs. His bedroom backed on to theirs. Within minutes, he was rewarded. Rula was hungry for her man, Gordon thought; she must have been waiting with scarcely controlled impatience for his return from work. She'd barely given him a chance to hang up his coat.

Not that Tomasz objected, by the sound of things. Gordon smiled fondly, his thoughts drifting back to Millie, and the way that bad luck with health and life's endless small frustrations had soured her. Yet right to the end, on the regrettably infrequent occasions when she allowed him to make love to her, she could lose herself in moments of shared ecstasy.

In her youth, she'd dreamed of becoming a singer-songwriter, a sort of Scottish version of Joni. But though she taught herself to play the guitar, her voice was shrill, and her songs tuneless dirges. She'd given up in disgust, but he kept trying to encourage her to go back to it. The very last birthday present he'd given her was *Taming the Tiger*. 'The Crazy Cries of Love' was a track that brought a smile to her lips, even during her darkest days.

And yes, those crazy cries of love kept coming from the other side of the bedroom wall, until suddenly another sound, alien and intrusive, jerked Gordon out of his reverie.

A slapping noise, accompanied by a yelp of pain.

Within moments, all hell was breaking loose. Tomasz shouted, Rula screamed. They might be playing a game, Gordon told himself. He and Millie had been known to experiment in the early days of their marriage.

But there was rage in the cries. He couldn't deceive himself. Whatever they were saying to each other in that strange language of theirs, there was no disguising either fury or fear.

A sharp crack was followed by a shriek of agony.

Then silence.

Fear paralysed Gordon. Should he knock on the wall, and ask if everything was all right?

Impossible. His throat was bone-dry, and he couldn't even manage a panicky squeak.

In any case, it was a bad idea. Rula and Tomasz were entitled to their privacy.

What was that? A muffled sobbing?

He squeezed his eyes shut, refusing to think the worst. A lovers' tiff, that was all, really nothing to lose sleep about. These things happened, they meant nothing in the grand scheme of things. Just bumps in the road.

Silly, perhaps, but he'd come to care about Rula and Tomasz. They'd never guess it, not in a thousand years, but he owed them a debt of gratitude. They reminded him of the best nights of his life. Strangers they might be, foreigners they undoubtedly were, but the very thought of Rula and Tomasz causing each other pain hurt him like the stab of a needle.

After a few minutes, more noises came, strange and unsettling. The sound of something dragged across a floor. Frantic panting, the violent slam of a door.

How could he help? He daren't embarrass them, or give himself away.

Time passed, he couldn't guess how long. He hadn't switched on the bedroom light, and so he lay on his bed in the darkness, thoughts racing around in circles like wild horses.

A clatter from outside roused him. He forced himself off the bed. After lying awkwardly, he had cramp in his legs, but he hobbled to the window as fast as he could. The curtains weren't drawn. In the moonlight he saw a dark figure on the other side of the boundary fence.

Low tubs of plants were scattered around his neighbours' garden, Gordon remembered. It looked as though someone had tripped over one of them. The figure bent down, and attempted to lift a long, heavy bundle. Something was rolled up – might it be a duvet?

Oh my God.

The dark figure looked around, as if in search of inspiration.

Gordon couldn't make out a face, but the figure's height and build was unmistakable. Tomasz, it must be.

And was that Rula, wrapped up in the duvet?

Gordon's gorge rose. He was skilled at deceiving himself, there were few better, but in an instant, he saw what had happened, even if he couldn't guess why or precisely how.

Otherwise, he was incapable of coherent thought. So was Tomasz, probably, as he moved towards the garage, like a man in a trance.

Surely he wasn't looking for a spade? Oh, no! Surely he couldn't contemplate burying the poor woman in a shallow grave in the garden?

An accident, it had to be. A lovers' frolic gone wrong? A blow struck in the heat of the moment? An attempt to stop her screaming, with horrific and unintended consequences? It was so easily done.

Should he call the police?

Gordon pictured that earnest, intelligent young man, in the prime of life, trapped inside a prison cell. They'd charge him with murder, and even if he got away with a conviction for manslaughter, his life would be destroyed. And for what? An innocent mistake, that's all. He and Rula loved each other with a passion, Gordon would swear it on his mother's life.

No, to give him away was unthinkable.

Tomasz disappeared into the garage and, moments later, drove his Vauxhall out into the open. He jumped out, shut the garage door and opened the car boot.

Gordon's eyes widened. So Tomasz had decided to dispose of the body somewhere else? What did he have in mind?

As Tomasz dragged the duvet and its contents to the car, Gordon allowed his mind to wander. Actually, it made sense. Tomasz was a clever man, he'd managed to overcome the terror of the tragedy quickly enough to draw a sensible conclusion. If he didn't want anyone to find out what he'd done, he couldn't bury Rula here. That would trap him in the house, make him a prisoner for life. He needed to get away, make a fresh start.

Anyone could make a mistake, Gordon told himself.

Tomasz might be thinking of the old quarry. The sides were steep and dangerous, and at the bottom there was now a small lake. Nor was that the only option. Plenty of lonely woodland in the vicinity, though you could never be confident that some inquisitive mongrel might not sniff out a shallow grave. And then...

Gordon shook his head. What was he playing at, trying to get inside the mind of an accidental murderer?

It took Tomasz a few minutes, but at last he managed to heave the duvet into the car boot, and secure the lid. He paused for a moment, breathing deeply, glancing up to the heavens, before climbing back into the car, and setting off.

Hurrying to the landing window at the front of the house, Gordon watched the Vauxhall crawl over the pot-holes. He guessed what was in his neighbour's mind. For all his impatience, he must drive with the utmost care. If he had an accident, if the car broke down, that would spell disaster.

Would Tomasz get away with his crime?

Yes, if Gordon had anything to do with it. He'd never tell a living soul what he'd heard and seen. What good came of crucifying someone for a moment of madness? People talked about the red mist descending, and it was perfectly true. Even the mildest of men were only human. And Tomasz, he knew this instinctively, was a decent sort. He'd been pushed too far once too often, and he'd pay enough of a price without the forces of so-called law and order destroying any chance he had of future happiness.

It helped that Rula didn't get out much. Apart from the people whose dogs she walked – and Gordon, of course, but he was no threat – nobody would miss her. If she was an illegal immigrant, the authorities mightn't know a thing about her. Tomasz could make up a story, and say that she'd left him without giving a hint about where she was going. If there were no anxious relatives to contend with, poking their noses in where they weren't wanted, it would work a treat.

Tomasz was wise to bury the body elsewhere. As long as he kept his nerve, he wouldn't find it hard to cover his tracks. He could pack in his job, and sell the house. He'd probably take a knock-down price, and Gordon was inclined to help him out by making an offer.

It wasn't purely a question of altruism, of lending a hand to someone who had hit a rough patch. After Rula and Tomasz, he wasn't sure he wanted any more neighbours. A new couple next door simply wouldn't be the same.

Sighing, he switched on the lights, and made his way down the steps. He'd not gone downstairs for a while, but instinct drove him to return to the dusty basement.

Standing on the uneven brickwork, he closed his eyes, as he always did down here. A habit, as much as a mark of respect.

"I'm doing the right thing, Millie, I know I am. You understand, don't you? There's no malice in him, just as there isn't in me. What happened…"

For a moment, the words stuck in his throat. He coughed, and tried again.

"You've always known, haven't you? I never meant to hurt you, just as he didn't want Rula to come to any harm. Tragic accidents, that's all they were. It wouldn't be right to pin blame on anyone, would it? To put that unlucky young man behind bars. You don't begrudge me my freedom, do you?"

"My freedom," he repeated. "Such as it is."

But she didn't answer, she never did. In the darkness of the cellar, all he heard inside his head was the sound he'd heard a thousand times before. Her crazy cries of love, becoming her crazy cries of terror.

WAITING FOR CORNELIA

Maxim Jakubowski

For all I know she might well, by devious means, have killed Leonard Cohen and David Bowie too. And many other musicians that I already knew of.

And now she's coming for me.

Even though I can't even read music, let alone play any instrument.

I had written a series of books, some years previously, in which the main character, a young woman called Summer, heavily into BDSM, also happened to be a classical violinist. Which had triggered memories of my teenage years, when my mother had arranged for me to attend a series of introduction to classical music subscription concerts every Saturday morning at the Théatre du Chatelet, by the river, which I had massively enjoyed. This was long before I fell into the grips of rock 'n' roll by way of folk music being Dylanised, and my life changed. I even saw the Beatles play at the Olympia on the occasion of their very first proper European tour. Not that I heard any of the tunes properly, as the majority female audience never ceased to scream loudly throughout, and my seat was at the back and John, Paul, George and Ringo were just a blur of animated silhouettes on the distant stage. Those were the years when a substantial percentage of my salary disappeared into my collection of albums. The sixties and seventies were expensive for me, but the music was worth every single penny I spent. Little did I know that I would one day in the future replace most of them with compact discs, although I would always draw the line at streaming, hoarder that I was at heart.

But I digress; that love of classical music never left me, even if I dipped my toes in – and then gave my heart – to the beat of rock. And conjuring Summer was a form of redemption, reigniting a forgotten passion. She interpreted Vivaldi, *The Four Seasons* becoming her pièce de résistance (and something of a leitmotif throughout her adventures between the sheets and the pages), and diverse violin concertos: Tchaikovsky, Mendelssohn, Max Bruch, Prokofiev. Her exploits (and sexual indiscretions) did so well in Germany that the publishers of the books there, who were part of a multi-national, even issued a CD of music from the books, by mining their extensive and prestigious back catalogue! On which I still get royalties today, though neither Beethoven, Mahler or the aforementioned composers do, which I find deeply ironic.

I'd briefly worked for a publishing house with close ties to the music industry, which provided me with great connections to the business – artists, agents, managers, promoters – which came in useful when I began reviewing books for *New Musical Express*, and would on occasion get commissions to write features on groups or musicians I took a liking to. In 1997, I was invited on a wonderful freebie and flown by a record company to New Orleans to cover a gig there by Jeff Buckley at the House of Blues on Decatur Street, with a view to, the following day, interviewing him for a lead feature. I didn't need to be asked twice, as the Crescent City was one of my favourite places in the whole world. I loved the atmosphere, the food, the smells and sounds of not only the sometimes overrated French Quarter, as well as the more upmarket Garden District. This was, of course, before Hurricane Katrina destroyed much of the city's outlying areas, and its atmosphere changed a lot, although I faithfully remain to this day both a fan and a sucker for those narrow streets, gumbo, crawfish boils and the juicy, fat, succulent oysters you are served at the Acme and most good eateries there.

I had been a great admirer of Jeff's late father, Tim Buckley, and still treasured his albums, still on vinyl in the collection in my attic, entranced by his sinuous and tender melodies. His son shared much of the same sound, although he was more bluesy and less tortured, but his talent and originality were undeniable and so full of future promise already.

I was standing at the House of Blues balcony bar, slowly sipping a long glass of Cola, waiting for Jeff Buckley's set to begin. The crowd below was restless, simmering with expectation. The opening act had been a forgettable local band who played the sort of zydeco music you could savour in every Bourbon Street bar, full of jagged rhythms and energy but not much good at feeding the soul.

My mind was elsewhere. As much as I'd wanted to come to New Orleans, it had meant a week away from a woman with whom I had been having a particularly emotional affair back in London, and I was afraid that the time spent away from her might dilute the intensity of what was inexorably happening between us. The fact that she was married was another factor contributing to my anxiety.

"You seem pensive..." An accent I found difficult to place. Not quite American, not that I was any good at distinguishing regional accents here. Maybe Canadian?

I turned around.

She was tall, her hair a Medusa-like growth of blonde curls, her eyes gravitating between grey and a pale shade of blue, her lips thin but sculptured, her cheekbones like a sharp angle new to geometry.

"Am I? Just nursing my drink and waiting for the headline act to take over the stage," I said.

"You're English," she remarked.

"Nowhere to hide," I replied. "I'm betrayed every time I open my mouth."

She smiled. She didn't appear to have a drink. I offered to get her something.

"I'll have what you're having," she said.

"It might disappoint you," I pointed out. "Just Coca-Cola, or maybe Pepsi; with all the ice they drop into it, it's not easy to know the difference."

"I don't drink alcohol either," she said. "So no problem."

I called the barman over, and ordered another round of Coke.

The musicians shuffled onto the stage a moment later so we were unable to get any deeper into a conversation. It was a good set, although I did feel that the production on Buckley's albums smoothed out some of the imperfections in his live delivery, which was often drowned in the jingly jangly clamour of his back-up band. And, of course, he was at times eerily reminiscent – in both looks and sound – of his father.

Arrangements had been made with his management to do an interview with Buckley the following day. We would meet for breakfast at the Café du Monde, off Jackson Square.

The crowds began filing out of the club. A breeze swept down the road carrying the scent of the Vieux Carré and the nearby river just a few blocks away. The young woman I had briefly conversed with at the bar had remained at my side throughout, seemingly as appreciative of the show as I had been.

"A nightcap?" she suggested as we began walking towards Canal Street. There was a mischievous glint in her eyes.

"I don't even know your name," I remarked.

"Is it important?" she asked.

"I suppose not." She was fiercely attractive but, for once, I had no urge to pursue another woman. All I could do was think of Kathryn and, even though my ethics were highly flexible, everything told me I was not ready for any one-night stand in a foreign city. I ached for Kathryn and desired no temporary substitute.

"It's Cornelia," she said.

"A nice name, unusual."

"I'm staying at the Monteleone; they have a lovely bar. Quite famous."

I was lodging off Bourbon in a small, boutique hotel called the St. Marie where my window looked out over an exiguous pool which I had never seen anyone swimming in since I had been in town, despite the oppressive heat.

"I think I'll pass, I have some work tomorrow," I informed her.

"You live in New Orleans?"

"No, just here to do some research," I pretexted. It was never wise to admit to music biz connections. "And you?"

"Tall me?" she grinned. "Oh, I'm just your average hit woman. Nothing remarkable about me. Unless you have a need for my services…"

I smiled. "Not in my line of work," I played along.

"So what about that nightcap?" she asked.

"No offence, but I'll pass. I'm in a…" I struggled to say the word as if it didn't quite define my situation with Kathryn. "…relationship."

"Pity," she said, leaning over and kissing my right cheek. I could feel her warmth and recognised her perfume: Anaïs Anaïs. It was the only fragrance I could actually identify as it was also Kathryn's. Some things you never forget. "Hasta la vista." She moved down the pavement with leggy strides and melted into the crowds migrating towards Canal Street and the big international hotels. It occurred to me that it was not the direction of the Monteleone.

The interview with Buckley the next day went well and I had managed to get some interesting quotes and background stories. He was both earnest and cagey, unlike many rock stars who created a persona behind which they could hide.

He had a couple of friends with him and as we were wrapping up suggested I join them. They were going for a drive slightly out of town. He wanted to swim.

"In the river," he said. "I have a deep mistrust of swimming pools..."

"How come?"

"Maybe I'll tell you when we get there, OK? But off the record."

I had nothing better to do. My flight to New York, where I was scheduled to spend a couple of days before returning to London, was not until the following afternoon. I always left some leeway when working on music features as both musicians and their managers were well known for postponing interviews on a whim, leaving you high and dry until they finally consented to meet. Anyway, the record company was paying my expenses.

Little did I know that we would have to drive for hours before Jeff decided which riverbank suited him best, and we ended up closer to Memphis than the Big Easy.

You all know what happened, of course. Yes, Buckley had had a few drinks before he waded into the Mississippi. But he appeared to be a good swimmer. His two friends and I had opted not to join him.

The small speedboat was racing southbound towards the middle of the muddy, brown river, although initially still some distance from Jeff Buckley's bobbing head. None of us observers thought it could become a problem, when it suddenly veered to the left, making a sharp turn and headed rapidly in his direction. I squinted. Saw a woman at the helm. A statuesque blonde. I immediately recognised Cornelia. I was momentarily struck dumb, while one of Jeff's friends called out to warn him – or the boat. Within inches of striking the lone swimmer I saw Cornelia violently steer the wheel leftwards as if to avoid him and roar away. But the wake of the speeding boat had disrupted the quiet flow of the river and an undercurrent must have taken hold of Jeff. We saw him struggling briefly and then his distant head disappeared under the surface.

It was reported as an accident; made the news all over the world. The tragic disappearance of a wonderful new talent, etc.... I never mentioned Cornelia specifically to the investigation. By then I was having doubts as to whether she was actually in control of the boat that might have been responsible for the drowning or it had just been a lookalike. The thought, though, haunted me for ages and I became the last journalist to have interviewed Jeff Buckley. Even made the *NME* cover. Not something I was proud to advertise.

Just a month after I got back to London, Kathryn and I broke up when she took fright at the way our affair was heating up and reaching not just our sexual parts but also our hearts, and confessed all to her husband. He magnanimously agreed they could try to patch things up and instigated a failed campaign to shame me publicly (he was also a journalist). Two years later, she had twins with him. Meanwhile I'd written a handful of stories in which every female character was a mirror image of her, as a way of both remembering her and torturing myself. But in some of the short stories, which I published all over the place, she began to look more and more like Cornelia. Both blondes, both tall. Oh, well…

Life went on. It always does, doesn't it? Even the worst mental pain fades, scars heal and wounds inevitably close.

A few years later, I was working on a feature for *Mojo* to commemorate the 50th anniversary of Jimi Hendrix's death and delving into a mass of archives, when I came across a set of photos spread across a variety of contact sheets which had been taken by a *Melody Maker* ringer and never actually used in the paper. According to a note stickered to the contact sheets the photos had been taken shortly after Hendrix had ceremonially burned his guitar at a concert at the Shaftesbury Theatre. They had been taken that same night at a since defunct trendy London club and showed Hendrix and a whole assortment of hangers-on drinking and sniffing lines of white powder around a recessed alcove table. Most of the protagonists seemed stoned or drunk or both. I could recognise one or two of the men, minor musicians of the times, signed to the same label as Hendrix, and the obligatory mini-skirted dolly birds who were part and parcel of the seventies rock scene.

Shuffling through the set of contacts I'd pulled out of the yellowing archival folder, images repeating ad infinitum with just variations of lighting and stances, my gaze suddenly focused on a set of similar pics in which another person appeared briefly by the table, initially standing and facing the group of revellers of which Jimi Hendrix stood at the centre. As if this new protagonist in the slow motion story the contact sheet was following with every successive click of the camera taking the pictures was just passing by and greeting the group before moving out of the frame. Just a half-dozen snaps. There was something familiar about the person, initially seen from the back, standard mini-skirt revealing long, lean legs, and a big head of hair the size of an Afro, but on closer inspection more of a wild mess of pale hair. I brought the contact sheet closer to my eyes and watched the scene unfold, frozen as it was, from small image to small image. The woman turned slightly, just enough of an angle for me to have a sideways view of her features in the final photo. There was no doubt it was Cornelia, the woman I had come across in New Orleans. Aside from the clothes she was wearing, the short skirt and a cropped white blouse, so typical of seventies London, she was an eerie replica of the Cornelia I'd met in 1997.

As if she hadn't changed in appearance at all.

What the hell was she doing there? She had no right to be. Less than twenty-four hours before the musician was found dead. It was a strange coincidence.

I shrugged the thought away. I must have been reading too many mystery stories, I reckoned. It must be someone different. Her mother, maybe? The dates might work.

Hadn't my good friend Mike Moorcock once written a short story called 'Dead Singers'? I actually looked it up a few days later: I had the title slightly wrong, it was 'A Dead Singer'. No plural.

But the seed of an idea had taken hold. For some time now, my literary agent Sarah had been suggesting I write a book about music. A couple of publishers had approached her to indicate they'd welcome any sort of proposal on the subject from me. And I was all too aware that my fiction was in something of a holding pattern, repeating itself, marked by the loss of Kathryn and, later, other paramours.

The thought occurred that a series of profiles of dead rock stars might find a good slot in the commercial market. Not particularly original, but maybe, as often happened when I wrote a book, the idea would strengthen as I progressed, links becoming more apparent, an overall mood coming to the fore.

I resolved to complete some further research before agreeing to such a project.

Within days, I found the Ian Curtis connection. He was a tragic figure, the singer of Joy Division who hung himself in his Manchester house in 1980, just as his band was about to become hugely successful and hit the big time. They actually changed their name after the sad event, and re-emerged as New Order, with phenomenal worldwide success. I was actually a great fan of both bands.

It was a blurry photo which had appeared, of all places, in *Smash Hits*. Taken at the Hacienda, it showed the group in conversation – and away to their left stood the mysterious Cornelia, casually puffing on a cigarette.

A nagging thought slipped to the front of my mind: how much had the impact of the death of Ian Curtis impacted on the band's later success? Would they have reached such heights of fame without the legend surrounding his passing?

And, apart from the other members of the group, who else benefited? Manager? Their record company?

Everyone knows that in the cases of artists, sometimes the adage 'better dead than alive' certainly comes into the equation, as the aura of death carries with it a twisted sense of romanticism that many find compelling.

And I recalled Cornelia's words, which I had always assumed were just another form of wit. That she just happened to be a hit woman.

I spent the following few months delving further into dusty archival papers in the vaults of the British Newspaper Library in Colindale, North London, or racing through microfilm records, as well as negotiating further access to the back issues of existing and defunct newspapers and magazines. I became a death-hunting detective.

My first focus of attention was the melancholy British folk singer Nick Drake, but after a couple of days treading over familiar ground nothing emerged that could raise suspicions. His suicidal tendencies had been much to the fore, and all the signs present in his lifestyle as well as his music and lyrics. A dead end, then.

I moved on to the death in a motorcycle accident of the American musician Duane Allman (of the Allman Brothers Band) in 1971, and within an hour or so my mind froze as I stumbled across a photo taken backstage at an unidentified gig just a few days prior to the tragic event – and there she was, right at the centre of a picture of the band relaxing in their green room, every participant holding cans of beer. She was unchanged, the only difference again the fact that she was dressed appropriately for the times: flared jeans, buckskin leather jacket with fringes à la Robert Plant in the heyday of Led Zeppelin, smiling broadly at the camera with one of the band's roadies wrapping his arm around her slender waist.

Jeezus… It was no longer a coincidence.

My mind was in turmoil, thinking of which deaths I should maybe investigate next. Were any of them genuine drug overdoses, which of course in the world of music would seldom evince too much curiosity or surprise? Which events had truly been accidents?

I also checked hit chart records. Yes, in every single case, the singer or the group's back catalogue had seen sales wildly surge in the aftermath of the death, long forgotten albums creeping back en masse into the hit parade, as fans with a ghoulish sense of devotion hurried to complete or renew their collections, making a lot of money indeed for many of the parties involved.

Indeed, I had myself quickly acquired a number of retrospective and expensive David Bowie box sets following his passing. Bowie? Surely not. It was well established that he had been suffering from cancer for some time.

And then I discovered a photograph taken on the rehearsal set of his *Lazarus* play in New York, and there was Cornelia, standing in a corner between some of the cast, wearing T-shirt and jeans, casual and impassive, seemingly looking into the lens like an angel of death, a bearer of black tides.

My heart tightened.

Until then, the tenuous connection between music and crime had been at best associational. Stephen King, Ridley Pearson, Scott Turow and other writers in the USA had formed a band called The Rock Bottom Remainders who occasionally performed at book fairs and festivals, while in the UK a similar project involving Mark Billingham, Val McDermid, Luca Veste, Chris Brookmyre, Stuart Neville and Douglas Johnstone had been known to make earnest appearances at similar events as The Fun Lovin' Crime Writers. And then South London noir writer Mark Timlin had in his youth been a roadie for The Who.

But this eerie connection between Cornelia and so many deaths was something else altogether.

Was I going mad? Seeing links where they did not in fact exist?

And if I overcame my serious reservations and did end up writing something about it, would I not be calling attention to myself and attracting undue scrutiny from what appeared to be a most devious and clever killer? Was I courageous enough?

I didn't think so.

Maybe I could just write a short story about it in the guise of entertainment, change the names and pretend it was all a witty fiction. I could call the hit woman Cornelia, say, under the influence of Cornell Woolrich, one of my favourite authors in the genre.

I pondered for weeks. But, as you'd expect, the decision was taken from me. You know how crime stories go: there is always a twist around the corner, something the reader doesn't expect.

These were now the days of the pandemic and lockdown, and publishing parties were a thing of the past. So now launch events were happening online, through the medium of Zoom. These lacked in immediacy but at least allowed for some form of promotional effort. I was sitting on my living-room sofa watching the author talking about her new novel, being interviewed by an unctuous critic dragged in for the occasion. I had read the book in question and found it lacking in energy and a tad repetitive. I distractedly scrolled all the small boxes bordering my laptop screen, checking out the other readers, fans, other authors and assorted members of the crime community attending virtually, their faces often draped in darkness, checking their backgrounds as the boxes moved along as people dropped in and out of the event.

And there she was: Cornelia.

Ever beautiful, not a wrinkle in sight, her hair a maze of royal curls, her cheekbones catching the light.

I peered at the screen, my nose inching forward.

As if she knew it was me, she smiled enigmatically and then, my heart halting on the spot, she actually waved briefly at me, acknowledging my online presence.

My stomach churned into a knot of aches, pains and anxieties.

I frantically looked around the laptop screen for the red box which would allow me to leave the event, eventually finding it and watching the myriad boxes and talking heads disappear in a flash, to be replaced by the normal landscape of my computer screen.

I was glued to the spot.

There was no doubt she had spotted me among the online participants.

Was there anything I could do now, and was her apparition at the virtual event coincidental or accidental?

My phone rang.

"It was nice seeing you briefly," she said. "But why did you leave so quickly?"

"I wasn't sure it was you," I pretexted.

"Oh, come on, don't insult my intelligence…"

Realisation dawned. "How did you get my number?"

There was a silence but I could almost hear her smile.

"Easy peasy," she finally said.

It was my turn to be quiet. I could hear music playing in the background where she was calling from. I even recognised the tune; it was a song by The Walkabouts, an American group I had once befriended and for which I had written the liner notes for a compilation CD of their best songs.

Now I knew it was all real and there were no coincidences involved.

"You've been doing some interesting work," she stated, her tone impersonal if friendly on the surface.

Damn! She even knew what I had been doing.

I was struck dumb as she stayed on the line.

Finally, "Hasta la vista."

It's now early morning. There is frost on the garden lawn outside, and the school-run traffic has begun on the main road outside the house. I have barely slept. I am still on the sofa. I'd like to listen to music, but can't seem to choose anything that might be right for the moment.

I've left the front door on the latch.

How will she do it? Gun, knife, rope, pills?

I'm waiting for Cornelia.

With thanks to Ernest Hemingway and Marc Behm

THE WATCH ROOM

Neil Daws

As a toddler, Abe had sat at the knee of his grandfather, fascinated by the jigs, reels and sea shanties the old man drew from his beloved fiddle. As he grew into a young lad, he learned the tunes by ear and his grandfather taught him the secrets of how to coax the best from the instrument. By the time his grandfather passed and left the fiddle to him, Abe knew every note, sound and nuance of that fiddle. Even at work around the lighthouse, he could recall the vibration of the strings beneath his fingers, the wood polished to a reflective shine, and the faint pine odour of bowstring rosin.

Abe's father doted on Luke, the younger son by two years, taking him on supply trips to the mainland and out fishing for pilchards, forever praising his good looks and physical prowess. What good that did in a lighthouse, Abe could never fathom, because Luke rarely did any work. It seemed to Abe as though their father was punishing him for the attention their grandfather had given him. He longed to visit the village fetes to play his fiddle there with the local group, but his father always refused permission. Instead, he'd take Luke out to Scallop Island to fish. After a while, he didn't much care what they got up to as long as they left him alone.

Then the time came when the old sod passed away, may his soul rot in hell, overlooking Abe as his natural successor to run the Stark Rock lighthouse.

Once the last shovelful of earth covered the old man's body, Luke took great pleasure in asserting his authority over Abe, taking whatever time off he liked and leaving Abe to operate the powerful lamps alone, a virtual prisoner in the lighthouse. Inevitably, their simmering animosity towards each other came to the boil and they exchanged blows, but Abe had long known he could never hope to win a straight fight against his brother. His father had been right about that, damn him. To gain any concessions, Abe needed to think smart, a skill lacking in his brother. Luke liked a wager, betting on anything from horse races to sheep shearing, and from bare-knuckle fights to the annual Pilot Gig rowing race. Against such an obsession, Abe found it easy to persuade his brother to bet on the toss of a coin with the winner going to the village and the loser manning the lighthouse.

And so it was that while Luke stayed home, seething at losing to his brother, Abe found himself at the village fete looking at the most beautiful creature he'd ever seen. From the moment Abe first set eyes on Rebecca as she wandered around the stalls on her own, he was smitten. He joined a group of men from the village to play some lively music to the revellers, his accomplished fiddle playing earning him appreciative pats on the back from the musicians. He also drew a smile from the watching Becca, as she asked to be called. His gentle and shy approach, offering to pay for a toffee apple, led to them spending the rest of the day together playing hoop-la, hook-a-duck and tombola. As if this wasn't magical enough, when she agreed to go to the village dance with him that evening, he felt like a dog with two tails. He found Becca's enthusiasm to see him again and be his sweetheart more uplifting and joyous than any sunset. Spending time with her made him feel ten feet tall, taller than his brother at least. Romance blossomed, or so Abe thought.

He should have known.

He couldn't remember whether it was Becca's idea to visit the lighthouse or his own, but he realised his mistake the moment they stepped up from the causeway to find Luke beaming at them. Beaming at Becca, to be precise. In fact, it might have been Luke's idea all along. However it came about, Becca and Luke got along like a ship under full sail, so much so that Abe couldn't be sure that either of them realised he was still there, in the lighthouse, in the same room with them. Then Luke asked Abe to check one of the powerful lamps, complaining that it had cut out the previous night and he couldn't find the fault. Abe was much better at that sort of thing anyway, wasn't he?

It took Abe the best part of an hour to find the problem and fix it.

Apologising, almost grovelling, at having left her alone for so long, Abe waited for the backlash, but Becca seemed not to mind. She said she'd enjoyed her visit but the time had come for her to go back to the mainland. Even as she assured him she'd come again, Luke took control. The rising tide had already covered the short causeway, the setting sun casting a purple glow across the sky from the west chased by navy blue from the east. Abe had to concede two things: Luke was the better rower, and it was Abe's turn to ensure the light shone as soon as the sun set.

Abe traipsed up several flights of stairs to the small Watch Room that nestled just below the Lantern Room. Being low-ceilinged, circular in shape and near the top of the lighthouse, he had always thought it resembled the inside of a hat box. From here, he was able to witness the progress of the ferry trip to the beach, which should have taken five minutes in calm seas, ten at the outside. Abe lost sight of the boat in the gloom and set the lamps flashing their warning, returning downstairs to prepare supper.

When Luke returned an hour and a half later, his excuse to the concerned and irritated Abe was that he'd escorted Becca to the village in the dark, then he'd had cramp in his fingers, making it impossible to grip the oars to row back. Abe let it ride, his anger subsiding. He would have walked with Becca too, and he'd experienced rowing cramp on many occasions. It was one of the reasons he'd never rowed in the village Pilot Gig against neighbouring Port Gilman. That and the embarrassing fact, common knowledge among the villagers, that he couldn't swim. Looking back, they must have thought him so stupid and gullible. Leaving them alone for so long, both on that day and a few times after.

Only a matter of weeks later, while Abe again tended the lighthouse, Becca and Luke announced their plans for a Christmas wedding in front of everyone at the Harvest Festival dance. The news stunned Abe into subdued silence. Luke took this to mean acceptance of the new status quo, and followed up with the revelation that Becca was pregnant.

Pregnant! That meant—

Abe punched Luke so suddenly, connecting just to one side of his brother's nose, that Luke had no time to throw up a defensive arm. The resultant bruising to Luke's left cheek and eye became almost as impressive as the initial gush of blood from his nose.

Abe knew why Luke didn't retaliate: he'd won anyway. Luke had the lighthouse, his girl, a baby on the way. What would Abe do now and where would he go? To remain a prisoner in the lighthouse, being laughed at and used as no more than a servant, would be unbearable.

That is when the idea crept into the back of his mind, grew and then festered like a boil waiting to be lanced.

As September passed into memory and November slid into December, Abe bided his time, planning and preparing, playing jaunty melodies to disguise his ever-darkening mood. His plan needed certain conditions to be met, both in weather and circumstance. His chance came in the second week of December as reports circulated of a big storm brewing in the Atlantic, the second of the season. Invariably, Luke left all lighthouse business to Abe, ignoring anything that interfered with his enjoyment of life, and had arranged to take Becca to the Port Gilman market for her to buy trinkets as Christmas presents. Abe saw his chance. He told Luke he must want to bore the underskirts off Becca if he was taking her to Port Gilman *again*. If she was still his sweetheart, he'd take her out to Scallop Island, a mile offshore, to watch the sunset. The gathering clouds were just right for a colourful spectacular. Abe could see Luke wavering so he bet him a night shift that he wouldn't be brave enough to row Becca to Scallop Island alone.

Luke said nothing, grinned and pushed his way from the room.

Abe heard his brother stomp down the many steps to the storeroom and listened to the recognisable sounds of him making ready for a sea trip. Then, taking up position in the Watch Room, Abe saw Luke reach the mainland in their old wooden rowing boat and stroll towards the village, returning to the beach with Becca less than two hours later. Abe almost smiled seeing Becca sitting so upright and stiff in the stern because her shopping plans had been curtailed, while Luke rowed them to sea. Abe climbed up to the narrow Window Walk outside the Lantern Room and waved to them cheerily as he pretended to clean the outside glass panes. With Abe always the one doing the lion's share of work, Luke never bothered to take notice of weather warnings.

Biding his time until the boat reached halfway to Scallop Island, Abe ran downstairs to the storeroom. The fishing net he'd been unpicking and retying into one long length of twine for weeks lay hidden behind wooden crates of tinned food supplies. Also hidden were a box of matches and a large hurricane storm lantern with a larger square of shiny tin fixed to it. About the size of a large hand-cloth, the tin had washed up on the rocks by the lighthouse a few weeks earlier. During one of Luke and Becca's many trips into the countryside, Abe had flattened the battered metal and polished one side until it gleamed like a mirror. Taking the lighthouse lamps as his inspiration, fixing the tin to the lantern made the reflected light brighter and visible much further than normal.

Abe slipped the matches into his pocket, put the twine into a hessian sack, picked up the lantern and set out on foot along the short causeway, conscious he had less than an hour before the tide began covering the path again. Reaching the beach, he turned away from the track to the village, instead climbing the increasingly steep path to the cliffs that ran above the rocks between the lighthouse and the Port Gilman breakwater. Having hurried and stumbled across the tussocky grass, Abe stopped at a point he'd marked weeks ago on a previous search along the cliff top. He'd worked out that a hundred yards would have to do, especially as he carried only four hundred yards or so of twine, representing many weeks of tortuous, finger-numbing work sat in his Watch Room prison.

Abe stood the heavy storm lantern on a flat rock he'd moved there for that purpose and weighted it in position, ensuring the polished tin was positioned at the rear to reflect the light towards the sea. He then removed the twine from the hessian sack, tied one end to the handle and began to run it along the cliff top, flicking it over the edge every few feet. Noticing the low, thick clouds becoming tinged with orange and pink, highlighting their dark, threatening hearts, Abe returned to the storm lantern and lit the wick. The tide had started lapping the edges of the lowest parts of the causeway, giving Abe a jolt as he realised time was running out. He took up the coil of twine again and continued to play it out along the edge, flicking as he went, and descended to the beach.

Abe had reached a crucial moment.

He uncoiled the remaining twine, splashing across the rapidly submerging causeway, and reached the lighthouse steps moments later. A length of frayed rope he'd found tangled on the beach the previous month dangled under the pull of a lead fishing weight from the Lantern Room's Window Walk railing. He removed the lead weight, tied the twine to the rope and hurried up the many flights of stairs to the Window Walk.

The sun had almost fully set and the wind from the fast-approaching storm had begun whipping the sea into a white-topped frenzy. Waves began thumping against the rocks, throwing spray into the wind before sucking back with a malevolent hiss. Rain drifted across in curtains, lashing against the lighthouse and stinging Abe's face. He coiled the rope as he pulled it up and tied the twine to the railing, barely able to see it looping towards where the lantern shone brighter than he'd hoped in these conditions. As waves crashed and foamed on the rocks, Abe tasted salt on his lips and prayed the wind, rain and sea would not conspire to pull the lantern off the cliff. He wiped his eyes and face with his sleeve, peering into the gloom, and could just make out the unnatural phosphorescent shape made by the sea foaming around the dark blob of a small boat. A glow above it rose and fell.

Luke's lamp.

Abe strained his eyes, watching the boat's slow progress as it rode each wave and plunged into the troughs behind. Then a pale shape outlined by the lamp's spectral glow appeared to stand, but was obscured quickly by another darker shape as the boat lurched. The boat stood on its end, bow skywards as the lamp arced away, and the two shapes merged with the black sea.

Abe watched the worsening storm for another ten minutes, just to be on the safe side, then began to pull in the twine. He saw the yellow light move and fall as his storm lantern toppled from the flat stone then plummeted over the cliff, the flame extinguished as it hit the sea. After what seemed an eternity, where waves and seaweed dragged and yanked the lantern, he noticed a different, constant pull on the twine. He looked down and smiled grimly as the lantern swung and bounced its way up the side of the lighthouse.

Abe untied the twine from the storm lantern and quickly reset the lighthouse lamps and clockwork mechanism in the Lantern Room. As it began flashing its warning to shipping, he descended into the bowels of the lighthouse, hid everything back in the storeroom, changed out of his wet clothes and lit a fire. Thankful to be warm and dry, he calmly cut himself some bread and leftover mutton and made some hot cocoa.

At dawn the following morning, Abe extinguished the lamps, breakfasted on hot buttered toast and tea, and was about to leave the lighthouse to report his brother missing when someone rapped three times on the door. Unused to visitors at the lighthouse, Abe hurried downstairs and opened the heavy storm door, to find PC Blythe standing on the steps brandishing his truncheon for another strike.

Surprise turned to shock.

Beside the constable stood the exhausted, blanket-swaddled but shivering figure of Luke, with red-rimmed eyes, downturned mouth and bedraggled hair. Abe thought his brother looked smaller than he remembered, his stature diminished somehow. PC Blythe spoke for the both of them, stating that a tragic accident had taken place the previous evening when Luke's boat had been driven by the storm onto the Stark Rocks. He and Becca had been thrown overboard, her skirts and cape dragging her beneath the pounding waves. Luke, despite being a strong swimmer, had barely managed to reach the beach himself before passing out. Regaining consciousness much later as the tide ebbed, he had finally staggered into PC Blythe's front garden, exhausted and sobbing, with tales of a phantom light that had lured them onto the rocks.

Abe had no need to pretend to look distraught. He had wished Becca's death, made it happen, but felt the pain of lost love no less, exacerbated in fact by the cruelty of Luke's escape. Abe told PC Blythe that he had feared for Luke's and Becca's safety as the storm approached and had lit the lighthouse lamps early to guide them home. When they failed to return Abe had no way to raise the alarm. The causeway was submerged, Luke had the boat and Abe couldn't swim. Imprisoned all night in the Watch Room, Abe was beyond suspicion.

Luke was never the same man after they found Becca's drowned body further along the beach that afternoon. He blamed himself for the loss of his love and his unborn child, spending his waking hours grieving in the living room, lying on his bed or crying as he sat in the Watch Room overnight, never venturing beyond the lighthouse walls.

Seeing his brother alive when he should have died on the rocks with Becca intensified Abe's pain, but to see Luke so broken and reclusive, now that brought great satisfaction and restored some balance. Abe still loved and missed Becca as much as Luke did, and their only fractured exchanges with each other revolved around her. Each knew how the other felt and that was strangely, disturbingly comforting.

Abe, for whom the lighthouse, especially the Watch Room, had become a prison when it passed to Luke, now found the small cell-like space beneath the Lantern Room a refuge. He looked forward to his nights spent alone in the tiny space and the many times he escaped there during the day to get away from his brother. There, he could play sad ballads and laments, replacing the jolly jigs and reels once played so joyously and effortlessly on his grandfather's old fiddle.

From that small, circular room he could see the village where Becca had watched him play his fiddle, the hill above where he had once picnicked with her, Port Gilman where they had walked hand in hand through the weekly market, Scallop Island where the first stage of his plan had come to fruition, and Stark Rocks where the treachery of his sweetheart and brother finally foundered and died.

Abe's prison.

Abe's refuge.

The Watch Room.

THE GHOSTS OF PEACE

Paul Charles

1

Another day begins the same, the things you do you'll do again. Well, then again… not quite.

Later on that evening – if only as a way of clearing his head – Detective Inspector Christy Kennedy pondered this thought as he walked down the rat run Delancey Street had become. He took a quick right into the lower part of Camden High Street, crossed the busy road and continued down the High Street to the majestic Camden Theatre.

As he walked into the theatre he realised his early-morning musing wasn't in the slightest bit accurate because here he was walking into a theatre which – one way or another – he had passed, either on foot or by car, on most of his days in Camden Town, but, until this very second, he had never ever ventured across its historic threshold.

As arranged, DS Dot King was waiting to meet him in the lobby and escorted her boss through the red velvet seated, gold-enhanced, four-tiered auditorium, towards the exit door to the right-hand, front lip of the stage. They turned quick right, up a flight of stairs, densely lined with framed posters and memorabilia celebrating the theatre's many nights of glory. They took the second door on the right and entered a smaller corridor with three doors on the left. This corridor and fixtures and fittings had been refurbished to a higher degree than the remainder of the theatre. The first two doors were shut. The third door was the hub of Camden Town CID and where the scene of crime officers were busy at work. They were all crammed into a plush, six-seated box, on the Royal Circle level, positioned to afford the occupants a perfect view of the stage proceedings. The polished-wood scents were sadly now tainted by the metallic tell-tale smell of blood.

Kennedy was briefed outside the box by his favoured bagman, DS James Irvine. Irvine was organising the SOCOs while Dr Leonard Taylor was, as meticulously as ever, examining the victim, who was slumped down in the prime seat in the box as if he was trying to glare through the two-and-a-half-foot-high wall of the box to continue viewing whatever had been occurring on the stage. So far Kennedy could view only the victim's pronounced monk's crown and strands of yellow-blond hair, which looked as if it had only recently been released from a ponytail in an effort to make the little go further. His apparent post-hippie style looked a bit like a threadbare and transparent curtain.

According to Dot King's wee pink notebook, the victim, Harry 'Happy' Champion, was known to the star attraction of the evening's performance, Hendi. All things considered Mr Champion's nickname was somewhat ironic. King had also discovered Hendi was not the name of a group but the name of the artist. Hendi was short for Henderson, as in Richard Henderson.

Kennedy carefully made his way deeper into the box to view Mr Champion in his final resting place. The victim was wearing a pair of immaculate Timberland boots and a blue checked flannel shirt worn out over his maroon-coloured corduroy trousers. He was clean-shaven with a bushy moustache, a more nicotined shade of yellow than his locks. His open brown eyes spooked Kennedy. He looked as if he knew exactly what had happened to him.

2

Dr Taylor acknowledged Kennedy's presence with a nod as he paused scribbling in his notebook. He sucked on the top of his green fountain pen, tapped his pen a few times on the notebook before quickly pointing the ink-soaked nib to a spot on the victim's neck.

"Too small for a bullet," Taylor explained, "and not enough blood and matter for the damage to be caused by a bullet," he continued, as he allowed his pen nib to trace – at a hygienic and evidence-protecting distance of a couple of inches – the diluted rust-coloured liquid as it disappeared under the collar of the victim's shirt. "Perhaps if his hair hadn't been quite so sparse, we would have missed it, and thought he died from natural causes while attending a concert."

"Perhaps," Kennedy replied, but very much doubted it.

"I'd say," Taylor volunteered, "the weapon of choice was a large nail, or a knitting needle."

"An ice pick?" Kennedy offered.

"'An ice pick would certainly have been sharp enough. A fatal stab wound of the neck and left innominate vein and arch of the aorta, resulting in an arteriovenous aneurysm which dissected the anterior mediastinum and ruptured into the left pleural cavity, where a massive hemothorax formed. The murderer appears to have known exactly what they were doing."

"An assassin?" Kennedy offered, translating Greek into Ulster-speak.

"Well, funny you should say so, Christy, but the first image that flashed into my mind would have been a World War Two French Resistance fighter, taking out a guard effectively and quietly during a cross-border raid."

Kennedy retained Taylor's vividly drawn image in his mind as he asked, "Any theories on the time of death?"

"A couple of hours at the max, I'd say," the good doctor, a man never scared of hazarding a guess, guessed.

"What time did the show go down?" Kennedy asked DS Dot King.

"Hendi went on stage at eight o'clock; he took an interval from nine o'clock to nine-thirty. The second set ran up to eleven o'clock when he left the stage, following three encores."

"So, somewhere during the nine to nine-thirty interval?" Kennedy asked.

"No," the rotund Taylor offered and then paused for thought. "I'd say that would have been too early. It's marginal but I would guess he died somewhere around twenty-two-thirty. I mean there was still some warmth in the body when I arrived in the theatre."

3

There was a bit of a racket outside the box and Kennedy could hear, "Sorry but I just need to let my team go, they've got another long day ahead of them tomorrow and..."

"I'll let you know when you can go, sir," DS James Irvine said, and then asked, "And you are?"

"I'm Lee Kingston," an affable-sounding voice replied, "Hendi's TM."

"TM?" Irvine asked.

"Sorry, yes, Tour Manager," Kingston replied, doing a fair impression of a giraffe trying to steal a view of the proceedings in the box. "I actually manage Hendi on the road, and I need to give our principal, his musicians and road crew an update so I can plan tomorrow's schedule accordingly. Who should I talk to?"

Once again he rose on the toes of his well-polished, black leather sensible shoes to steal another look into the box.

"Aye," Irvine said, as he put his hand gently on the back of Kingston's black pinstriped jacket and nudged him towards the outer door. "That would be me in the interim. My superior Detective Inspector Christy Kennedy is currently busy with the body."

Kennedy was impressed with his DS's kid-gloves approach. He figured it was due to the fact the tour manager was very well turned out in his black pinstriped suit and black collarless shirt buttoned up to the top. He had one of those classic all-England, football star hairstyles, a bit like Harry Kane, but with highlights. If anything he looked more like an off-duty, trendy vicar than one of these rock-and-roll types.

"OK… wow, it's a strange one I know, but that's by far the best Sean Connery accent I've ever heard. Where in Scotland are you from?"

"Edinburgh," Irvine admitted.

"Where in Edinburgh?" Kingston pushed.

"Fountainbridge, quite close to Sean's birthplace in fact."

"Unbleedin' believable," Kingston gushed.

"Look, my DI is examining the body with the pathologist. Following the examination, we'll start the questioning," Irvine offered.

"Right, DS, I see. Well, the questioning shouldn't take very long because my band and crew were on stage in front of twelve hundred people when Happy passed."

"Had you seen him before the show?"

"Happy had just enjoyed some private time with Hendi after the soundcheck. They were still nattering away together in catering. Then we all saw him in the band dressing room before the show. He was… well, what can I tell you? He was always happy. I escorted him up to Hendi's private box just before showtime; I didn't see Happy in the Ligger's

Lounge afterwards. The next thing I know we're told we can't leave the venue because Happy has died."

"Did your band know Happy – Mr Harry Champion – well?"

"Hendi had known him since they were teenagers."

"Oh?" Irvine said, his eyebrows arching into another question.

"Yes, they were both from Bangor, a seaside town about thirty minutes outside of Belfast," the tour manager began. "They formed a prog-rock band in the seventies called White Eyes."

"I should be making notes," Irvine said, realising that King was currently with Kennedy.

"Perhaps, it's a long story, James," Kingston said, and on noting Irvine twitching with obvious discomfort, quickly added, "Sorry, of course I meant to say DS Irvine. So anyway, White Eyes made the trip to London and secured a record deal. The first couple of albums didn't exactly set the world on fire, but they gigged non-stop. Their shows were very dramatic, very visual and they started to build up a loyal following.

"For their third album they decided to do a concept album based on a thirty-minute suite, *The Ghosts of Peace*. In fact Hendi closed the show with *GoP* tonight. Sorry, *GoP* is our in-house name for *The Ghosts of Peace*. This album was what is known in the business as *a sleeper*, as in the buzz spread by word of mouth. The more they toured the more it sold and eventually – we're talking about a year after the release date – they released a single 'The Fight for Peace'. Like the album, the single was about war and peace. Hendi believes the only way you can find peace is through war, and if you're not prepared to do evil you'll never succeed in doing good. Good and evil are similar extremes, which is why it's always better to stick in the middle ground. Not everyone's cup o' cha, I know, but the single was a five-minute version of the album, enjoyed excellent radio-play, sold well, and made the top ten. *GoP* secured number one in the album charts and the first two albums also charted.

"The band became massive. They were set to become bigger than Pink Floyd, but then Hendi split the band and started recording and touring under his own name. He had a few chart albums but nothing as successful as *GoP*. Happy returned to Bangor. He hadn't been on our radar for years. It's a strange one, I know, but recently there was talk of White Eyes reforming for a mega world tour, but… well, nothing so far. I guess tonight has put an end to that."

"Oh-kay," Irvine offered.

"Look, Ja— sorry, DS Irvine… as I said, I'm not sure how much we can help you, the band were on stage, in front of twelve hundred witnesses who have long since gone. But when the box office opens tomorrow morning I can get you a copy of the ticket manifest with the contact details of everyone who purchased tickets."

4

"There comes a time," Dr Taylor announced to no one in particular, "when one just has to accept that there is little else one can accomplish at the scene of the crime, particularly in such a confined space. Therefore on such occasions it's best to retire to the mortuary for a closer examination of the remains. I'd say such a time has now arrived."

Kennedy nodded his approval, leaving Irvine's SOCOs to apply their fine-toothcomb search to the corridor just outside the box.

Kennedy took the opportunity to sit on the wall of the box with his back to the auditorium and view the box from this angle.

"Was there a chance," Kennedy asked Lee Kingston, "a member of the audience might have made their way up into the box?"

"Not without the appropriate and certified passes," Kingston replied, flashing one such pass hanging around his neck on a lanyard. "On top of which there would have been two separate security checks cramping the style of any potential interlopers. I can show you the route."

"That would be very helpful," Kennedy replied, appearing distracted.

Kennedy continued sitting on the low wall and considered this information. He noticed for the first time that as well as the entrance door to the box there was also a second door. Suited up in a white baggy evidence-protecting outfit – which did tend to make all the SOCOs look like pandas – he walked across the box and opened the second door. To the right was a toilet and a hand basin, with a mirror above the sink. The middle wall housed a unit complete with sparkling clean glasses for wine and spirits. Beneath were two cupboard doors which revealed a small built-in fridge – with milk and mineral water – plus tea and coffee-making equipment and a rack for wine bottles. On the floor to the left of the door was a small Arts and Crafts table with two matching chairs. The third wall housed an ornate floor-to-ceiling mirror and two large framed posters, one proudly proclaiming a White Eyes two-week run of sold-out shows in this very theatre, and the other with FRUUPP plus special guest White Eyes in this theatre back in 1976.

"Would you like me to lead the way from the box to downstairs now?" Kingston asked, as Kennedy was considering the vanity aspect of the large mirror in the anteroom.

Kennedy nodded to DS King to join them. They pretty much retraced the path along the inner and outer corridors and then down the stairs Kennedy had climbed earlier.

"So there would have been a security guard between the foot of the stairs and the entrance of the auditorium," Kingston advised, detouring from King's original track, "but then there would also have been one at the pass door to the hallowed backstage area, which is just through here.

"I've spoken to both security guards and they said there was no one they let through to Mr Henderson's private suite, apart from Mr Harry Champion. No one else passed the security. They reported that Mr Champion did not make his way backstage or into the auditorium bars during the interval. House security swept the entire building before the public were allowed access to the venue."

"Which means that no one could have been hiding in the box from earlier?" Kennedy asked.

"That's what I'm implying," the tour manager said.

"OK," Kennedy said, "I'll go and chat with Mr Henderson..."

"He likes to be called 'Hendi'," Kingston cautioned.

"I'll go and chat with Hendi, and DS King and DS Irvine can interview the band and crew and we'll compare notes later."

5

"Yeah, I've heard of you," the lanky Hendi announced warmly, "you're the boyfriend of Nealey Dean, the actress. She's a very beautiful woman, so she is. We tried to get her for one of our vid shoots. Sadly we couldn't work it out. Our schedules conflicted, so they did."

Kennedy's instinct was not to like the guy, but that was until he remembered Nealey Dean had informed him the majority of celebrities try to find a route, a short-cut connection if you will, to move to a less superficial conversation. The fact that Hendi had introduced the potential link was a sure sign he was attempting to make some kind of connection, and prolong the conversation beyond the standard couple of lines offered to fans and taxi drivers.

"Yeah, I don't think she can find the time to do as much as she would like to," Kennedy replied, hoping he wasn't discourteous to either Hendi or Nealey Dean.

"She's clearly very selective, so she is," Hendi replied immediately. Like Kennedy's reply, Hendi's was also open to interpretation. "I get that, I really do, which is why we felt it would be a major coup if we could have secured Nealey for our video."

Kennedy was struggling to find a way, without appearing rude, to start this interview. His hesitation led him into even more troubled waters.

"How did youse two hook up?" Hendi asked, as he moved from leaning on the doorpost to sitting on the ancient radiator in his dressing room. From the scuff marks on the wall above the radiator it looked like this was one of the singer's favourite resting places.

"Well, I met Nealey through a colleague of mine," Kennedy offered, admitting the truth but without giving anything away. He chose this point to pull his notebook and pen from the inside of his Harrington jacket. The manoeuvre had the desired effect.

Hendi withdrew a pocket watch on a gold chain from his waistcoat pocket, looked at it without really looking at it, and then yawned.

"I'm sure DI Kennedy won't keep you long," Kingston offered, clearly reading Hendi's signal while making to leave the dressing room.

Hendi nodded to his TM just as the door was about to close, then walked over to him and whispered something. Kingston nodded and disappeared behind the closed door.

Hendi, with a wave of his hand, invited Kennedy to sample the grand catering spread. The catering seemed to be guarded by a life-size mannequin on wheels, dressed in what Kennedy assumed was Hendi's stage costume.

Kennedy opted for a bottle of still Ballygowan mineral water while Hendi popped an 8Greens effervescent tab into a glass of the same.

"I believe you knew the victim?" Kennedy stated, elated to have finally started the interview.

"Well, yes, of course. Happy is… Happy was a big part of my history," Hendi replied, in a voice more Anthony Hopkins than Liam Neeson.

"We formed our first group together. They were called White Eyes, so they were."

"They split up?" Kennedy said in a conscious interruption, keen for a career highlights version.

Hendi paused, his annoyance obvious. He removed his thick black-framed glasses. His look was transformed: his eyes looked smaller and sunken into his skull due to the lack of the magnification of his lenses. He used the thumb and forefinger of his right hand to squeeze either side of his nose as he drew in a large breath.

Kennedy studied him. His look, Kennedy guessed, had been carefully moulded to create the persona he wished to project – very much the old-style theatre manager cum actor, cum director. He wore a mid-height felt top hat which was so dark blue it looked black. If it hadn't been for a lapis lazuli-topped hat pin, the hat would have looked less out of place in a jumble sale than on the crown of a self-celebrated grand entertainer. Salt-and-pepper shoulder-length hair escaped below the brim of his hat and flowed over his high-collared, dazzling white shirt. His shirt had matching cuffs protruding from his crimson military, bum-freezer jacket. With Hendi's tight blue trousers and calf-length leather boots, Kennedy couldn't work out if the performer was going for the Colonel Custer's Cavalry or D'Artagnan's Musketeers persona.

Hendi clocked Kennedy glaring at his jacket. He put his glasses back on and his on-stage character returned.

"I'm sure you realise that the jackets were this red so blood spilled on the battlefield wouldn't alarm your compatriots. One of the main themes of *The Ghosts of Peace*, which was White Eyes' breakthrough album, is there's no chance of peace without spilling blood. But anyway that's for a future, and longer, conversation. I still have an ambition to have it made into a movie, so I have. Where were we?"

"You were just starting to tell me how well you knew Mr Champion?"

"Yes, well, very well in fact. So then we'd our big album. We toured that to death for about two years. We were all burnt out and the band broke up. The other lads including Happy returned to Bangor. I stayed in London. Then, wouldn't you know it, but I started to enjoy a rather successful solo career."

"Did Mr Champion not want to continue with the band?"

"You know, the truth is that we didn't officially decide to break up.

We just needed a rest from the road and a break from each other. Then I decided to try something else and before I knew it, ten years had passed and it became my career and my life."

"Did the original members stay in touch?"

"Not really," Hendi began and paused; he paused just like it had been in a script. "You see, when you're the front man in a band, there tends to be a bit of resentment from the other band members. You know, all that attention and adulation? So we just drifted apart. It was one of the joys of my life, though, that in recent months Happy and I were in touch on a regular basis."

"Can I ask you if the band members of White Eyes shared the income equally?"

"I've just come to realise how different a crime feels when you knew the victim," Hendi announced, now sounding more Hannibal Lector than Anthony Hopkins, and laying down a marker that he much preferred to remain in his 'moment' and avoid Kennedy's direct questions.

"You were about to tell me if all your fellow band members shared the income equally."

"Well, here's the thing; I wrote all the songs, so I did, and produced all the records... so..." He seemed to be thinking better of his intended answer, and changed tack to, "but our solicitors, Lyons and Cullen, would have all of that information."

"From what I can gather, you were actually on stage when Mr Champion was murdered?"

"Yes, lucky enough in front of 1,287 witnesses."

"Did Mr Champion have anyone... who would have wanted to... to do him harm?"

"I'm not sure I can best answer that for you," Hendi started, "but I do remember he had a big problem with drugs during our last couple of years in White Eyes. I remember hearing he was having payment troubles with his drug dealer."

Lee Kingston reappeared as if on cue.

"Ah, look, I really do need to get home to my bed or I'm going to be short-changing tomorrow's fans, so I am. But your people know how to get me if there is anything else I can help with. In the meantime," Hendi said, taking something from his tour manager, "I wanted to gift you this. It's a copy of the White Eyes CD, *The Ghosts of Peace*. I've included an extra one in the hope that you might pass it on to Miss Dean for me. Please tell her I'm a big fan and I'd love to meet her and perhaps explain my plans about making this into a film. I'd very much like her to star opposite me in it, so I would."

Kennedy was experiencing a multi-level shock reaction.

"I, ah… well… Miss Dean is on location at the moment, but I will get a copy to her agent," was all Kennedy could manage to come up with.

Hendi reacted as if Kennedy had just smacked him across the face with a wet fish. The performer stormed out of the dressing room without another word.

6

King and Irvine could not believe Hendi had blatantly tried using a murder investigation to indirectly pitch a movie project to Kennedy's girlfriend.

"He'd have been after a front page in the *Camden News Journal* if you'd still been dating Ann Rea," Irvine offered.

Kennedy laughed, but this evening he'd already thought twice how handy it would have been to have his journalist ex-girlfriend here, for her invaluable insider knowledge on the music business.

"But does it put him in the frame as a suspect?" King asked.

"Well, no matter how much we might have wished for that, we have to remember…" Irvine offered.

"Hendi was on stage in front of several hundred witnesses when Happy met his sad end," Kennedy said, and then repeated the meagre information he had gleaned from Hendi. "So what did youse two learn while I was being granted my audience with Hendi?"

"OK," King started, opening her notebook, "I've learned that Richard Henderson always considered this theatre, the Camden Theatre, to be the spiritual home of his music. He and Harry Champion originally formed White Eyes in Bangor, their Ulster home town. When they moved to London, back in the late seventies, they originally settled in nearby Chalk Farm, just across the road from the Roundhouse, in fact. The first time Richard stepped on the stage, as a support act to Belfast band FRUUPP, he felt at home. He felt as if he'd arrived. The fact that White Eyes, as a band, had played a flawless gig – their first flawless gig – would have had a lot to do with it. But that night after he walked from the stage, Richard knew something big, something cosmic even, had clicked and he knew with all his heart and soul that his band was going to happen. He'd been saying as much for a year or so but acknowledged, to himself at least, that was all just Ulster bravado. That night the ever-present unacknowledged niggling doubt literally just evaporated."

"Sounds like you were interviewing Hendi's PR person," Kennedy announced, careful not to make it sound like a criticism.

"As good as," King admitted. "Lee Kingston was clearly toeing the party line. Anyway, Henderson bought the theatre, literally for a song, in the nineteen-eighties, if only to permanently banish the enemy, disco music" – here King paused to add some air quote marks – "from its 'hallowed stage'. He based his complete operation – management, promotion, publishing, rehearsals, touring equipment and props – in the theatre building and took advantage of its high-street frontage to have a café, ticket agency and merchandising shop selling mostly, but not exclusively, Hendi and White Eyes material."

King stopped and flicked through some pages in her notebook, looking for something else.

"Well, I sought out the longest-serving member of the road crew," Irvine started, as King and Kennedy visibly cocked their ears, "a chap by the name of Gene Alexander, a no-nonsense Ulsterman, and he confirmed that our friend Hendi broke up White Eyes at their peak. Hendi – being the singer and frontman – believed, like Peter Gabriel did with Genesis, he could be a brand beyond the band. Just like Genesis, the remaining members of White Eyes decided they would continue as a band without Hendi. However, unlike Genesis, White Eyes discovered the original band members, Hendi and Happy, had registered the band name under a partnership where both of them had to agree usage of the name. Hendi was unhappy and blocked the remaining musicians from continuing. According to Gene, Happy was the most naturally talented in White Eyes, both as a musician and as a writer."

"Could the band not just have tried to continue as they were and pick a new name?" King asked.

"Good question," Irvine offered through a smile. "Well, I certainly thought so, so I asked the question myself and was told that they tried to, but during rehearsals of Happy's new material, they ran out of money before they could get a deal. Happy went to Hendi and asked him for what he felt were his overdue songwriting royalties and recording royalties. According to Gene, Happy wrote all the music and helped Hendi with the lyrics but Hendi still took the lion's share of the publishing income. Hendi claimed the songwriting and recording royalties were working their way through the infamous pipeline, and they weren't due for another twelve months. However…"

"I was expecting a 'However'," King claimed.

"However… Hendi, for old times' sake, offered to help Nom de Plume, the name of Happy's new band," Irvine continued. "Sadly, this is not a Happy-ever-after tale. Hendi told fellow songwriter and *friend* that he would give him £100,000…"

"OK," King said, "here comes the 'but'."

"But… in return he wanted Happy to sign over all his rights to the White Eyes material, meaning Hendi would receive all monies White Eyes earned forever and a day, and Hendi would be the only songwriter listed on the credits."

"But of course Happy turned him down," King said.

"'Well, no, actually. Happy took the money, signed over all his rights to the songs and spent the money recording an album on spec and financing the band until the mythical record deal arrived.

"Everyone who heard the tapes of the album proclaimed it to be the best thing they'd ever heard. All the record labels were offering great deals for Nom de Plume's debut album, which they were going to call," Irvine paused to check his notes, "*Inside My Mind, Looking Out, With My Eyes Closed.*"

"But…" King interrupted.

"None of the record companies would agree to the deal unless the band's name was… White Eyes."

"And Hendi could legally block them from using it," Kennedy offered. "From the way you're telling the story, we should have been expecting Hendi to be the one found dead, with us questioning Happy as our prime suspect."

"Well, you see, this is where it gets interesting," Irvine continued. "A couple of years ago, what with all these heritage acts, like The Stones, Fleetwood Mac, Genesis, Beach Boys etc. reforming for very successful world tours, the three main worldwide promoters, Live Nation, 3A and AEG, had started bidding against each other for these mega tours. The remaining three bands they were trying to entice out on the road again were Dire Straits, The Kinks and White Eyes. We're talking about world tours for a fee somewhere north of one hundred million pounds."

"You're kidding," King gushed.

"Not at all. Every time Hendi said, 'No, thanks', one of the promoters would come back with a higher offer." Irvine continued. "Eventually, several months ago Hendi made contact with Happy and attempted to persuade him to either reform White Eyes or, at the least, allow Hendi to do the tour with his own backing band but using the White Eyes name."

"So at least Happy was getting his own back," King said, sounding more content with that revelation.

"Well, my new best mate, Gene Alexander, told me that Happy was willing to do the tour under the name White Eyes, *but* only if all the original members were involved. If any of them didn't want to do the tour, or couldn't tour for health reasons, then the missing musicians should still receive their fair share of the pot. On top of that, Happy wanted back the rights to his White Eyes songs and he wanted his record royalties backdated so he could recoup all the money he felt had been stolen from him."

"And Hendi said what?" King asked.

"Well, that's why Happy was over in London. He and Hendi were trying to reach an agreement. Funny enough, Hendi was resisting giving Happy back his credits more than giving Happy a token of the money he was owed."

"Good on Happy," King said.

"And what exactly does all of that mean?" Kennedy asked himself as much as his two colleagues.

"Well, it means the crew's nickname for Hendi seems fair after all," Irvine offered.

"I feel I'm going to regret this," King started, "but I'll bite. What is the crew's nickname for Hendi, then?"

"The crew call Hendi, Dick Shit."

"Dick Shit?" King repeated, sounding like she felt she was missing something.

"OK," Irvine said, "Hendi's name is Richard Henderson. His father and his grandfather were also called Richard Henderson, so Hendi is

Richard the Third or Richard the Turd, aka Dick Shit."

"Gross!" King protested, but then she joined the other two in a quick chuckle.

"Not gross," Irvine claimed, "just crew humour."

7

Kennedy found himself, for some reason, figuring that when he visited the theatre during the day (rather than at performance time) it would be bright with natural light. When he walked into the theatre the following morning, via a quick detour to Lyons and Cullen where he picked up a useful piece of information, he discovered the auditorium was in total darkness with nothing but a ghost light on the stage. He wandered around the theatre considering its history, as had been relayed by team Hendi.

The Camden Theatre had been built in 1900 by Walter Wallis. The theatre was threatened with demolition in the 1970s, but reopened in 1977 as The Music Machine, a popular venue for the punk movement. In 1982 Hendi became the owner and changed the name back to the Camden Theatre. Along the way, Charlie Chaplin, The Rolling Stones, The Clash, Coldplay and Prince (for a secret late-night show) had all appeared on the stage Kennedy was now staring at.

Kennedy could hear voices coming from backstage and he moved in that direction. He wanted to walk the venue at his leisure. He accepted his prime suspect had the perfect alibi at the time of the murder. In fact Hendi had 1,200-plus witnesses. Kennedy's other major problem was: how could anyone have reached the box without passing the two security guards?

8

The access door from the auditorium to backstage seemed to be locked. Kennedy tapped on it and eventually it was opened from the inside.

Kennedy flashed his warrant card to the gentleman who opened the door.

"Oh, so you're DI Kennedy," the genial middle-aged man with a grey buzz hairstyle offered, "I spoke to your colleague yesterday evening."

"Ah, you'd be Gene Alexander?" Kennedy offered, while shaking the roadie's hand, "I… ah, wanted to walk around the backstage area and the dressing rooms again, please?"

"Well, your warrant card trumps our backstage-pass privileges any day of the week," Gene admitted. "I'll walk you around if you want."

"That would be perfect," Kennedy smiled. "I'm interested in how you can get from the backstage area to the box where Mr Champion's body was discovered?"

"Just one route really, here… let me show you."

Gene Alexander, mostly keeping his hands deep in the pockets of his blue denim boiler suit, led Kennedy back along the route he'd taken the evening before.

"So there's no way I can get from the stage to the box without getting through the pass doors and two security checks?"

"None at all," Gene confirmed. "That's Hendi's private box and he doesn't want either his guests or himself being pestered by mere mortals."

The helpful roadie walked Kennedy all around the venue to prove the point.

"'The band and crew were all on the stage during the performance last night?" Kennedy suggested.

"Correct."

"At any point in the performance did any member of the band leave the stage for a costume change or anything?"

"Not at all," Gene replied, immediately.

"So they were all in your eyeline for the entire time?"

The roadie laughed.

"What? What have I missed?" Kennedy asked, more bemused than excited.

"It's just that when you asked your question, I immediately thought, if I say all the band were in my view all evening, I would be immediately promoted to the prime suspect."

They both eyed each other suspiciously.

"Well?" Kennedy asked, finally breaking the moment.

"OK. Technically I saw the band members on stage all evening…" Gene started, looking like he was choosing his words carefully.

"But?" Kennedy prompted.

"But… Hendi has this raised platform, stage left, a two-metre cube, and he has a quick-change gazebo area on the same level, which joins his performance platform directly to his dressing room. So…"

"So?"

"So, technically he would have been on the stage but…"

"But he'd have been out of your view?"

"Correct."

Kennedy loved the one-word positive replies.

"Does Hendi have a dresser?" Kennedy asked, enjoying a flashback of one of Tom Courtenay's towering performances.

"No," Gene replied, through a knowing smile. "All Hendi's spaces – dressing room, quick-change area and his theatre office, all of them are sacrosanct."

"How often would Hendi use his gazebo in the course of a performance?"

"Well, if we include his entry and exit that would make four times in total," Gene replied, visibly counting them off.

"Apart from his stage entry and exit, what would the two other occasions have been?" Kennedy asked.

"Right… so towards the end of the first half, just before he takes a bow up there, the band starts up 'Janet Planet', the final song of the first half. It's a FRUUPP song, but Hendi has been performing it in the set since the very first night he played this theatre. The fans love it and it always enjoys a phenomenal reaction. As the band starts into it, Hendi nips into the gazebo, removes his cloak and returns to his platform in shirt and trousers to sing the first verse."

"How long would he be out of view at that point?" Kennedy asked, as he remembered Dr Taylor had assessed that Harry 'Happy' Champion died after the interval.

"Twenty seconds at the most," Gene replied.

"OK, and the remaining instance?"

"The beginning of the second half is the *GoP* suite, it's half an hour long and…" Gene stopped, looking lost in another thought.

"And?" Kennedy prompted.

"I just remembered that he acknowledged Happy's involvement in the music for the first time tonight in his introduction. He said, 'Here's a little number Happy Champion and I happened upon all those years ago in White Eyes'. At the mention of Happy and White Eyes the audience went berserk. Hendi nodded for the band to start. Hendi started singing and when they got to the War section, where the band musically projects the 'battle' section of the song, Hendi retreats to his platform. He was dressed mostly in black. The battle rages on as he remains motionless on the platform. Genuine war images flash up on the screen, the fighting, the death, innocent victims…

"As the battle draws to a close the band play a very pastoral section of music, which serves as a backdrop to the statistics of war. It's incredibly moving. The numbers, the lives, the costs. The music has always been the same but Hendi continuously updated the visuals and the stats to include the latest worldwide conflicts. Unnoticed by the audience, Hendi nipped back into his quick-change area for his most dramatic change of the evening. He was off stage for a minute at the most. Before the final song in the suite, 'We Will Remember Them', Hendi, in a flash of lights, fireworks, smoke and mirrors changes from his black stage outfit to his white outfit. He's all in white, apart from his black top hat, of course – he always wears his black hat. Mind you, it does have a white feather…"

Gene Alexander suddenly stopped mid-flow and clicked the fingers of his right hand, which made a rare appearance from the security of his trouser pocket. "I've just remembered something. Usually there would be a white eagle feather in his top hat, but last night when he changed to his white outfit he was featherless. Anyway… as all the smoke and flashing died down, the UV lights came on and gave his white outfit a spiritual glow. As in… the battle is now over and peace reigns."

"OK," Kennedy offered, using a moment of silence to take it all in.

"And there's absolutely no route a member of the audience could find into the box?"

"Correct," Gene confirmed. "Joe Public still can't find a way into the box."

"Can I examine the guest box again, please?"

9

Kennedy led the way through the six seats in the box and opened the door to the anteroom he'd discovered the previous night. Something had caught his eye, but he couldn't put his finger on it. Today, though, what had caught his unconscious eye had traversed that difficult divide into his consciousness.

It came as a result of him continuously asking himself the same question, 'What is wrong with this picture?'

And the answer in the end was very simple.

Every square inch from floor to ceiling of the outer box, and the toilet and lounge in the anteroom, was spic and span. The only flaw was that one small section of the floor-to-ceiling mirror was smeared, with grubby palm marks, midway up the mirror on the left-hand edge. As Gene looked on, Kennedy – still in his evidence-protecting outfit – pushed the mirror at the grubby point. Nothing happened. The detective felt totally deflated, embarrassed even. He pushed the mirror close to the grubby hand marks again, this time with a bit more force. Then he heard the wee *click* he'd been hoping for. The mirror gently opened back into the anteroom.

Right on cue Gene produced a Cree Q5 Ultra-fire torch and said, "Yeah, roadies, like the constabulary, get one of these with our passing-out badge," and they headed off along a very narrow, dark and dingy corridor, up a tiny staircase with a very low ceiling. It was at this point that Gene's torchlight happened upon a solitary white feather on the tread of the first step. Kennedy snared it in an evidence bag. They proceeded along another flat section of the corridor, veering to the right. Then they dropped down another low-ceilinged staircase and...

... and came to a dead end in the corridor. Sadly, they did not discover a door handle or any such convenience. There was, however, a finger-size cup-hook attached to the left-hand side of the end wall. Kennedy pulled the cup-hook towards him. He heard the magic *click* and the door sprung away from them.

"Ah, behold, it's Dick Shit's private quarters, I assume," Gene Alexander proclaimed.

10

When Hendi arrived at the theatre just after lunchtime, Dot King arrested and transported him to North Bridge House. Within the hour Hendi, together with his solicitor, Lionel Lyons, DS Dot King and DI Christy Kennedy were in the interview room.

DS Dot King cautioned Hendi, who behaved like a tolerant teacher might with his students. He was wearing his signature top hat, minus its signature white eagle feather. Hendi removed his top hat, placing it on the table in front of him. He kept saying, while leaning into the microphone recording the proceedings, "I have 1,287 people who will swear that they saw me on stage at the time poor Happy was being murdered."

"When we start off our investigations we have three main questions we endeavour to answer," Kennedy started off, trying to ensure he imposed some shape on the proceedings. "Who did it? Why did they do it? How did they do it?"

"Those 1,287 witnesses, will testify I'm not the 'who'."

"Well, we'll get to that eventually," Kennedy started back up again. "First off, let's deal with why you did it. Briefly, you cheated Harry Champion out of his songwriting credits, recording royalties and income from his share of White Eyes publishing royalties."

"Oh, come on, man, not that old backstage roadie's story again," Hendi protested flamboyantly. "Check my paperwork, man, it's all legit, so it is."

"You then blocked Happy's chance of his own recording career," Kennedy said, and raised his hand in a stop sign to Hendi's protests. "When you left the band, you refused to let him use the name White Eyes. Years passed; three major promoters start to bid for a comeback White Eyes world tour. The offers were so phenomenal you tried to persuade Happy to do the tour. But you both jointly and equally own the rights to the band's name so you need Happy to sign off on the deal. He agreed on condition you gave him back his songwriting credits and rightful share of the publishing and recording royalties owed from all the years you'd been cheating him. He also wanted all of the original band members to have their share of the comeback tour profits.

"You won't agree to any of his conditions. During the negotiations, you check with your solicitor to see what would be the case if you were deceased and Happy wanted to do the tour as White Eyes. Of course, the question you were really asking was: if Happy died, could *you* do the tour as White Eyes?

"So that was why Happy was murdered. Next we get to how.

"You invited Happy to London as your guest to further your talks. During last night's performance Happy sat alone in pride of place in your private box.

"After the interval, during the battle section of White Eyes' suite, you, under the pretence of changing from your black outfit to your white outfit, disappeared into your stage-side gazebo. In effect you had your white outfit completely hidden under your black cloak. But you didn't immediately return to the stage. Instead you subtly wheel your mannequin, dressed head to toe in black, onto your performance platform. This is during the raging battle sequence with only the shadows and darkness – with just your mannequin stand-in visible – so no one realised you were no longer on stage.

"During this section you sneaked – via your secret corridor – into the anteroom of the box. Your signature white feather was knocked from your top hat and fell on the stairway in your secret passageway." Kennedy paused to produce the white eagle feather secure in its evidence bag. "You crept up behind Happy and assassinated him by stabbing your hat pin into his neck."

At this point in the proceedings, Kennedy won the grab for Hendi's hat. He replaced it with a warrant he passed to Lionel Lyons, who nodded the paperwork was in order.

"This five-inch hat pin with its proud lapis lazuli blue crown – normally used to secure your signature eagle's feather to your top hat – will contain Happy's DNA," Kennedy claimed. "You returned back along your secret passage. You were back in position in time – under the distraction of the war visuals, fireworks, smoke and lights – to switch places with the mannequin on your performance platform, by subtly wheeling it into your gazebo. You were then in perfect position to simply remove your black cloak and transform yourself into the prophet of peace, the man in white, and, thanks to the UV lights, a spiritual being."

Hendi seemed to bask in the pomp and glory of being considered a spiritual presence.

"Inspector Kennedy, I wonder if you could do me a massive favour," Hendi started, sounding like Sir Anthony Hopkins in search of an Oscar, "and pass an important message to Miss Nealey Dean for me. Could you please tell her I believe I am soon going to be in a position where I will be able to dedicate a lot of quality time to work on my script for the *Ghosts of Peace* movie project, so I am."

NO MORE 'I LOVE YOU'S'

Paul Gitsham

A DCI Warren Jones short story

Tuesday

The crash from the rear of the house jerked the couple awake.

"What was that?" the woman asked, clutching her husband's arm.

"No idea," he grunted, fumbling for his glasses on the bedside table as he opened the CCTV app on his phone. "Nothing on the cameras, and the alarm hasn't gone off."

He swung his legs out, scrabbling for his slippers. "I'll go and have a quick look, but it's probably just a fox knocking a bin over. You know how sound travels when we have the windows open."

He tapped his phone again and every light in the house flicked on.

A quick circuit of the semi-detached property revealed nothing amiss; doors and windows secure. He rewound the security footage, playing it at full speed; nothing obvious for the twenty minutes before they were woken. He was contemplating whether to return to bed, when he heard sirens in the distance. Moments later, the front room was splashed with flashing blue lights.

"There's an ambulance," he called up the stairs. "It's pulling into next door."

* * *

"You have got to be kidding me. Annie Lennox?" groaned Detective Inspector Tony Sutton as the car radio kicked in.

Beside him, in the driver's seat, DCI Warren Jones gave an evil grin as he reversed out of his space in Middlesbury police station's car park. "A bet's a bet, DI Sutton."

"Come on, back me up, Moray," pleaded Sutton, turning to the young detective constable squeezed into the backseat. "It's one thing to force me to listen to his God-awful music, but it isn't fair that you have to suffer too."

"Actually, I quite like a bit of Eurythmics and she's a great solo artist," said Ruskin. "Alex and I even had some at our wedding."

"Don't remind me," muttered Sutton.

"I seem to recall that you and Marie got up on the dance floor to 'Walking on Broken Glass'," said Warren.

"Well, my dear wife is a wonderful woman, but her taste in music is almost as bad as yours. *Sir.*"

"Oh, dear, you only call me that when we're in the office or you're sulking," teased Warren. "What's annoying you more? That I was right about Johnny Stanwick blaming his girlfriend instead of doing a no-comment interview, or that because I was right, we get to listen to my choice of music in the car for the next month?"

"Yeah, well, I still can't believe he was stupid enough to try and lie. He should have listened to his solicitor."

"So, what would we be listening to if you'd won, Inspector?" asked Ruskin.

"Radio One," interjected Warren. "DI Sutton is down with the kids, you know that, Moray. He's probably their oldest listener."

"Piss off," grumbled Sutton, as Warren negotiated a roundabout.

But Warren wasn't ready to let it go just yet. Seven years of putting up with Sutton's barbed comments about his love of eighties and early nineties pop music, and he was going to make the most of a rare opportunity to gloat. Besides which, he'd been saving some ammunition…

"It's funny you should blame Marie, I seem to recall that it was you that dragged her onto the dance floor."

"Only because I know she likes that song," protested Sutton.

"Really? Because that's not what I heard," said Warren.

"I don't know what you mean," said Sutton, suddenly suspicious.

"In fact, I believe that Marie has no opinion either way about Annie Lennox or the Eurythmics, but you have a whole box of original LPs that you keep in the spare room."

Warren adopted a stage whisper, addressing Ruskin in the rear. "Apparently, DI Sutton used to have a bit of a thing for her back when he was a young man."

"That's bollocks," said Sutton.

"Are you suggesting that Marie was lying when she spoke to Susan? Or perhaps you think that my wife made up the whole story? Should I ask them?"

Sutton gritted his teeth. He'd teamed up with Warren in enough interviews to know when his boss had expertly backed someone into a corner. "Oh, it looks like we're here," he said, just as the satnav announced that they had reached their destination.

"To be continued," said Warren, parking behind an ambulance with its doors open, and its lights off.

*   *   *

"As you can see, the rope was threaded through the eyelet that the window hook slotted into, and the end was tied to that wooden beam." DC Karen Hardwick was wearing plastic overshoes and gloves as she stood on the threshold between the kitchen and the conservatory. The body of the late Laetitia Wainwright-Burke lay splayed on her back, a crudely fashioned noose loose around her neck, a wooden chair lying on its side.

"The house is Grade II listed, so they're stuck with this old-fashioned wooden conservatory," she continued. "Very pretty, but it's single-paned glass, so freezing in winter and boiling in summer; the skylights provide ventilation. They use a hook on the end of a wooden pole to open and close them. Remarkably, the eyelet took her weight; rather it was the window frame that gave way."

Warren agreed with Hardwick's observations. Up close, he could see that the wooden frame was rotten; the bolts that attached it to the frame of the conservatory had ripped through the soft timber. He estimated that the heavy frame had fallen the better part of four metres, hitting the unfortunate Mrs Wainwright-Burke before the glass shattered on the concrete floor.

"Not much blood from the cuts," observed Sutton.

"So, she was dead by the time the skylight hit her," said Ruskin. He looked at the woman's swollen features. "Bloody hell, what a way to go."

*   *   *

"Why are we here?" whispered Ruskin to Hardwick, once they were out of earshot of Warren and Sutton. "Or more importantly, why are *they* here?" He nodded towards the two senior officers taking a seat in the spacious living room. "Since when did two detective inspectors, one of them a chief inspector no less, attend what looks like an open-and-shut suicide by hanging?"

The two constables were heading out of the front door to speak to the next-door neighbour.

"Since the Chief Constable was phoned at six o'clock this morning to tell him that the wife of one of his golfing buddies had killed herself," replied Hardwick. "It also doesn't hurt that Mr Wainwright-Burke is a wealthy business owner, prominent philanthropist, generous patron of the arts and, rumour has it, contemplating a run for Parliament."

"Ah. The extra-special service," said Ruskin.

"Exactly," said Hardwick.

*　　*　　*

Pale-faced, his eyes a swollen red, Carlton Wainwright-Burke was asking the exact same question of Warren and Sutton. He peered at them over the top of the steaming cup of coffee that a kind-faced family liaison officer had handed him.

"It's just a courtesy," said Warren. "We're here to help expedite matters. We appreciate that this must have been a tremendous shock, so the sooner we can work out what's taken place, the quicker we can leave you in peace to mourn the loss of your wife."

"Why don't you tell us, in your own words, what happened?" suggested Sutton.

Wainwright-Burke leaned forward in his chair, placing his mug on a hardwood coffee table. He gave a shiver.

"You are welcome to put some more clothes on first," suggested Warren. The man was barefoot, with just an expensive-looking navy dressing gown covering the boxer shorts that were the only thing he was wearing when the police had arrived.

"No, it's OK, I'll be fine," the man's voice was gravelly, his wide vowels betraying his upbringing on an east London council estate. "I just want to get this over with, you know…" He cleared his throat. "I went to bed about eleven. Letty stayed down here to finish her drink and her book," he pointed towards the far end of the room. A pair of green leather wing-backed chairs sat either side of another coffee table, in front of a wall of floor-to-ceiling bookshelves. A paperback book lay face down, its pages splayed open, next to a glass tumbler and an empty whisky bottle.

"We call that end of the room the library," he smiled weakly. "An in-joke; it sounds more posh than 'the end of the lounge with the bookcases'." The smile faded. "Anyway, I fell asleep immediately. I was dead to the world until I heard a loud crash. I realised Letty wasn't beside me, so I jumped up and raced downstairs." He covered his mouth with his hand. "The light was still on in the library, but Letty wasn't in there, so I went out to the conservatory… and that's when I found her…"

He took a shuddering breath. "I'm sorry," he mumbled, rubbing his face with the baggy sleeve of his dressing gown.

"No need to apologise," said Warren. "Continue in your own time."

Eventually, Wainwright-Burke resumed. "It was obvious that she was dead. I mean, you can just tell, can't you?" He looked at the two men, who nodded. They'd seen enough over the years to understand what he meant.

"But anyway, I had to try." He gave a quiet snort. "Forty years since I was in the Scouts; I remembered to check her pulse and clear her airways and even pumped her chest to the rhythm of that Bee Gees song like Vinnie Jones does on the TV advert, but I never even thought to ring for a bloody ambulance…"

He placed his face in his hands, his shoulders shuddering.

"From what you've told us, it sounds like there was nothing else you could have done," said Warren gently.

"So, what happened next?" asked Sutton, once the man had regained control.

"I finally realised it was no use, so I went back inside and used the phone in the hallway."

"Did you return to the conservatory?" asked Warren.

The man shook his head. "No, I couldn't…" He looked at the two men imploringly. "I didn't want to see her all… you know… does that make me a bad husband, not being with her one last time?"

"No," said Warren softly. "You should try and remember her the way she was."

"Can I ask if it was normal for you to go to bed before your wife?" asked Sutton eventually.

Wainwright-Burke was silent for a few moments, picking at a loose thread on his sleeve. He gave a sigh. "I suppose it will all come out eventually," he paused, choosing his words carefully. "My wife was not a well woman. She had been having problems for a while." He looked towards the end of the room. "She would often sit up late, drinking." He lowered his eyes. "Quite often, I would come downstairs and find her passed out in her favourite chair."

"I see," said Sutton quietly. "Can I ask how long this had been going on?"

"A couple of years. Her mother passed away unexpectedly and it completely knocked her for six." He let out a puff of air. "But if I'm honest, she'd been drinking too much before then," he shrugged. "At first it was just a bottle of wine a couple of nights a week, then it was most nights, maybe with a couple of G&Ts. I tried to speak to her about it, but we just ended up arguing. A few months ago, I persuaded her to go to her GP. He prescribed some anti-depressants and tried to get her to attend counselling. She promised she'd cut down, but the neighbour across the road came over and said that they'd started finding bottles that weren't theirs in their recycling bin…"

He rubbed his nose on his sleeve. "I should have pushed harder, I know," his voice caught. "I let her down…"

Glancing at Sutton, Warren stood up, snapping his pocketbook closed.

"Mr Wainwright-Burke, we are both very sorry for your loss. You're obviously in shock and I think we have everything we need for now, so can we ask you to come into the station in a couple of days for a formal interview?"

The man agreed, his eyes fixed firmly on the table in front of him.

"For my piece of mind, would you let the paramedics check you over?" asked Warren. "Just to make sure you're OK?"

Wainwright-Burke nodded silently. Warren stepped out of the room and fetched a paramedic from the kitchen; Mrs Wainwright-Burke wouldn't be needing his services.

That seen to, the two detectives showed themselves out; they met Hardwick and Ruskin returning from the house next door.

"We've got a statement and a preliminary timeline," said Ruskin.

"That could be useful," said Warren as they got into the car. Hardwick had hitched a lift in a patrol car earlier and so joined Ruskin on the backseat for the return journey.

By now Warren had his phone out. "I want the full works," he said when Detective Sergeant David Hutchinson picked up. "I need a CSI unit down here ASAP and the area secured. Get door-knockers out and tell Mags to source any domestic CCTV or dashcam footage for the last couple of days. Ask Professor Jordan if he can do the post-mortem as a priority."

Beside him, Sutton was also on his mobile. "Rachel, it's me," he said to DS Pymm. "Can you get the ball rolling on warrants for mobile phone records for the deceased and her husband, and pull all their financials? Also, call Mrs Wainwright-Burke's GP and get a copy of her medical records."

The two men continued with their instructions for a couple more minutes before finally ending their calls.

"I'll let DSI Grayson pass on the good news to the Chief Constable," said Warren, with a grim smile, as he started the engine, the car filling with Annie Lennox's 'No More "I Love You's"'.

"I'm sure he'll be delighted," said Sutton, grimacing at the music. "Mind you, I wouldn't be surprised if the Super has actually played a round or two with Mr Wainwright-Burke over the years."

Behind them, Ruskin exchanged a bemused look with Hardwick.

"Sirs, are we missing something?"

*　　*　　*

"We have a timeline," said Mags Richardson, early that afternoon. She started playing a black-and-white video on her screen.

"This is from their next-door neighbours' security camera. Unfortunately, it doesn't overlook the Wainwright-Burke's house, but watch what happens."

The footage was sharp, infrared lighting producing a clear image of the driveway. The neighbour's car, a boxy Range Rover rendered a light grey in the monochrome video, sat squarely in the centre of the picture. The time stamp in the top right-hand corner clicked over to 04:12. Suddenly the vehicle's rear lights flared.

"According to their statements, the couple were asleep at the rear with the window open and were both woken by the sound of a loud crash from somewhere out the back. The husband used an app on his phone to turn on all the lights before going downstairs to investigate. The curtains in the front bedroom were open, so what we're seeing is the light illuminating the safety reflectors on the rear of the car. The 999 call was received at 04:19, and the ambulance arrived in just under four minutes."

"That matches what Mr Wainwright-Burke told us," said Sutton.

"Thanks, Mags," said Warren. He walked across the room to where DS Pymm, their officer in the case, sat partially hidden behind her horseshoe arrangement of computer monitors. "What have you got for us, Rachel?"

"Mobile phone records for both of their handsets. I'll need more context about their daily lives if we're to spot any numbers or call patterns that raise suspicions, but I've run all their contacts through the databases and none of them match persons of interest. It looks as though they used their mobiles mainly for social and family calls, although Mr Wainwright-Burke also received some business calls. The house had two landlines; the one which he used to call the emergency operator on and then another which seems to have been for work. All the numbers we've traced from the business line appear to be customers or suppliers."

"What about location data?" asked Warren.

"We've gone back ten days so far. Both phones were in the house from early evening onwards last night, and every other night this week. Mr Wainwright-Burke's phone was either in the house during working hours, or out at Middlesbury Leisure Centre, which I believe is a client. He returned home every day for about forty-five minutes around one o'clock. His wife's phone was at home most of that time, and there was heavy usage of the business landline during working hours."

"They maintain swimming pools, don't they?" said Ruskin.

"Yes, they pretty much have the market cornered in this part of the world," said Sutton, who'd spent a productive hour on the internet. "They do everything from fitting thirty-foot pools in back gardens to cleaning and servicing leisure centres with fifty-metre training pools and family splash zones."

"That's right, they've grown it from scratch over the past thirty years," said Pymm. "Carlton Wainwright-Burke is the public face of the company but Laetitia was the one with the business acumen. I'd say he was out and about, while she ran the company from home."

"So that was it?" asked Warren.

"Yes. It looks like Mr Wainwright-Burke did the supermarket run last Thursday; however, his wife went to the corner shop about two o'clock every day. There and back, leaving about ten minutes after he returned to work."

"Stocking up on liquid refreshments," said Warren.

"That's it, as far as movement of their phones goes," said Pymm. "Home or work, with the occasional trip to the supermarket to liven things up. No outings to restaurants or pubs, or even to see friends." She gave a sigh. "Either they left their phones at home when they went out on the razzle, or they lead an even more boring existence than I do."

"Or he was ashamed of her drinking in public," said Warren quietly, feeling a brief wave of sadness. It was clear that while the couple had much going for them publicly, Laetitia Wainwright-Burke at least had been troubled, and her husband had helped her hide it from the world.

*   *   *

The post-mortem was scheduled for early evening. Warren and Sutton headed down the A1 to the Lister Hospital, where Professor Ryan Jordan ran the local morgue. The traffic was heavy, and so Sutton was treated to almost an hour of top-shelf eighties classics. "I knew there was another reason you wanted me to come with you," he groused as he stared out of the window.

"I don't know what you mean," said Warren, taking the opportunity presented by stationary traffic to use the steering wheel to join in the drum solo on Phil Collins' 'In the Air Tonight'. He smothered a grin when he noticed that despite his protestations, Sutton's left foot seemed to know the exact rhythm.

"As soon as this is all over, you and Susan are coming around for dinner and you will listen to every Stormzy track on Spotify."

"Sorry, Tony, I'll try and be more considerate on the way home. I downloaded some A-ha that we can listen to if you prefer?"

"I'd rather walk."

*   *   *

"Come on in, gentlemen," the American-born Home Office pathologist greeted the two detectives when they'd finished changing into their scrubs. "I know you wanted a rush job, so I started without you."

"Sorry, Prof, the traffic was a bugger," said Sutton cheerily. Beside him, Warren waved a weak greeting. He hated autopsies at the best of times, but he'd realised too late that he didn't have his jar of VapoRub in his jacket pocket. Sutton had taken great pleasure in smearing a liberal dose underneath his own nose after Warren had stubbornly refused to accept his offer of some of the mentholated ointment in exchange for silence on the drive home. He glared darkly at his old friend; he could have sworn he'd placed the jar in his pocket earlier that day. As he recalled, Sutton had handed him his suit jacket as they left his office to head down to the car park…

At least Laetitia Wainwright-Burke was fresh.

"I received the deceased's medical records an hour ago," said Jordan. "They are consistent with my findings so far." He pointed towards a brown mass sitting on a metal tray. "I'll need to send samples off to histopathology to be certain, but a gross physical inspection reveals early-stage alcoholic liver cirrhosis. I've drawn some bloods for toxicology, but when I opened up her stomach it was filled with brown liquid that smells a hell of a lot like whisky."

"Would she have been in a fit state to hoist herself up on a chair and hang herself?" managed Warren; without the protection of the VapoRub, he'd noticed the smell the moment he'd approached the body.

"No way to be certain until I've got the blood alcohol results back."

"What about cause of death?" asked Sutton.

"Well, that's where it gets interesting. She died of asphyxiation, caused by strangulation."

Warren had thought as much; her swollen face had indicated that.

"The vertebrae are intact and correctly aligned, so definitely no hangman's drop. If she was lucky, the pressure on her carotids would have rendered her unconscious in a few seconds. If she wasn't so lucky…"

"And those marks are consistent with the rope that was tied around her throat?" said Warren, pointing at the ugly-looking welts.

"Yes, definitely. You'll need to see what the DNA results and the fibre analysis show, but there were plenty of trapped skin cells between the strands for comparison, and I collected a number of what look to me like hemp fibres from the wounds. It's unfortunate that her husband loosened the noose, but it can't be helped."

"So, she died from strangulation, after she hanged herself," summarised Sutton.

The crinkle of Jordan's eyes telegraphed the smile behind his mask. "Like I said, that's where it gets interesting…"

Wednesday

Wednesday was another beautiful day. By the time Warren called the mid-morning briefing to order, there wasn't a cloud in the sky and the building's elderly air-conditioning system was wheezing into action.

"Fill us in on what you've got for us, Rachel," said Warren, after appraising the assembled team of the previous evening's autopsy findings.

"WB Pool Services has been undergoing a cash crisis for the past couple of years," said Pymm. "Most of their turnover comes from large clients like leisure centres, but it seems that after many years of repeat business, several have opted not to renew their contracts. WB's income has dropped by almost eighty per cent from where it was two or three years ago."

"Any idea why?" asked Sutton.

"Not yet. I'm going to call some of their former clients and see if they can shed some light."

"Karen, where are you with the insurance company?" asked Warren.

"I'm waiting for a call back," she replied.

"Moray?"

"Same. Andy Harrison managed the scene, he's promised me a preliminary report on what else he's found in the next hour or so, and the rush job on the DNA is due in after lunch."

With little else to report, Warren dismissed the meeting. Grabbing his empty mug, he headed for his boss's office. Superintendent John Grayson had a coffee machine that served the best brew in the building – perhaps he'd take the hint and offer him a refill.

★　　★　　★

"I haven't spoken to Carlton in ages," said Grayson as he leaned back in his chair. "I last saw him when we played a few rounds in a charity match a couple of summers ago."

"Was his wife there?" asked Warren, enjoying the rich aroma drifting out of his mug.

"Yes. Letty didn't play herself, but she enjoyed the social side of it. We were raising money for muscular dystrophy as I recall and she was due to run the auction. I remember it, because she dropped out at the last moment and Refilwe stepped in."

Grayson's wife, a prominent international human rights lawyer, didn't share her husband's passion for golf either, but was an active supporter of several charities.

"Any idea why?" asked Warren.

"The official story was that she had a sudden migraine, but I spoke to Refilwe afterwards and she was rather cagey about the circumstances. My wife is the most honest person I've ever met, but she's a master at changing the subject when she wants to. I have my suspicions."

"Letty was drunk," stated Warren.

"I think so. She was rather boisterous when we broke for lunch and I got the impression that the large G&T she was drinking wasn't the first of the day. If she carried on while we played our second round… well, who knows what state she was in by the evening?" He shook his head. "All very sad."

"Any idea what the Chief Constable's thoughts are on the matter?" asked Warren cautiously. It was well known that DSI Grayson's golfing circle included several of Hertfordshire Constabulary's most senior officers, although his attempts to parlay those relationships into one final promotion before retirement had been resisted so far. Warren was also well aware that the Chief Constable was friends with Carlton Wainwright-Burke. Warren didn't think for one moment that there would be any improper interference with his investigation, but it wouldn't hurt to know what level of scrutiny he could expect.

Grayson gave a half-smile. "Don't worry, Warren, he is watching with interest, 'but has complete confidence in your team's ability to uncover the circumstances behind this unfortunate tragedy'. In other words, go where the investigation leads and let the cards fall as they may. He has no intention of getting his hands dirty over this."

"The thought never crossed my mind, sir."

★　★　★

"The DNA is in," announced Ruskin, when Warren returned to the main office, "and CSM Harrison has sent over his preliminary scene report."

"That matches what Prof Jordan suspected," said Sutton, reading the DNA results over Ruskin's shoulder. At Warren's prompting, Ruskin switched to the scene report. Warren scanned quickly down the email until he found what he was looking for.

"Well, well, isn't that interesting," he said.

"Can I play as well?" called out Pymm from behind her desk.

"The more the merrier," said Warren.

"Good, because I just had some very illuminating conversations with three former clients of WB Pool Services."

Pymm relayed what she'd been told.

"I think it's time we got that formal statement," said Warren.

★　★　★

Carlton Wainwright-Burke was dressed in chinos and a long-sleeved, white shirt, open at the neck. His muscular body, with its golden tan and broad shoulders, could pass for that of a man a decade or more younger than his fifty-three years. But his pallid face was drawn, and the purple smudges under his bloodshot eyes made him look decades older.

"Thank you for coming in today, I realise that this must be the last place you want to be at such a difficult time," began Warren. "The interview is being recorded, and you have the right to stop it at any time or request legal advice. I'm sorry that it's so uncomfortable in here, the air-con in this building is on its last legs."

Wainwright-Burke acknowledged him with an inclination of his head.

"We just need to clear up some details," said Sutton. "Can you see if we have the sequence of events correct?"

"Yes. Anything I can do to help," said Wainwright-Burke, leaning back in his chair.

"OK," said Warren. "You went to bed at approximately eleven p.m., leaving your wife, Laetitia, downstairs with a drink and a book?"

"Yes."

"Is this your normal evening routine?"

"Yeah, I like to get up early. Letty... well, she isn't a morning person."

"Forgive me, but would it be fair to say that your wife is an alcoholic and it wasn't uncommon for her to remain downstairs if she drank too much?"

"Yeah."

"Would you say that your wife was drunk when you left her?" asked Sutton.

Wainwright-Burke paused. "She was getting there," he conceded eventually.

"According to what you told DI Sutton and I, and the attending officers, you were woken up by a loud crash at approximately four a.m.?"

"A little after, I think, but yes."

"And you immediately ran downstairs?"

"Yeah, I jumped straight out of bed."

"You didn't get dressed first?" asked Sutton.

"No, I sleep in my boxers this time of year."

"Before you found your wife, what did you think caused the noise?"

He sighed. "I thought she'd had a fall. She's done it before; got up to go to the bathroom and tripped."

"Because she was drunk?"

"Yes. Look, my wife was ill, do you need to keep banging on about it?"

"I'm sorry, the more detail we have in your statement, the fewer questions the coroner will need to ask at the inquest," said Warren.

Wainwright-Burke flinched, but nodded.

"You found your wife in the conservatory. She was lying on the floor, with a rope around her neck and a broken skylight on top of her?" continued Warren.

"Yes." Wainwright-Burke's voice was a pained whisper.

"Did you go to her immediately?" asked Sutton.

"Of course."

"And what did you do?" asked Warren, his tone gentle.

"The rope was digging into her neck, so I loosened it," he gave a shuddering breath. "I could see that she was probably dead, but I couldn't just leave her." He pushed his knuckles into his mouth. "I couldn't give up without a fight," he managed. Eventually he looked up, his gaze imploring. "Please don't tell me she would have survived if I'd remembered to call for an ambulance sooner?"

"No, Carlton. The pathologist says she was already dead, there was nothing else you could have done," said Warren.

The man's eyes closed and some of the tension in his shoulders eased.

"Based on your next-door neighbours' statement, we believe the skylight fell in at roughly twelve minutes past four. The emergency services logged your call at nineteen minutes past, which suggests that you tried to revive your wife for about seven minutes."

He shrugged. "I guess. Everything is a bit of a blur."

"I understand," said Warren. "The ambulance arrived a little under four minutes later and a patrol car a minute or so after that. Where were you during that period?"

"After I made the call, I sat on the stairs and waited."

"Did you get dressed?"

"No."

"Did you go back into the conservatory?"

"No, I already told you this."

Sutton took over. "We have a recording of the 999 call. The operator asked you to double-check that your wife wasn't breathing and then come back to her, but you hung up the phone. Why did you do that?"

"I don't really remember," he said.

"So, you didn't check that she was alive?"

"No, I couldn't bring myself to see her again," he looked at the two men directly. "You said yourself, she was already dead. I could see that."

"Of course," said Warren.

"How long have you and your wife run WB Pool Services?" asked Sutton.

Wainwright-Burke blinked at the sudden change in topic. "Um, thirty years? We started it a year or so after we got married." His bottom lip trembled. "We started small, just me and a couple of lads digging pools in back gardens. The plan had been for me to supervise the jobs, and Letty to do the paperwork. We figured that way we could start a family; Letty could work from home and raise the kids at the same time."

"But that didn't happen?" asked Warren gently.

"No. We couldn't... Anyway, the business expanded, and I hired more workers. We had a lean few years during the nineties' recession, but we bounced back and I went into partnership with a local outfit that serviced commercial pools; leisure centres, schools, universities, that sort of thing. When the owner of the firm retired, he accepted my offer to buy him out."

"But you continued working from home? You didn't hire any office space?" said Sutton.

"No need. We have a unit on the industrial estate to store our supplies, but we use a recruitment firm specialising in construction workers to hire contractors on a job-by-job basis, so all we really needed was a spare room." He shrugged. "It keeps us flexible and reduces the overheads." He frowned. "Look, what does this all have to do with my wife's death?"

"Just painting a picture," said Warren.

"How is business these days?" asked Sutton.

"Um, OK, I suppose."

"Are you sure about that?" asked Warren. "It's just that according to your business accounts, your turnover has reduced significantly in the past couple of years."

"How do you…? Yeah, OK. We've been going through a bit of a slow patch. But I've been looking at some new opportunities to expand, so we'll recover. It's happened before."

"It didn't happen during the 2008 financial crash," said Sutton. "As you said, most of your business comes from commercial contracts with public bodies. I'm sure some of your private clients may have decided that a pool in the back garden was a luxury they couldn't afford, but the local sports centre still had to stay open and keep the pool clean and safe, so you weathered the downturn pretty well, all things considered. Those customers remained loyal."

Wainwright-Burke said nothing.

"We spoke to a number of your former clients, to ask them why they had decided not to renew their contract after so many years," said Sutton. "What do you think they said?"

Wainwright-Burke remained silent, his jaw working.

"According to one, 'the professionalism that they had come to expect from WB Pool Services had declined markedly, to the point that they could no longer rely on them to deliver the services that they need'. They cited examples of missed maintenance visits, essential cleaning supplies not being delivered or incorrectly billed, and phone calls or emails either not being answered or not dealt with properly."

"Your wife's drinking was affecting her work, wasn't it?" said Warren.

"Yes." Wainwright-Burke's shoulders slumped. "It was my fault. I've always left that side of the business to Letty. When she became…. ill, I should have paid more attention. I could have employed an admin assistant; just a couple of days a week to keep things ticking over while she got better. But she was so damn proud, she never said anything. By the time I realised what was going on, we couldn't have afforded to pay someone even if we wanted to."

"And how did that make you feel?" asked Warren.

The man said nothing for so long that Warren was about to ask the question again.

"Angry. At first. We'd built that business for decades, and we were about to lose it all because Letty was too drunk to keep on top of things. I'm fifty-three and suddenly I'm digging bloody swimming pools again," he sighed. "But then I realised that it wasn't all her fault, I was at least as much to blame as she was. She wasn't just some co-worker with personal problems, she was my wife. The only woman I've ever loved." He gestured dismissively with his hand. "When we married, we didn't have a pot to piss in, and I never thought we'd be as wealthy as we are… were. It was never about the money. We loved each other when we had nothing and we'll still love each other if we lose it all, we've just come full circle." He snorted. "If anything, it was a good thing. It finally forced her to face up to her problems… Oh, Christ, Letty…" he put his head in his hands, his shoulders starting to shake. "Why did you do it, my darling?" his voice thick with emotion. "We could have got through this. Together, we can deal with anything."

"I think now would be a good time to take a short break," said Warren.

★   ★   ★

Warren and Sutton headed back to the office, while Carlton Wainwright-Burke headed outside for a smoke.

"Any news, Karen?" asked Warren.

"Yes, Allianz just got back to me. They confirmed what you suspected."

Warren took her pocketbook and scanned through her notes.

"Prof Jordan just phoned," said Ruskin. He handed over his own pocketbook.

"Bingo," said Warren.

*   *   *

The interview restarted after twenty minutes. Again, Wainwright-Burke declined a solicitor. In deference to the sweltering heat in the interview suite, Warren and Sutton had loosened their ties and rolled up their sleeves.

"Your business needs a substantial cash injection to stay afloat, doesn't it?" said Sutton. "You've remortgaged your house, but you're still short. That's quite a mess your wife has left behind."

"She was ill," snapped Wainwright-Burke. "Alcoholism is a disease. I didn't blame her. I couldn't... for richer, for poorer, that's what I promised." He gestured towards the two men's hands. "You're both married, you must understand that."

"So divorce was never an option?" asked Warren.

"Of course not. I told you, we started with nothing. If we ended up with nothing – well, we're just back where we started. As long as we had each other, we could survive anything."

"I understand," said Sutton. "Besides, bankruptcy and a failed marriage... not the best credentials for someone thinking of standing as an MP, are they?"

"Now hold on a minute..." started Wainwright-Burke, his face flushing.

"You and your wife had substantial life insurance policies, I believe," said Warren. "More than enough to save the business."

"Oh, come on!" protested Wainwright-Burke. "We've had those policies for over twenty years, they were a condition of the original bank loans. We've paid the same premium since we started, and I've never changed the terms or the size of the pay-out. Anyway, Letty dealt with the paperwork," he sniffed. "Besides, she committed suicide. They don't cough up for that."

"Actually, that's a myth," said Sutton. "The standard suicide clause expired years ago. They'd pay out in full."

"But then you know that already, don't you, Carlton?" said Warren. "As you say, your wife dealt with all the paperwork, and always has done, but six weeks ago, you set up your own online account with Allianz and downloaded the terms and conditions of your policy from their secure document server. There was no need for you to change anything, as you could see that the policy would still pay up."

"This is ridiculous," snapped Wainwright-Burke. "And offensive."

"Have you had any work done on the conservatory recently? It's a very old structure, I'm sure it takes a lot of maintenance," asked Sutton.

Wainwright-Burke's eyes narrowed. "Yes, I have someone come and have a look every few years."

Warren opened a file folder and removed a series of printed photos. "What about the skylights?"

"Of course."

"There are three skylights. Single-glazed windows in a wooden frame."

"Yes, we looked at getting them modernised, but the house is listed." He shrugged. "It's a bit of a pain, but it comes with owning an old property."

"The rope that your wife used to hang herself was threaded through the eyelet that the window hook fits into for opening and closing the middle skylight." Warren pushed a photograph across the table. "We were a bit surprised that the eyelet could take your wife's weight – she was a small woman, less than seven stone, but it's still a lot of force on something with only two screws attaching it to a piece of wood. But another two screws were added – recently, judging by the lack of tarnishing."

"I told you, we had somebody come and do some maintenance a couple of years ago."

"Any idea why they only reinforced the centre skylight?" Warren placed another two printouts on the table. "The others just have the original two screws."

"No idea."

"Perhaps we could ask them?" suggested Sutton. "Do you have a name?"

"Not off the top of my head."

"Can you explain why only your fingerprints are on the eyelet and the window frame?" asked Warren.

"No," said Wainwright-Burke.

Warren pressed on quickly. Any minute now, the man was going to wise up to his predicament, start 'no commenting' and ask for a solicitor.

"How long would you say it took you to get from your bedroom to the conservatory after the crash of the falling skylight woke you up?"

"Thirty seconds? Maybe less?"

"Well, here's the thing," he said. "When the chair that your wife was standing on was kicked over, the drop wasn't long enough to break her neck. Your wife died of strangulation."

He pushed another set of photographs across the table.

"These were taken during the post-mortem. You can see that there are contusions on the neck consistent with a ligature. We have her skin cells embedded in the fibres of the rope, and the bruising was caused in the moments before her heart stopped. Cause of death was strangulation by that rope."

"Well, there you go, then."

Warren turned another photograph over.

"This shows the rear of her neck. You can see that there are bruises here, also. Again, they would have been formed pre-mortem."

He removed another image. "Your wife had a noose around her neck. That would have caused the bruising on the front of her neck as she was strangled. But the noose didn't kill her."

On cue, Sutton turned his chair away from Warren, and handed over his tie. Warren moved behind him and wound the tie once around Sutton's neck.

"Instead, we believe that the same piece of rope was actually placed around her neck from behind as she sat passed out in her favourite chair."

Warren pulled the two ends of the tie, and the silk material tightened around Sutton's throat.

"The rope crushed her windpipe and compressed her carotid arteries, causing bruising similar to what we'd see if she hanged herself. But it also caused bruising and abrasions on the rear of the neck that wouldn't have occurred with such a crude noose."

"This is madness. What are you saying?"

"Your wife had a blood alcohol content so high she could never clamber on a chair, tie a noose, thread the rope through that eyelet and secure the end to the wooden beam for support. In fact, she was probably barely conscious. She did put up a bit of a struggle – the skin cells under her broken fingernails tell us that; a DNA test will identify exactly who they came from." He looked pointedly at the man's long-sleeved shirt, still neatly buttoned at the wrists despite the uncomfortable temperature in the interview suite, which had been steadily rising ever since Warren had turned the air-conditioning off shortly before the man had arrived.

"You see, we think you killed her in the lounge – sorry, 'library' –

after letting her pass out from drinking too much. You then took the rope, made a crude noose and rigged it up, before carrying her out to the conservatory – not difficult for a man who digs swimming pools for a living. We believe the plan was for you to leave her dangling, get undressed and go back to bed, ready to 'find' her in the morning. She'd have been there all night, hanging from the rope that killed her."

"No, you've got it wrong, I would never hurt her."

"You screwed up," said Sutton. "You reinforced the eyelet on the skylight, but didn't think to check the strength of the wooden frame. The moment you kicked the chair over, her weight tore it down. You're lucky it didn't hit you on the head. If you had really jumped out of bed and run to her the moment you were woken by the sound of the skylight crashing down, you'd have been there in time to loosen the noose before she died of strangulation."

The man before them had turned a faint green. "I want a lawyer," he managed.

"I think that's a very good idea," said Warren. "Carlton Wainwright-Burke, I am arresting you on suspicion of murder…"

★   ★   ★

It was all over by ten p.m. The Crown Prosecution Service had authorised charging, and Carlton Wainwright-Burke had been led to a cell, to spend the first in what was certain to be many more nights behind bars.

"At least he admitted it in the end," said Sutton. The team were gathered in the office, preparing to go for a celebratory pint.

"He knew he'd messed up," said Warren. "And when we confronted him with what they found in his laundry basket during the search, the game was up."

"Something I have to ask," said Grayson, shrugging on his jacket. "You and Tony knew from the outset that he was guilty, long before the autopsy and the forensics came back. What tipped you off?"

Warren smiled. "I'll let DI Sutton answer that. After all, he's the big Annie Lennox fan."

Grayson looked bemused.

"Her 1992 hit, 'Walking on Broken Glass'," Sutton replied with a scowl. "He claimed to have jumped out of bed, wearing nothing but his boxer shorts. Then he gave her CPR. We know that's true, because of the damage to her ribs and sternum. But the skylight had smashed and there were shards of glass everywhere."

"There's no way he could have walked across that floor, and knelt down to give her first aid, without getting cut," continued Warren. "He was barefoot when we interviewed him. I spoke to the paramedic who checked him over, who confirmed that his knees and feet were fine but that there were scratches on his forearms. The CSIs looked at his dirty clothes and found tiny fragments of glass embedded in the knees of his jeans and the tread of his slippers, plus some on the carpet in the bedroom, so we knew that he was lying about not being dressed when he found her."

"Great work," said Grayson. "All of you. First round is on me," he announced.

As the team filed out, Warren turned to Sutton, a smile playing on his lips.

"I hope you have some pound coins for the jukebox."

AND THE BAND PLAYED ON

Peter Lovesey

> *'Casey would waltz with a strawberry blonde*
> *And the Band played on.*
> *He'd glide 'cross the floor with the girl he adored*
> *And the Band played on.*
> *But his brain was so loaded it nearly exploded*
> *The poor girl would shake with alarm.*
> *He'd ne'er leave the girl with the strawberry curls*
> *And the Band played on.'*

Grandpa's thin, reedy voice wasn't loud, but we couldn't shut it out, however hard we tried. He stopped singing and smiled. Some of the family tried to smile back. Our dad sighed and rolled his eyes. Gemma, my youngest sister, who was six and would say anything that came into her head, spoke for all of us. "Grandpa, I'm tired of that song."

Our mum shushed her and told her she was only tired because it was past her bedtime. That was enough to send Gemma into the other room where the TV was.

I wouldn't say so in front of my family, but everyone was pissed off by the song. Grandpa didn't know. He was going to carry on singing it until he dropped dead. Mum sometimes said he was getting slow on the trigger, which was putting it gently. He hadn't said anything worth hearing for months. The worst of it was that he remembered every word of the song and it was one of those catchy tunes that stayed in your head.

"Who was Casey, anyway?" I asked Mum. I knew I wouldn't get a sensible answer out of Grandpa.

"I've no idea, Josh," Mum said, "and I don't really care."

"Someone ought to know."

"It's only a song. Does it matter?"

Sarah, one of my three sisters, said, "It's creepy."

"Why?"

"That line about his brain being so loaded it nearly exploded and the poor girl shaking with alarm. At a dance? I don't get it and I don't like it."

I did some scrolling. "Grandpa's bit is only the chorus."

"Don't you dare sing it," Dad said.

So I simply read them the words. "'Matt Casey formed a social club that beat the town for style and hired for a meeting place a hall. When payday came around each week, they'd grease the floor with wax and dance with noise and vigour at the ball...' It's like a story."

"Crap lyrics," Becky, my oldest sister, said.

Dad frowned at her and said, "Language."

"There's no other word for it." Becky was seventeen and thought she knew everything.

I carried on reading out what was on my phone. "'Each Saturday, you'd see them dressed up in Sunday clothes—'"

"Shh. You'll start him off again," Mum said.

So I took a quick look at the last part and gave them the gist of it in my own words. "At midnight they all push off for a late meal except Casey, who tells the band to keep playing so he can carry on waltzing with the strawberry blonde. Finally they get fed up and play 'Home, Sweet Home' and he thanks them and now the blonde is his wife."

"Is that it?" Becky said.

"More or less."

"Sappy stuff."

"It's old-fashioned," Mum said to her. "A bit sentimental, but people were in the old days."

"What's a strawberry blonde, anyway?" my middle sister Sarah, who was sixteen, asked.

"Something between a true blonde and a redhead," Mum said. "You can get it with modern hair colouring, but it must have been rare when the song was written."

"Eighteen-ninety-five," I told them, thanks to Wikipedia.

"What colour was our Grandma's hair?" Sarah asked.

"That's got nothing to do with it."

"I've never seen a photo of her."

"That's enough," Dad said. "Change the subject." He never spoke about his parents and he didn't encourage us to ask. We didn't even know we had grandparents until Grandpa turned up at our house one afternoon when I was twelve and off school getting over chickenpox. I was the one who went to the door. This shabby old guy with no teeth was carrying a bag Mum called a holdall, and I thought he was selling stuff at the door. He was wearing a thick overcoat on a belting hot day in June. He asked if my parents were in and I shouted for Mum and waited. She came out from the kitchen and he grinned at her and said, "You must be Hazel. I'm Richard's father."

Richard is my dad's name. Mum went white. She told me to get upstairs to my room. I sat at the top of the stairs and heard her say in a strange, strained voice, "You'd better come in." She took him through to the back. Going by the noise the cups and saucers made, she was making him tea, using the tea service she only ever got out for visitors. Normally she drank from a mug with *Best Mum in the World* written on it. I couldn't hear what was said because she had shut the kitchen door. I was stuck in my room for the rest of the day and when my sisters came home they got sent upstairs as well. Dad got in as usual about six and we all stood on the landing and listened. There was some shouting, but we couldn't work out what was going on.

After about two hours, Mum came upstairs and told Sarah she would have to move out of her room and sleep on the spare bed in Gemma's room. Sarah didn't kick up a fuss, thinking it was for one night only. She didn't know it was permanent. We were told the old bloke was our grandpa – Dad's father – and he would be using Sarah's room from now on. Luckily for me, it wasn't my room he was given. I'm the boy in the family and not supposed to share with girls.

It was Becky who found out the truth from Mum. Grandpa had been living in a place called Wormwood Scrubs for nearly twenty years.

A prison.

Bit by bit, Becky found out more. She knew she wouldn't get anything out of Grandpa or Dad, but she got to work on Mum. She wasn't supposed to tell us what she found out, but of course she did. What's the point of knowing a secret if you can't have the pleasure of breaking it to your kid sisters and brother? She wanted to see our scared faces and, most of all, mine.

I got the shakes when I first heard.

Our grandpa was a murderer. Our own flesh and blood.

Once you've done a murder, that's it. You can't change who you are by doing time in prison. You're still a murderer when you come out. You stay a murderer for the rest of your life.

He didn't look like a murderer, not to my way of thinking. He was old and ordinary, thin, toothless, a bit pathetic.

He had shot a man, a well-known gangster, and buried the body on Oxshott Common. He'd been sent to prison for life but they'd let him out when they decided he was no danger to anyone else.

How could they know he wasn't dangerous?

Now I knew what he'd done, he didn't seem harmless at all. I tried not to show it, but I was so spooked I wished it was me who was sharing in Gemma's room. I didn't like being alone at night anymore. I lay awake listening for my bedroom door to open. Sometimes I heard him go to the bathroom humming his song about the strawberry blonde. Like I said, he was confused and he could easily have opened my door and climbed into my bed. As for that song, it was *my* head that was so loaded it nearly exploded.

Part of me wanted to know more about the murder and part of me didn't. My sisters seemed to lose interest, or else they decided to shut out the horror. I asked Becky if she'd heard anything else and she told me to get a life. I sensed that even if she knew anything she wouldn't tell. She'd had the pleasure of seeing me scared witless and she couldn't top that. I was on my own.

I wasn't going to ask Mum. I could see how uncomfortable she was. She never called Grandpa 'Dad'. She called him Nick, like he wasn't family.

One evening we were watching an old black-and-white film on TV, Grandpa dozing in the best armchair, the rest of us following the story, which was called *Strangers on a Train*. Dad said it was a Hitchcock and they were always good. The baddie was a character called Bruno. I won't bore you with the story. Quite early, there's a scene in a fairground with a young woman called Miriam enjoying a ride on a merry-go-round with two boyfriends. Suddenly they all start singing the words to the music and you see Bruno sitting on one of the wooden horses near them joining in.

I heard the tune first and thought it was familiar, and when they sang the words I could have kicked myself. Of course I knew what it was.

'And the Band Played On.'

Dad frowned and looked across at Grandpa, who was still asleep. My sister Sarah started giggling and so did the others until Mum put her finger to her lips. Everyone was relieved when Grandpa slept right through the scene.

What none of us realised was that Grandpa's song was a theme that kept coming back when the tension was ramped up. Bruno strangles Miriam, and guess what you hear on the soundtrack? Mum grabbed the remote and turned the sound down because Grandpa was stirring.

"Do we have to watch this?" she asked.

"I want to know what happens," Becky said. "I'm enjoying this. It's cool."

Dad didn't say anything and Grandpa settled down again, so we stayed watching.

And then – would you believe it? – there was another scene on the merry-go-round and the music was playing again. Same tune, Grandpa's song. Guy, the goodie, chases Bruno through the amusement park towards the turning carousel. A cop takes a shot at Bruno but misses and hits the guy in charge of the ride. Guy and Bruno jump on the ride and get into a wrestling match between the moving horses. The suspense gets worse because the mechanism is out of control and the whole thing turns faster and faster. The music gets quicker and louder, too, insanely quick. A kid is almost flung off and Guy breaks off the fistfight and saves him. On the fairground an old toothless bloke looking awfully like Grandpa says, "I can handle it," and squirms under the wildly spinning base, worming his way on his stomach towards the controls in the middle. When he gets there and slams on the brake, the whole merry-go-round comes off its moorings in a screaming, smoking wreck.

We were so caught up in the drama that we'd forgotten about Grandpa. He jerked into life and shouted like he'd been shot.

Mum grabbed the remote and switched to mute. "It's all right, Nick. You were having a bad dream."

Dad said, "I think he's pooed his pants."

"Ooh, yes," Gemma said, pinching her nose.

We never saw the end of that film.

Not long after that, I started sleepwalking. One night I woke up standing at the top of the stairs without any memory of how I got there. Another time, my sister Sarah heard the floorboards creak outside her room and screamed. Maybe she thought it was Grandpa coming to murder her. It wasn't. It was me on another sleepwalk. Her screaming woke me up. It woke everyone up except Grandpa.

With all this going on, my schoolwork suffered. I wasn't paying attention and I was getting into fights. Up to that time I'd always had good reports and got on well with the other kids. The Head decided I needed to see a shrink. This Mrs Bailey asked me loads of questions about what was going on in my life and at home. She invited Mum and Dad to meet her later, just the two of them.

I don't know who was more embarrassed when Dad spoke to me the next day. I thought he was going to talk about puberty and stuff, which the shrink had brought up. I didn't need telling about sex – least of all from my own father. But he was on a different tack altogether.

"I've never said much to you about my childhood, Josh," he said. "It wasn't a good time and I prefer to block it out, but I can tell you're going through some kind of crisis yourself – the sleepwalking and the troubles at school – and Mrs Bailey thinks I should be more open with you than I have. Did you know I was fostered as a child?"

I shook my head.

"This concerns Grandpa as well," he said. "He wasn't much older than you when I was born. Fifteen, to be precise. He got a girl of the same age into trouble, as they used to say. Know what I'm talking about?"

I nodded.

"They were only schoolkids, too young to marry. She wasn't on the pill. Because of their religion, her parents insisted she had the baby, which was me. So I'm illegitimate." He paused. "There's another word for it, an ugly word."

I knew what it was, but I wasn't going to say so, not to my dad.

He started again. "My birth mother – I suppose we can call her your grandma – didn't want any more to do with me. She'd done what her parents expected and given birth to me and that was it. Being a baby, I didn't know anything about it until later. I had to be fostered. I was with several different families while I was growing up, some good and some not so good. I didn't know it at the time, but Grandpa felt responsible and took an interest in where I was and who I was fostered with. As I got older, he sent me small amounts of money sometimes and postcards from places overseas, like Aden and Malta. After the scandal of the pregnancy, he'd left school and joined the Air Force as a boy entrant. He did about twenty years in the RAF and got to be a flight sergeant and had several postings abroad."

Dad had stopped. I was taking it in, understanding so much more now about my father's silences whenever anyone mentioned the past. And his need for a settled family life. But it wasn't helping me much. My head was still overloaded. "How did he get to be in prison?"

"You know about that?" Dad said, sounding relieved that he didn't have to break it to me.

"Not much," I said. "He killed someone, didn't he?"

"An evil man, a well-known gangster called Fred Odell, who almost certainly killed several people himself or ordered his gang members to kill them. Nobody shed any tears over Odell's death, but someone had to be brought to justice for it, and that was Grandpa."

"Why?" I said. "How come he shot this gangster?"

"It was while he was stationed at RAF Uxbridge. This was before you were born, before your older sisters were born. He was in his mid-thirties by then and he'd not been out with a woman since his schooldays. Some of his Air Force mates insisted he went into London with them for an evening out. He had the bad luck to meet Odell's daughter Annie in a dance hall. She was not much over twenty, a natural blonde and pretty. That damned tune was playing, the one he's always singing. They got on well and met a few times more and he was in love with her.

"He found out too late who her father was. Odell disapproved. He wasn't allowing his daughter to go out with a man fifteen years older than she was, so he warned him off, but your grandfather wasn't having it. He took to carrying a gun, for self-defence supposedly, but one evening he went back to Odell's house at Oxshott with Annie, escorting her home, as blokes did in those days, and her father caught them snogging in the front porch. There was a row and threats and Dad took out the gun and fired five shots into Odell's chest. Then he drove out to Oxshott with the body and buried it along with the murder weapon. Unluckily for him, Oxshott Common isn't the quiet spot he thought it was. He was seen by two separate witnesses walking their dogs. One got the number of his car and phoned the police."

"Was he in uniform?"

"I don't think so, but they found him easily enough. He didn't go into hiding or anything. He was arrested the next night coming out of a London dance hall, the Hammersmith Palais, with Annie Odell, the girl he loved. The police had tipped off the press and it was front-page news, a picture of him with Annie at his side, eyes wide with fright. That's how I found out. He confessed and pleaded guilty when it came to court. He didn't have much choice. He couldn't pretend it had been accidental or anything. He'd buried the body and the gun. If you murder someone, you get a life sentence, no argument. He did almost twenty years in prison."

"Did you visit him there?"

"No. I couldn't face it. There was no contact. I scarcely knew him anyway. What could I have said?" Dad stopped speaking for a moment and ran his hand through his hair. "I suppose I should have manned up and gone there. He'd made efforts to keep in touch with me when I was growing up. I didn't respond, didn't visit him at this low point in his life and now I regret it. What happened after he came out on parole isn't very clear because his mind has gone, as you know. He was sleeping rough on the streets for at least a couple of years before he turned up here out of the blue. There was drinking and drugs, I'm sure. The heroin rots your teeth. Everything he owned in the world was in one bag and most of it was so filthy it had to be binned. None of it was personal except for one small photo he'd kept. You know the rest."

"What was the photo?"

"It was of Annie Odell, the girl. Has any of this helped?"

I nodded. "I think so. There is one question: did you ever get in touch with your mother?"

Dad sighed. "I tried. I managed to trace her. She'd married, divorced and married again to quite a successful man, an architect. I wrote to her. But she refused point blank to meet me. She wrote one sentence back saying that her past was a closed book. The only link I have with my start in life is Grandpa. I'll see that his last years are comfortable."

"Thanks for telling me, Dad. Appreciate it."

I wasn't scared of Grandpa any more. I almost respected him. He'd shot a famous gangster and taken his punishment. He'd earned the right to walk free again.

The sleepwalking stopped and my schoolwork improved. I wished I could have talked to Grandpa about the experiences he'd had, but he was off his rocker. I bought a small gilt frame for the precious photo of Annie, the gangster's daughter, his strawberry blonde. I think he appreciated that. He watched me fitting it into the frame and it stayed beside his bed for the rest of his life.

He lived two more years and died peacefully.

Dad made the funeral arrangements, just a short service at the crematorium. We didn't expect anyone to be there except our family, but Grandpa sprang one more surprise. Almost every seat was taken. One of the papers had got the story and printed a column headed, *FRED ODELL'S KILLER PASSES*. Three of his old RAF buddies came. Five or six of our neighbours. Two ex-prisoners and their wives. A retired prison officer. A couple who ran a refuge for homeless people. Someone from the Alzheimer's Society.

I found myself sitting next to a silver-haired woman in a dark blue coat with silver frogging and black gloves. She was wearing expensive perfume. Her face was faintly familiar. She said, "Are you family?"

"His grandson, Josh."

"And are those your parents at the front?"

"Yes."

"After the service, there's something I'd like to say to you. Would you mind? I won't be going back to your house for the tea and sandwiches."

"If you like."

It wasn't a religious service. There was a humanist guy who took us through the ceremony and admitted he hadn't known Grandpa personally. We had a couple of readings and some taped music, including 'Flying Home', played by the RAF big band, Shades of Blue, and the RAF March Past. Dad gave a short address and skilfully managed to say nothing about the two worst episodes of Grandpa's life, and finished by inviting everyone back to the house. Then we had the bit called the committal when the curtains closed around the coffin.

Do I need to tell you which music was played for his send-off? It was only the tune, but I was thinking the words in my head, imagining that last dance he had with Annie at the Hammersmith Palais before he was arrested. Did they dance to their tune? Was that why he never forgot it? Those troubling words – 'His brain was so loaded it nearly exploded and the poor girl would shake with alarm' – drew tears from my eyes.

There was plenty of handshaking outside the crematorium and we looked at the wreaths people had sent. The whole thing was so much more touching than I expected. All these people cared enough about Grandpa to have come to his funeral, ignoring the huge mistakes he'd made.

I'd forgotten the woman who had spoken to me, but she appeared at my side and thanked me for waiting. She drew me aside as if she didn't want anyone overhearing her.

She said, "Your parents were good to him, taking him in and making his last years peaceful."

I agreed with her.

But that wasn't all she wanted to say. "There's something I'd like your father to know, but I won't be speaking to him myself. He doesn't know me. Would you mind telling him that the headline in the paper was cruel and got it wrong? Nick was never a killer."

"No?" I'd heard what she said and wasn't overimpressed. I thought she meant he wasn't a professional gunman. I guessed she'd been moved by the service, as I had. There were marks under her eyes where the liner had moistened and run.

"He didn't fire the fatal shots, Josh. He wasn't there."

"What?" I listened up, startled.

"Fred Odell was a monster. He abused his own daughter for years, touched her intimately when she was only a child and forced himself on her before she even reached her teens. When Nick started seeing her, Fred was jealous. He said if she didn't break up with Nick, he'd have him killed. She was shattered. It was the last straw. She shot her own father with one of his guns. Then she phoned Nick in a panic and told him what she'd done. He came to the house and calmed her down and took the body away and buried it. That's how he was caught and mistakenly accused of the murder."

"You're talking about Annie?" I was so dumbstruck I repeated what she'd just told me in case I hadn't heard right. "Annie killed her own father?"

"And your grandfather served a life sentence to protect her. Not that she showed much appreciation. She married someone else, stupid woman. There's gratitude!" She rested her black-gloved palm lightly against my chest. "Promise me you'll tell your father what I said."

"Yes – but who are you? He's sure to ask."

"He doesn't need to know."

Before she turned away, I recognised her. The face was older and more lined than the face in the photo I'd framed and, like I said, her hair was white, but I'm certain she was my grandpa's strawberry blonde.

4 x 3.3

Ragnar Jónasson

He measured the room once more. There was little else to do, the silence was driving him crazy.

Four steps, almost exactly, by just over three steps, perhaps three and a third.

It would never be an exact science.

By now he had lost all track of time, but somehow he managed to keep his composure. He had never been claustrophobic, his tolerance in that respect was high, but even those barriers would be breached at some point by the never-ending flow of silence.

Inexplicably, he had woken up in here.

Sometimes he would sleep so soundly, so wonderfully soundly, that waking up, almost unconsciously, had the feel of a new birth. No sense of time or place, for a brief and beautiful moment. This had been the exact feeling, but the beauty of it had very rapidly turned to utter fear.

He hadn't fallen asleep since, but perhaps he had been locked in the room for more than twenty-four hours. It was impossible to know.

At first he had assumed it was either a practical joke or some sort of a game; was he supposed to figure out how to escape?

It was definitely a game. Someone else's game, and there was no escape.

He had been out drinking with a friend, but he couldn't remember how or when the night had ended.

However, he now had this unspeakable feeling, magnified by the only sound he could hear; the thundering echo of his ever-accelerating heartbeat.

What bothered him the most was who this particular friend had been: the guy he had lied about to the police years ago, resulting in the friend spending time in jail, for no reason.

He had of course apologised, repeatedly, and they had put aside their differences, or so he thought. But now he wasn't so sure.

The lies had been instinctive and horrible, and he had regretted them ever since.

Perhaps this was his friend's ultimate revenge.

A cruel joke for cruel lies.

Funnily enough, at this moment he didn't miss the warmth and sparkle of the sunshine, or the salty scent of the sea. Most of all he missed the sounds, any sounds. The noise from the street, the indistinguishable voices at the bar, the unexplained sounds of the night-time in his house, the simple ticking of a clock. His wristwatch was missing.

He was afraid.

The silence scared him.

But what scared him the most was knowing how long his friend had been in jail, completely innocent: 433 days.

To be read while listening to 4'33" by John Cage

A DEATH IN FOUR PARTS

Shawn Reilly Simmons

1

The knock came just as Xavier Mendoza put pen to paper for the first time that day. It was an old-fashioned way of composing music but the fastest means of transferring the notes from his mind into something people would understand. He flung the felt-tipped pen at the grimy window of his third-floor walkup as the music slipped away from him. There was more knocking and then his chair legs scraped the kitchen floor as he heaved himself from the table and lurched towards the apartment's door.

"What is it now?" Mendoza seethed as he swung it open. "I am working, as if you didn't know."

Ruby stood in the doorway, a foil-covered bowl in her hands. "I brought soup. You have to eat."

Mendoza sighed. "I have no time. I have a deadline to meet." He gazed at the bowl and couldn't remember if he'd stopped working to eat the night before, or between which hours he'd slept.

Ruby moved through the narrow doorway, clutching the bowl tightly. She glanced into the kitchen at his unruly stacks of paper, jagged notes scrawled and then discarded onto the floor. "You can eat the soup while you work." Ruby was a slight woman with pointed features and small feet. Mendoza thought about the mice that scurried across the floor of his mother's basement whenever she came calling. He'd seen Ruby's bare feet a few times, and much more of her too, but not recently. Not since the commission that had come out of the blue for a new Xavier Mendoza composition.

He took the soup from her just as the door across the hall opened, revealing his bleary-eyed neighbour, just waking up at half-past noon.

"For the last time, keep it down out here!"

"Go back inside, mole," Mendoza growled. "Before I shine more light on you."

"Shut up, old man," his blinking neighbour snorted before retreating into his dark apartment. A moment later the wail of an electric guitar pressed its way into the hallway.

"Thank you for the soup, Ruby," Mendoza said, raising his voice over the noise. "I would invite you in but I must have a draft of this composition completed before Monday and it's…"

"Thursday?" Ruby asked, as if she wasn't sure.

Mendoza looked at her, alarmed. "It can only be Tuesday, no?"

Ruby dropped her eyes to the floor and shook her head. "I hope you like the soup."

The guitar came to a sudden stop and the mole man banged loudly from inside his apartment door, causing Ruby's shoulders to jump beneath her faded sweater. She'd told Mendoza she'd danced on Broadway once, but he wasn't sure if she meant in a show, or along the sidewalk. He hadn't thought to ask her much about how she ended up living at Musica, the apartment building designed to house the city's struggling artists at a rent they could afford.

Mendoza's lip curled as he glared at the closed door, then down at her. "Go away, now. Please. I can't work in all this madness.

2

The mewling of a cat on the fire escape woke Mendoza. Raising his head from the kitchen table, his cheek flat against the scarred wood, he tried to remember when he'd decided to put his head down and sleep. The cat rose on its back legs and scratched its paws at the glass, trying to find a way into the apartment. Mendoza watched it for a few minutes, wondering why it would want to.

A low groan escaped him as he attempted to stand, dull pain radiating through his limbs, his mouth brackish from stale coffee and old soup.

Mendoza groped the wall for the light switch then stumbled to the sink, drinking metallic-tasting water directly from the faucet. When he first moved to the city he lived in a very different part of town. He never could have pictured just twenty years later living in a place like Musica, accepting charity in every form it could be given. His debut symphony as a young composer was a runaway success, gifting him every luxury he could imagine, and a lifestyle all too easy to get used to. When he couldn't quite top that first work of staggering genius, his phone stopped ringing as often, and eventually his commissions dried up along with his accounts. By the time his third divorce was settled, the music in his mind had stopped playing. As hard as he tried, he couldn't force the notes to reveal themselves. Stephens, his former business manager, recommended he move to Musica, telling him it was an artists' refuge, a place for Mendoza to reinvigorate his creativity, surround himself with fellow musicians, and stop focusing on romantic entanglements and rediscover his muse. Mendoza wondered how much other bad advice he'd taken from Stephens over the years.

Standing up from the sink, Mendoza looked towards the window. The cat had moved on, spooked by the light, or the groaning man inside. He did not notice the trail of blood leading from the kitchen into the hallway until he turned back to the table to continue his work.

3

Mendoza worked until dawn. The music in his mind vibrated his skull, and it was all he could do to keep his hand moving as fast as the notes were revealed. When he closed his eyes, he could see them sliding by on the insides of his eyelids. His pulse skittered as he worked, and he pressed his free hand to his chest to make sure his heart was staying on the inside. The long-neglected fire inside him was lit, and Mendoza stoked it relentlessly through the morning hours, burning from the inside out, until he collapsed from exhaustion onto the kitchen floor, sheets of music falling around him.

He wept with relief and curled his legs into his chest, having reached the end of his composition. The gift that had abandoned him so many years earlier had returned. He'd created something just as good, if not better, than his debut. He was saved.

The blood on the floor had dried to a dark red. Mendoza sat up on the linoleum and wiped the tears of joy from his face. Ruby's thin knock sounded at the door.

Mendoza sighed and picked himself up from the floor. The pain he'd felt the night before had been replaced by a tight elastic feeling in his limbs. He walked stiffly to the door.

"More soup, Ruby?" Mendoza asked, looking down at his neighbour. He kept the door mostly closed, only sticking his head through the gap into the shabby hallway. Ruby looked more alive, less like a mouse and more like the cat scratching at his window.

"Have you seen Cruz?" Ruby asked.

"And who might that be?"

She glanced at the door across the hall.

"Ah, Cruz," Mendoza said through the gap. "I will say with every pleasure, no, I have not."

Ruby slid her eyes through the gap. "He owes me."

"A debt you might have to consider irretrievable," Mendoza said.

"Can I come in?" Ruby asked, her bony fingers pinning back her thinning hair over her ear.

"Sorry," Mendoza said. "It's a bit of a mess in here right now. Work and all. Raincheck?"

Ruby gave him a smile, revealing a gap where a tooth used to be before her fingers moved to cover her mouth. Mendoza closed the door before she could say anything else.

Mole man's body was still in the bathtub. Cruz, apparently his name.

Mendoza wondered how long it would take to cut him into smaller pieces and flush him down the toilet. Maybe he could feed some of him to the fire escape cat. Or maybe he'd take a little bit of him out every day in sandwich bags and drop him in different dumpsters around town.

Surely no one would miss Cruz, a man who never emerged from his dingy apartment in this forgotten wasteland of a building while the sun was shining. Mole man was some kind of musician, Mendoza supposed. He'd heard him returning late at night, drunkenly banging his guitar case against the banister as he navigated his way up the stairs, waking Mendoza up more often than not.

Mendoza didn't remember confronting Cruz during the night. He was in the throes of a creative frenzy, where nothing mattered besides getting the notes out of his brain and on to paper. He'd tried to picture finding Cruz out in the hall, envision the rage it must have taken to crack the man's rodent-like skull. Which is apparently what happened. He'd found no blood on his own hands. Mole man's end had brought about a new beginning, had relit Mendoza's creative fire.

Mendoza closed the bathroom door and went back to the kitchen. The composition needed to be put into order and read through again.

4

Mendoza slipped into his one remaining suit on Monday morning. He was overjoyed at the prospect of moving out of Musica and getting back to his previous life. This time he would be more appreciative, more cautious, less inclined to fall in love and entrust his fortune and gift to everyone who came into his orbit. His new composition was his ticket out of his current misery.

He glanced at Cruz in the tub as he finished brushing his teeth. "You and I are both out of here soon, old boy."

The familiar knock on the door caused his mood to slip briefly. "Ruby," he muttered under his breath as he stepped from the bathroom.

"I just wanted to wish you good luck," Ruby said. She stood in the hallway in a silk nightgown, one thin strap slipping from her shoulder. Mendoza opened the door wider, allowing her to enter. She slid her arms around his neck and kissed his cheek. He was tense at first, but then felt himself relaxing as she pressed her flesh close to his.

"Odd time for a social call," Mendoza murmured. "And attire."

"I knew you had that big meeting today and just wanted to wish you well," Ruby said, pulling away from him and heading towards the kitchen. "You finished your work?"

Mendoza glanced over his shoulder at the bathroom, and at the faint trail of blood under his feet. He'd tried to wipe it up, but he could see places where he'd missed in the morning light. "It's done."

"Good," Ruby said. "Coffee?"

Mendoza watched the silky gown press against her bony frame as she moved around the kitchen, making a pot of coffee and glancing at the neat stacks of music on the table. "I'm going to have to go soon, Ruby. I don't think I'm coming back. Ever."

Ruby frowned as she poured a cup of coffee and set it on the counter near him. He watched as she slid open a drawer and pulled out a knife.

"From what I've heard, you've always been lucky," Ruby said. "Cruz, on the other hand. He ran out of luck."

Mendoza glanced at the knife in her hand. "What do you mean?"

Ruby set the knife on the counter and went to kiss him. Mendoza pulled away from her.

"Stephens can't wait to get his hands on, well, this." Ruby gazed at the stacks of music on the table. "He's been angling for your big comeback. His well ran dry right along with yours until he landed this deal. He did come up with a few new tenants and a little extra cash for me to get to know you better."

"Stephens?" Mendoza said as a loud knock sounded on the door.

"He's very generous. With your money. Ask your ex."

"You know Stephens?" Mendoza said numbly, backing away from her.

"A dead composer's work is more valuable than a live one's. Add a murder scandal on top of it…? Sorry, but you're an easy mark. I do like you, Xavier. I'm glad you finally finished your work. Your time at Musica is over."

Ruby picked up the knife and stabbed herself in the stomach, bright red blood spreading its way across the pale silk gown as she fell to her knees.

"Police, don't move."

Mendoza watched Ruby fall to the ground as the police officers pushed their way into his apartment.

"He stabbed me," Ruby said.

Mendoza could tell she was going to be fine, the smile obvious behind her eyes. She'd only be a dancer, never an actress.

The officer closest to Mendoza raised his club, and everything went dark.

BOMBAY BLUES

Vaseem Khan

1

The body was slumped forward, still seated on its padded bench, face down on the keys, one arm dangling below, one held crookedly in his lap. It was obvious from the damage to the back of the skull that death must have been instantaneous, the bullet's impact thrusting him forward onto the piano.

Blood had splattered across sheet music held open on a carved wooden stand.

Persis turned to the hotel manager, a small man with receding hair and a pencil moustache. He dabbed at his sweating jowls with a sodden handkerchief. Despite the ceiling fan, the room was sweltering. Bombay was caught in the grip of the hottest summer in a decade. Many had already perished.

But none like this, she thought. "Who found him?"

The manager coughed uncomfortably beneath her gaze. His name was Sharma and he had been the one to call the Malabar House station some twenty minutes earlier.

"Elsa," he said. "She's one of our maids. She came in to clean the bathroom –" he pointed at the adjoining door – "saw him and…" He tailed away.

"What time was that?"

"Nine-fifteen."

"That's very precise."

"Don was on his regular break from his set. Every evening from nine to nine-twenty. I noted the time when Elsa came to fetch me."

"So he was murdered in that fifteen-minute window." It wasn't a question, but he nodded anyway, and wiped his forehead.

She wondered what it would do for the Taj's reputation once word got out that one of the world's most famous jazz musicians had been murdered in the hotel. No doubt many would flock to the place because of the notoriety.

She turned back to look at the body of Don Rollins.

She'd seen him in the newspapers, of course. Who hadn't?

Over the past two decades Bombay had become a magnet for jazz musicians, particularly black American pioneers of the genre, fleeing persecution in their homeland. Bombay had laid out the welcome mat and now every club or hotel worth its salt boasted its own resident quartet, quintet or – in the case of the Taj – a nine-piece extravaganza led by the now-late Rollins.

Independence may have been three years in the past, but thousands of foreigners remained in the city, congregating in the hotel's grand ballroom each evening with the Indians who, not so long ago, had been at their beck and call.

Or, at least, with the better class of Indian.

The Taj's doormen, towering Sikhs to a man, had strict instructions to keep out the riff-raff.

Some things hadn't changed with the changing of the guard.

The door opened behind them and Archie Blackfinch walked in, his black doctor's bag swinging by his side.

The tall, dark-haired Englishman nodded at Sharma, then smiled warmly at Persis, green eyes crinkling behind black-framed spectacles.

She looked away, not wanting him to see her expression.

Blackfinch, a crime scene specialist with the Metropolitan Police in London, had spent the past year seconded to the Bombay force – at their request – helping to establish a forensic crime lab in the city. He and Persis had successfully worked several high-profile cases together. Something had passed between them during that time and now the dominant emotion engendered by his presence was confusion. She'd fought too hard to qualify as India's first – and, to date, only – female police Inspector to throw it all away on an affair of the heart.

Besides, Blackfinch's oddities made him as infuriating as he was attract—

"Is that who I think it is?"

"Yes," she said.

He whistled, then set down his bag, dropped to his knees, unearthed a pair of gloves and snapped them on.

"Mohammed, set up the camera."

She hadn't noticed Blackfinch's young assistant enter. The rake-thin boy looked barely old enough to be wearing long trousers. His head was weighed down by a ridiculous stack of Brylcreemed hair. A moustache looked scrawled on with a crayon.

They waited as he set up his camera and tripod and photographed the body, and then the rest of the scene, the flashbulb popping loudly in the small room.

Once he was done, Blackfinch moved forward and gently lifted Rollins's head, examining the wounds.

"He was shot twice, one bullet in the back of the neck, one in the skull. He was shot at close range."

"How do you know that?" asked Sharma.

"Stippling," said Blackfinch, pointing with a gloved finger. "The gunman set the muzzle at the base of his neck."

"What does that mean?"

"Two things," said Persis. "The gunman wasn't sure of his aim; he took no chance of missing. And Rollins probably knew his killer."

"Why do you say that?"

"Because he turned his back on him."

"He was lost to his music," mused Blackfinch. "The killer simply walked up and shot him. A small-bore weapon, judging from his wounds. A .32, perhaps."

"We've found the gun," said Sharma.

They both turned to stare at him. He reached into his pocket and took out the weapon, wrapped in a handkerchief.

"Why did you move it?" Persis practically shouted.

Sharma quailed. "It was on the floor. I could hardly leave it there. What if someone else had happened to walk in?"

She glared at him.

"It doesn't matter," said Blackfinch. "I doubt we'll find any evidence on it. The only reason for the killer to leave it behind is because he knows we can't trace it back to him."

"You think he wore gloves?" said Persis.

"It would make sense." A thought occurred to him. "There'll probably be some blood droplets blown back onto the killer's clothing. Or, at the very least, his sleeves."

He continued searching the victim, rummaging in the pockets of the dead man's jacket.

He held up a short square of white card, scanned it quickly, then handed it to Persis. It said:

To my darling Sweet,
How do I love thee? Let me count the ways…
From your heart's Desire.

"Elizabeth Browning," she said. "It's the opening line from 'How Do I Love Thee?'"

"I wonder why he kept this," said Blackfinch. "I mean, I'd guess he gets a lot of such messages."

Sharma spoke, "Yes. He is very popular with women."

"This one meant something," thought Persis aloud.

She turned to Sharma. "We'll have to interview everyone."

He blinked at her. "There's almost two hundred people out there."

"Then we'd better get started, hadn't we?"

2

The interviews took less time than the hotel manager's concern had warranted.

The short timeframe for the killing meant that very few had had the opportunity, let alone the means or the motive.

Rollins had left the stage for his break at nine, handing the reins to his protégé, a trumpet player named Duke Fernandes – a Goan of Portuguese extraction. Duke's real name was Gerard. As a rising star on the jazz scene, he'd kept the evening's guests firmly in their seats.

The few that *had* stepped out from the ballroom had alibis for those crucial fifteen minutes.

As she completed her interviews, Persis was surprised at the number of women openly weeping. She knew that Rollins had a reputation as a charmer; he was a handsome man, with a loud personality and the wild habits to match. Legend had it that he'd slept with the wife of a prominent white politician back in his home state of Louisiana and had been run out of town. Fearing for his life, he'd toured Europe, spending six months in Paris and London before ending up in Bombay.

One man – middling height, rotund, dressed in an ill-fitting tuxedo – took particular exception to her questions. "Do you know who I am?"

"No."

"Sen. I bankrolled this show." He waved a lit cigar at her.

"You knew Don Rollins?"

"Very well. He was a great musician. His death is a real loss." He didn't sound as if he was grieving. "He was teaching my daughter to play piano." He pointed his cigar at a strikingly beautiful young woman, no more than nineteen, tall, with thick black hair and large eyes. "Said she has a real gift for it. I suppose I'll have to find someone else."

Her name was Akanksha and she was inconsolable, leaning against her mother for support as if she might faint at any moment. Persis found the whole thing overly dramatic.

She watched as her father led the girl away, the man's irritation barely held in check.

The girl's mother, Radha, apologised. "You know how impressionable girls can be at that age."

Persis didn't know. She'd never been the impressionable type.

Having completed the interviews, she released the guests, watching as they ran for the exits.

Within the hour, news of Rollins's death would have raced around the city, if not the country. By tomorrow it would be front-page news.

The pressure to solve the crime quickly would fall squarely on her shoulders.

3

"Yes, I hired him," said Pickett, plucking the cigarette from his mouth and waving it at her. "Worst damned decision I ever made."

The American shifted in his seat, scratching at his beard.

Persis was surprised by the admission. Samuel Pickett was the band's manager, a short, fat man reeking of sweat and tobacco.

"Why do you say that?"

"The man was incorrigible. Women, booze, gambling. He had more vices than the Devil."

"Did that affect his performances?"

"No. He was one of those strange cats who played better the drunker he got. Besides, the crowd loved him. He could have pitched a piano at their heads, they'd still have adored him. It's the reason I took him on."

"I thought the Taj hired him."

He chuckled nastily. "*I* brought Rollins to India. Found a sponsor willing to bankroll a nine-piece band. Negotiated the deal with the Taj. Drummed up publicity, made sure we were the hottest ticket in town."

"But Rollins was putting all that at risk with his behaviour?"

"The way he was carrying on, our sponsor was just about ready to give us the boot."

"Who *is* your sponsor?"

"Indian guy by the name of Sen. Rohan Sen. One of these types born with a tin ear but wants to be held up as a patron of the arts."

Sen. The man she had interviewed in the ballroom.

"He was in the audience."

"Yep. Planned on giving Don a dressing down after the show."

"Sen was going to fire Rollins?"

He puffed on his cigarette. "Sen's not the type to get his hands dirty. If he wants someone's bones broken he pays people to do it."

"Perhaps he paid someone to scare Rollins straight. Perhaps the plan went wrong."

His eyes narrowed. "Tell me, what's it like in this la-la land you live in? But I guess that's what happens when you let women put on a uniform."

She coloured, but bit her tongue. "I suppose you were angry with him too. Rollins, I mean. He was about to cost you a lucrative contract."

He snatched the cigarette from his mouth, reddening. "What are you getting at?"

"Where were you between nine and nine-fifteen?"

"Right here. In this office."

"Alone?"

"Who else would there be?"

"So you have no alibi?"

He staggered to his feet. "I don't have to listen to this."

"Your office is just yards from Rollins's dressing room."

"So is the fire exit at the end of the corridor. Has it occurred to you that anyone could have walked in off the street and shot him?"

"Why would someone do that?"

"Because celebrity is catnip to the nutcases. Look at what happened to your Gandhi fellow."

He rhymed *Gandhi* with *candy*.

She didn't bother to explain that Gandhi's assassination had come in the wake of the sectarian violence engendered by Partition, at the hands of an Indian nationalist who believed the Mahatma was pandering to the country's Muslim minority.

"Did Rollins have any enemies?"

"Sure. Show me a man in the spotlight who doesn't."

"Anyone specific?"

He shifted on his feet, but said nothing. Something about his manner told her that he was holding something back.

"If you have any information you must tell me. Otherwise, I can always take a closer look at *you*."

He let his cigarette fall to the tiles, crushed it under his shoe. "It's probably nothing. A few days ago, he and Duke got into an argument. Almost came to blows. I heard Duke say he'd kill him."

"Duke Fernandes?"

He nodded.

"What were they fighting about?"

"I couldn't make out. After I broke it up, they wouldn't say." He shrugged. "But, hey, they're musicians. It's par for the course."

"You must have *some* idea."

He hesitated. "I can guess."

4

"Don was my mentor. Why would I threaten to kill him?"

Duke Fernandes was still dressed in his performance outfit, a baggy zoot suit with two-toned shoes. He had removed his trademark Fedora, revealing close-cropped black hair.

"Rollins made an improper advance towards your wife."

His expression froze. Behind him the woman in question, Mary Fernandes, straightened. "Who told you that?"

"That's not important. Is it true?"

Mary glanced at her husband. "It was a misunderstanding. Quickly cleared up."

"You'd be surprised how many misunderstandings lead to murder."

"You can't possibly think Duke had anything to do with Don's death?"

Persis turned to face Duke. "The hotel manager says you left the stage during the time Rollins was on a break."

He frowned. "I stepped backstage for a smoke. I was barely gone for a couple of minutes."

"Rollins's dressing room is just along a corridor running from behind the stage. You could have gone to his room, shot him, and returned within two minutes."

His face was thunderous. "I had nothing to do with Don's death."

With that, he stormed out, Mary Fernandes following on his heels.

*   *   *

Persis turned to face the third person in the room, so far silent. He was a tall, black man with a mournful look, sat on a low sofa like a praying mantis, a saxophone resting between his knees.

His name was Jerome Jackson and he was the band's most senior member.

"Mr Jackson—"

"Call me Jerome," he said.

"Jerome. Is there anything you can tell me about Don Rollins's death?"

"I can tell you that Mary's lying to you."

"Please explain."

He lifted his saxophone and blew a succession of short notes. "Couple of days ago, I walked in on her and Sweet—"

"Sweet?"

"Don. Sweet was his nickname."

Something about this struck her. The note. *To my darling Sweet.* "Please continue."

"They were, how can I put this, all over each other."

"Were they having an affair?"

"Affair is too grand a word. Sweet – Don – didn't go in for that sort of thing. He was more the love-'em-and-leave-'em type. You dig?"

She paused. "Did Mary leave the stage between nine and nine-fifteen?"

"Now that you mention it… She stepped out for a few minutes to go powder her nose."

He played another long note on the saxophone. "Don was a legend, but he wasn't what you would call a stand-up guy. He started off as a blues singer, then he got the jazz bug. Practically invented a lot of the new sounds coming out of the South. He was a real virtuoso, an improviser like no one else I've ever played with. I suppose the success went to his head. He thought he could do just about anything and there'd never be a bill to pay afterwards. It's a shame he's dead, but I can't say I'm surprised at the way he left the stage."

5

She found Mary Fernandes in the hotel's Harbour bar, nursing a gin.

There was no sign of Duke Fernandes.

"When did your husband find out about your affair with Rollins?"

Mary leaned back on her stool, her sequinned evening gown shimmering in the chandelier lights.

"He didn't find out because there was nothing to find out."

"You were witnessed in a passionate embrace with Rollins. Please don't waste my time by denying it."

Her eyes widened, but she said nothing.

Persis waited.

Mary took a gulp from her glass, then smoothed down the front of her dress. "It was a mistake. We'd both had too much to drink. Duke and I had had a huge fight… Don just leaned in and kissed me. I let him. I regretted it immediately." She was close to tears. "I swear to you, nothing happened."

"Why were you and Duke fighting?"

"He's insanely jealous."

"Of you and Rollins?"

Mary shook her head. "No. Of Don. Don had a natural talent. He never needed to work at it. Duke spends every waking minute practising, composing. When Samuel hired him for the band he thought his time had finally come. In many ways, it has. But it's not enough for him. He can't stand the way Don gets all the adulation. The papers refer to him as Don's protégé – but the truth is Don didn't teach him a thing. Don was never that kind of man."

Persis pulled the note from her pocket. "Did you send him this?"

Mary scanned it quickly. "No."

"Do you know who did?"

"Don used to get dozens of these every night."

"But this was the only one he kept in his pocket." She paused. "Was there anyone he *was* in love with?"

Mary smiled wanly. "It would take quite a woman to have made Don Rollins fall out of love with himself."

6

"It has to be the husband. This Duke chap. He had motive *and* opportunity."

Roshan Seth, Superintendent of Police, and her boss, prowled his office, a glass of whisky sloshing in his hand. Seth, like the rest of them, had ended up here because he'd fallen afoul of those who now ran the Indian Police Service.

In Seth's case the accusation was that he'd executed his office a little too zealously under the country's erstwhile masters. Memories ran deep. As soon as the new regime took over, just three short years ago, Seth had been shunted to Malabar House, one of the city's smallest stations, tucked out of sight – and mind – in the basement of a corporate building, and populated with the unwanted and the undesirable.

Persis had qualified for a berth by the simple expedient of being a woman.

"I disagree," she now said.

"Well, do you have any better leads?"

"Not yet."

"You have witnesses who saw him leave the stage at the time Rollins was murdered. He hated the man. What more do you need?"

She set her peaked cap back onto her head. "I need to be *sure*."

7

By the time she reached home it was past midnight. The bookshop was dark; her father had gone upstairs. She knew he'd probably have fallen asleep on the sofa waiting for her, his wheelchair set to one side, Akbar, her Persian tom, curled up beside him.

He never went to bed until he knew she was safely home.

Growing up without a mother or siblings, Sam Wadia had always been her closest companion.

She knew he would have left the shop unlocked. He'd never bothered to lock it, not even during the years of the Quit India movement, and the darker days of Partition, when protesters and rioters would surge down the alley, stopping only to hurl a brick through the shop's glass frontage.

The Wadia Book Emporium bore its scars with grace.

Above the façade, twin stone vultures roosted on a plinth, ever-present reminders of her Parsee heritage: their real-life counterparts were essential to the process of *excarnation*, the eating of the dead, placed in the Towers of Silence, at the very heart of the city. In Bombay's heaving mix of religions and cultures, the Zoroastrians had long ago carved a unique niche.

Inside the shop, the familiar smell of books, old and new, rose up to greet her.

She switched on a light, then went to the poetry section.

Quickly, she found the volume she was looking for.

Flicking through the pages, she stopped at Elizabeth Barrett Browning's 'How Do I Love Thee?' She took out the note they'd found on Rollins, and set it beside the book.

She read the poem, searching for some meaning, some clue as to why he would have kept it with him.

But there was nothing.

Frustrated, she looked again at the note. *To my darling Sweet…* Sweet. What had Jerome Jackson said? That 'Sweet' was Don Rollins's nickname. She supposed the opening line was a play on words, a saccharine greeting specifically addressing Rollins.

What if the same might be applied to the last line?

From your heart's Desire.

Desire.

Could that be the name of a female admirer? Or a nickname?

Desire…

And suddenly it came to her, a flash of insight that lifted her from her seat and sent her back out into the night.

8

The whitewashed mansion stood proudly atop a hill in the exclusive Malabar Hill area, palm trees swaying out front, and a brace of guards sitting on stools by the gate.

She was let in by a house servant and led to a drawing room where, in due course, she was joined by the three members of the Sen family: Rohan, Radha and their daughter Akanksha.

Sen's annoyance was obvious. "What the devil do you mean turning up here in the middle of the night? I've a good mind to call the commissioner."

Radha put a hand on her husband's arm. "Let us hear what she has to say. Perhaps she has an update on Don's death."

"Yes, madam, I do," said Persis. She took a deep breath. She knew that she was gambling – to a certain extent. "We know that Rollins was killed between nine and nine-fifteen. This means only a handful of people had the opportunity to murder him. In such cases we try to narrow down our list of suspects by looking at motive.

"Don Rollins was not a pleasant man. He was selfish and arrogant. Because of this there are many people who might have wanted to harm him. But my own belief is that his killer is right here in this room."

Sen stared at her, then roared: "Have you lost your mind? Are you suggesting *I* killed the man?"

He could not have been more enraged if she had accused him of killing Gandhi.

"You, your wife and your daughter were seated at a private table. *They* both left to go to the washroom just after nine. You were left alone. You told me earlier that you hadn't left your seat, but the fact is that no one else can verify that. With everyone's attention on the stage, and no one else at your table, you might have slipped out for a few minutes."

"This is going to cost you your job!" Sen hollered. His face was red and he looked on the verge of apoplexy.

Persis relented. "But I don't think you killed Rollins."

She took out the note and turned to the two women. "*To my darling Sweet, How do I love thee? Let me count the ways… From your heart's Desire.*"

She looked directly at the girl. "Desire. The meaning of the name Akanksha in Hindi is desire. You wrote this note to Rollins. You were in love with him. He seduced you. He may even have fallen in love with you. That's why he kept the note, while discarding similar ones."

The girl stared at her, white-faced, then burst into tears, smothering her face with her hands.

Behind her, her father collapsed onto the sofa. "You – you…!" But words failed him. The horror of the picture Persis had painted had overwhelmed him.

"Inspector," said Radha, "you cannot possibly be suggesting that my daughter killed Don Rollins. May I remind you, we were both in the washroom together when he was killed."

Persis ignored this and turned to the girl. "Akanksha, when you were in the washroom, did you go into one of the cubicles?"

The girl took an age to respond, then nodded.

"How long were you in there?"

She blinked. "About five minutes."

Persis turned to Radha. "Plenty of time for you to slip out, walk to Rollins's dressing room, kill him and return before she even noticed that you were gone."

For a moment, the woman seemed speechless. "I suppose you have some proof to back up such a wild accusation?"

"Your clothes. Microscopic particles of Don Rollins's blood and residue from the gunshot will have blown back onto your clothing. It won't take long for us to find them. You made the mistake of walking right up to him and shooting him. You were nervous of missing your mark. My guess is that you haven't fired a weapon in anger before."

Radha blinked and then her shoulders seemed to slump. Guilt had that effect on people, Persis knew, particularly those unused to carrying it.

"I had to do something," she murmured. "He was ruining my daughter. Who will marry her now?"

It was a question Persis could not answer.

India in 1950 may have become a sovereign nation, but in many ways it was still a victim of its past. Social attitudes hadn't changed that much, even in a city as cosmopolitan as Bombay.

But that wasn't her problem.

She stepped forward. "Radha Sen, I am arresting you for the murder of Don Rollins."

BIOGRAPHIES

Abi Silver

I have been writing stories for as long as I can remember. Growing up with a house full of books (my parents were teachers), I was inspired from an early age to believe I could join the ranks of my heroes. But I accept that I probably could not have produced 'The Pinocchio Brief', the first in my Burton & Lamb series of courtroom dramas, without my experience as a lawyer to guide me along the way.

My stories feature the dynamic legal duo of Judith Burton (more experienced, sometimes acid-tongued) criminal barrister and Constance Lamb (younger, determined and more circumspect) solicitor, who defend suspects accused of a variety of serious crimes set in contemporary London.

In every story, quite apart from the challenges of the case itself, there's a new and topical issue which must be tackled, whether it's lie-detecting software or the filming and livestreaming of trials for public consumption. But Judith and Constance take it in their stride, as they must, if they are going to find justice for their clients.

abisilver.co.uk
@abisilver16

Alison Joseph

Alison Joseph is a London-based crime writer and radio dramatist. She was born in North London and educated at Leeds University. After graduating she worked as a presenter on a local radio station, then, moving back to London, for Channel 4. She later became a partner in an independent production company and one of its commissions was the series *Through the Devil's Gateway*, about women and religion, presented by Helen Mirren.

Alison has written about twenty-five radio plays and adaptations, including the Sony award-winning abridgement of Captain Corelli's Mandolin. She is the author of the series of novels featuring Sister Agnes, a contemporary detective nun based in South London, as well as a crime novel about particle physics, featuring DI Berenice Killick, called *Dying to Know*. She is the author of three novellas featuring a fictional Agatha Christie as a detective. Her new series stars Malone, a London-based detective from Galway. Alison was Chair of the Crime Writers' Association from 2013 to 2015 and is a founder member of the Killer Women collective.

alisonjoseph.com
@AlisonJoseph1

Andrew Taylor

Since my first novel, *Caroline Minuscule* (1982), I've written nearly fifty more, mainly for adults but a few for children. They include the Dougal Series; espionage thrillers; the Lydmouth novels (set in the 1950s); the Roth Trilogy (filmed for TV as *Fallen Angel*); *The American Boy* (a Richard & Judy bookclub choice about the boyhood of Edgar Allan Poe); historical crime novels including *Bleeding Heart Square* and *The Scent of Death*); and, most recently, the Marwood and Lovett series set in Restoration London, which began with *The Ashes of London*. My most recent novel, the fifth in this series, is *The Royal Secret* (April 2021).

I review for *The Times* and the *Spectator* (I was the *Spectator*'s crime fiction critic for ten years. I inaugurated the CWA New Writing Competition, which became the CWA Debut Dagger, in 1998. I've also edited *The Author*, the journal of the Society of Authors, and written its regular Grub Street column since 2004.

andrew-taylor.co.uk
@andrewjrtaylor

Antony M. Brown

Author of the *Cold Case Jury* true crime books, Antony also writes fiction in his *Crime & Mystery Hour* series – short eBooks of crime fiction and essays designed for discerning but time-pressed readers. He is also co-founder of Wow-Vinyl, a website dedicated to the 'golden years' of the British chart single (1977–85), which inspired his short story.

coldcasejury.com
wow-vinyl.com

Art Taylor

Art Taylor is the author of *On the Road with Del & Louise: A Novel in Stories*, winner of the Agatha Award for Best First Novel. He has won three additional Agatha Awards, an Anthony Award, a Macavity Award, and three consecutive Derringer Awards for his short fiction, and his work has appeared in *Best American Mystery Stories*. He also edited *Murder Under the Oaks: Bouchercon Anthology 2015*, winner of the Anthony Award for Best Anthology or Collection. He is an associate professor of English at George Mason University, and he contributes frequently to the *Washington Post*, the *Washington Independent Review of Books*, and *Mystery Scene Magazine*.

arttaylorwriter.com

Brian Price

Brian Price is a chemist and biologist who retired from the Environment Agency in 2016. He is the author of *Crime Writing: How to write the science* and runs a website offering tips on science for crime writers (crimewriterscience.co.uk). He is an avid reader of crime fiction and has also written a number of short stories, one of which was a runner-up in the Weston-super-Mare Literary Festival 2019 and another was shortlisted in the Chorley Writers Circle competition in 2018. He taught science and technology courses for the Open University for twenty-six years. Previous books include *P for Pollution* and *C for Chemicals* (with Mike Birkin). His first crime novel is *Fatal Trade*.

brianpriceauthor.co.uk
@crimewritersci

Cath Staincliffe

Cath Staincliffe is a bestselling, award-winning novelist, radio playwright and the creator of ITV's hit series, *Blue Murder*, starring Caroline Quentin as DCI Janine Lewis.

Cath's books have been shortlisted for the CWA best first novel award, for the Dagger in the Library twice and twice for the Short Story Dagger, winning in 2012. She was a winner of the WGGB Best Radio Drama Award in 2019. Cath's Sal Kilkenny private eye series features a single-parent sleuth working the mean streets of Manchester. Her debut *Looking For Trouble* was serialised on Woman's Hour on BBC Radio 4. *Trio*, a stand-alone novel, moved away from crime to explore adoption and growing up in the 1960s, informed by Cath's own experience. *Letters To My Daughter's Killer* was selected for Specsavers Crime Thriller Book Club in 2014 and featured on ITV3's Crime Thriller Club. Cath also writes the *Scott & Bailey* novels based on the popular UK TV series. Cath created the probate detective series *Legacy* for BBC Radio 4 and guest writes on the *Stone* police drama.

Her recent stand-alone novels examine the impact of crime on ordinary families. *The Girl in the Green Dress* was inspired by her experience as the parent of a transgender child. Cath's latest book, *Running out of Road*, is a race against time, played out in the brooding wilderness, the limestone gorges and gritstone edges of the Derbyshire Peaks when eleven-year-old Scarlett is abducted on her way home from school. Cath is one of the founding members of Murder Squad – a group of Northern crime writers who give readings, talks and signings around the country. Cath was born in Bradford, Yorkshire, UK and now lives in Manchester, Lancashire with her family. You can follow her on Twitter, where she hangs about when she should be busy writing!

cathstaincliffe.co.uk
@CathStaincliffe

Catherine Aird

Catherine Aird is the author of some twenty-six detective novels and volumes of short stories, many of which have appeared in translation and one made into a film. She has also edited several biographies, produced a number of local histories, and written a *son-et-lumiere*, a video, etc.

Born in 1930 and educated in Huddersfield in the West Riding of Yorkshire, she has lived since the war in a village in east Kent, where for many years she took an active interest in local affairs as well as acting as a dispenser and receptionist in her father's general practice.

She was made an MBE for services to the Guide Movement and awarded an Honorary MA by the University of Kent at Canterbury. She is currently working on another detective story featuring Inspector

C.D. Sloan, while a third collection of short stories is in the course of publication.

catherineaird.com

Chris Simms

Chris Simms has worked in airports, nightclubs, post offices and telesales centres. Along with nominations for Crime Writers' Association Daggers and the Theakston's Crime Novel of the Year award, Chris was selected by Waterstones as one of their '25 authors for the future'.

The idea for his debut novel, *Outside the White Lines*, came to him in the early hours of the morning while broken down on the hard shoulder of the M40. His series of DI Spicer novels – psychological thrillers set very firmly in Manchester – follow the police detective's fortunes as he pursues mad, bad and deadly individuals through the city's ever-changing landscape.

More recently, he has launched a new series featuring DC Sean Blake – an inexperienced young detective fighting to establish himself in the close-knit Serious Crimes Unit of Manchester's police.

Chris says he is drawn to books that give insights into unusual minds. The twisted desires of Frederick in John Fowles' *The Collector*; the tormented thoughts of Scobie in Graham Greene's *Heart of the Matter*; the violent urges of Francie in Patrick McCabe's *Butcher Boy* are all books Chris states had an influence in shaping him as a writer.

chrissimms.info

Christine Poulson

Before Christine Poulson turned to crime, she was a respectable academic with a PhD in History of Art and had written widely on nineteenth-century art and literature. Her book, *The Quest for the Grail: Arthurian Legend in British Art 1840–1920* (Manchester University Press, 1999), was shortlisted for a Mythopoeic Award for non-fiction. During her career as an art historian, she worked at Birmingham Museum and Art Gallery and at the William Morris Society at Kelmscott House, London. Later she was a lecturer in Art History at a college in Cambridge.

The city of Cambridge and the surrounding Fens, with their unique and sinister atmosphere, provided the setting for her first novel, *Dead Letters*, published in 2002, which featured literary historian and accidental sleuth Cassandra James. *Stage Fright*, the second in the series, came out in 2003, and *Footfall* in 2006. *Invisible*, a stand-alone suspense novel, was published by Accent Press in 2014. Christine's short stories have appeared in CWA anthologies, *Ellery Queen's Mystery Magazine*, and elsewhere. 'A Tour of the Tower' was shortlisted for a Short Mystery Fiction Derringer Award. In 2018 she was shortlisted for the Margery Allingham Prize and the CWA Short Story Dagger.

Deep Water, published by Lion Hudson in 2016, is the first in a series set in Ely and the biotech industry, and features scientist Katie Flanagan and patent lawyer, Daniel Marchmont. *Cold, Cold Heart*, the second in the series, sees Katie taking up a research post at an isolated base in Antarctica where six months of darkness are about to begin and the ten-strong team are about to become nine. In the third, *An Air That Kills*, Kate goes undercover in a high-security research lab where the scientists are as deadly as the diseases.

christinepoulson.co.uk
@ChrissiePoulson

David Stuart Davies

David is a writer, editor and performer, the author of fourteen published novels and several non-fiction works.

He is a member of the national committee of the Crime Writers' Association and edits *Red Herrings*, their monthly publication. He is a member of the Detection Club and the Baker Street Irregulars. He also edited the crime fiction magazine *Sherlock* from 1996 to 2006.

David's latest novel is *The Scarlet Coven*, a 1936 New York thriller with a supernatural edge. He has also created two modern series of crime novels, featuring wartime London private detective Johnny Hawke and 1980s Yorkshire noir Detective Inspector Paul Snow.

davidstuartdavies.co.uk
@DStuartDavies

Dea Parkin

Dea Parkin, Secretary of the CWA, has been an Associate Member since 2012 and owns and manages editorial consultancy Fiction Feedback.

Fiction Feedback was established in 2008 and provides top-quality developmental and copy-editing as well as critiques for novels, novel extracts and short stories. The focus is on crime and historical fiction.

Dea writes short stories and has had several shortlisted or placed in competitions. She is writing or redrafting several novels, and in 2015 published a short collection of poetry called *Any Other Business*.

fictionfeedback.co.uk

@deawriter

Jason Monaghan

I love writing, I love mysteries and I love to uncover the secrets of the past. A sense of time and place is crucial to a novel, and is at the forefront of the new series of thrillers set in the 1930s which I'm currently writing.

I was born in a Yorkshire village from a line of miners and steelworkers, and as is often the case in my generation I was the first in my family to go to university. I gained a PhD from the London Institute of Archaeology, specialising in Roman pottery and working on various excavations and shipwreck projects. Ultimately becoming Director of Guernsey Museums, I've also been able to maintain a steady output of non-fiction books plus the historical novel *Glint of Light on Broken Glass*.

I travel widely, and as frequently as I can, liking nothing better than hitting the open road in my Jeep with the top open and a Country and Western soundtrack. My writing, adventures and digs provide ample material for my blog and Facebook page.

monaghanfoss.com/

@jasonthriller

Kate Ellis

Kate Ellis was born and brought up in Liverpool and studied drama in Manchester. She is married with two grown-up sons and lives in North Cheshire. She worked in teaching, marketing and accountancy, none of which she particularly enjoyed, before discovering that writing crime fiction was what she'd wanted to do all along!

Before 'turning to crime' she first enjoyed literary success as winner of the North West Playwrights Competition in 1990. Her keen interest in history and archaeology features strongly in her books. Described by *The Times* as 'a beguiling author who interweaves past and present', she has written twenty-five novels featuring black archaeology graduate DI Wesley Peterson and his Liverpool-born boss DCI Gerry Heffernan and five crime novels with a supernatural twist featuring DI Joe Plantagenet – as well as a standalone historical mystery, *The Devil's Priest*, set in Tudor Liverpool, which is now available on Kindle. Kate has also written an historical trilogy set in the aftermath of the First World War. She also writes short stories and has been shortlisted twice for the CWA Short Story Dagger and for a Barry Award in the USA.

Kate was elected as a member of the Detection Club in 2014 and was awarded the CWA Dagger in the Library in 2019.

Her latest Wesley Peterson novel is *The Stone Chamber* and the latest in her Joe Plantagenet series is *Walking by Night*. The final book in her trilogy set in the North West of England shortly after World War One is *The House of the Hanged Woman*, now out in paperback.

kateellis.co.uk
@kateellisauthor

L.C. Tyler

L.C. (Len) Tyler is a British writer of comic crime fiction. His Elsie and Ethelred mysteries feature Ethelred Tressider, a crime writer, and Elsie Thirkettle, his literary agent. L.C. Tyler was raised in Essex and read geography at Oxford University before going on to study systems analysis at City University in London.

He worked for the British Council before becoming Chief Executive of the Royal College of Paediatrics and Child Health, then a full-time writer. His Ethelred and Elsie series has twice been nominated for an Edgar Award in the US. *The Herring in the Library* and *Crooked Herring* both won the Goldsboro Last Laugh Award at Bristol Crimefest. He has published a number of short stories in magazines and anthologies, including the CWA's *Guilty Consciences*. His latest crime series is set in the seventeenth century and features the lawyer John Grey. He is a former Chair of the Crime Writers' Association.

lctyler.com
@lenctyler

Leo McNeir

Leo McNeir is the author of the series of crime novels with a waterways setting featuring Marnie Walker, her lover Ralph Lombard, her close friend Anne Price and several others. He doesn't guarantee that all the characters, even some of the central core, will feature in every book. Some of them may get bumped off from time to time. That's crime fiction for you!

leomcneir.com

Martin Edwards

Martin Edwards received the CWA Diamond Dagger, the highest honour in UK crime writing, in 2020. His recent novels include *Mortmain Hall* and *Gallows Court*; the latter was nominated for two awards. In 2018 he received the CWA Dagger in the Library, awarded by UK librarians, for his body of work. He has won the Edgar, Agatha, Macavity (twice), and Poirot awards in the USA, and the CWA Short Story Dagger, the CWA Margery Allingham Prize, and the H.R.F. Keating award (twice) in the UK. His latest Lake District Mystery is *The Crooked Shore*, published in 2021. The series began with *The Coffin Trail* (shortlisted for the Theakston's prize for best British crime novel) and includes *The Arsenic Labyrinth* (shortlisted for the Lakeland Book of the Year award). He has written eight novels about Liverpool lawyer Harry Devlin, starting with *All the Lonely People*.

The author of about seventy short stories, he has also edited forty anthologies and published ten non-fiction books, including a study of crime scene investigation techniques and real-life cases. A well-known critic and writer about the crime fiction genre, past and present, with *The Golden Age of Murder* exemplifying his knowledge of crime fiction and its authors in the 1920s and 1930s, Martin is President and Archivist of the world-famous Detection Club and a former Chair of the CWA. He is also series consultant to the British Library's highly successful series of crime classics, and has published *The Story of Classic Crime in 100 Books.* and *Howdunit,* two more award-winning books. Martin is currently also Archivist of the Crime Writers' Association and editor of its annual anthology.

martinedwardsbooks.com

Neil Daws

Neil Daws has been a decent waiter, an average baker and a pretty good printer but most notably a diligent civil servant, retiring in 2015 after thirty years, twenty spent in security and counter terrorism. Other short-term jobs taken many years ago include enthusiastic tin-rattler for the Royal National Institute for the Blind, a dog-fearing leaflet distributor and a sticker-on of cork tiles in a hotel foyer.

Enthralled by real-life tales of adventure and exploration (Sir Ranulph Fiennes is one of his heroes – although cutting off frostbitten fingers with a hacksaw seems a bit extreme), he became a hiker, skier, lover of travel, history and maps, and is a long-standing Fellow of the Royal Geographical Society.

An alumnus of the Curtis Brown Creative writing school, he achieved Highly Commended in the Blue Pencil Agency's First Novel Award 2019, where he met his agent, Nelle Andrew of Rachel Mills Literary (RML).

He is finally making use of his Open University psychology degree and interest in history, especially World War Two, to write historical crime featuring serial killers and all manner of unsavoury people. His debut novel, *A Quiet Place to Kill*, was published by Thomas & Mercer in September 2021.

neildaws.com
@NeilDaws59

Paul Charles

Paul Charles was born and raised in the Northern Irish countryside. He is the author of the acclaimed Detective Inspector Christy Kennedy series. The most recent title, *A Pleasure To Do Death With You*, is the tenth in the series. He is also the author of two Inspector Starrett Mysteries set in Donegal and a couple of music-related novels, namely *The First of the True Believers* (2002), which uses the story of the Beatles as a backdrop, and *The Last Dance* (2012), set in the legendary Irish Showband scene of the late 1950s and the early 1960s. Charles may be unique in that not only was he around in the sixties, but he also remembers the decade vividly.

The Lonesome Heart is Angry, a rural mystery set in the Ulster countryside of the 1960s, was published in 2014.

paulcharlesbooks.com

Paul Gitsham

Paul Gitsham started his career as a biologist: after gaining a PhD in molecular biology, he worked in laboratories in Manchester and Toronto, before retraining as a science teacher. Along the way he had spells as the world's most over-qualified receptionist and spent time working for a major UK bank, ensuring that terrorists, foreign dictators and other international ne'er-do-wells hadn't embarrassed the institution by managing to deposit their ill-gotten gains in a Children's Trust Fund.

Paul's final school reports from primary school said that he would never achieve anything if his handwriting didn't improve; a somewhat kinder note urged him to become the next Roald Dahl. If anything, his handwriting has got worse and, unless Mr Dahl also wrote police procedurals under a pseudonym, he has failed on both counts.

Paul is the author of the DCI Warren Jones series, soon numbering eleven entries. The latest in the series is *Out of Sight*.

paulgitsham.com
@dcijoneswriter

Peter Lovesey

Peter Lovesey has published forty-one novels and five collections of short stories since he joined the CWA in 1969. His work has been adapted for radio, TV and film and translated into over twenty languages. His first novel, *Wobble to Death*, won the Macmillan/Panther first crime novel prize of £1,000 and featured Sergeant Cribb, a Victorian policeman, the first of an eight-book series that was televised by Granada in 1979-80, starring Alan Dobie as Cribb.

He has written three other series, one featuring Bertie, the Prince of Wales, as an inept amateur sleuth, and two with modern police: Hen Mallin, a female Chief Inspector, and Peter Diamond, a detective superintendent with Bath CID. The long-running Diamond series has won two Silver Daggers and a number of American awards, including the Anthony, the Barry and the Macavity.

Peter won the Silver Dagger for *Waxwork* in 1978 and the Gold Dagger for *The False Inspector Dew* in 1982 and in 2000 he was honoured by the CWA with the Cartier Diamond Dagger. In 2018 the Mystery Writers of America made him a Grand Master. He is also a Grand Master of the Swedish Academy of Detection and a winner of the French Grand Prix de Littérature Policière. He was Chair of the CWA in 1991–92. His son Phil is also a crime writer and both father and son have won the CWA Short Story Dagger.

peterlovesey.com

Ragnar Jonasson

Ragnar Jonasson is the author of the bestselling Dark Iceland series, set in and around Siglufjörður, and featuring Detective Ari Thor. He was born in Iceland and works as an Attorney at Law and writer in Reykjavik. Before embarking on a writing career, Ragnar translated fourteen Agatha Christie novels into Icelandic. Ragnar is the co-founder of the Reykjavik international crime-writing festival Iceland Noir.

ragnarjonasson.com

Shawn Reilly Simmons

Shawn Reilly Simmons is the author of seven novels in the Red Carpet Catering Mystery series and of over twenty published short stories. Shawn's stories have appeared in the Malice Domestic, Best New England Crime Stories, Bouchercon, Crime Writers' Association, Writers' Police Academy, and *Writers Crushing Covid-19* anthologies.

Shawn's short story 'The Last Word' won the Agatha for Best Short Story, and she also won the Anthony Award as co-editor of the anthology in which it appeared, *Malice Domestic 14: Mystery Most Edible*.

In addition to writing, Shawn also serves on the Board of Malice Domestic, and is Managing Editor at Level Best Books. She is a member of Sisters in Crime, Mystery Writers of America, the International Thriller Writers, and the Crime Writers' Association in the UK. She lives in historic downtown Frederick, Maryland, with her husband, son, and French Bulldog.

shawnreillysimmons.com
Facebook: @ShawnReillySimmonsAuthor
Twitter and Instagram: @ShawnRSimmons

Vaseem Khan

Vaseem Khan is the author of two crime series set in India, the Baby Ganesh Agency books set in modern Mumbai, and the Malabar House novels set in 1950s Bombay. His aim with these books is to take readers on a journey to the heart of India, showcasing both the colour and darker aspects of this incredible country. The first novel in his historical crime series set in 1950s India, *Midnight at Malabar House*, features India's first female police detective and is shortlisted for the CWA Historical Dagger 2021. The second is *The Dying Day*, published in 2021, and described by M.W. Craven, CWA Gold Dagger winner, as '*The Da Vinci Code* meets post-Independence India.'

His first book, *The Unexpected Inheritance of Inspector Chopra*, was a *Times* bestseller and an Amazon Best Debut. The second in the series, *The Perplexing Theft of the Jewel in the Crown*, won the 2017 Shamus Award for Best Original Private Investigator Paperback. The third, *The Strange Disappearance of a Bollywood Star* focused on India's movie industry, and the fourth, *Murder at the Grand Raj Palace*, was described by *Publisher's Weekly* as 'the best entry in the series to date'. The fifth is called *Bad Day at the Vulture Club*.

Vaseem was born in London in 1973, studied finance at the London School of Economics, before spending a decade on the subcontinent. He returned to the UK in 2006 and has since worked at University College London for the Department of Security and Crime Science. Elephants are third on his list of passions, first and second being great literature and cricket, not always in that order.

vaseemkhan.com

@VaseemKhanUK

FLAME TREE PRESS
FICTION WITHOUT FRONTIERS
Award-Winning Authors & Original Voices

Flame Tree Press is the trade fiction imprint of Flame Tree
Publishing, focusing on excellent writing in horror and the
supernatural, crime and mystery, science fiction and fantasy. Our
aim is to explore beyond the boundaries of the everyday, with
tales from both award-winning authors and original voices.

•

Other titles available in this series:
Vintage Crime

You may also enjoy:
The Sentient by Nadia Afifi
Junction by Daniel M. Bensen
Interchange by Daniel M. Bensen
American Dreams by Kenneth Bromberg
Second Lives by P.D. Cacek
The City Among the Stars by Francis Carsac
Vulcan's Forge by Robert Mitchell Evans
The Widening Gyre by Michael R. Johnston
The Blood-Dimmed Tide by Michael R. Johnston
The Sky Woman by J.D. Moyer
The Guardian by J.D. Moyer
The Last Crucible by J.D. Moyer
The Goblets Immortal by Beth Overmyer
The Apocalypse Strain by Jason Parent
The Gemini Experiment by Brian Pinkerton
The Nirvana Effect by Brian Pinkerton
A Killing Fire by Faye Snowden
Fearless by Allen Stroud
The Bad Neighbor by David Tallerman
A Savage Generation by David Tallerman
Screams from the Void by Anne Tibbets
Ten Thousand Thunders by Brian Trent
Two Lives: Tales of Life, Love & Crime by A Yi

•

Join our mailing list for free short stories, new release details,
news about our authors and special promotions:

flametreepress.com